BY ROSALIND LAUER

LANCASTER CROSSROADS
A Simple Crossroads (novella)

A Simple Faith

A Simple Hope

A Simple Charity

SEASONS OF LANCASTER
A Simple Winter

A Simple Spring

A Simple Autumn

A Simple Charity

A Simple Charity

A LANCASTER
CROSSROADS NOVEL

Rosalind Lauer

BALLANTINE BOOKS TRADE PAPERBACKS
NEW YORK

A Ballantine Books Trade Paperback Original

Copyright © 2014 by Rosalind Lauer

Published in the United States by Ballantine Books, an imprint of Random House, a division of Random House LLC, a Penguin Random House Company, New York.

BALLANTINE and the HOUSE colophon are registered trademarks of Random House LLC.

All scripture taken from *The Zondervan KJV Study Bible*. Copyright © 2002 by Zondervan. Used by permission of Zondervan Publishing House.

LIBRARY OF CONGRESS CATALOGING-IN-PUBLICATION DATA
Lauer, Rosalind.
A simple charity : a Lancaster crossroads novel / Rosalind Lauer.
pages cm.— (Lancaster crossroads)
ISBN 978-0-345-54330-1 (paperback)—ISBN 978-0-345-54331-8 (eBook)
1. Widows—Fiction. 2. Lancaster County (Pa.)—Fiction. I. Title.
PS3612.A94276S533 2014
813'.6—dc23   2014024915

Printed in the United States of America on acid-free paper

www.ballantinebooks.com

246897531

Book design by Karin Batten

For my dear editor Junessa Viloria,
insightful and brilliant.
Thank you for believing in my characters.

PART ONE

Everyday Miracles

For now we see through a glass, darkly; but then face to face:
now I know in part; but then shall I know even as also I am known.
And now abideth faith, hope, charity, these three;
but the greatest of these is charity.

—1 CORINTHIANS 13:12–13

1

*T*he purple of dusk still cloaked the sky as Fanny Lapp lifted her five-month-old son from the infant seat in the buggy and cooed to soothe him. "I know, I know. It's too early to be awake. You can sleep when we get inside." Shifting the little one onto her shoulder, she walked the small path bordered by red and yellow pansies and knocked on the door.

Today promised to be a warm one, with the wonderful good blessing of a new baby for Lizzy and Joe. Seeing a child into the world was the sweetest delight a person could know—though it came with its inconveniences. When she had agreed to cover for Anna Beiler for a spell while the midwife went to visit her family in Florida, Fanny had not imagined herself traipsing through the night with her own baby in tow. How quickly she'd forgotten that babes came into the world on their own schedule, whether it be stretched over three long summer days or as quick as a teapot comes to the boil.

First-time mothers could be a trial, not knowing what was to happen, but Lizzy King was different. Maybe because Lizzy knew about the dark patch of sorrow and grief Fanny was working through. Or maybe because it had taken this couple longer than most to be blessed in this way.

The door was opened by Lizzy's husband, Market Joe, a young Amish man with a broad, friendly face and thick black-framed glasses. "It's Fanny," he called to his wife, opening the door wide. "Come." With the excitement and nervousness of a first-time father, Joe scampered over to his wife, who stood leaning over a chair, breathing through a contraction.

Stepping inside, Fanny smiled at the young man and his wife. Ah, how dear they were to her heart! Although Joe and Lizzy King were not family, Fanny felt a special attachment to the couple, who had shared her family's fears and grief after the tragic car accident six months ago. Joe and Lizzy had been in the van with Fanny's husband, dear Tom, who had been taken by Gott.

The house smelled sweet, of cinnamon and sugar. "Someone's been baking," Fanny said.

"Lizzy made cookies, in the middle of everything," Joe said. "And you brought little Tommy this time. Come. We've got a place for the boy." He scrambled back behind Fanny to close the door.

"Lizzy." Fanny rocked Tommy back and forth as she made a quick assessment of Lizzy, who wore exhaustion on her pale face. A midwife had to learn much from the first look at a mother, especially since a husband often did not pass along details of his wife's condition when he called in a fit of jitters. Instinct told Fanny that the baby was still a good two hours away. "Looks like you're coming along fine."

"You were right about staying on my feet." Lizzy gripped the top of the ladder-back chair so firmly, her knuckles were white. "I baked a batch of snickerdoodles. That got things moving along."

When Fanny had come out last night around ten o'clock, Lizzy had been resting in bed, still in the very early stages of labor. Since Lizzy's pains had been nothing more than occasional cramps, Fanny knew she need not stick around. She had left the couple with instructions that Lizzy do some walking, and a promise that she would return before dawn.

Fanny felt her son's head stirring on her shoulder as she spotted a pile of quilts set up on the living room floor.

"We made a *Budda Nesht* for Tommy," Joe said.

"Looks cozy." Fanny squatted down beside the nest of blankets and placed her son in the center of the thick bedding. His lips formed a pout, then opened slightly as a look of peace softened his face. Covering him with a soft blanket, she bent down to kiss his forehead. "Sleep well, *liebe*."

"It's good you returned." Joe stood at Lizzy's side, rubbing her back. "She's been walking and standing most of the night, just like you told us, Fanny."

"Good. I knew you would follow advice. You're a good patient, Lizzy."

"Maybe not so much. I'm sorry for getting you out here last night, with the baby not really coming yet. When everything started, I got a little scared."

"It was no problem at all," Fanny said, comforting the younger woman. "The first baby usually takes its time, but this is all new for you. I liken it to a road you never traveled before. You need directions and a companion at your side. Joe has taken good care of you. Now it's my turn."

With her little one tucked away, Fanny took charge of the situation. The house was tidy, but Lizzy looked tired, and she needed to be strong for the pushing part of labor. "You go into the bedroom and change your clothes. The walking has helped your labor to progress, but now you need some rest."

As Lizzy waddled into the bedroom, Fanny turned to Joe and asked if Doc Trueherz was on his way. Fanny was happy to help Amish mothers bring their babies into the world, but the doctor was always in charge.

"I called, and Celeste said Dr. Minetta was coming."

"Not Doc Trueherz?" Lizzy paused in the hall, strain showing in her face. Most everyone liked Henry Trueherz, the country doctor who had served the Amish for years.

Joe readjusted his black-framed glasses on the bridge of his nose. "The regular doc's gone to the city. This Minetta fella is filling in."

"He's a good doctor, too," Fanny said, holding back her concerns. Both times she had encountered Dr. Minetta, she had been assisting Anna, and both times he had been late. Most doctors were not familiar with the farm roads and unmarked lanes of Lancaster County, which Doc Trueherz knew well from twenty years of making house calls. Dr. Minetta had arrived so late to one of the births, the baby had already been diapered and wrapped. Fanny hoped he would be prompt today.

Fanny sent Joe out to the buggy to tend to the horse and fetch her things—two heavy cases of supplies and medical gadgets that Anna had loaned her. As she washed her hands at the kitchen sink, Fanny was startled by her reflection in the window with the dense night still behind it. Her tawny hair was neatly pulled back under her white prayer *Kapp,* but her cheeks seemed hollow, her eyes wide and round like a wise old owl. My, oh my, but she could use a good night's sleep. She was beginning to understand why Anna was always yawning at quilting bees. Ah, but to hear a baby's first cry, to bundle an infant in flannel and hand it over to the mother—those sweet moments were worth a little lost sleep.

In the bedroom, Lizzy had changed into a robe that stretched over her wide belly and had slipped fluffy socks on her feet. Her white prayer kapp hung from a peg on the wall, and her golden blond hair was unpinned, still twined in a braid that ran down her back. The bed was already covered with a mattress pad and clean sheets.

"Look at that. The bed's all ready to go. Now we just need your baby to come," Fanny said as she motioned Lizzy to sit on the bed.

"We've been waiting so long," Lizzy said as she scrambled back on the mattress, then quickly looked away. Amish women didn't usually talk about such things—pregnancy and the like—but certain things had to be told to a midwife or doctor, and Fanny knew how Lizzy and Joe had waited. Most Amish women had their first babies within a year of marriage, but Gott had given Lizzy and Market Joe a different path. Lizzy was in her mid-twenties and having her first child.

Fanny propped up some pillows and had Lizzy lean back. Smoothing a hand over the young woman's forehead for a quick temperature check, Fanny was relieved to see Lizzy relaxing between contractions, drawing in a breath and sinking back against the pillows.

"No sign of fever, and it's good for you to close your eyes. You're going to need strength for what's ahead."

"Where do you want these bags?" Joe asked from the doorway. He hung back sheepishly, knowing a man's place was not in this bedroom right now.

"Right here." Fanny pulled one of the heavy bags close to the bed, thanked Joe, and sent him back out to the kitchen. "Why don't you go put some water on to boil," she told him. The tradition of boiling water was steadfast during Amish home births, though the most practical use for it was making tea.

Guiding her hands over Lizzy's taut belly, she felt the baby's head pointed down and securely engaged. "All good. Let me count the baby's heartbeats." The listening piece of the stethoscope was cold, so Fanny rubbed it with her palm. "Don't want to send you and the baby jumping," she teased.

"I'm not going anywhere," Lizzy murmured.

With the cup of the stethoscope pressed to Lizzy's belly, Fanny found the rapid thud of the infant's heart. Using a stopwatch from Anna's black bag, she counted the beats. "A hundred and forty," she said aloud. "A good, strong heartbeat."

Lizzy smiled, though her lips thinned as a contraction took over. "Ah, Fanny, I need this baby to be born," she said, wincing. "Please! Give me my baby now!"

Fanny helped Lizzy move to her knees so that she could rock her way through the wave. Tears glimmered in Lizzy's golden eyes as she searched the room for relief.

"Look at that calendar over there. What a lovely picture. Looks like Niagara Falls. That's it."

"I didn't think it would . . ." Lizzy moaned. "I didn't think it would hurt so."

"No one knows until it happens," Fanny said gently, but she doubted that Lizzy could hear her. Although Lizzy had been told what to expect from her dutiful visits to the clinic in Paradise, Fanny found that all the well-told stories and directions flew out the window when a woman was in the throes of labor. A midwife's simple words and calm explanations could wash over a woman in labor like a warm balm. Fanny stayed by Lizzy's side until the pain subsided and Lizzy closed her eyes again.

"The contractions are getting closer. I'm going to send Joe to watch for the doctor. You rest."

"Got to go." Lizzy pushed herself up on her elbows and edged off the bed. "I need the bathroom." She took two steps, leaned forward, and gave a cry of pain. She gathered her robe up and peered down at the linoleum floor. "My water."

"It's clear. That's a good sign, and it also means that your baby will be here soon."

"Oh, Fanny, it's taking so long and I'm about spent." Lizzy dropped down to a squat, her head resting against the bed. "This little one will never come."

"Your baby will come." Fanny smoothed a strand of blond hair away from Lizzy's forehead. "They always do." She helped Lizzy to her feet. "Off you go. After that, you come back in here. This room is your little cocoon, ya? We'll spin a warm, soft nest of love around your baby as it comes into the world."

Lizzy gave a wan smile, then headed down the hall as Fanny quickly fetched a rag to wash the floor. Although Fanny was experienced in assisting with home births, she didn't want to overstep her bounds. Where was that doctor?

Keeping a calm way about her, Fanny cleaned up the floor. In the kitchen, she started two cups of tea brewing. Joe asked how it was going, and she told him there was time to go down the road to get someone in the family to cover for him at the King family's cheese stand in the city. Joe wanted to be here when his baby was born, but he was a bit squeamish about hanging around now. "Go," Fanny told him. "Take my buggy if it's still hitched up. And keep a lookout for the doctor when you're on your way back."

Inside the bedroom, Lizzy was curled on her side. Fanny helped her up to a sitting position and handed her a cup of honeyed tea with a dose of blue cohosh, an herb that stimulated labor.

"*Denki.*" Lizzy sipped gratefully. "The doctor . . . he should be here soon, ya?"

"He's probably trying to find his way on the back roads." Fanny perched in the chair beside the bed. "I do wish we had a birth center here. That's how things are done back in Ohio. All the doctors and Amish know where to go when the time comes. Makes for fewer mix-ups, and it can be a lot of fun, women together with their newborns for a few days."

"That sounds like a very good thing, Fanny. Let's pray on it. Maybe someone will build one before I have the next baby."

"That's thinking positive," Fanny said. It would be a wonderful thing for mothers in this town, but who would build such a place? Her mamm used to say that if you want something done, you'll do it yourself. That got Fanny thinking about the old carriage house at home. Would it be possible?

"Oh, here comes another." Lizzy put the tea aside and focused on the picture of the waterfall. Her face was puffy from strain, but she didn't complain.

Fanny recognized that look, the turning point when a woman realized she must give herself over to the pain, trust it, ride it out. She put her teacup down and blotted Lizzy's face with the cool cloth.

"*Geh lessa.* Go with it." She spoke in their first language, though she doubted Lizzy could hear her. The dear young woman was caught up in the shifting tides of intense labor. Fanny tended to Lizzy quietly as the pain ebbed and flowed. This was the bulk of Fanny's duties: watching and waiting, soothing and cleaning up.

Not so long ago, Fanny herself had been attended by Doc Trueherz and Anna when Tommy was born. When Fanny's labor pains began, her heart had been heavy with sadness over Tom's death. But the minute she held the baby in her arms and kissed his wrinkled brow, she had recognized the blessing of family that Gott had granted her.

Every day she thanked Gott for her family. The older ones, Caleb, Emma, and Elsie, worked all day at their jobs and helped keep the household running smoothly. What would she do without them? And then there were the little ones. Will had his rambunctious games, Beth was Fanny's little helper around the house, and Tommy was a bundle of joy. How Fanny loved being mother hen to her brood of chicks!

Lizzy let out a small cry, then scraped in a deep breath and moaned quietly as the pain took her. Turned toward the wall, the young woman was withdrawing, finding her way. For now, it was best to let her be. Willing Lizzy to blossom with the pain, Fanny slipped out of the room to check on Tommy. He was up on his little fists, rocking and crooning.

"Time to eat, little one." She took him into her arms and sat down in a rocking chair. His eyes soaked up her face as she smiled down at him and got him nursing. "Such a good boy, plucked from your crib in the middle of the night without a fuss," she cooed. Of course, babies didn't seem to care much where they were, as long as Mamm was near.

She ran a thumb over the crease in his little forehead. "What have you to worry about?" she teased as he nuzzled into her.

The sound of the creaking bed inside reminded her of dear Lizzy, and Fanny flashed back to her first time, when she gave birth to Will. At the time, her husband, Thomas, had been the knowing one, having had three children with his departed wife.

For the most part, Amish women went through the paces quietly when they had their children. And that was a good thing, with so many women having ten and twelve children. Fanny had seen her grandmother Martha, who was a midwife in Ohio, handle them with a steady gaze, a minimum of words, and a firm hand.

Rocking gently in the chair, Fanny warmed over thoughts of the large family she had left behind. As a girl, she had been content to help out at the birth center in Sugar Valley. She had been happy as a lark with her family and friends there, until she had fallen for David Fisher, who had been visiting from Pennsylvania. Hard to believe that was more than ten years ago.

When David had asked her about Sugar Valley, she had told him that it was a good stretch of Gott's acres. "Everything I love is here in Sugar Valley," she had told him.

"Not everything," he'd said. "I'll be heading back home next week, and I don't want to go without you."

Verhuddelt though it seemed, it had felt right as rain to follow him back here to Lancaster County and get married as soon as wedding season allowed.

The Fisher clan was a family of bakers with a successful shop in the town, but her David had wanted to work the land. He had been handy with machinery and good with animals—apt skills for a farmer. They had been living in a small outbuilding on the Fisher farm, saving up for their own house, when David died in a farming accident. She had been hanging wash outside on the line when she got the word. And suddenly, in the blink of an eye, she was an Amish widow living in a settlement hundreds of miles from home.

Although the community had supported her, she had not been comfortable living on their charity, and with her marriage so new, she never felt completely accepted by David's family. Although the words were never said, she sensed that they were disappointed David didn't choose a wife from here in Lancaster County. The family was never cruel to her, but she didn't have a friend among them.

Fanny had been making plans to return to Sugar Valley when the bishop had asked her to help out a family in need. Widower Thomas Lapp needed a woman to come in and do some cooking and cleaning and minding his young ones, seven-year-old Elsie, ten-year-old Emma, and Caleb, just coming into his teen years.

Fanny had accepted because it was the charitable thing to do, and she'd stayed because the children had won her heart, along with their kind, thoughtful father.

A gray cloud of grief had hung over her, but Fanny had learned how to occupy her hands to ease her mind. As months went by, her heart began to mend, and Tom and the children kept her on her toes. One year after David's death, to the day, Tom came into the quiet kitchen while she was cutting vegetables and the children were off doing chores. His muscular arms were brown against the blue of his shirt, and instead of taking his usual seat at the table, he had stood behind her, his hat in his hand.

"It's time that we talk, Fanny." She turned to find his eyes gleaming, his fingers pinching the brim of his hat nervously. "I haven't said anything until now, out of respect to David, may he rest in peace. But I want you to know that I believe Gott sent you to us. You're like a part of the family now. And I'm asking if, well, if you ever see fit to court again, I'd like to be on the top of your list."

Fanny told Tom that she hadn't planned to court again—and she held true to that plan for a few weeks. But as time passed, she had realized that, in large and small ways, Tom Lapp had become a good friend to her. A dear friend. And though she tried to push him away, after a year of working in his household, he had already found a place in her heart. He didn't pressure her, but he was always there by her side, kind and good.

"How is it that the carrots have all this space, and yet they grow right against each other?" she had asked Tom one day as they worked together in the garden. "See this?" She held up two fat carrots that had twined so close, they were nearly one.

Tom had stepped over the broccoli and come to kneel by her side as he examined the tangled carrots. "Maybe carrots are like people," he said, pushing back the brim of his hat so that she could see the glimmer in his eyes. "No one should be alone. People could spread out over the land, and yet, we live together. A community, a family. A couple."

With a broad smile, she put the two carrots in her pail. "I was only talking about vegetables, Tom."

"I know. But I've been looking for a way to talk about this, and carrots are as good as any." He took her hands in his, capturing her eyes. "Marry me, Fanny. You know I love you, and you're already a mother to my children. *Kumm* now. Can't you find room in your heart for an old widower like me and three children who need you?"

It wasn't the first time he had asked her . . . but somehow, that day, she did find the room in her heart and the courage to say yes. Thankfully, the children were at school, so no one was there to see the two of them kissing in the garden, promising love and faith in the narrow rows between fat bunches of broccoli.

Dear Tom! Somehow he had found the twisted, narrow path to her heart.

Placing the baby on her shoulder to pat out the gas, Fanny rose. She patted Tommy's back as she walked to the bedroom for a quick peek. Lizzy was breathing her way through a pain.

They exchanged a few words, the short language of labor, and Fanny returned her son to the front room. She swayed back and forth over the budda nesht, lulling him to sleep. How she loved this little one! "Your father was a good man," she whispered. "I wish you could know him, little Tommy. But it was not part of Gott's plan."

She and Tom had enjoyed eight good years of marriage before he passed, and Gott had blessed them with three children, as well as Tom's three, whom Fanny was still raising as her own. Getting old, those three, but she smiled as she thought of their little family. It was up to her to manage the household now—a big job, but Gott never gave a person more than she could handle. Fanny's heart was still heavy, and there was no getting over the emptiness Tom had left behind. But Gott had blessed her with wonderful children.

Setting Tommy back in the budda nesht, Fanny returned to the bedroom, where Lizzy lay on her side, her eyes focused on the picture of the waterfall. All was good.

Just then Lizzy was jolted from her resting place with a fitful cry. She rolled to her knees on the bed, lost in a strong wave.

That was when Fanny noticed the dark stain on the plastic sheet. The once clear waters had turned brown, the color of dried leaves in October. That meant the baby was in some trouble. Without wasting words, she tended to Lizzy, then went to find Joe.

Fanny tried to calm her racing heart with measured steps to the kitchen. A panicked midwife was no help to anyone.

She was relieved to see Joe was back, pacing. "Is the baby coming?"

"Soon, but there could be a problem. We need the doctor, Joe. A doctor or nurse, and there's no time to waste. Go now, and find Doc Minetta."

He pressed his straw hat on his head. "Is Lizzy all right?" he asked, his eyes growing round with alarm.

"I'm more worried about the baby. If you can't find Dr. Minetta, call Doc Trueherz's office again. Tell Celeste we need help and—" She stopped short of telling him to call an ambulance. There wasn't an emergency. Not yet.

"I'll call the doc's office. And I'll get folks out on the road to watch for him and send him our way." As Joe hustled out the door, Fanny pressed her hands together at her chin and said a silent prayer that Gott would bring this baby to them in good health.

Then, with a deep, steadying breath, she turned and went back inside to tend to Lizzy.

❧ 2 ❧

Meg Harper beat the hollandaise sauce with a whisk and paused to take a taste. Too much lemon? It wasn't awful, but something had gone wrong in the prep, and instead of a smooth, fluffy sauce, curdles swirled in the liquid. Not very appealing.

"Remind me to pick up some hollandaise mix next time I get into Philly," she told Shandell, who was spooning fruit salad into bowls for diners in the next room.

"Does that come in a mix?" Shandell asked.

"It must. Maybe it even comes in a boil-in bag or a spray can." Meg spooned the tasty but mediocre hollandaise over two poached eggs and garnished it with enough parsley to distract and disguise.

"What is hollandaise, anyway? Did it start in Holland?" Shandell asked. The teenage girl was quick with the questions, but she was learning fast about every aspect of running the Amish country bed-and-breakfast.

Meg shrugged. "All I know is that it can be delicious when prepared properly. Which this is not."

"Don't be that way. Everything you make is delicious," Shandell said.

"This from a girl who spent a month in a cave."

"A shack, not a cave," the former runaway corrected Meg. "And from what I've seen, you're a good chef. Did you go to cooking school?"

"Plenty of school, but not for cooking."

"What did you study?" Shandell asked. She didn't realize that questions mining the recent past made Meg bristle.

"This and that." Meg handed over the egg plate, and Shandell added it to her tray. Meg wasn't ready to talk about her real profession—her calling. Or at least she had always thought that she'd been called to deliver babies, until an early morning last winter that shook loose the foundation of her life.

"For real. I know you and Zoey both went to college. I'm signing up to take some classes at community college in the fall. What did you major in?"

Meg bit her lower lip. Shandell Darby was a sweet kid, but Meg was sick of defending herself, trying to give a complex situation a simple summary. For now Meg was content to be impersonating a cook at her sister's inn.

"We'll talk later. Right now I've got some veggies to chop for an omelet, and you'd better get that out before it gets cold," Meg told Shandell, who hoisted the tray and hurried out.

Meg was amazed at the way cooking could fill your mind and suck up your time. The prep work, the whisking of a delicate sauce, the art of cracking eggs. Cooking was the engine that kept her pistons going these days, and though it was a methodical lifestyle, she was glad for the impetus to get out of bed each morning. She slid the omelet onto a heated plate and added a ruby red sliced strawberry to the corner of the dish. She was removing two fluffy waffles from the iron when her sister Zoey popped in, waving a few handwritten pages in the air.

"Success! I've got Amish recipes." Zoey and her husband, Tate, owned the inn, and their mission was to provide guests with a taste of Amish living. "Real authentic recipes from the Amish girl next door. Well, I guess she's not really a girl. I think she's eighteen or so, but she's a little person, and there's something youthful about her. Elsie Lapp . . . have you met her?"

"I think I've seen her in town. She runs a shop, right?"

"That's right. And her sister Emma is the Amish schoolteacher and her mother, Fanny, has some midwife training." She pushed a strand of blond hair out of her eyes. Zoey had thick, naturally curly hair that refused to be tamed by gels and dryers. It hung in a cloud around her heart-shaped face. "You and Fanny should meet. You have the midwife thing in common."

Meg tucked her thumbs under the straps of her bib apron. "I'm a cook now. Besides, Amish midwives aren't interested in talking shop. The Amish tend not to want to talk about pregnancy and birth. I think they find it embarrassing, and they don't usually need much coaching. When it comes to birthing, they seem to be born experts."

A proud smile lit Zoey's eyes. "I love it when you revert to your old self. I miss the confident Meg."

"She's gone," Meg deadpanned. "I had to give her up with the medical license."

"Ha, ha, not so funny. The investigation still hasn't been resolved, and the suspension is only temporary. Speaking of . . . what's the latest on that?"

"No news is good news," Meg said, cutting off the topic. "Look at you, Miss Congeniality. Just two months here and you've got the skinny on the Amish women next door, names and occupations. You've really made some inroads in this community, and that's not easy." Meg had delivered babies for some Amish families in Butler County, and she knew firsthand how difficult it could be to gain their trust. "What's your secret?"

"I just turn on the old Harper family charm," Zoey said with a twinkle in her eyes. "And they seem to get a kick out of it when I speak German. I told you that exchange program to Stuttgart would pay off one day."

More likely it was Zoey's genuine kindness that won them over. Meg liked to give her sister a hard time, but at the end of the day, no one had a heart as big as Zoey's. "What kind of recipes did she give you?"

"Breakfast foods. Some one-dish wonders. There's creamed eggs. Bacon-and-egg bake. And here's one called egg-in-the-nest. Doesn't that sound quaint?"

"As long as no twigs and branches are involved." Meg moved close enough to read over her shoulder. None of these simpler dishes called for hollandaise or poaching skills. "And a breakfast pizza? Snap. Looks like we've been serving the guests way too fancy breakfast fare."

"Who knew? Do you think you could whip one of these up tomorrow?"

"I'll give it a try." Meg glanced at the kitchen clock. "How did you extract these from poor Elsie so early in the morning? Half of our guests aren't even out of bed."

"These Amish folks keep early hours. Early to bed and early to rise. Elsie is already out there hanging a load of laundry before she goes into town to the shop. She said that Fanny is off delivering a baby. Isn't that exciting?"

"Mmm." Why did Zoey always push her to the one thing that brought her pain? Meg couldn't let her thoughts go there, to the earnest memories of so many new babies sliding into this world—232, to be precise. A midwife always kept count, each one so special. But now, the memories were blocked by a twisted, thorny memory that made her bristle when she tried to get past it.

Meg picked up one of the recipes. "We've got all the ingredients for the bacon-and-egg bake. Tomorrow I'll give it a try. One size fits all. It'll be a relief to have something simpler to prepare for breakfast. Something that matches my skills. I've been faking it, trying to master these sauces and scones."

"Fake, schmake. The guests love your breakfasts," Zoey assured her. "I wouldn't even think of changing the menu if we weren't committed to offering a real-life Amish experience. Just yesterday the Albees told me breakfast was their favorite part of their stay, and all the—"

"Please, spare me the false praise." Meg held up a hand to stop her sister. "We both know cooking is not my thing, but I appreciate your finding a place for me here and pretending that you need me." Meg had been at the inn for almost two weeks now, and she was feeling stronger and steadier every day.

"We do need you," Zoey insisted. Her lower lip was puffing out in that expression that came over her when she was bossing her little sister around. "You know there's a place for you here as long as you want it. Far as I'm concerned, I'd be happy to have you here forever and always, and I know that Tate feels the same way."

"Well, let's not push it."

Zoey reached across the island to touch her sister's arm. When Meg looked up, concern shone in her sister's eyes, crisp and blue as the sky. "Honey . . ." Zoey's voice was low, almost a whisper. "I don't ever want to have to pull you out of a dark bedroom again."

"And I don't want to be pulled," Meg responded. "That's behind me now."

"Just saying. If I find you backsliding, I'm going to kick your butt."

Meg gave a soft laugh. Her sister was pushy—always had been—but Meg's emotional shutdown had been one time when Meg had needed a kick in the pants. These days the depression still nipped at her heels, but more and more she was beginning to feel like she could stay one step ahead of it.

With a lull in the breakfast prep, Meg peeled off the hairnet that reminded her of the lunch ladies in grade school and fluffed her bangs. It felt good to release her long red hair as she stepped out on the patio. Zoey followed with two mugs of coffee, and they sat in two of the Adirondack chairs and stared off over a fenced field of weeds and wildflowers, over distant barns and silos that blurred into purple hills. Earlier in the morning a haze had lingered over the distant hills and fields like floating lace, but now sunshine had broken through. Meg leaned into the warmth, grateful for another beautiful summer day. They were chatting when the pounding of a horse's hooves turned their heads. An Amish buggy was coming up the lane toward the inn, moving at a swift pace.

"Someone's in a hurry," Zoey observed.

Meg was sure she had never seen a horse and buggy move that fast. "Do you know the driver?"

Zoey squinted. "Can't say that I do, but it's hard to see inside the buggy."

Mugs in their hands, the women went around the side of the house to the small parking lot beside the old red barn. The driver halted the horse and quickly hopped out. He was a young man, thirtyish, with a dark beard and black square-framed glasses that would have been nerdy ten years ago but now were the height of fashion.

"Hello, there," Zoey said in that hearty voice that made friends of strangers. "Oh, we've met. You run the cheese stand in Philly, right? Market Joe, what can we do you for?"

"My wife needs a doctor, now, and Betsy King told me you have one here." He removed his straw hat, revealing dark hair and a face drawn with exhaustion. "A guest. You have a doctor staying here."

"Dr. Nelson? Oh, no, sorry. He and his wife checked out yesterday."

His disappointment was palpable. "Ach."

Meg had to look away as she did the math. Worried young Amish man plus wife in need of a doctor; in her experience, that added up to labor and delivery. She hoped that her sister didn't give her up.

"Why don't you call Dr. Trueherz?" Zoey asked. "You can use our phone, if you like."

"Already talked to Celeste. Doc's out of town."

Meg saw his worry, the sweat on his brow, the tightness around his mouth. "There must be a doctor on call," she said.

"There is, Dr. Minetta, but he couldn't find his way. Still over in the next county, and Lizzy's in poor shape. Fanny told me to find a doctor, now."

"Fanny? So your wife is having a baby?" Zoey pressed a palm to her heart. "Oh, my gosh. And the regular midwife is out of town, too."

The man was looking back toward the road, eager to return to his mission.

"Do you want us to call an ambulance for your wife . . . for Lizzy?" Meg understood his distress, but there was no other choice. In a town like Halfway, the nearest licensed physician was often miles away.

"Nay . . . no ambulance. I'm to find a doctor, right away. There's something wrong . . ." He grimaced, looking away. "Trouble with the baby."

Mouth gaping open, Zoey turned to Meg with a silent plea, but Meg shook her head. No, she couldn't. Not now.

"Meg. Come on, now. It sounds like there are complications and you know you can help."

Oh, no. No, no. Meg wanted to go back into that bedroom upstairs, draw the shades, and hide for another few weeks. "I can't do anything. I'm under investigation, and I'm not even licensed right now."

Zoey nodded at the Amish man. "Do you think Joe here cares about your issues with the nursing board? No, he doesn't. His wife is having a baby and she needs your help. These people need you now."

Meg made the mistake of looking over at Joe. Holding his straw hat with both hands, he stared at her as if she were an answer to his prayers.

"Please, miss. Will you help us?"

The plaintive look in his dark eyes cracked her shield of resolve.

"Look, Joe. I'm not a doctor. I'm a midwife, but I'm not licensed to deliver babies at the moment. Besides that, it's not good to jump in on a case at the last minute."

"Meg?" A quiet panic glowed in his dark eyes, round as quarters. "Please, kumm. Help Lizzy. Bring us our baby."

The plea was like rain to a parched traveler in the desert.

Bring us our baby.

She had thought she might never have the chance to partake in such a miracle again, and here was a desperate situation, luring her back.

"Okay." With her apron still on, Meg strode toward the man's buggy, while behind her Zoey chattered on to Joe, singing Meg's praises, calling her a gifted midwife and a miracle worker.

"Wait." Meg paused midstride. "My bags . . . my equipment." She turned to Zoey. "In the back of my car." Although she was on the skids with the medical board, she still carried her bags in her trunk. Toting the equipment was second nature to her.

"Of course." With all the aplomb that had escaped Meg, Zoey pointed out the garage to Joe and told him to bring the buggy there and help Meg load her equipment.

The sight of the heavy cases tugged at an emotion Meg had buried inside her. Joe lifted them into the buggy as if they were light as a feather.

And then they were off, the powerful horse trotting Meg toward what she was sure would be the second biggest mistake of her life.

3

A cocoon of peace and calm. Fanny told herself that she had to keep her wits about her and maintain this quiet haven for Lizzy. Right now, Fanny's only relief was knowing that Lizzy was too preoccupied to sense the danger in the moment. The young woman didn't notice that Fanny was quivering beneath her tranquil smile.

The baby was in trouble. Fanny had told Lizzy that the heartbeat had slowed, and this dark discharge was not a good sign. Lizzy had borne the news bravely, but what else could she do, riding the fury of a contraction?

As Fanny wiped off the plastic sheets yet again, she wondered what was to be done to help an infant in distress. She had seen this a few times before, but since she had only been a helper, she wasn't sure what to do. The doctor had always taken over, working the cord loose or moving the mother by ambulance to the hospital for . . . what? What did they do at the hospital to help the mother and baby, besides surgery, of course? Ach, she couldn't know these things without being a doctor herself.

As Lizzy rested through a lull, Fanny wiped the woman's forehead with a cool cloth and listened for the welcome sound of a car coming up the lane. A medical doctor. *Please, Gott in Heaven, send us a doctor.*

Sending up a silent prayer, Fanny told Lizzy she was doing just fine. When Lizzy squeezed her fingers, Fanny stayed by her side as another pain came and went. Sometimes, that was all a person could do, keep company and pray.

Lizzy wouldn't believe it now, but the pain would become a distant memory after the baby was born. And the joy of having a newborn in the house! Fanny remembered cold winter nights when she and Tom would snuggle in their bed, tucked in a nest of blankets with a baby between them. Tom had been a patient father, good at consoling the little ones when they whimpered. How she'd loved hearing him speak to them or sing "This Little Light of Mine" in his winsome, smooth voice.

"This little light of mine . . . I'm gonna let it shine . . ."

Fanny closed her eyes for a moment, picturing the kind, gentle man she had expected to spend the rest of her life with.

Oh, Tom! We still miss you so!

A meek little cry brought Fanny back to the birthing room.

"When will my baby be here?" Lizzy asked in a voice weak from exhaustion.

"Soon, liebe." Fanny checked the baby's wavering heartbeat again and wondered what Anna would have done. When it came to helping mothers give birth, Anna had seen it all. A wonderful good midwife to this community for more than forty years, Anna had delivered Fanny's three children with the help of Doc Trueherz. Fanny longed for someone else to take the lead here, but wishing wouldn't make it so.

Wishing was a waste of time, but the power of prayer was endless. Again, she prayed silently, asking Gott to bless this mother and child. Fanny knew that Lizzy and Joe had been married for many years, longing for a child all that time.

Pressing a cloth to Lizzy's forehead, Fanny recalled the couple's wedding some six years ago. Tall, square-jawed Joe was nearly a head taller than Lizzy, a fair-haired girl with warm amber eyes. Two young folks with love in their eyes.

Even before that, Fanny had known Lizzy through David's family, as Lizzy was one of David's nieces. Just a teen when David had died, Lizzy had been so thoughtful during that difficult time when some of David's family had suggested that Fanny return to Ohio. David's sister Dorcas and his mother, Joan—oh, those two had probably thought they were being helpful, but they had made Fanny feel like a burr on the coat of the Fisher family. But not Lizzy. Lizzy had brought Fanny baked goods and even knitted her a scarf, which Fanny still wore on cold winter days.

And then, Gott had brought them even closer in the accident. Although Fanny missed Tom every day, she was grateful that the others had been spared. Lizzy was the closest thing that Fanny had to a sister here in Halfway.

Dear Gott, have mercy on this young couple and bring them a healthy baby.

With a moan, Lizzy scrambled onto her knees. "I need to push."

It was time. Fanny could only do her best; the rest was up to the Almighty.

4

*H*umidity rose from the road in a steamy promise of a hot day as the Amish buggy rushed Meg into the center of a crisis. Was she about to revisit the same dire situation that had put her midwife practice in jeopardy? A likely possibility. Oddly, she felt serenity at being called to help with the thing she knew best, and a little excitement at the speed Market Joe had reached with the buggy. The vehicle jostled over bumps in the road, but the horse seemed to like having its head, taking the road at a fast trot. Meg didn't mind the speed, though it did worry her that the vehicle had no seat belts.

Thinking ahead, she tugged off the kitchen apron and pulled her hair back with an elastic from a pocket of her shorts. She needed to be ready for whatever stage of labor this woman was in.

Lizzy. Meg knew her name but not much else. When she worked with a client, she wove a delicate relationship with the mother through weeks of prenatal care. She knew her medical history and gained her trust. The bond between midwife and mother was an important part of the difficult dance of labor and delivery, which could be exhausting for everyone involved.

Meg didn't like coming in at the eleventh hour—especially after the Collier case, which had turned tragic after Meg had taken on a desperate woman at the last minute.

She shot a look at the nervous Amish man beside her. "I need you to fill me in on your wife's medical history. Has she had a baby before?"

"No. This is our first."

"And you said she has a doctor. She's been seeing him for regular prenatal checkups?"

"Ya. Doc Trueherz, and the Amish midwives. She saw Anna in the beginning. In the last month, Fanny began to pay us visits, seeing as Anna was going away."

So Lizzy had been seeing a doctor and a midwife; that was a relief.

"Do you know the problem with the delivery? Is she bleeding?"

"That I don't know. Fanny just told me that the baby might be in trouble."

"A slow heartbeat?"

"You have to ask Fanny."

She took her cell phone from her pocket and checked—two bars. "Should I call an ambulance while I still have reception?"

"Nay. Fanny didn't ask for an ambulance."

Well, maybe that was some consolation.

The road was a dark ribbon cutting through fields and looping up and down hills. All the planning in the world couldn't account for the barriers that fell in a person's path; Meg was learning that lesson in spades. She held on to the vinyl seat and prayed for a positive outcome.

The buggy moved quickly to the outer edge of Halfway, zipped by a cornfield, then turned into a lane that led to simple clapboard houses. Joe pulled up in front of a plain white house with yellow and red pansies providing bright bursts of color along the front porch. Joe halted the horse, and Meg quickly jumped to the ground. She grabbed one case and told Joe to bring the other as she moved briskly along the path. Even before Meg reached the porch, an Amish woman appeared at the screen door.

"Please, kumm."

"You're Fanny?" Meg put her equipment down inside the door and followed the woman down a narrow hall. She kept her voice level, knowing that loud voices or whispers could aggravate a laboring woman. "Tell me what's happening."

Fanny knew the basics, and she had accurately recognized the signs of fetal distress.

As Fanny filled her in, Meg washed her hands and tugged on latex gloves. At the bedside, she leaned in close to make eye contact with the patient. "Lizzy? My name is Meg and I'm here to help you deliver your baby."

There was puffiness around Lizzy's golden eyes, but it was clear that she understood. A quick exam revealed that she was fully dilated and already pushing.

"Every time she pushes, the baby's heartbeat goes down," Fanny explained, even before Meg could attach the fetal heart monitor from her bag.

"The cord might be wrapped around the baby," Meg said, shifting into midwife mode. She handed her cell phone to Joe and asked him to get an ambulance here. She could see that the labor was too far progressed to get Lizzy to a hospital, but the crew would have special equipment to aspirate fluid and meconium from the baby's bronchial passages. Meg had learned the hard way, from that terrible winter night, that an ambulance can save a life.

In the meantime, Meg had to help this young woman have her baby, now.

She slipped a mask on Lizzy's face and started the oxygen flow as another contraction began. Fanny held Lizzy's shoulders as she pushed, and the baby's head crowned, but then receded as the contraction ended. Fanny was right; the contraction had made the baby's heart rate dip dangerously low.

Meg warned Lizzy, then reached in to check for a tangled cord. The baby's head was right there, firm as a sweet potato. Easing her fingers along the head, Meg found it—the umbilical cord looped around the baby's neck. Straining, she worked to pull the rubbery cord of flesh over the head just as another contraction began.

This time, when Lizzy pushed, the baby's head slid into Meg's palm. Coated with slick meconium, the baby looked more like a rough sculpture. Meg had Fanny hand her the suctioning tool. The Amish woman was intuitive—a great help at a time like this.

"We want to get as much of this muck out as we can before the baby starts breathing," Meg said as she suctioned the baby's mouth, filling the portable container with brown sludge. When Meg pushed the suction tube into the tiny nostrils, the infant wrinkled its face and tried to turn its head away.

"Oh, so you don't like that?" Meg let out a laugh, delighted by such a healthy reaction. "Your baby is a feisty one." Then she continued sucking on the mouthpiece until the nostrils were clear.

"Okay, Lizzy." Meg looked up at the weary faces of the Amish couple. "One more big push and your baby will be here."

With one solid push, the rest of the baby slid out, so fast that Meg was grateful to have the bed beneath her arms. "It's a boy, and a slippery little thing, too!"

"Such a long cord," Fanny observed as Meg unwrapped the tangled cord from the baby's chest and shoulders.

Meg agreed. "No wonder it was tangled."

As the couple exchanged words of delight, Meg clamped and cut the cord, and Fanny whisked the infant away in blankets she had warmed in the stove. "Don't clean him up yet," Meg told Fanny, explaining to the three of them that rubbing stimulated breathing, and they wanted to keep the baby's respirations shallow until the paramedics were able to check his lungs and bronchial passages. She emphasized these instructions to Fanny, realizing that the Amish woman would be the one to explain the situation to the paramedics. For her own sake, Meg knew she'd best lam out of here before any medical officials arrived. With a case pending against her and her license at risk, she knew it would not look good to be delivering a baby.

Tending to Lizzy and the afterbirth, Meg listened to Joe's suggestion of names, Fanny's cooing, and the indignant cries of the baby, who certainly seemed to have clear lungs despite the meconium.

"He's determined to holler," Fanny told Meg.

"I'm not worried about that. His lungs sound healthy to me." Meg spared the infant a glance and smiled.

A healthy baby had been born at her hands today.

Baby number 233.

She had worried that it might never happen again, and just when she'd been about to give up, an Amish stranger had come riding up the road to the inn.

∞

Out in the main room, the mood was jubilant. Lizzy rested on the sofa, her face lit with delight as Fanny placed the baby boy in her arms. Leaning in behind his wife, Joe spoke to the baby, who turned toward his father's voice, dark eyes alert.

"Ya, that's your dat, little one," Lizzy said, looking fondly from her son to her husband. "What shall we call you? What do you think, Joe?"

"I think Gott has blessed us with a good son."

"I meant about his name," Lizzy said, and they laughed together as Fanny teased them about not being prepared.

The sight of the happy couple with the baby in their arms brought tears to Meg's eyes. After delivering more than two hundred babies, she was still in awe of the miracle of birth. She had always thought she was meant to help women deliver their babies at home, but the case against her shattered those plans and dreams. She had thought she was at the end of a road, but in fact, she'd been waiting at a crossroads.

Meg smiled as she packed up her equipment. The tension that had gripped her had drained away, leaving a bubbly, giddy feeling of jubilation. She knew she should call her sister to come get her. She had to get out of here. But the desire to stay and bask in the glow of a new life was irresistible.

As she closed up her case, she saw that Fanny had done a thorough cleanup in the bedroom; the bed was covered with fresh sheets and a quilt, and the plastic sheets were out of sight. Fanny appeared at the bedroom doorway.

"Meg, do you want a sandwich or some lemonade?"

"No, thanks. I was just thinking that you do excellent work," she told Fanny.

"Oh, it's nothing, and it brings me so much joy to be nearby when a baby is born. Every new baby is like a new sunrise, bright and so hopeful."

"That's a beautiful image—a new sunrise." Meg patted Fanny's shoulder. "You were a big help. Thank you."

"I just do what I can. It was a good thing that you came when you did."

Meg lugged her equipment out to the living room, where the couple now sat together on the sofa. Lizzy was singing softly to the newborn, and Joe held another baby, with the formed features and alertness of a six- to eight-month-old. With a beautiful shock of dark hair, pale, chubby cheeks, and a gummy smile, this baby was fully engaged with the world around him.

"And who are you?" Meg asked.

"This is Tommy, Fanny's little one. He slept through everything."

"You're a happy guy," Meg teased.

Joe jumped up, cradling Tommy in one arm. "Let me carry that out for you. I'll take you back to the inn."

"No need to do that. My sister will come for me," Meg said. She didn't want to tear Joe away from his newborn baby.

"It's no trouble, after all you did for us. Fanny said you were sent from Gott, and she's right."

"God does work in mysterious ways. But I can get home on my own. Sit. Enjoy your new family."

"If you're sure, then I'm happy to stay a bit with Lizzy and John." A wide grin lit his face as he deposited her case near the door and looked fondly toward his new son. "That's his name."

"John is a good, strong name."

Just then Fanny came in bearing a tray of food. There was a large bowl of cornflakes topped with icy purple gobs—a concoction of frozen grape juice, popular among the Amish. The plate held a sandwich stuffed so fat, the top slice of bread was teetering off to the side. "There you go," she said, setting the tray on the table. She took her son from Joe and kissed his fat cheeks, cajoling him in Pennsylvania Dutch. Despite the stern appearance of the Amish to the outside world, these folks had much love and affection for their children.

"It all looks good, Fanny." Dimples appeared when Lizzy smiled over the tray of food. "I'm so hungry, I think I could eat a hundred sandwiches." Lizzy nodded to Meg. "Do you want to hold him before you go? We sure do appreciate everything you did for us, bringing us our baby, safe and sound."

"I'm glad it all worked out." Tears stung Meg's eyes as she leaned down and took the small bundle into her arms. "Hey, little man.

You certainly came into the world with a roar." The mottled baby writhed and turned his head, alert and healthy. *Thank you, Lord, for this bright new life.*

With so many feelings welling up inside her—relief and joy, pride and fear—Meg knew she had better hand the baby off before she started bawling all over him.

Thankfully, Joe, ever the proud father, swept him out of her arms when the sound of trucks rumbled outside on the street. "Kumm, John. The rescue squad is here to see you."

Meg swiped at her eyes as she turned to face the front window. The paramedics had arrived, and here she was, on the scene with all her equipment. She looked toward the kitchen, wondering if she should try to slip out the side door, but what would she do outside, hide in the carriage house? She had no car, no way to escape without attracting attention to herself. She decided it was best that she stay. Besides, she wanted to make sure the medical team understood the baby's needs. But just before Joe opened the door, she wheeled the oxygen tank out of sight behind the sofa. No need to leave the evidence of her involvement out in plain sight.

Two of the volunteers on Halfway's fire and rescue squad were Amish, and Joe was so pleased at the prospect of showing them his son that it was hard to wrest the infant away for the respiratory check. Meg worked with one of the paramedics, an older man named Scott, who proved to be experienced with newborn care. He quickly maneuvered a thin, flexible tube into the baby's bronchi—and got nothing.

"Clear as a whistle," Scott said. The minute he removed the tubing, John let out a wail of protest.

"I don't blame you one bit," Meg told the baby, "but it had to be done."

"Time to clean him up?" Fanny lifted the baby from the stretcher and carried him off. "Oh, ya. We'll get you clean in no time."

Tension drained from Meg as she watched them disappear down the hall. It had been a nightmarish delivery, but everything was fine now. A healthy baby and mother. Why, then, did she want to cry?

The medical team said their good-byes and packed up, their booming voices, heavy boots, and intrusive equipment receding. The invasion was over but for one uniformed man—a cop. In the excitement, Meg had not even noticed that a police officer was here.

He was a tall man with a calm demeanor and steely gray eyes. "You've made my day, and my shift just started. Congratulations, folks." He had a warm smile for Lizzy and Joe. "Your first baby, right?"

"Ya," Joe said. "A boy, and we named him John. Do you want some lemonade, Jack?"

"That'd be great. Looks like another hot day," the deputy said.

Why was he sticking around? It was clear that he knew Joe, but they wouldn't be close friends. Was this cop planning to question Meg's involvement?

As Joe went into the kitchen for drinks, the officer turned to Meg. "I don't think we've met. Jack Woods."

"Meg." She made a conscious choice not to give her last name.

"You're a friend of Lizzy and Market Joe?" His silver eyes were earnest and his tone so friendly that Meg didn't want to lie to him.

"She's a midwife," Lizzy said, pausing with her spoon in the air. "Meg helped bring our baby."

"Well . . ." Meg stammered. "I was asked to help at the last minute. I did what I could."

"I thought I knew all the midwives in the area. Let's see, there's Anna Beiler and Fanny here . . ."

"I'm just visiting," Meg said. "Helping my sister out at the Halfway to Heaven Bed and Breakfast. Do you know Tate and Zoey Jordan?"

"Sure. Tate's becoming a regular at the hardware store in town, and Zoey, she's like a walking, talking chamber of commerce."

"That's my big sister. We used to say, 'Telephone, tell-a-zoey,'" Meg said, warming to his friendly manner. In another place and time, she would have enjoyed a conversation with Jack Woods. Despite his size, he had a gentle manner that suggested protection and calm, a smile that said everything would be all right. "So you're part of Halfway's extended family," Jack told her.

"I guess I am." Meg smiled up at him, wishing she didn't need to keep kicking the truth under the rug.

Just then Joe came out with a pitcher of lemonade and a stack of paper cups. Fanny was right behind him with the baby, and Lizzy clucked over how sweet and fresh baby John now smelled. Joe took John, while Fanny sat beside Tommy, who was now content to watch from his portable chair.

"So was Dr. Trueherz here earlier?" asked Jack.

"Doc is in the city." Lizzy popped a slice of salami into her mouth and licked her fingers.

"There was another doctor on his way . . . Dr. Minetta," Fanny explained. "I guess he got lost, since he doesn't know these parts too well. I'm telling you, if Dr. Trueherz was around, he would have been here quick as a wink."

"There's no replacing Henry Trueherz," said Jack. "Those other guys don't understand what it takes to be a good country doctor. Doc Trueherz is great on the fly, and he's got a rep for forging through blizzard conditions to make a house call." He turned to Fanny. "How long have you worked with him?"

Fanny shook her head. "Oh, I'm just stepping in for Anna. All I can say is, thank Gott you were here, Meg."

"Oh, you were handling it well until I arrived," Meg said, dropping to the floor to play peekaboo with Fanny's baby. Much as she liked Jack, she wished that she might open her eyes and find him gone, out of her hair.

Fortunately, Joe and Lizzy were distracted by their baby. "And now, our baby is here," Lizzy said with a happy sigh.

"I suppose one of the docs will help you get the birth certificate," said Jack.

"I reckon," Joe said, though it was clear that no one here was concerned with the paperwork.

"You'll want to ask your doctor about that at your next checkup," Meg advised. "It can be really hard to get a birth certificate if you wait too long."

"I'll ask Dr. Trueherz," Lizzy said. She put the empty plate on the tray and reached for her baby. "Kumm, dear one."

The conversation was interrupted by a knock on the door. Fanny looked out the window and sighed. "Dr. Minetta."

A balding gentleman with a gray mustache and a small frame opened the door and spread his arms dramatically. "Your baby is here. Wow! I knew I was late, but I didn't think I'd miss everything."

"Here he is." Lizzy smiled up at him, her cheeks pink with pleasure. "Healthy as could be."

By the grace of God, Meg thought.

"These country roads aren't well marked, and I don't usually make house calls—that's Dr. Trueherz's passion. So it was a routine delivery?" the doctor asked.

"Oh, no, it was a different sort." Fanny clamped a firm hand on Meg's shoulder. "Won't you step into the kitchen with the doctor so you two can talk about medical things?"

Meg knew that Fanny's question was a discreet request not to discuss details of the labor and delivery in front of the men. Truly, Lizzy herself didn't seem interested in knowing why John had had a difficult birth; she was simply overjoyed that he was here at last.

Inside the kitchen, Meg recounted the birth as Dr. Minetta listened with admiration. "The cord was wrapped around the neck and chest, causing deep decelerations with every contraction in the last half hour." She told him that they had suctioned the infant's mouth and nasal passages, and that the paramedics had followed up but found the bronchi clear.

"Nice work." He patted her shoulder. "You make my job easy. I'm just going to check the mother and baby, and then I'll be on my way."

Meg nodded, relieved that he didn't ask her name or background. She really couldn't afford to go on record with this. He probably assumed that she worked with Dr. Trueherz.

With Fanny, Lizzy, and the baby in the bedroom for the doctor's exam, Meg decided it was time to make her exit. She raised a hand and smiled at Joe. "I'm heading out."

He nodded, scrambling to take one of her cases out to the front porch. "Thank you, Meg. We're very grateful."

Meg leaned down to cluck for Tommy, who indulged her by babbling in return. She ruffled his downy hair and picked up the oxygen tank, hoping to escape without anyone paying attention to her equipment. "Officer Woods, nice to meet you."

There was mystery in his smile as he watched her cross the living room. She had made it to the screen door when he snagged her.

"Hold on. Do you need a lift?" He held the door for her. "I didn't see any cars out here."

"Her sister is coming to get her," Joe answered from the front porch.

In truth, she hadn't even had a chance to call her sister yet, but with the cop here, the impulse to separate herself from the scene of the birth was strong. "I was just about to call for a ride," she said.

"No way. Don't make Zoey come out here when I can give you a ride." Jack pointed a thumb toward the police vehicle. "The inn is right on my way."

"I'd appreciate that." Meg was too tired and a little too intrigued to deny his generous offer. Besides, nothing was far out of your way in a small town. And social butterfly Zoey would give him a hard time for not giving her a ride. In a heartbeat, they loaded her home birth kits and oxygen tank into the back of his police cruiser and were on their way.

"So Zoey's sister is a midwife," Jack said as they turned onto the road. "Whereabouts do you live?"

"The Pittsburgh area. I've been down here to help Zoey and Tate get the inn on its feet and . . ." How much should she tell him? "The thing is, I'm taking a break."

"A break from being a midwife?"

"Yes, and if you've been wondering why I was dodging your questions, it's because I'm not licensed right now." There. She'd said it. Though she sensed that she had nothing to fear from Jack Woods. "And for full disclosure, I'm under investigation for a birth that ended tragically." There . . . she had said it aloud, given herself up. "Are you going to file charges or arrest me?"

"What? Why?" He seemed mildly amused.

"Because I delivered a baby without a license."

"Around here, that's not a license we usually check for. Driver's license, yeah. Hunting license, sometimes. But I've never busted a midwife. I'm just glad you were there, Meg, with the cord tangled and all that. Not being a husband or dad, I don't know much about childbirth, but I do know that things can go horribly wrong."

She ran her fingers along the seat belt across her chest. "So . . . I don't have to worry about you reporting me to the board?"

"Hell, no. The way I see it, you were at the right place at the right time. Divine Providence, if you believe in God, and I do. The Lord meant for you to be here today, and I'm grateful for that. I know Lizzy and Joe are, too. It's all good."

Meg pinched the seat belt and stared out the window as she

tried to process the conversation. So he wasn't going to get her in trouble. Well, sure. He was a cop, not the Pennsylvania State Nursing Board.

"Hurray and hallelujah," she said aloud.

He laughed. "What's that?"

"I'm extremely relieved. Right now I'm in so deep with this case, I know the tiniest impropriety will end my career, and it's really important to me to get my license reinstated."

"From where I stand, you do your job well. Dr. Minetta seemed to agree."

She sighed. "Too bad he's not on the nursing board."

"So you've been away from the profession for how long?"

"Two months, give or take. The incident happened in March, when that ice storm hit Pittsburgh. The board didn't take action for a while after that, not until the client made a complaint."

"Do you miss it?" Easy conversation was one of his gifts. He always had a way of making people relax. "The baby business?"

"Every day. I miss the connection I form with the mother, the different language we speak during labor. And the babies . . . ushering in a new life." Again, she was misting over. She took a deep breath. "It's the best job in the world."

"I hear you. In my job, there's good and bad and in between. But I envy you, focused on new life. That's cool." He turned from the road to smile at her, his eyes gleaming with pride. "You know, I delivered a baby once. Came upon a car on the side of the highway; the woman, her name was June, she couldn't make it to LanCo General in time. So I was the labor coach of last resort."

She chuckled. "I'm sure she was glad to have another human being to help her."

"Now, I have to admit I was a little squeamish at the idea of it all, but once I got in the car with her, well, there was no turning back, if you know what I mean."

She nodded. "She needed you, and you rose to the challenge."

"Of course, it was mostly the dispatcher who talked me through it, but it was an amazing experience. Life-changing. I'll never forget it. June and her husband, they text me photos of the kid sometimes."

"Isn't it fun to see them grow up? I stay in touch with most of my clients." She thought of the bulletin board of photos at home—her kids. Well, not really, but it looked like they were going to be the only kids she would ever have.

"So what I'm saying is, I think your job is really cool. Amazing."

She shot him a look. "I can honestly say that I've never heard that from a guy. Most people I meet think my job is weird. Like I'm some hermit lady who concocts potions in the woods and keeps expectant mothers away from technology."

He snickered. "Not surprising. Back in colonial times, many of the women accused of being witches were actually midwives who knew about herbs and home remedies."

She nodded. "Most people don't know that."

"History 110 with Dr. Hoppes," he said.

"Oh, now you're showing off," she teased. She was enjoying the easy banter, but already they were pulling into the parking lot of the inn. Meg felt a pang of regret. She enjoyed talking to Jack Woods, and she was sorry it had to end. He was attractive, with his surfer blond hair and silver eyes. So comfortable in his own skin, Jack had eased her mind with his sense of humor and love for people. In another time and place, she would have asked for his number, but here . . . this was a temporary stop for her.

He got out of the cruiser to help her lift out the cases. "Need some help getting these inside?" he asked.

"I can manage. I'm used to lugging them around, but I really didn't think I'd be using them again this soon."

"Well, lucky for all of us you had this stuff handy. Lucky that you were here." He lowered the forty-pound case next to her feet and stood facing her, just a breath away.

Meg felt a wild impulse to rise up on her toes and reach for his shoulders and press her lips to his. She wanted to kiss him, right here in front of the inn in the light of day, with her sister most likely spying from one of the front windows. She felt herself veering toward the heat of his body, but he abruptly stepped back. "I'd better head out. Got to keep a lid on this town. You know how it is; without a police presence, folks'll be jaywalking up and down Main Street."

She had forgotten that he was working. Wow. She had almost kissed an on-duty cop and compromised his professionalism. "Thanks for the ride," she said.

"I hope to see you again, Meg. If you're staying awhile, I could show you around. Hook you up with some of the best Amish cooking in Lancaster County, not to mention some whoopie pies and soft pretzels."

"I'd really like that, but . . ." The thought of spending time with Jack was very appealing, but responsibility tugged her back to Pittsburgh. "I've got to get home. I see that now."

"So we'll keep in touch." He held one hand to his face, pinky and thumb sticking out. "I'll call you."

She picked up one of the cases. "You don't even have my number."

He paused at the door to the vehicle. "Trust me. I know how to do detective work."

As she watched him drive away, she felt lighter. The path ahead was going to be bumpy, but at least now she knew which road to take.

5

No one answered the third time Zed Miller knocked on the door at the Lapp house. Moving off the porch, Zed tipped his straw hat back and looked up at the two-story home. The curtains didn't move, and there wasn't a sound from within. He knew that Caleb would be at the sheep ranch and Elsie would be in town, running the Country Store. But where was the rest of the family? Fanny had asked him to come by this morning and take a look at some renovations that needed to be done.

He went around the side and saw that both buggies were gone from the garage. Hmm. Nobody home.

Zed walked out to the old carriage house, a ramshackle building with two boarded-up windows that resembled missing teeth in a weathered face. Although neglected and battered by time, the structure had good bones. He had been here more than a year ago, helping Tom and Caleb patch up the roof. Holding his hand to the brim of his hat to ward off the sun, he could see the signs of their work, where new black shingles were mixed in with the faded gray. The three large bays for carriages had been designed for buggies, but they hadn't been used that way for years, since the Lapps housed their buggies in the newer garage next to the house.

The door creaked as he pushed it open and stepped into the cooler air. The interior was just posts and pillars and a dirt floor. A pile of fresh lumber stood in the center of the space. He tested the steps of the wooden staircase to the right as he climbed, passing through dust motes in the sunlight from a broken window. Ya, the staircase was good. Upstairs was a basic attic that could be used for storage. *A very hot attic,* Zed thought, wiping sweat from his brow as he headed back down the stairs. A Dutch door led to a small stable area in the back of the building, where horses had once been kept. Someone had planned the building well, but that had been many years ago. He wondered what the Lapps wanted to do with it now.

Figuring that someone would be back soon, he went around to the back of the house where a pale green table and chairs sat in the inviting shade of a thick box hedge. It was cooler back here in this small yard, such a peaceful place for a quiet moment. This was one of the things he had missed in his time away from Halfway, years spent trying to find the spark of life out among the English. Taking a deep breath of honeysuckle-scented air, he tossed his hat onto the table and scraped back his brown hair. If working here was to be part of his punishment, Zed was a lucky man.

Zed was here by order of Bishop Samuel, who had told him that he needed to show with his deeds that he was ready to join this Amish community that had been the home of his youth. Zed left Halfway during his *Rumspringa,* and he had stayed on the outside for many years—too many years. And now that he had come home, he found it wasn't so easy to pick up where he had left off. He had been a young man when he left, and now, at twenty-nine, nearly thirty, Zed found that his childhood friends were married with children of their own. He was far too old for youth events and far too solitary for gatherings of couples and their children. In a community that followed rules and traditions, he was the odd man out.

Each week in the sessions with the bishop to prepare for baptism, Zed felt a sharp awareness that he was the old man of the group. Bishop Samuel had said flat out that Zed would be the oldest man he had ever baptized. No one in the group had commented, but later, Elsie Lapp had tried to mend the hole inside him. Little Elsie. She'd been a child when Zed had left, but even then she'd been jolly and sweet, a bright, smiling flower. After class, Elsie had patted Zed on the arm with a knowing smile, telling him not to concern himself with age. "You are at the exact right place at the right time," she'd told him. "I know that because I know that Gott doesn't make mistakes." It was true, Zed knew that. But he hadn't been able to shed the awkwardness of being on the outside for so long. He had made the Englisher mistake of trying to find himself when he should have followed the Amish way, losing himself in his community. He had grown accustomed to English folk talking about the things they wanted—so many wants.

Zed grunted. It was good to have the modern world behind him, good to be home, even if he was still on the outside. But he was taking the classes for baptism, and Elsie and Rachel were in the group. Zed had gotten to know them in the weeks and months after the accident, and now he was grateful to see their friendly faces at the weekly classes with the bishop.

Leaning back in the chair, he realized it was a bit shaky and gave it a look. Loose bolts. He could tighten this up. All the chairs could use a bit of tending.

He fetched his tool kit from the buggy and set to work in the backyard with a screwdriver and wrench. The bolts tightened easily, and he tested the first chair. Good and sturdy. These chairs, this table, they were plain and simple, durable and strong. He knew the Lapp family had sat around this table in good times and bad, taking

their supper out here on hot nights, cleaning strawberries or string-
ing beans. From the brushstrokes on the side of the table, he saw
that it had been here a long while, standing the test of time.

But back among the English, such a table would have been
pushed out to the trash heap by the curb. Abandoned for a shiny
new replacement.

Just like me, Zed thought. He had been replaced for a newer
model. It had taken him a while to sort it all out, but finally he had
turned back to the community he'd grown up in. Now he saw
the Amish with new eyes.

He started tightening up the other chairs. From beyond the fence
came the low rumble of a passing truck, and he realized the yard
backed up to a road. An endless road. Zed had learned that one road
always led to another, and when you had a vehicle and money for gas,
you could keep rolling until the day you died. He had been down
those roads, driving an eighteen-wheeler. It was long hours, but he
didn't mind the work, and in the beginning, the journey was just
what Zed was looking for. To go to another place, with palm trees
and sunshine or mountains and snow—that had been his way of getting away from himself. In a new place, hundreds of miles from Halfway, he had thought he would be a new man—confident and free
from the Ordnung, the rules that dictated everything from what a
man could wear to when he could marry. But as the years wore on,
he began to see that he could never get away from himself.

Why had he stayed out so long among the Englishers? He wasn't
so sure. There was some *Hochmut*—pride—that had kept him from
admitting to himself that he had made a mistake in leaving.

And what had drawn him away in the first place?

Cars.

The answer still brought a hot flush of shame to his cheeks when
he thought about it. He had told his parents that he wasn't ready to
join the church just yet, and they had let him go with a sad nod. He

did not mention his fascination with cars and trucks and engines, but they had to know. After all, he had left behind a broken-down Jeep that he'd spent hours tinkering with during his early rumspringa. There was something about driving a vehicle, being in control of a loud, powerful engine, that had held Zed in awe. Driving made him a man, or so he thought.

With the help of a Mennonite cousin who gave him a place to stay, he had gotten his license and a good job as a truck driver. He made enough money to pay for what he needed—at least until he'd met Jessica. An Englisher, Jessica described herself as a plain country girl, but she was far from plain. She was always shopping at malls or paging through magazines, trying to find the shoes or lip color that would make her feel good about herself. Zed used to ask her why she didn't feel good as she was, but her response was always a little smile and a nudge on the shoulder.

In the years that he courted her, she began to buy clothes for him, too. Blue jeans and striped shirts. Expensive leather shoes. But Zed had no interest in the clothes. Broadcloth pants and a simple shirt suited him just fine. Too bad it took him so long to find that out. That was when he realized that he would never fit in with Englishers. He didn't talk or think like them. He would never belong there.

It had been a long, hard lesson. He immediately saw that Jessica bought clothes and jewelry to fill the hole in her heart. It took him longer to realize that he was doing the same thing with his interest in cars and trucks.

After he had returned to Halfway, Zed had tried to hire on with an Amish contractor. Although there would be no more truck-driving for him, he was good with his hands, a capable carpenter. But no one would hire him. Some Amish folks had been so cold, you would have thought he was under the *Bann*. People knew he had turned away for a long time; they weren't so quick to welcome him back with open arms, that much was clear. He knew he would have to prove himself to them, show them that he was here to stay, that he wanted to be a part of the community.

For now, he would have to work without pay. Amish charity. He didn't mind that so much, and he was glad to help the Lapps, his family.

Sometimes Zed still found it hard to believe Thomas Lapp was gone. When Zed had returned to Halfway, Tom Lapp was one of the few men who would look him in the eye and give him work. Tom and Fanny had been close to Zed's parents, Rose and Ira. And somehow, Gott had seen fit to put Zed in the van with Elsie and Tom Lapp on that terrible night last winter. From that day on, Zed and his parents had kept a close watch on Tom's family, vowing to step in if they ever needed a helping hand. Zed figured it was the least he could do for Tom's widow.

With the chairs fixed, Zed closed up his toolbox and walked past the hedge, where sparrows darted in and out. Bees bounced along the honeysuckle, and the warm breeze brought the scent of cut grass. This was one of the things he had missed, trapped in the cab of his truck: the sight and smell of the land. The simplicity of a wooden fence built to keep boundaries.

He was ready to obey those boundaries now—the Ordnung, the church rules, the customs that were like Amish law. Submission was the key to *Gelassenheit,* bowing to the Almighty.

As he leaned into the buggy to replace his tool box, the sound of a horse's hooves on pavement caught his attention. A buggy was coming down the road. The kapp of its driver seemed white as snow in the stark sunlight.

Such a familiar sight; another comfort of being home. It was good to wake each morning to the language and manner he was accustomed to.

Even if he did wake up in his old bed in his parents' house. Twenty-nine was too old for that, and he was eager to find a place of his own as soon as he could get a job and save some money.

Not that his parents minded having him. "It's good to have you home, Zed," his mother always said, "but I know it's just for a short time. Before you know it, you'll be leaving for your own place with your wife." Mamm liked to remind him that he would be expected to take an Amish wife after he was baptized in the fall.

"Wife?" Dat always teased. "Don't put the cart before the horse, Rose. He needs to find a willing gal first."

"And what Amish woman would have me?" Zed would answer, poking fun at himself. "I'm like the apple that fell off the cart on the way to market—a little scarred and hard to sell."

That usually made Dat laugh, though Mamm would swat away the comment as if it were a pesky gnat. Zed couldn't tell his mother that he had already encountered a few interested young women. Becca Yoder always came over to talk with him after church, but talking with her was tedious work, like digging up potatoes. And he knew what Mamm was doing when she sent him to the bakery each week for a loaf of bread. Rose Miller spent plenty of time in town; she could have easily made the purchase. The bread wasn't nearly as important to his mamm as getting Zed to talk to Dorcas Fisher, a woman Zed had grown up with who was still single and at least thirty. Zed had always avoided her as a kid, hearing the way she criticized other children at school, and the stories she told. Dorcas still liked to gossip. These days the Fishers' bakery had more news than *The Budget,* the local Amish newspaper.

There was no shortage of unmarried women. It was Zed holding things up, his thoughts still wrapped up in the life he used to have . . . the woman he used to love.

A woman who had chosen another. Although Jessica was married with a child, living a hundred miles away, Zed had trouble chasing her from his mind. Sometimes it was hard to move down the road when the heart lagged so far behind the head.

6

*S*uch a glorious day! Fanny smiled through her weariness as Flicker's hooves tapped the asphalt road. Despite all the obstacles, a new baby boy had been born. Another sweet child in their community! Ah, but Gott had truly blessed Fanny, allowing her to help deliver new babes.

Squinting through the heat shimmering up from the black road, Fanny tried to identify the man walking around her house. Not Caleb, but Zed Miller. How could she have forgotten? Bishop Samuel had told her Zed would be coming out this morning to take a look at the old carriage house with an eye toward repairs. Caleb and Elsie would have gone to work, but where were Emma and the young ones?

He met her in front of the buggy garage, tipping his hat back as she brought the horse to a halt.

"Zed, I'm sorry to keep you waiting. I just came from Market Joe and Lizzy's, where there's a new baby boy in the house. John King."

"Good news. I'm sure they're both full of joy."

"They are. You should stop by on your way home. They'd love to see you." Fanny knew Zed had a special bond with Lizzy and Market Joe, ties wrought in the highway accident.

"I just might."

Fanny turned around to check on Tommy, but Zed was already reaching into the backseat of the buggy, lifting out the infant chair as if it was light as a feather. Zed was a strong man, with nut brown hair and thoughtful eyes. A handsome one. If he had stayed in Halfway during his rumspringa, Fanny had no doubt that he would be long married with a family of his own. He was a bit on the quiet side, like his father, but that never concerned Fanny, who saw peace and grace in the silent moments in life.

She lifted Tommy into her arms and straightened his little shirt. The baby jutted out his lower lip and stared at Zed curiously.

"He's getting big." Zed offered a finger, and Tommy gripped it and smiled.

"I see that no one was home to greet you. I thought Emma and the little ones would be here."

"I was able to get into the carriage house. There's some long work ahead, but the building is solid. Good bones. What sort of shop do you want to make it?"

Fanny stepped down from the buggy as the horse nickered. "That is a very good question. Tom used to talk of a carriage shop, but Caleb doesn't seem so interested in it anymore."

"Either way, the siding and roof need some more work first."

"That would be good, for starters." She shifted Tommy onto her hip. "Would you mind unhitching the horse for me, Zed? And then we could talk inside, with something cool to drink. Not even noon, and the sun is high."

He nodded and began tending to the horse as she carried Tommy into the house.

When Zed came into the kitchen fifteen minutes later, Fanny had put out some fried chicken and potato salad, and she insisted Zed sit and eat. "At least have a glass of lemonade. My hungry brood should be back any minute. Until then, we can enjoy the peace and quiet."

He considered for a moment, then hung his hat on the hook and took a seat at the table.

"I guess you know your mamm has been worried about you," Fanny said as she opened a jar of pickles. Zed's mother, Rose, a cousin of Tom's departed wife, had always been close to Tom's family. "She said you're having trouble finding work."

"I am. I drove a truck for seven years, but I can't do that anymore."

"You were gone such a long time. Rose feared that you'd been lost to the community."

"Lost without a map," he said. "But I'm back to stay. Only I'm finding it's not so easy to join the flock. No one wants to hire a man who's left his community behind."

"That's not right." A church member would be shunned for leaving, but Zed had not been baptized before he left. "You were never under the bann."

"But people can turn a cold shoulder against a man who's not a member of the church. They think I'm unreliable."

She shook her head. "Some folks do have a way of thinking the worst." Fanny had learned that firsthand, having been widowed twice. She knew certain people thought her sad circumstances were her fault. As if she brought bad luck to men or even worse, as if Gott had punished her by taking her husbands. Such cutting, hurtful thoughts. She wished that people thought about the sharp edges of their words before they let them spill out in gossip. "Have you thought of working for the English? Lunch pail work?" Many Amish men traveled by van to work on job sites or factories owned by Englishers.

"The bishop thinks I should stay with Plain folk for now. I appreciate your family taking me on for some work."

"There's plenty around here," Fanny said. "And we've saved some money to pay you a modest salary."

"I can't take your money," he said. "We're family."

Amish extended families could include two hundred people or more. Zed's mother had been a cousin of Tom's first wife. That meant Zed was related to Caleb, Elsie, and Emma, but not Fanny. "Family or not, you must be paid for your work. A man must make a living."

He held up one hand. "Not this time. You know Bishop Samuel sent me here. He wants me to work in the community as punishment for leaving."

"Did you come here to find work, then, or to get back in the bishop's good graces?"

He shrugged. "Both."

They both chuckled. They agreed that the family's money would be put toward supplies for the renovation. When the work was done, Zed hoped to get a paying job based on his work here.

As Zed started a list of necessary repairs on the carriage house, Fanny sensed that he would be an easy person to have around. It was the fact that her family was now a community charity that made her a bit uncomfortable. Unfortunately, it was necessary. They needed help right now, and it would be better to build a business than to just keep taking money. Now and again Fanny was paid as a midwife, but only when Anna was away. The Country Store brought in some steady income and there was Emma's teaching salary, too, though Fanny couldn't count on that forever. Emma and her boyfriend, Gabe, were coming of age, and Fanny knew they'd be wanting to get married next year. Still, Gott would provide for her little family. They would not starve, but it was tough making ends meet at times.

As Fanny ate a piece of cold chicken, Zed explained that the bishop hadn't made it so easy for him to return to Halfway's Amish community. There would be no slipping back into place. "But I'm getting closer. Inch by inch. Right now I'm getting the training for baptism. Did Elsie tell you? An old man like me is in class with eighteen-year-olds. They must think I'm an odd duck."

Fanny laughed. "Come on, now. You're not that old, are you?"

"I'm twenty-nine, nearly thirty."

"The same age as me, although I feel so much older than that." Fanny was not even thirty and she had outlived two husbands. "Gott has given me so many wonderful lifetimes already."

"Now, Fanny, you sound like my grandmother, and she's twice your age."

She took a bite of chicken and smiled at his gentle teasing. "I'm not a mammi, but I do wonder where the years go. In the blink of an eye, the older ones went from children to full grown, all with work of their own now."

"But you still have them here."

She nodded. "I'm happy to have a houseful." Her children filled her days and nights with joy. Emma, the teacher, was such a good storyteller, so willing to share her knowledge and wisdom. Caleb, Tom's oldest, had proven himself as the man of the house—strong, fair, and kind, just like his father. Dear Elsie had been blessed with the small body of a little person and the big heart of a giant. Fanny often looked to her for patience when she became frustrated trying to juggle chores and responsibilities. The three older ones had been born to Tom and Rachel, but Fanny continued to raise them as her own.

And what a help they were with the young ones! When the family was around, baby Tommy was never at a loss for someone to pick him up and tote him around the house, narrating chores like the cooking of dinner or the feeding of chickens. Will and Beth looked up to their older siblings, who had already taught them so much. Will loved fishing and repairing things with Caleb, and Beth enjoyed standing on a stool beside Elsie to help with the dinner dishes each night after supper.

"Family is such a blessing," Fanny said.

Zed nodded. "I'm sorry I spent so many years away from mine."

"So I reckon you heard the story behind our needing some help here?" Fanny asked.

When Zed shook his head, she told him about the day two weeks ago when she had helped Caleb buy wood from the lumberyard. "We were loading the new two-by-fours into the old carriage house, when I got clumsy. I gave Caleb a nasty poke by accident. And then I tripped and fell forward. The long piece of wood fell with me—right into one of the windows." She waved off the concern on his face. "Ach, everyone was fine. But I learned that I wasn't cut out to do that sort of work."

"Then Samuel has sent me to the right place."

As they talked, Fanny thought of how Bishop Sam put people and jobs together. Some folks were uncomfortable around the stern bishop—a graying bear of a man—but Fanny had always been able to face his owlish eyes and growling voice with a smile, just as she had been quick to abide his decisions. She would follow the bishop's instructions and hire Zed.

"Who's here?" came Will's voice as he burst into the kitchen, bare feet pattering on the linoleum. "Ah, it's you, Zed. Caleb said that was your buggy."

"It is."

"And where were you off to?" Fanny asked.

"To town. We all went to drop Elsie at the shop and pick up Caleb for lunch. And while we were there, Emma bought us cookies from the bakery."

"Cookies from the bakery," Beth repeated, putting her chin on the table and staring up at Zed. At four, she was a smaller, chubby-cheeked version of her mother, with reddish brown hair and flashing blue eyes.

"Did you save a bite for me?" Zed asked.

"Nay. We gobbled them up," Will said.

"All gone," Beth agreed.

"You would think these two never had a snickerdoodle before." Emma nodded at Zed as she came in and placed a fresh loaf of bread on the counter.

Caleb was right behind her, and he spoke with Zed about the hot weather as he took a seat at the table beside him. Caleb would need to eat quickly and get back to work at the Stoltzfus ranch, though the rest of them could take their time.

As the men talked about repairs to the carriage house, Fanny sent the children to wash their hands, then sat them all at the table. They bowed their heads for a silent prayer of thanks before helping themselves to cold chicken, potato salad, pickles, and the fresh bread Emma had bought at Halfway's bakery.

"The Fishers always do a good job," Fanny said as she buttered a slice, "and it's nice not to heat up the kitchen with baking this time of year." Biting into the bread, she thought of the folks she had once counted as family. Joan Fisher, her former mother-in-law who still ran the bakery staffed by her daughters and nieces, reminded Fanny of a hardworking donkey—slow, steady, and stubborn. Joan always seemed to be on the brink of a bad temper, but Fanny suspected that she would be in a stormy mood, too, if she had to be at the bakery before three A.M. every day. Sometimes Fanny saw Gott's wisdom in moving her away from the bakery business, as Fanny was an adequate baker, but her heart just wasn't in kitchen work.

"Tell us about the little baby!" Will said, interrupting Fanny's thoughts.

Everyone was delighted by the news of Lizzy and Joe's newborn, and Fanny promised to bring Beth and Will along to visit when she went by tomorrow to check on Lizzy.

"So, Zed here is asking me what we want to do with the carriage house," Fanny said. "And I didn't have the answer."

"It would be good to finish it with a bathroom and kitchen," Caleb said. "Like a Doddy house. We might need it down the road."

A Doddy house was a small, complete home where grandparents lived on family property. Fanny suspected that Caleb was thinking that down the road, he or one of his sisters might need a starter home after they married, and it was a good plan. Gabe King had been courting Emma for quite a while now; they were probably next in line to marry. Elsie was becoming inseparable from Ruben Zook, and though Caleb never brought anyone around, Fanny knew from his late nights out that he was courting some lucky girl. In the next few years, there were bound to be more new babies in the family.

"That might be an expensive renovation," Emma said.

"Could be," Fanny agreed. "I wonder what that might cost."

Zed rubbed his clean-shaven jaw. "I can ask around and get some prices for you."

"We should turn it into a zoo," Will said. "And we can fill it with tigers and bears and elephants. And then we wouldn't have to travel so far in a van to visit the zoo in Philadelphia."

"And who will feed the tigers and bears?" Emma asked.

"I can do it," Will said. "I'll toss the animals some meat with a pitchfork."

"I can give the elephants peanuts," Beth offered, her youthful face aglow with the notion of a backyard zoo. Dear little Beth had not even been to the zoo in Philadelphia yet, but one of her favorite picture books was about a trip to the zoo, and she knew that elephants were one of Gott's creations.

Fanny smiled at the children's creativity. "Wouldn't that be fun? Too bad we don't have the space for wild elephants. We have to be content with our horses and chickens."

When the light meal was finished, Zed went off to survey the barn with Caleb.

Fanny was rinsing plates in the sink when she saw the two of them cross the yard. There was something reassuring about the way Zed walked, sure and smooth, like thick molasses. Zed would make a fine husband for a very lucky Amish girl. Such a good young man with a heart of gold. Oh, he was still in the doghouse now, but the shadow of his life with the Englishers would fade over time. Soon all the single women in the community would see Zed as a right fine catch. Fanny had a flash of Zed being followed by a row of his own little ducklings, and she wiped her hands on a towel before dipping down to hug Beth and tickle little Tommy. Ya, she wished Zed the joy of children.

"Do you want Gabe to help with the carriage house?" Emma asked as she dried a fistful of forks and knives. "He told me he could find the time."

"That would be wonderful. I think we're going to need lots of spare hands." *And it's a good excuse for you to have Gabe here at the house,* Fanny thought with a secret smile as she watched her oldest daughter stack the forks in the drawer. It was tempting to tease Emma, but Fanny didn't want to ruffle the very serious young woman's feathers. Besides, Fanny understood the sweetness of true love. When you were inside the wondrous bubble, you didn't want folks on the outside poking at you.

With the dishes done, Fanny yawned, thinking of the chores not even started yet.

"Did Lizzy and the baby have you up all night?" Emma asked.

"I got some sleep. And, Emma, you have to see the baby. Such a cute little thing, with a crown of blond hair like his mother."

Smoothing down the edges of her apron, Emma smiled. "I'm so happy for Lizzy. A baby boy, you said?"

Fanny nodded as she imagined Emma with a baby of her own. That wouldn't be far off now ... just a few years. A knot of emotion grew in Fanny's throat at the thought of dear Emma caring for a babe of her own.

So many changes! This family had endured such sadness this past year. Fanny prayed that the changes ahead of them would be for the better. Weddings and babies ... many babies, Gott willing.

Emma offered to tidy the bedrooms upstairs, and Fanny set to sweeping the downstairs. She had told Lizzy to go easy on the chores for a few days. New mothers here in Halfway had to be reminded of that. They didn't get a little break, like the women in the birth centers back home in Sugar Valley.

Such fond memories Fanny had of that place! Fanny's grandmother had turned the Doddy house into a little retreat with beds and cribs—a place where all the Amish women in Sugar Valley used to go to have their babies. "Going to Martha's," a mother would say, and she'd meet the doctor there and get a bed to stay in for three whole days while Martha and her helpers cooked meals and cared for the baby. Women loved going to Martha's.

Curious about the women who always left Martha's happily, each with a baby bundled in her arms, Fanny had made excuses for peeking into the building behind their house. She brought cookies and apples. She offered to sweep the floor or wash the windows. Mammi put her to work, giving her light chores and letting her wait on the mothers or change diapers. Then one day, two women were having their babies at the same time, and Fanny was allowed to stay and help. She had watched in wonder as Mammi tended the women with soothing words and warm cloths on their foreheads. She witnessed pain, but few complaints. And when a baby finally slid into the doctor's hands, Fanny was hooked. This was a miracle she longed to be a part of, again and again.

Now, as she swept the crumbs and dirt into a dustpan, Fanny wished once again that there was a birth center close by, here in Lancaster County.

At a lull in Lizzy's labor, Fanny had spun her tale about the birth centers back in Ohio. Lizzy had said it sounded wonderful good, and Joe had wished they had a place like that here in Lancaster, so the docs would know right where to go when they were called. It was a very good point that Joe made. If they had a place like Martha's here, a birthing center . . . would Anna take to it? The midwife was in her sixties, slowing down a bit. She might like a place closer to home, even walking distance from her house.

With Tommy on her hip, Fanny headed out to talk with Caleb and Zed about a new possibility for the carriage house.

7

The adrenaline rush of delivering Lizzy and Joe King's baby was still thrumming in Meg's veins as she stowed her equipment in the back of her car. Add to that the bubbly joy of attraction to a tall, handsome man, and she had half a mind to dance up the inn steps, Ginger Rogers–style. It was nice to meet someone like Jack, even if it was just a short interlude. Sometimes small moments sparkled like stars. Little gems you could put into your pocket to save for the sad times when you needed them.

She went into the kitchen looking for her sister, but found Shandell scrubbing down the countertops.

"Meg!" The young woman flung her arms in the air with a gaping look of shock. "Oh, my gosh! Zoey told me you had to leave the breakfast service to go off and help Fanny deliver a baby. I couldn't believe it. How'd it go?" Shandell could never be faulted for lack of enthusiasm.

"There were a few complications, but it all worked out fine."

Meg poured herself some hot water from one of the urns they kept in the cubby beside the kitchen. "Lizzy and Joe King have a sweet baby boy."

"Lizzy and Joe King? I think they're Rachel's cousins. I'll bet Rachel's family is thrilled. The Amish love babies. And you delivered him? Or did you help the doctor? How did that work?"

"The doctor couldn't make it in time. So, yeah." Dunking a tea bag in her cup, Meg cracked a smile and chuckled. "I did it." After all the angst, all the fear that it would never happen again, she'd delivered a healthy baby. The personal victory was sweet.

"I didn't know you were a midwife." Shandell tossed away the bunch of paper towels and came around the counter. "Why didn't you say anything?"

"I was on a break." Meg faced the young woman, wondering how her sister had managed to find such an earnest, clearheaded employee. That was the luck of Zoey; she had that blithe, unblinking enthusiasm that seemed to attract others of the same ilk.

"So, wait. That's why you were here, working as the cook. Kind of like a working vacation?"

"I was trying for the vacation part, but as you can see, my sister doesn't believe in idle time. And where is Zoey?"

"She made a run into Paradise."

Meg took a sip of her tea, thinking of how Zoey had saved her from that dark room . . . saved her from herself. And today, pushing her into that buggy with a worried expectant father, Zoey had forced her to face her fears.

My sister should have gotten a degree in psychology.

"So, the kitchen is done for the day," Shandell reported. "Zoey asked me to check out our store of eggs and cheese and stuff, and we're good to go for tomorrow. I transferred those Amish recipes to cards and put them in this drawer." Shandell opened a drawer to show Meg, and that's when the realization swiftly hit Meg.

She wouldn't be here for breakfast tomorrow.

She had to get back to Pittsburgh, back into the thick of the problem. No one was going to step in and fix it for her; she needed to buck up and do it herself.

"Someone else is going to handle breakfast," Meg said. "I'm going upstairs to pack. It's time for me to get back to my job in Pittsburgh." *Time to see if I still have a job in Pittsburgh.*

Shandell closed the drawer with a confused expression. "Who's going to cook for the inn? Can I give it a try?"

Meg shook her head. "You'll need to talk with Zoey about that, but I think she'd be happy to give you a shot at it." She lifted her cup to Shandell in a salute. "Thanks for all your help here. You have a great attitude, Shandell."

The young woman smiled. "Now I just need the credentials to back it up, but I'm working on it. I'm on track to get my GED by the end of summer, and then community college in the fall."

Meg opened her arms wide to give Shandell a hug, and then proceeded upstairs to pack.

⚭

"I am sorry to see you go, but I get it." Zoey was perched against the pillows of Meg's bed, wiggling her toes so that she could admire her glittery pedicure. "So you're not mad at me for making you go and deliver that baby?"

"I'm always annoyed at you for something," Meg admitted.

Zoey arched one eyebrow as she folded her arms across her chest. "The joy of sisterhood."

"But going to help was the right thing to do." T-shirt in hand, Meg perched beside her sister for a moment as she recalled the happy couple curled up on the sofa around their baby. They had needed her today. Although Fanny might have been able to untangle the cord, the Amish midwife's kit did not contain suctioning tools to clear the baby's airways. Childbirth could be complicated. Sometimes, serious intervention was necessary.

"I wish you could have seen them—a new family. Once we cleaned the baby up, you could see his crown of golden hair, just like his mother. And a little button nose. And Lizzy and Joe were all over him, talking and cooing and cuddling. A newborn is such a magnificent thing—a true miracle. In all the turmoil over my investigation, I lost sight of what really matters."

"That is so beautiful!" Zoey pressed a hand to her throat. "You're getting me all choked up."

"Being there this morning, I knew what I had to do. All the training and experience, it was at my fingertips. I'm good at what I do."

"Yes, you are. When my time comes, you're the one I want yelling at me to breathe and relax so that I don't break every bone in Tate's hand."

"I care about my patients. I keep up with the latest technologies and developments. I'm not afraid to call an ambulance and transport to the hospital when a patient needs it."

"That's right, honey." Zoey patted Meg's shoulder. "You have always done the right thing. Even when I tried to keep you from telling Dad who ate all the Oreos, you had to confess. Moral and honest to a tee."

"The charges against me are wrong," Meg said, folding the T-shirt in her lap. "I didn't break protocol for the Collier baby. I called for transport to the hospital, but the ambulance couldn't get through."

"I was wondering when you were going to tell me about that nightmare case." Zoey's lips were pursed now, about as serious as she ever got. "Tell me about it. I've been dying to get your side of the story."

The icy desolation of that terrible night came rushing back to Meg. So far she had only told her sister a few details—that she had been called to the scene by a neighbor of the pregnant woman, who didn't know her well at all, but had taken pity on her.

"She's owned the place for about a year now," the neighbor had told Meg over the phone, "but I've only seen her a handful of times. Didn't even know she was expecting a child until she called the house and woke us up. My husband called 911, but the local rescue squad is clearing a crash on the bridge. There's black ice everywhere. They don't think that they'll be getting out here anytime soon. I saw from the phone book that you live in the area. Maybe you can get here." The neighbor, Nora Landers, said she was going to stay with Ms. Collier: "But I'm not much good to her. I'm no doctor."

Meg had told Nora she would try to make it out to the Collier place, but made no promises in this weather. Hanging up, she fell back against her pillow, teased by the temptation of warmth and sleep.

Deedee Collier was not her responsibility. Most midwives did not take on clients already in labor. A good midwife worked with a mother throughout her pregnancy, developing a relationship and monitoring her medical condition. Meg had no obligation to brave the bad weather to serve Ms. Collier.

But as she rolled over in bed, her eyes wide open, she felt a tug of sympathy. Denying this woman help seemed ruthless. She couldn't ignore the pang of duty deep inside.

"So I got dressed," Meg told her sister. "With all-wheel and studded tires, I figured I could make it. I drove out to Deedee Collier's place at the end of a dirt road that was like an Olympic luge run. It was treacherous. Even my Subaru was slip-sliding around. But I made it—only to find complications. Deedee was semiconscious; her vitals were weak. The baby was breech, and the fetal heart rate was slow. There's no way of knowing how long it had been that way, but it's a sign of fetal distress. She needed a C-section. I called 911 again, and was told it would be at least two hours. That was going to be too late, so I went to bring my car closer to the house, figuring that Nora and I could load Deedee into the backseat and I'd drive her there myself. But I slipped on the porch steps and fell hard on the ice. So hard that I saw stars and blacked out for a moment. Such a terrible night." Meg told her sister that no state allowed a midwife to perform a cesarean, with good reason, and that had been what Deedee needed. With tears dripping down her cheeks, Meg had worked to keep the mother alive while the baby slipped away, a light gone dark before it had a chance to shine in the world.

"The ambulance didn't arrive until after sunrise. They transported Deedee to the hospital for a C-section. The baby was stillborn."

"That's pretty different from the story that aired on the news," Zoey said. "They made it sound like you were a home-birth fanatic, that you and Deedee had made a pact to refuse help from any outside sources."

Meg shrugged and pushed off the bed. "The media puts their own spin on stories." She dropped the T-shirt into her open suitcase and added her hairbrush to her cosmetics case.

"So you didn't do anything wrong. You've always said that every birth plan has an emergency option—a way to get to a hospital or a doctor. It's not your fault that Deedee Collier wasn't prepared for the worst."

"It's not. But as a medical professional, I'm held to a different standard. The board needs to make sure that I'm not a rogue midwife with an inflated view of her skills."

"Why don't you get the facts out there?" Zoey asked. "The true story."

"It's not my place to divulge a client's information. Besides, I'm under investigation, and Ms. Collier keeps threatening a lawsuit."

"It sounds to me like that woman doesn't have a chance. She had no prenatal care, and you did call for help. Even the neighbor called for help. What is wrong with those damned reporters? They just give people like Deedee Collier fuel for the fire."

"Collier probably wouldn't win a lawsuit. She has a history of diabetes and alcohol abuse. But even when she backs down, after the investigation is resolved and I'm cleared, the real tragedy is that a baby didn't make it."

"You're right. That's the sad part." With a deep breath, Zoey leaned back on the pillows and pressed one palm to her belly. "So why the sudden rush to get back to Pittsburgh? I thought you were going to stick around here until things blow over back home."

"That was my plan, and it's tempting, but today I realized that I'm wasting my talents in the kitchen. You know that Bible verse about letting your light shine? It may sound corny, but when I'm delivering a baby, that's when I'm shining. God blessed me with the understanding and instinct and skill to do it well. If that's where he wants me to be, then I figure I'd better clear up this mess and get back to my calling."

"Can't you let it be for a few more weeks?" Zoey asked. "You've got nowhere else that you have to be right now, and Tate and I need the help. I need a cook right now, and down the road, I'm going to need a midwife."

This time, her sister's comment tweaked Meg's attention. "Zoey?" She looked down at her sister, reclining on the bed, and suddenly it was clear. "Are you pregnant?"

"It's about time you figured that out. Why do you think I've been downing all that milk and doing all this nesting, decorating every room in this inn?"

"That's wonderful. The best news ever!" Meg wedged beside her sister on the bed to give her a hug. "Ohmigosh!" she squeaked.

"I know, I know, I know!" Zoey shrieked in response as she rocked her sister back and forth. As Meg leaned back, Zoey pulled her smock tight over her belly. "And you couldn't tell? I'm eight weeks along. Haven't popped yet."

"I thought you were just dressing more modestly to match the look of the Amish inn. And you and Tate were going to wait. You said you wanted to get the business set up first."

"The doctor warned us that waiting was a bad idea, especially with my endometriosis."

"I know how that is." Meg and her sister suffered from the same condition, a disorder that could hinder conception.

"When the doctor told us that it was now or maybe never, we thought we should throw out the long-term plan and get going. So . . ." Zoey patted her belly. "Are you sure baby Jordan can't convince you to stay on?"

Meg put her hand over her sister's and looked into her eyes. "I'm so happy for you, Zoey, but I gotta go now."

Delivering the King baby had opened a window to the future. Now she knew what she had to do. No more sitting in a dark room, and no more hiding in her sister's kitchen. It was time to fight back; time to press her case and persist until she got justice. She was sorry for Deedee Collier and her infant, but sometimes doctors and nurses lost patients through no fault of their own.

It was time to face the music . . . time to take her life back.

"But I'll be back in plenty of time to help with baby Jordan," she promised her sister. "Just take your vitamins, keep up with your prenatal care, and start reading. Call me if you have any questions about anything."

"You know I will." Zoey went to the closet and tugged Meg's two summer dresses from their hangers. "Don't forget these."

"Right. My vast collection of dresses. I'm going to need them when I meet with the nursing board." Meg strapped down the clothes in her suitcase and zipped it shut. "If I forgot anything, I'll be back for it. When are you due?"

"January."

"Then I'll be back before Christmas." That meant that Meg wouldn't be able to take on many new clients in Pittsburgh if she got her license back; she would want a clear schedule so that she could commit herself to being with her sister. "That'll be a real vacation for me. In the meantime, I've got some great books to loan you."

"I've already got a slew of maternity books on my nightstand, and I've been seeing Dr. Trueherz. Everyone here loves him."

"Well, I hope he has a better GPS than the doctor on call today."

Zoey kissed her sister's cheek and patted her shoulder. "I'm not worried. I've got an expert midwife in the family."

Her words brought tears to Meg's eyes. What would she do without her sister?

Promising to return in December to be by Zoey's side, Meg packed up her car and headed back home to mend her broken life.

8

After a few days of rain, it felt good to be out in the yard, soaking up fresh air and sunshine. Zed had moved his worktable outside the carriage house, and Fanny smiled as she walked by on the way to the garden. He'd been working here a week now, and yet somehow it seemed as if he'd been here for months, measuring and sawing and hammering, working steadily around them.

Morning coffee was a pleasure with Zed, who brought a measure of calm to the noisy, bustling kitchen. He was quick to pick up Tommy when he was fussing or to set Will straight when the boy taunted his little sister. In the shelter of the Lapp home, Zed showed himself to be thoughtful, smart, and strong. Not at all the painfully quiet man folks talked about! She had worried about having an outsider in their home every day, but Fanny found that she was glad to have Zed here, and it was clear that he felt right at home with them.

Bent over the workbench, Zed pumped the saw with steady

strokes. She saw determination and strength tempered by a simple peace. Whatever turbulence had sent him off into the English world had been long resolved, that much she knew. Lots of folk were curious about why Zed had left their community and what he'd done out there, but not Fanny. She was interested in what had drawn him home again: the love for Gott and his family, the desire to live simply in Gott's footsteps.

She waited as he cut through a plank until the end piece dropped away.

"Will you be having lunch with us?" she asked. "There are tomato and cheese sandwiches and a salad from the garden."

"That sounds delicious." He blew the wood dust away, then rubbed the edge with his fingers, testing it. "I brought a cooler, but let me know and I'll join you. I'll never turn down something fresh from the garden."

She nodded at the wood. "Now where will that fit in the big jigsaw puzzle?"

His dark eyes softened as he held up the board. "What do you think?"

"I think I'm better at assembling jigsaw puzzles that sit on the kitchen table. Putting together a whole house? Not so much."

"But it's just one piece at a time, the same as your puzzle. Step by step. It's easy as making a cake. You just follow your recipe."

Fanny glanced up toward the roof of the carriage house. "That is quite a large cake you're working on, and I never had to saw and hammer to make a cake rise."

With a gentle smile, he tucked the wood plank under one arm. "Kumm. I'll show you where this fits in."

The piece of wood was part of the new frame for one of the windows, which Zed planned to install the next day.

"It will be nice to have new windows," she said. "There's something sad about windows that are all boarded up. Like missing teeth. The building had a crooked smile."

There was amusement in his eyes. "In a few days your carriage house will be smiling again." He fitted the board snugly into the opening, hammering it into place.

I could stand here and watch all morning, Fanny thought. It was a wonder, the way things took shape under Zed's hands. Gray, soft chips fell away. A simple board was pared into shape and hammered into place, forming a clean, new window frame. He was quick to clear away the rotten wood and wise enough to know what to leave alone. She wanted to linger, to watch, but chores wouldn't get done on their own.

"We'll eat in an hour or so," she told him, heading off to check on the children. Fanny paused at the edge of the garden to watch Will and Beth lean close to tug on a tall weed that had insinuated itself in the center of their tomato patch. The rains that had kept them out of the garden the past few days had nurtured more than the vegetables.

"Did you loosen the soil?" Fanny called. "That'll help it come out more easily."

"I can get it," Will insisted, clenching his teeth as he gave another pull.

"It's stubborn, Mamm," Beth announced.

"Sometimes they don't want to let go." Fanny glanced over at the garden tools Will had fetched from the shed. "Where's the spade, Will? The one you like to use?"

Will shrugged. "It's gone, Mamm. I think a robber stole it."

"A robber?" Fanny pointed a shovel at the base of the green shoot and stepped on it with her sneakered foot. The blade of the shovel sank into the soil. "Now why would a robber take our garden spade?"

"Because he's a thief," said Will. "That's what he does. He takes things."

"Mmm. And why would he take the spade and leave everything else in the shed?" Fanny asked as she wiggled the shovel to loosen the weed.

"I don't know." Will shook his head. "I guess he needed to do some digging."

Will's story was quite creative, but the boy needed to know that it was a sin to lie. She had never come across this problem with Caleb or the older girls. Will was an unusual flower in the garden, to say the least. Sometimes she worried that he misbehaved out of grief over his dat. She understood the sorrow, but she had to teach her son to handle it in an honest way. Fanny kept quiet as she pulled out the shovel and watched the children descend on the weed and remove it with a final tug.

"Got it!" Will held it up proudly.

"I got it, too," Beth said.

"It's nothing to fight about. There are plenty more weeds to pull, though none quite as tall as that one." She set Will to the task of weed pulling and gave Beth a basket to collect the fat tomatoes that had fallen from the vine in the storm. Some were still green, but they could be pickled or sliced, breaded, and fried for a tart and tasty dish. The hour passed quickly and the children gleefully carried buckets of weeds to the compost bins on their way back to the house.

After everyone washed up, they brought the lunch things out to the little green table in the shade by the box hedge. During the meal, Fanny brought up the subject of the missing spade, and Will repeated his story about how a robber had stolen it from the shed.

Zed held a sandwich aloft and studied Will with thoughtful eyes, though he reserved comment.

"That would be such a shame. It was your favorite garden tool,"

Fanny said as she poured Zed more lemonade. Will had often pointed out how the small spade fit his hand just right. In fact, last time they gardened she had let him use the spade to play farmer, with the promise that he would return it to the shed by the end of the day.

"I know." Will looked down at his paper plate. "I feel sad."

"Well, if someone else needed that spade so much that he stole it, then Gott bless him." Zed spoke in a quiet voice, without accusation. "I hope he uses it to grow some food to fill his belly."

Will's lower lip jutted out as he nodded.

∽∾

The matter of the missing spade was dropped until the next morning, when Zed appeared at the door, hands behind his back.

"Good morning," Fanny said, looking up from the counter where she was cutting up leftover chicken for a salad. "Would you like coffee?"

"A cup would be nice." Zed remained in the doorway, looking over at the table where Will and Beth were finishing bowls of cereal. Tommy raised his hands from the tray of his highchair and gurgled a greeting.

Zed touched the baby's cheek, then turned to the children at the table. "Funny thing happened this morning. I was walking around the back of the carriage house when I found this on the ground." He held up the spade. Its blade was now orange with rust from sitting in the rain.

Handing Zed a mug, Fanny noticed that Will's face had turned a rosy shade of pink. "That looks like our spade," she said. "Doesn't it, Will?"

The boy crumpled over the table. "It is our spade. I left it out in the rain, and now it's all rusty. I'm sorry, Mamm."

"But what about the robber?" Beth asked.

"There was no robber." Fanny's gaze remained steady on her son.

"I made that part up, because I knew it was my fault the spade got ruined. I was supposed to put it away."

"That's right," Fanny said. "And now you understand why it's a sin to lie."

Will stared into his cereal bowl. "It made my tummy ache. And after I made up one story, I had to keep lying so you wouldn't find out what I did."

"My mamm used to tell me that one lie brings the next," Fanny said.

"And now the spade is ruined," Will said sadly.

"Maybe not." Fanny took the hand shovel from Zed. "You see how this part is covered with rust? The rust eats away at the metal. If we don't get the rust off, it will weaken the blade until one day, it will break. But there's a way to fix it." She handed it over to her son. "That will be your chore."

"How do I do it?"

"White vinegar," Zed said. "The metal part needs to soak overnight. Then you'll take a wire brush to it. Go on out and get a bucket and I'll show you."

Will dropped down from the table, gripping the spade. Then, like a gust of wind, he blew out of the kitchen. Through the kitchen window, Fanny saw him running toward the shed.

"He got out of here fast," Zed observed.

"Probably trying to stay ahead of a punishment." Fanny turned to Zed, grateful for his calming presence. "Thank you. With you showing him how to fix the spade, I think the lesson will stick better."

"I'm happy to do it." Zed picked a cherry tomato from the salad and popped it in his mouth. "There's nothing like a garden tomato."

She nodded, still concerned about Will. "Sometimes I wonder if Will misbehaves to get extra attention. He never got into trouble before his dat died."

"That may be true. Or he might just be a normal boy who gets into mischief. If it is about missing Tom, there's really no way of explaining things to Will, is there?"

She leaned over Tommy to kiss the top of his head. "That's true. None of us understands Gott's plan."

"He'll be fine." Zed drank down the last of his coffee. "This home has taught him much about love. He'll figure out the importance of honesty, too. Now . . ." He put his mug in the sink. "Do you have any white vinegar?"

As Fanny fetched the vinegar, she realized what a blessing it was to have Zed here for Will's sake. There was so much a boy needed to learn from a man, and Zed was a willing teacher. They were all benefiting from Zed's many acts of charity. Gott worked in wondrous ways.

PART TWO

Into the Crossroads

Verily, verily, I say unto you,
That ye shall weep and lament,
but the world shall rejoice:
and ye shall be sorrowful,
but your sorrow shall be turned into joy.

—JOHN 16:20

9

*T*here was contentment in the rhythm of quilting. Fanny let her hand pause a moment as she gazed fondly over the other women, their white-capped heads bent over the quilt. A cloak of peace had fallen over the garden at the Stoltzfus house, where a quilting bee was in progress. The charity quilt had already been completed, and Lovina had started the women on a second project. Pressing the needle through in short, regular stitches, Fanny looked across the table and noticed Anna Beiler watching her. A curious smile pinched the older woman's face.

"Such relaxing work, I'm about to doze off," Fanny said aloud, stifling a yawn. "It's a good thing you're back, Anna. It wouldn't be possible for me to be a midwife and enjoy gatherings like this."

"There's plenty of time in the day when I've got an empty house at home," Anna said. "If I'm out late tending to a mother, I take cat-naps all day long."

"Well, I'm relieved to have you back," said Fanny, "and I know I'm not alone."

"We all missed you, Anna," agreed Lovina Stoltzfus, hostess of the event. "How are your daughter and her family?"

Anna told the women about the wedding festivities in the Old Order Amish community where her daughter lived. "Two weddings a week, while I was there," Anna said. "I was invited to three of them. Wonderful good receptions. But weddings in late June—it just doesn't seem right." In most of Lancaster's Amish communities, November was the traditional month for weddings, but in Ohio, where Fanny had grown up, weddings happened in June and November.

"I think I would like having two wedding seasons in the year." Lovina's daughter Annie spoke with a bright smile. "Sometimes, it's hard to wait until November."

"Are you telling us you're waiting?" rasped an elderly woman, Nell King. It was no secret that Annie had been courting Jonah King. "So we can expect a wedding here in November, then."

A few women chuckled as Annie's hands flew to her face to hide the rosy blush of embarrassment on her cheeks.

"But I didn't say that," Annie insisted. It was traditional for wedding plans to stay within the family until the couple's engagement was announced in church.

"It's all right, child," Anna said. "Anyone with eyes can see that you and Jonah King are two peas in a pod."

Annie lowered her head in deference to the older midwife, who caught Fanny yawning. "Don't fall asleep on us now, Fanny."

"Still catching up on my rest. How do you keep up, Anna? Running here and there, often in the middle of the night."

"There's little joy in hitching up a horse in the dark of night," Anna agreed.

"I know how that goes." Joan Fisher's dark brows arched down in a bad-tempered expression. "We're out hitching up the buggy most days at three A.M. It's gotten so I can put the harness on with my eyes closed."

Some of the women chuckled, but Fanny ducked her head and tended to her work. She had learned that it was best to avoid David's mother—best to dodge his entire family as much as possible. Sometimes it still prickled to be around them—a constant thorn in her side.

When David had died, there had been some talk about his life being spared had he gone into the family bakery; it was verhuddelt talk, as far as Fanny was concerned. The bishop had clamped down on the gossip, but once the word was out, it did its damage like a slug in the garden. Nowadays, Fanny counted her blessings that the bishop had helped her move on from David's family. Oh, the Fishers had disapproved when she had taken up with Thomas and his children, but once Fanny and Tom had married, their displeasure had faded.

"Baking is an early business," Lovina commented.

"Early to bed, early to rise." Joan's stern brown eyes caught Fanny's for a moment until Fanny quickly looked down at her stitching. "It's not a bad way of life."

"At least you keep regular hours," said Anna. "I go at all times, in all weather, and I'm not a youngster anymore. I've grown weary of fighting winter's snow and ice. That's why I think your idea is a good one, Fanny. A birth center that I could walk to, that would be right good."

A smile welled up inside Fanny at the midwife's kind words. When Fanny first mentioned the notion to Anna, the older woman had liked the idea, but her stoic expression had left Fanny wondering if Anna would support a birth center.

"What's that, now?" Lovina asked. "Do you mean a clinic here in Halfway?"

"Not quite," Fanny answered. "This is just a place for women to have their babies."

"Our town had a birth center, back in Ohio," said Mary Yoder. "Most Amish women went there."

Pausing with her stitching, Fanny explained how her grandmother had converted their Doddy house into a place for women to go to have their babies. "We'd like to do the same with our carriage house, once we get it fixed up. It would be a place for women to come and stay a couple of days."

"Imagine, getting off your feet for a few days," Lovina said with wonder in her voice.

"My sister says it's very good indeed," added Mary. "Every woman gets a bed and good food and plenty of back rubs for a few days. I wish we had something like that here."

"You see, Fanny?" Anna peered over her spectacles. "There's a real need, and you know that business would be good. There's plenty more babies to be born. I can barely keep up anymore."

The women were enthusiastic, the conversation brimming over with questions about how it might come to be. Even Joan nodded in agreement. Fanny beamed with pleasure.

"So you can tell Caleb that my husband will lend a hand if he needs help on the carriage house," Lovina offered. "Aaron is good with repairs."

"Denki," Fanny said gratefully. "I'll tell Caleb about the offer. Right now Zed Miller is doing a lot of the work, and he's quite handy."

"Well, that explains one mystery," said Dorcas Fisher. "I was wondering why Zed Miller is spending so much time at your place."

"That's right." Fanny lifted her gaze cautiously to her former sister-in-law, and then quickly stared back at her stitching. Although Fanny harbored no malice toward Dorcas, she tried to steer clear of the woman who had dropped her like a hot potato after Fanny went to work for Thomas Lapp, soon after David's death. Many of the Fishers thought it was disrespectful to David for Fanny to take such a job, but at that time she had no choice. The Fishers had no work for her at the bakery, and she had suddenly found herself a woman alone, without any income. When the bishop had suggested that she care for Tom and his children, Fanny had jumped at the chance to do what she did best—running a household and taking good care of other folk.

"Are you keeping an eye on Zed Miller now, Dorcas?" Lovina asked in that smooth way she had of turning a conversation.

"I could be." Dorcas lifted her chin, a bit defiant. Thirty-two and never married, Dorcas Fisher was a hardworking woman with strong opinions. Fanny had always felt a little sorry for her not having found a husband, but what man wanted to tangle with an angry bull? "I know Zed's been out to Fanny's place because he told me. The past two weeks, when he comes into the bakery, that's where he's spent the day."

"I heard he's getting baptized," said Sally Reil, another widow, with ten children. "It looks like Zed has come back to us for good."

"Let's hope so," Dorcas said as she tugged a stitch through. "Zed is just the kind of man we need around here. A bit older and wiser."

Although Fanny kept quiet, she did agree. For single women in their thirties who were looking for a husband, it was slim pickings. A man like Zed was like a breath of fresh air.

"He's right around your age, isn't he?" Lovina asked Dorcas.

"Give or take a few years." Dorcas grinned. "I'm beginning to think there's a reason he comes into the bakery every Tuesday. I know he likes my bread, and we all know the best way to a man's heart is through his stomach."

The women chuckled over the harmless comment, but Fanny felt a little sick at the thought that Zed might have eyes for Dorcas

Fisher. That shouldn't matter to her at all, but somehow it did. Shaken, she kept quiet until Dorcas prodded her.

"So if you're seeing Zed Miller day in and day out, you know him best. Tell us about him. What's Zed really like?"

"It's hard to say." Fanny pressed her lips together, stalling.

She could tell them how he bent down so that he could be eye-to-eye with the children when he spoke to them.

She could tell them about the slow drawl of his movements, full of care and purpose. Nothing was rushed or hurried, and yet so much got done. In just two weeks, new windows had been popped in and secured. Rotted beams and trim had been replaced, all under Zed's skilled hands.

Or she might share how much she enjoyed his quiet presence, how it was the perfect complement to their active house, bustling with rambunctious children and determined young adults. Zed seemed equally comfortable whether holding the baby or teaching Will how to swing a hammer or discussing how to install plumbing with Caleb.

There were oh so many things she could tell them about Zed, but Fanny knew that each little detail would reveal too much. Her words would tell them that she was growing attached to this man.

Fortunately, she was saved when Lovina jumped in.

"Come now, Dorcas, you're asking Fanny to talk about someone behind his back, and gossip is a sin."

"Is it gossip when we're saying nice things?" Dorcas asked, her brows raised in a sweet expression.

"There's not much to say about a man as quiet as Zed," said Becca Yoder. "I've tried to get him talking a few times, but he's silent as a stone."

Some of us don't need to fill the quiet spaces with chatter, thought Fanny.

"There's nothing wrong with a quiet man," said Lovina.

"I wouldn't know," Mary Yoder said with a wink. "I can't get my Eli to shut up."

Their joking eased Fanny's tension for now, but as the women chatted, she took note of the single women in the room who might be interested in Zed. Maybe she felt stirred out of a need to protect him, like an older sister taking care of her brother. Ya, that was it. A good sister—nothing more.

10

Seated in a lone chair that was surrounded by the thirteen-member nursing board, Meg felt as if she were facing the fire and fury of the Wizard of Oz. The panel of nurses and laypeople was intimidating due to the mere fact that they outnumbered her. Add to that the vindictive style of Peter, one of the registered nurses on the board, and Meg felt her knees knocking together under the table.

Surrender, Dorothy.

Meg wiped her damp palms on her thighs, trying to calm herself with a little perspective. The inquisition was almost over; soon it would be behind her, and that would be a relief.

Only two weeks had passed since she'd left Halfway. On her way back to Pittsburgh, Meg had stopped in a gas station and put a call through to the state nursing board about scheduling a hearing. They had agreed to hold an emergency session, though the first possible date had been two weeks away, which had seemed like an eternity.

Ending the call, she had noticed a text message from an unknown number.

This is Jack Woods. Got your digits from Zoey. Tell me that's okay or else I'll bug off.

Joy rippled through Meg from head to toe. Jack was geographically undesirable, but it was nice to be courted. Besides, she was in need of a friend. She texted back with news that she had just scheduled a hearing with the board and was eager to set things straight.

You go, girl, he shot back. *And the truth shall set you free.*

That had been the first of Jack's texts of wisdom. A few times a day, he sent her words of wisdom, Amish proverbs or Bible verses. He wrote things like *You can't keep trouble from visiting, but you don't have to offer it a chair* and *Let it shine!* Jack's upbeat text messages lifted her spirits.

In response, she sent him photos of her kids—the babies she had delivered, who were now toddlers or in grammar school. Since she was unable to practice, she used the time to connect with the families she had served. It was always a wonder to see the older versions of the babies she had delivered, to see the toddlers as they learned to walk or the older ones as they tossed a football in the yard with siblings. That had made those two weeks fly by.

Although she kept sipping water, Meg's mouth was dry and pasty. She wondered if the doctors on the medical board noticed the way her lips stuck together when she tried to speak, making a ridiculous smacking sound.

"We've gone over your statement, Ms. Harper." Peter was picking on her again. She couldn't see his eyes because of the silver glare on his spectacles, but his crankiness came through loud and clear in his tone of voice. "Quite frankly, I don't understand why you thought you could handle such a high-risk case. The mother was overweight and diabetic. No prenatal care. What was your reasoning for agreeing to the home delivery?"

"Ms. Collier was not a typical client for me." Meg explained how she worked with her clients throughout their pregnancies, how she kept charts on them and came to know their medical profiles and personal lives. She was grateful to see a few of the nurses' heads nodding when she emphasized that a trusting relationship between mother and midwife was key to a smooth delivery.

"Unfortunately, Ms. Collier was determined to have her child at home, with or without medical assistance. Afterward, I learned that she had not seen a medical professional for her diabetes for two years, and . . ." There was an embarrassing catch of emotion in her voice, and Meg cleared her throat and went on. "As you know, Ms. Collier did not receive prenatal care. I don't condone this. But I made the choice to try to help her when her neighbor called me and reported that the local paramedics probably would not make it to the scene in time."

Her statement was followed by silence and a silver-spectacled glare from Peter. Was it a sympathetic silence? Meg didn't know what to make of the fact that most of the people facing her from the board table did not look her in the eye. Were they looking away out of disapproval, or simply bored with the proceedings?

"Ms. Harper?" A female nurse named Judith, a small woman with blond hair that was a sharp contrast to her black blouse, spoke up for the first time. "The sequence of events you describe in this case is nightmarish. Quite frankly, I don't know what I would have done if I'd been in your situation. Can you tell us what time you called 911 and what stage of labor Ms. Collier was in at that point?"

Meg answered as truthfully as she could, trying to keep the fear she'd experienced that night and her subsequent resentment of Deedee Collier from her voice. There were a few more questions, many of them covering the very same information she had provided in her account of the birth. Had they not read her report, or were they trying to trip her up? Meg didn't know if the board had a psychological strategy for these hearings, but she tried to stay focused and honest. There was too much at stake here to let herself cave in to the emotions that tugged at her from all directions.

At last, the commissioner sitting at the center of the dais held up her hand and asked if there were any more questions. When there was no response, Audra Machen asked Meg to step out of the room while they deliberated.

Outside in the waiting room, Meg couldn't bear to sit. Hugging her folder of notes to her chest, she paced from the glass door to the sofa and back again. In her heart, she had known that it was time to push this issue with the board, time to have the hearing and get her license reinstated. The dust had settled and the issues were clear now. They would see that she had handled the situation with the correct medical protocol. Wouldn't they?

Her stomach sank as she began to think of the worst-case scenario. What if they didn't reinstate her license? She needed a backup . . . a plan B. Oh, no, no. She couldn't bear to give up the one profession she was made for.

Just then the door to the boardroom opened, and Audra summoned her back inside. Meg followed, not even trying to read into the poker-faced expressions of the thirteen people staring her down.

The commissioner began with an explanation of the emergency session, how it was important to put a licensed practitioner back to work as soon as possible if a complaint turned out to be unfounded.

Meg stared down at the floor, not sure where this was going.

"In this case, the expedient hearing proved worthwhile, because we have found that the charges do not have foundation. We are reinstating your license, without reprimand."

Meg lifted her chin, her heart dancing. "Thank you," she said, but some of the members of the board were already out of their chairs, collecting papers. For them, this was business as usual. But for Meg, it was the end of an extraordinary nightmare.

Half an hour later, Meg was still in a pleasant daze as she rode the elevator down from the sixth floor. The commissioner had shown her to the administrative office, which issued licenses, and the woman there helped her through the paperwork to update her profile and reinstate her license. She was in good standing now, free to practice as a midwife anywhere in the state.

"Congratulations on being reinstated."

Meg turned to the other woman in the elevator. It was one of the board members, Judith. "Thanks. I'm sorry I didn't notice you there. I'm still in a daze. The last few months have been crazy."

"I'll say. We don't see cases like yours too often. You really went through the wringer. I know it must be extremely difficult to be under investigation, but our job is to protect the patient, first and foremost."

"I understand that. I really do," Meg agreed. "Practitioners need to be monitored. The standard of care is important."

"I work for an ob-gyn now," Judith went on, "but I was a midwife for a few years." She let out a small laugh. "The hardest four years of my life, but also the most fulfilling."

Their eyes met, and Meg nodded. "I'm hooked."

"I sensed that about you."

"I'm glad to be able to practice again. But I'll never forget this case. I'll never forget Deedee's baby when I saw him at the hospital. Even stillborn, he was . . ." Meg's voice cracked with emotion. "He was perfection."

Judith bit her lower lip, nodding. "I lost a baby, too. It did me in. I was never able to go back to being a midwife with the same confidence. I admire you for getting back on that horse."

"Like I said, I'm hooked."

They were in the lobby now, lingering by the elevator. Judith opened her arms wide and folded Meg into a warm embrace. "Good luck to you, Meg. Go forth and bring lots of healthy babies into the world."

Meg hugged Judith, taking her words as a mission. A responsibility. A prayer.

৪ 11 ৪

*S*uch a sight! Remy King sat beside her sister-in-law Mary, each woman cradling a newborn in her arms. Fanny leaned back against the kitchen counter and clasped her hands together, delighted to have helped deliver both these babies. Last week she had spent a good day helping Mary Beiler and her husband, Five, give birth to their first, a boy named Nathan, and now today, Remy and Adam's baby, Esther, had come into the world, blinking her eyes and screeching like a little chipmunk. Named after Adam's mother, Essie was a feisty little thing!

Doc Trueherz had made it to the house in plenty of time to take care of the hard part. Dear Remy had pushed for so many hours, she was about spent. But Fanny had made up some herbs to give her strength, along with a light snack of toast and cheese to give her a boost, and that seemed to do the trick. Remy, who had been so pale during labor, now sat smiling with a pink radiance on her cheeks.

Adam King nodded at his wife and sister, who had become best friends over the past two years. "Now we'll never be able to separate those two."

Fanny and Doc Trueherz laughed along with Adam, who could not take his eyes off his wife and child. The two young mothers sat side by side on the daybed in the King kitchen. Each woman's face glowed with love as she spoke gentle words to the infant in her arms. The room was filling up with family, who gathered round to coo over the new arrivals.

"I wish my parents could have seen this day," Adam said wistfully. "My dat would have been all smiles."

"And your mother would have been delighted," Dr. Trueherz said. "Esther loved babies."

"But Gott had other plans." There was no bitterness in Adam's voice; only a touch of sadness for the parents he'd lost nearly three years ago. This family had seen difficult times, especially that first year after Levi and Esther King were killed. But their passing had brought oldest son Adam home from rumspringa, and in a turn of events that surprised most everyone in these parts, he had fallen in love with an English girl who turned Amish, Remy McCallister. She had been a reporter of some sort, but she'd been willing to give up her job and her car and belongings to live Plain. Adam and Remy married and took charge of the household with seven young children left behind. And now, praise be to Gott, Remy and Adam had added a new baby to the King family.

Although Fanny hadn't known Levi and Esther King well, she had mourned their deaths along with the rest of the community. After such a sad time, it made days like this all the more festive to see the family growing. It reminded Fanny that she wasn't the only one to have lost people she loved dearly. Most everyone had come across a sad patch in their journey, but a person had to keep on going down the road.

"Babies, babies, everywhere!" Adam's teenage sister Susie clapped her hands together in glee.

Little Katie climbed up on the daybed and leaned over Remy's arm to peer into the bundled cotton blanket.

"Say hello to the new baby," Remy said.

Leah, Susie, and Ruthie leaned in close, cooing and chattering, while Gabe and Jonah teased Adam about too many girls outnumbering the boys in the house.

"I'd better get going," Doc Trueherz said, tucking his stethoscope into his black case. "We need to pace ourselves, Fanny, with three more due in the next week."

"Mmm." Fanny pursed her lips, not wanting to speak of such things in public. Indeed, September had brought a rash of births—seven already, and the month wasn't even over yet. "It's too much for one woman to handle," Anna had told Fanny two weeks ago. Fanny had been delighted to be a midwife for half the women on Anna's list. It was wonderful to be present with each new miracle. Fanny would have offered to help Anna years ago, but back then she thought the older woman wouldn't want a newcomer like her taking away business.

"These two will enjoy playing together," observed Leah, Susie's twin.

"They'll be close, getting to spend so much time together," Fanny agreed, looking up at the clock. Nearly three P.M. If she left now, she would be home in plenty of time to prepare some supper for her family. It had been wonderful good having Emma at home during the summer, but now school was back in session, and all three of the older ones spent their days at work. The evening meal had become one of Fanny's regular chores, and she enjoyed cooking for her family and checking in with Zed. Often, after she popped a casserole in the oven or gathered vegetables from the garden, she would go out to the carriage house and talk with Zed, admiring the progress he'd made that day or talking through possibilities for the renovation.

"I'd best be going, too," Fanny said.

"I'll go hitch up your buggy," Simon offered, ducking out the door. A true horse lover, that one.

"Can I get one of you big, strong men to carry my black suitcase out to the buggy?" Fanny asked.

"I'll do it," Gabe said, darting into the other room to get the case of medical instruments and supplies. What a good young man he was, strong and quiet, but a little wild and fun-loving at times, which was what Tom's daughter Emma needed.

Fanny went to say good-bye to the new parents. Adam and Remy wanted her to take some cookies, and the children wanted to give her apples and cheese and rhubarb from the garden. She agreed to take some cookies for the children and cheese from the King dairy, but left the rhubarb, telling them she had a garden full of it.

Outside the stables, her buggy was waiting with Flicker hitched up. But instead of Simon, Gabe stood there rubbing the horse's neck. At nineteen, he was a tall young man, and in his black pants and blue shirt, he looked like he could use some meat on his bones. Fanny would have Emma find out what he fancied so that she could bake him something tasty.

"You got my bag all tucked away?" Fanny asked.

"It's in the back." When Gabe faced her, she could tell he was skittish. His Adam's apple moved up and down as he swallowed nervously, turning away to cough.

"Are you all right, Gabe? Having trouble with allergies?" Why would Gabe be nervous around her? She had known this young man for many years, even before he had started courting Emma. And by the time he became Emma's beau, she and Tom were very comfortable with Gabe.

"Friends first," Tom had once said of Emma and Gabe's relationship. "Emma and Gabe will be a very good couple, because they started as friends." Fanny remembered exactly where they were when they had that conversation. She and Tom had been in their room on a Saturday night, preparing for bed, when they'd heard the clip-clop of a horse's hooves receding down the lane—a telltale sign that Gabe had just left with their eldest daughter. "Emma was a sympathetic ear for Gabe when his parents were taken," Tom explained. "That's a solid foundation for good things to come."

"Is that how you courted me, Tom?" She had removed her kapp and unraveled her braid, leaving waves of brown hair spilling over the bodice of her white nightgown. "You gave me work when I needed it, a chance to take care of three wonderful good children, and while I had my guard down, you showered me with kindness and love and became my best friend."

"Oops! Now you know my secret. But the kindness came first." He came up behind her and pulled her against him, one arm around her growing waist, another sweeping the hair from her neck so that he could plant a kiss there. "The love came later."

Pushing back the intimate memory, Fanny drew in a breath to clear her head, and the pungent smells of fresh hay and manure reminded her she was standing outside a stable, and she was supposed to be calming a nervous young man. "What is it, Gabe? It can't be all that bad, now."

"It's been eating at me for a while." He took off his black felt hat, raked back his gold hair, and then replaced the hat. "There's something to ask you, and it's a rough question." His gaze finally rose to meet hers, and in that moment, her breath escaped her because she knew.

He would be asking for Emma's hand in marriage, and the question would open a wound that had been healing ever so slowly. The pain of losing Tom but eight months ago was still fresh at times. Although Fanny knew he was gone from this earth, there were still times when she mistakenly thought she might find him at home, or when his words and laughter came to her so vividly, she found herself answering him. Of course, she knew Gott had taken him. She remembered that every day.

"You know I don't mean any disrespect, Fanny. You lost your husband and Emma lost her dat, and there's nothing I can say to ease the pain. But Emma and I want your permission to marry in November," Gabe said solemnly. "Now that I'm baptized, we're both in good standing in the church. The bishop says there's nothing to stop us, but we want your permission, Fanny."

Her heart was beating so hard, she could hear the rushing sound in her ears. "You want to marry *this year*?"

He nodded solemnly, swallowing hard. "I know it's soon after her dat's passing, but wedding season comes but once a year, and we're ready to marry now."

"Not even a year. November won't be a year after Tom's death," Fanny said, thinking aloud. She didn't mean to blurt it out, and she didn't mean to criticize Gabe, but a year was the usual mourning period for family members. The girls were still wearing black to church, and Fanny wore her black dress every day. It was still a time of sorrow, and a happy event like a wedding would feel wrong when the heart was still swollen with grief.

"Aw, Fanny, don't look at me that way. This is a good thing, Emma and me. We want to be man and wife with Gott's blessing, but we want your blessing, too."

The initial shock wore off, leaving her in a daze. "A wedding . . . in two months?" It wasn't nearly enough time to plan such a big event, and Fanny couldn't imagine herself or any of her children rising to the occasion with their hearts so burdened with grief. "There's not enough time to put together a reception."

"We can have it at our farm, and we'll rent a wedding wagon, like Adam and Remy did. But don't worry about those things. We can pull it all together. Just as long as you think it's still respectful to Tom."

Her eyes stung as tears threatened. How could this wedding possibly be respectful to a man who had passed so suddenly just months ago? She could not tell Gabe what he wanted to hear.

"Can you wait until next year?" she asked again, her voice hoarse with emotion.

"We can wait, but it doesn't seem right to us."

She turned away from him and climbed into the buggy. "Give me some time to think about it. A week." *A week to think of a kind way to let you and Emma down easy.*

Gabe nodded. "A week, then." His eyes watched pensively as she called to the horse and looked toward the highway.

Biting her lip as the buggy rolled down the lane, she took in a deep, ragged breath. It was only when she reached the end of the lane with the shelter of trees and bushes behind her that she let the first sob rush from her throat.

∞

On the drive home, Fanny kept trying to put the matter out of her mind. She looked to the golden fields and trees that were just beginning to take on the glowing hues of autumn. She tried to let the patter of the horse's hooves feed a little song in her head . . . something from church.

But the song that came to her was the one Tom used to sing to calm the children. *This little light of mine, I'm gonna let it shine. Let it shine, let it shine, let it shine . . .*

A band of emotion squeezed her chest at the memory. "Dear Tom, they want to wash you away. They want to pretend you are long gone and everything is fine."

The grip on her heart tightened.

What a relief it was to turn into the narrow lane that led home. She would have Emma swing over to Rose Miller's to pick up the children when she got home; right now, it would upset them to see their mamm broken up and crying.

She climbed out of the buggy and began to unhitch the horse. Flicker nickered, nuzzling Fanny gently. "What is it, girl?" The horse's large eyes brimmed with sympathy. "You know something's wrong, do you?" Pressing her head against Flicker's neck, Fanny breathed in the scent of warm horse and fresh hay. "I don't know what to do." The horse tried to console her, but only Gott in Heaven could lift the burden that weighed on her heart.

As she led the horse to water, Zed came around the side of the carriage house. Golden September sunlight outlined his tall, straight figure topped by a wide-brimmed straw hat. She nodded at him and turned to the horse, hoping to hide her tears.

"I think the problem with the door is finally solved," he said. "Kumm, take a look."

"Good." Fanny's voice squeaked. She swallowed hard over the knot in her throat. How much had Zed seen?

"Is everything all right?" His voice was low and thick with concern.

"Mmm." She couldn't bear to face him. Best to change the subject. "I have good news. There's a new baby for Adam and Remy King. A little girl named Essie."

"That is good news. The community is sure growing." He dropped the hammer into a loop on his tool belt and stepped back. "I'll be out in the carriage house when you want to have a look."

"I'll take a look now." She gave Flicker a pat and followed Zed, gazing down at the gravel path.

She was grateful that he didn't turn to stare at her puffy, sore eyes or poke her with questions right now. That was one of the reasons Zed was so easy to have around the house; he understood the necessary spaces between words, the healing quiet that had the power to nourish the mind and ease the heart.

The door that had been a problem for years was a wide six-paneled slab of wood. Tom had tinkered with it for years, but no matter what he did, it swelled shut in the heat and humidity of summer. In winter, the doorjamb never seemed to line up with the latch.

"I know we wanted to save this," Zed said, one big hand on the knob. "But I wanted to make sure we could make it reliable before we close off the big carriage doors with drywall." He turned the knob, and the old door glided open without a creak or groan.

"I don't think I've ever seen this door move without a battle." Fanny closed it and opened it herself. Not a moan or creak, and it latched easily. "How did you do it?"

"It wasn't the door that was the problem. The framing was rotten and shifted. Taking in moisture and swelling in the hot weather. And in the winter, the hinges would start sinking in the soft wood. So I pulled out the framing and put in all new wood. It's level now." He stood back, hands on his hips, as Fanny swung it open and shut.

She let out a grateful sigh. "It's wonderful good, Zed. Tom struggled with this door so many times, every season. He used to say he was good at fixing a wheel, but not so much a . . ." Her voice broke as sudden tears filled her eyes, blurring her vision. In her mind, she saw Tom staring up at the top hinge, scratching his head. She covered her face with her hands and sobbed.

"Fanny, Fanny . . ." Zed's gentle hands gripped her shoulders and led her into the building, to a workbench, which he dusted off with one hand.

Gratefully, she sank down and drew in a quavering breath.

"It's not easy, is it?" His voice was ever so soft as he lowered himself to a tool chest beside her. "Gott takes away someone we love, and life goes on all around us while we keep looking for them. That's how it was when my grandmother passed. I was young, just a kid, but I kept expecting to see her baking in the kitchen or chasing me out of the bathroom or scolding me to redd up my room."

She swiped at her damp cheeks and mustered the courage to face him. There was no wall of judgment in his eyes, only sympathy. "That's how it is. The mind plays tricks on us, doesn't it? But this isn't about the door you fixed. Something happened today that put Tom in my mind, and I can't stop thinking that his memory is being swept aside like dried leaves."

"Folks will tell you to move on. They think it's for your own good." He lifted his chin and stared at the shaft of light from the window, where dust glittered in the air. "It's hard to suit other folks, though we try, don't we?"

Fanny sniffed. Many times in the past few weeks she had confided in Zed about personal and family matters. Whether it be her worries about Will not wanting to mind her or the carriage house costs staying under control, Zed had always listened to her concerns and shared his good advice. "That's just what I'm facing now." She told him of the question Gabe had posed this afternoon—how he and Emma wanted to marry this wedding season. "They're good, responsible young people, Emma and Gabe, so very much in love, and good friends for many years. But to marry so soon, while we're still mourning Tom . . ." She swallowed back the thick knot in her throat.

"Did you ask them to wait until next year?"

She nodded. "But they want to marry now. I understand that, I truly do. They've been courting long enough. But I don't think I have a celebration inside me right now. They're looking to me for approval and joy, but I have none to give. It's wrong to cast away mourning so soon. It's disrespectful to Tom's memory."

"It does seem wrong." Zed rubbed his knuckles against his chin. "But nothing is all wrong. Even a broken clock is right at two times during the day."

"What can I do? If I put myself in Emma's shoes, I wouldn't want to wait."

Zed leaned forward and wiped sawdust from the knees of his pants. "I take it that Tom knew about Emma and Gabe? He knew they were courting?"

"Ya. And he was happy that they were friends first. Tom thought friendship was the right foundation to build a marriage on. And he said it did his heart good to know that his Emma had found a man who would make her happy. Tom liked that Gabe was a good dairy farmer. He thought Emma needed a man who would get her out of the schoolhouse now and again."

"So if the decision was up to Tom, he would have told Emma and Gabe to go ahead and get married."

A feathery sensation tingled up Fanny's spine as his words sank in. "Well, ya. Tom would give his blessing. He was looking forward to the two of them getting married."

The silence of the old carriage house echoed with the answer: *Tom would give his blessing.*

Fanny straightened, pushing back her shoulders as she drew in a breath. "Oh, Zed, you're right. Tom would want them to marry." She bit back her lower lip, wanting to rein in her emotions now that she knew what she needed to do.

The answer was plain as could be; she had just needed Zed's help to look in the right direction.

"Zed . . . what would I do without you?" The words were out before she realized what they might imply—that she had grown attached to Zed. But wasn't that the truth? In just a few weeks she'd come to trust Zed with her thoughts and worries. He was a friend in every way.

Fortunately, Zed was not fazed by her enthusiasm. Thoughtful, he stared into the shadows of the old building, as if measuring the space in his mind. "You would have chosen that road sooner or later," he finally said. "I just lit a lantern in the dark."

 ⬡⬡

That night at supper, Fanny felt a strong resolve deep inside as she lowered her chin to pray. *Thank you, Father, for this gentle peace.* She marveled at how a decision that had caused her so much anxiety earlier in the day now seemed clear as a summer sky.

As platters and bowls of ham, mac'n'cheese, green beans, rolls with butter, and corn were passed around, Fanny let her gaze linger on her dear family.

Caleb bore the responsibility of oldest son well, handling repairs and family matters with the same calm patience his father had possessed. It was hard to believe that the boy who used to shadow Tom all around the house had grown into a man. Fanny knew he sorely missed his father, but she was glad for the bond he had found with Zed.

Always ready to bubble over with laughter, Elsie brought a ray of sunshine to the gloomiest day. Her love of people was reflected in the shelves of the Country Store, where Elsie promoted the various crafts of Amish women—everything from lavender soap to birdhouses to paintings. Although a bit shy of Englisher folk, Elsie had overcome that fear to make the shop a Halfway destination for Englisher shoppers.

Fanny realized that Will was still adjusting to his school schedule, and she vowed to have patience with the boy, who was feeling his oats lately. Emma had only good reports from school, but by the end of the day it seemed that Will's good behavior had run out. In the after-school hours before Caleb returned from the Stoltzfus ranch, Zed did a good job of channeling Will's wild antics into projects. When Will had taken to beating back weeds with a stick, Zed showed him how to use the weed whacker. It was a blessing to have a man around who understood what it was like to be a boy.

Watching Beth spoon a clump of macaroni and cheese into her mouth, Fanny realized the only time Beth stopped talking or humming was when she was eating. In the past year Beth had gone from repeating a few words to being a regular chatterbox, and Fanny enjoyed hearing her low, squeaky voice narrate the day. It warmed her heart to look down and see her little girl working the big broom or practicing stitches. They grew up so fast.

Strapped into his high chair, Tommy yammered a bit as his little fingers closed over Cheerios. Now that Tommy was eight months old, there was not a trace of that tiny bundle everyone had passed around last winter. He'd become an expert crawler and quite heavy, too. Fanny loved talking and singing to him all day long, especially now that he answered her by cooing right back.

And then Fanny's gaze shifted to the daughter who would be leaving soon. Emma sat tall, her hair pulled back tight under her white kapp, as she told them of an assignment her youngest pupils had completed that day. Always neat as a pin, Emma set a wonderful example for her scholars and her younger siblings. It was hard to think of gathering here at the supper table without Emma and her stories of her scholars at school. She would be missed.

"I'm learning how to spell 'joy,'" said Will. "But I keep forgetting: What does it stand for again?"

"J is for 'Jesus first,'" Emma answered. "O is for 'Others in between,' and Y is for 'You are last.' J-O-Y. You can practice writing it after supper, if you want."

Leaving the food untouched on her plate, Fanny spoke. "When I was about to leave Adam and Remy King's today, Gabe stopped me to ask a question."

Although the little ones kept eating, Emma, Caleb, and Elsie grew wide-eyed and silent. Fanny turned to Emma, who had pressed a hand to her throat, looking a bit startled. "He said you two want to get married in November."

Emma nodded. "Yes, Mamm. But we wanted to make sure it was all right with you. We'll still be mourning Dat, I know, but ... Gabe and I, we don't want to wait."

"He told me as much." Everyone at the table was quiet now. Even Tommy had stopped babbling to stare at a trio of peas. "I told Gabe I needed some time to think about it, but I've made my decision." Fanny paused, then gave herself a push, much like the gentle nudge Tom used to give her when she was being stubborn. "Tom wouldn't have wanted you to wait. I know that your happiness was far more important to him than the mourning period. Seeing as this is what your father wanted, I give you my blessing."

Elsie gasped in delight, and Caleb's jaw dropped.

"Oh, thank you! Denki!" Emma's eyes narrowed; she had a habit of squinting when she smiled. "You know we wouldn't do it without your blessing."

"You'll be blessed by Gott, and you know your father would've given his blessing, too."

"So you're marrying Gabe?" Caleb teased his sister. "He's a good one for you, Emma. He'll get your nose out of those books."

Elsie clapped her small hands together and steepled her fingers under her chin. "We have a wedding to plan, and November is so soon!"

"I know it's not much time, but somehow, we'll manage," said Emma.

"When is the wedding? Can I come?" asked Beth.

"It will be in November," Elsie told her. "And of course you'll be there. All our family and friends will be invited."

"That's good." Beth tore off a piece of roll. "But I'm wondering who's getting married?"

With that, the room filled with soft laughter. Fanny breathed a sigh of relief as she took in the happy faces of her family. She had made the right decision, difficult as it was, though she had come close to saying no to these lovebirds. Thank goodness Zed had been here to steer her right. Good, wise Zed.

12

Four days later, Zed Miller had to duck beneath the low brim of the tent as he filed out of church with the other men for the first time in his life. His baptism at the beginning of the month had earned him the privilege of sitting in the men's section. He smiled to himself, remembering how, as a boy in church, he had looked over at the men and wondered what it would be like to sit among them. Back then, he never imagined that it would take him so long to become baptized. He grabbed his hat from the assortment of black felt hats stuck onto the pikes of the fence and smiled as he pressed it onto his head. Gott was good.

It was the last Sunday in September, a bright and sunny church day with golden autumn light that glowed soft in the trees. The Almighty's handiwork was all around him in the blue sky with clouds thin as spun sugar and bursts of color from crimson maples to orange beech trees and yellow oaks. There was joy in the air, joy in the faces of the children sharing the leftover church cookies, joy in the lilting voices of women and the laughter of young boys.

These were the touches of home that were so ingrained in Zed, so much a part of him, that he wondered how he'd ever had the guts to leave. Here in Halfway, there was a rhythm to the days and weeks and changing seasons. A time for every purpose under Heaven.

Following his father, Zed joined a group of older men who talked of dry weather and the early corn harvest. Though not a farmer, Zed listened and nodded. This was his purpose under Heaven—living Plain and doing carpentry in Halfway. And over the past few months, since he'd started renovating the Lapps' carriage house, Zed saw his purpose blossoming. All the while he'd been hoping for a job with a contractor to keep him busy, but instead, he'd found solitary work to quiet his mind and a good family to warm his heart.

Each morning he rose before dawn, glad to be on his way. Fanny was always the first out to the carriage house with a thermos of coffee and an invitation for Zed to join the family for breakfast. It was usually a simple meal—oatmeal and fruit or biscuits and eggs—but Zed was nourished by the conversation. He was the last child living with his parents, Rose and Ira, and he missed having a big brood gathered around the family table.

There was always plenty to talk about at the Lapp table. Caleb was learning the ins and outs of tending to the Stoltzfuses' sheep. Emma shared stories of her young scholars at the one-room schoolhouse. Elsie asked advice on how to handle the growing business at the Country Store. Beth offered her own tales before dutifully helping their mamm clean up the kitchen. Most mornings, Will came out to the carriage house, where Zed was happy to assign him a task and teach him a thing or two about building. And Fanny . . . Fanny was loving tenderness, steely determination, and soft humility all woven into one beautiful cloth.

Trying to keep one ear on the men's conversation, Zed lifted his gaze to search for her in the clusters of folk waiting to eat. The sight of Will playing by the Beilers' woodpile brought a smile to his face. The boys were making a game of climbing onto the tree stump and jumping down. He looked toward the house, and there she was. The ribbons of her white kapp were tied under her chin as she carried a large platter of bread out to the serving table. That quiet smile, he knew it well. Time and again he longed to kiss those pink lips, to part them and taste the sweetness there, the way he and his friends used to suck the sweetness from a honeysuckle blossom.

He turned away, taking a breath to clear his head.

A quiet man by nature, Zed tended to watch others and soak up the things that were left unsaid. With Fanny Lapp, there were so many things under the surface: A deep sadness for her husband Thomas. A delight in each baby she brought into the world. And an endless well of support for her family.

Zed knew she was lonely, but she never said a word about it. And he didn't push. Instead, he looked to the reddish sheen of lamplight on her hair, the glimmer of her blue eyes, the joy of her gentle laugh, like leaves shimmering in the wind.

He knew she was in mourning still. She had loved her husband, and she needed time to heal the heart.

Which made Zed's feelings for her all the more forbidden. It wasn't proper to court a widow so soon after her husband's death. But Gott help him, he savored the moments they had together, and when they were apart, he couldn't stop thinking about her. As each day unraveled at the Lapps', Zed shared so much of his life—his search, his disappointments. She understood how he'd become lost among the English, and she supported his earnest efforts to join the Amish community. There was no condemnation or judgment in her clear blue eyes; only charity, pure and simple.

A firm hand clamped on his back, bringing Zed out of his reverie. His father leaned in close, a gleam in his eyes. "You don't have to stick with us old-timers," Ira said quietly. "Go. See your friends."

Zed enjoyed hearing the tales of the older men, but lately Ira Miller was always pushing Zed off to be social. Dat was determined that his youngest son find a wife, and soon. "Almost thirty, Zed?" he teased around the house. "You're no spring chicken anymore."

Nothing Zed said could calm his father's worries. "Are you waiting to fall in love, son?"

I have found love, Zed always wanted to answer, although he wasn't sure she felt the same way.

"Because that will happen over time. The important thing is to find a good friend. A woman you respect."

I've found her, Dat, but she's not ready to take a husband.

Zed's father shifted from foot to foot. "Besides, you need to find Bishop Samuel. He wants to talk with you," Ira said.

At least that would give Zed someone to search out in the crowd. Ya, he'd be content to find his friends, to sit with James Lapp and Caleb or talk with Ruben. But some folks gave odd looks when they saw a man as old as Zed passing time with younger ones.

"I'll go find the bishop, then." Zed turned on his heel and was headed toward the tables when he discovered Becca Yoder and her friend Sarah Eicher watching him from the garden a few yards away. His heart sank. Becca was always swooping down on him, an eager bird looking to feather her nest.

"Nice day," he said, nodding at the young women, their faces lit with bright smiles.

"So warm for September," Sarah said. "Did you hear the crickets chirping last night? They chirp faster when it's warm outside. That's a fact." Sarah was a bit of a chatterbox, and her detailed accounts of weather and events often made it into the Amish paper.

"Ya," Zed said slowly, "we can learn a lot from Gott's creatures."

Sarah babbled on about how the noises of frogs and donkeys

predicted rain. "You know the saying? 'If the donkey blows his horn, it's time to house your corn.'"

Becca laughed softly. "That one always makes me chuckle. Do you think it's true, Zed?"

"Don't know. I'm not really much of a farmer." As he spoke he scanned the area for the bishop. Once again, his eyes lit on Fanny, who was now talking with two Amish women, both of them cradling newborns. Her smile was bright enough to light the darkest night. That's how Fanny was when she was around the babies. She had told Zed that she was drawn to being a midwife because it gave her a chance to see miracles over and over again.

"But you've been around donkeys," Becca prodded.

"Ya. My parents have one." He tore his gaze from Fanny and faced Becca's broad, smiling face. He didn't want to disappoint her, but her attempts at courtship would go nowhere. Couldn't she see the wide chasm between them? No amount of smiling could build a bridge across that divide.

"Zed? There you are," called a female voice.

Zed was beginning to feel like a cornered animal when he recognized Dorcas Fisher traipsing up the grassy incline, a basket on her arm. "I've been looking all over for you."

"You found me," he joked, though no one laughed.

Becca's smile had disappeared, and she and her friend wore bland expressions that might have been cast in stone as they studied Dorcas. In the eyes of those single women, the tall woman from the bakery was fierce competition.

"These are the last of the church cookies I baked. Folks like them so much, it's hard to keep any around for after church." Dorcas extended the basket toward Zed. "I wanted to be sure you got a taste before they were all snatched up."

His stomach wrenched at the thought of sweets right now. "Maybe later, Dorcas. They look good, but I haven't had a sandwich yet."

His answer seemed to please Becca, but Dorcas thrust the basket closer to him. "But you have to try one. Everyone loves this recipe. It's not just the chocolate chips; I add coconut, too."

"Is that so?" He picked up a cookie and held it aloft. He would have liked to hand it to one of the children playing Frisbee on the lawn, but Dorcas faced him squarely, like a simmering bull. He took a bite and smiled. "Very good."

Dorcas nodded. "I knew you would like it. Sometime when you come into the bakery for bread, you can try some of the other cookies and pies."

"Denki." He swallowed hard, searching the yard and house beyond for an escape from these three single maidens. In the line of men descending the porch step, he spotted Bishop Samuel. "And there's someone I need to speak with." With a polite nod, he ducked away.

As he moved from the garden path to the grass, Zed felt Fanny's eyes upon him. She sat on a bench by the fence with some other young mothers. Tommy was in her arms, chewing on a rubber toy. She had seen him talking with the women, but he saw no jealousy in her expression. Only grace.

He smiled, and her face brightened for a moment.

How he wished he could go to her and sit beside her on the bench. Talking with Fanny wouldn't be the chore it was with Becca and Dorcas. Words and quiet pauses flowed between them like a fresh, clear spring. But it would be wrong to spend time with her here on a church afternoon, with the whole community around. Folks would cluck and whisper at the sight of a single man enjoying the company of a widow in mourning.

Zed made his way over to the bishop, who brought him to meet one of the Amish builders in their community, Tim Ebersol.

"Samuel mentioned that you're good with a hammer," Tim said, tucking a thumb under one suspender. "And I'm looking to take on some workers. You interested in a job?"

A job with an Amish builder ... it was exactly what Zed had wanted, until he had started working for Fanny. He lowered his chin, not wanting to appear proud. "That sounds like right good work," he said. "I could start as soon as I finish doing the renovations on the Lapp carriage house. That'll be December, I reckon. Maybe January."

"Mmm." Tim's discontent was obvious as he ran his hand up and down the suspender strap. "That's a ways off."

"I took the job on in the summer, and I promised to see it through." Zed met the older man's steely eyes. This was one thing he would not back down on; he wouldn't leave Fanny's family in the lurch.

"I need to expand my crew now, but it's a good man who sees a job through to the end." Tim nodded. "A job worth doing is worth doing right. Let me know when you're free to work, and I'll find a place for you."

"So the new center will be open in December?" Bishop Samuel's steely eyes were magnified by his spectacles. "It will be helpful for the women to have a place right here in Halfway. Keeps friends and family closer to home." He gave Zed a brusque nod. "You're doing a good thing for the community, Zed. It's good to have you back."

The bishop's words, the job offer from Tim, the steadfast woman he shared his days with—all these things lifted Zed's mood on this golden September day. After all this time, it was a fine welcome home.

❧ 13 ❧

"What are all these people doing, going out to eat the night before Thanksgiving? Aren't they supposed to be home thawing the turkey and cracking nuts and all?" Jack held the door of Molly's Roadside Diner open for his sister, Kat, who was moving a little slower now that the baby was almost due.

"Quite a crowd," Kat agreed, weaving between a group grabbing their coats and a couple studying the menu to speak with the Amish hostess. "How long for a table for two?"

"Probably half an hour," the young woman said. "Want to leave your name?"

Kat shook her head no, but Jack intervened.

"Jack Woods." He smiled, recognizing the Amish girl. "Hey, Susie-Q. How's it going?"

Dimples appeared as she smiled, acknowledging one of Molly's regulars. "Good, Jack. Have a seat and I'll call you."

"You know, we could go someplace else," Kat said, waddling away from the reception counter.

"No, we can't. Molly has the best fried chicken for miles around. Good food—that's why it's crowded. Besides, I need to get me some pie. Don't you want some pumpkin pie with whipped cream?"

Kat let out a sigh. "My doctor will kill me."

"You're eating for two," he said, guiding her to the vinyl bench that lined the window.

"That's a myth. Apparently the baby wants milk and vegetables and protein. I'm the one who wants the pie."

They were tucked away behind the overstuffed coatrack, which was fine by him. Although the department was okay with it, Jack didn't like going out to eat in uniform. Sometimes customers were scared to see the dark shirt and gold star, worrying that something bad was going down. Other times, folks hounded him with complaints about traffic tickets or questions about the fine points of the law. People saw a uniform and forgot that he was human, too. A guy had to eat.

"And I'll be seeing plenty of pie tomorrow at Nanna's." She unwrapped the checkered knit scarf from her neck. "You sure you won't go with me, Bug?"

Stirred by the childhood name inspired by his wide, penetrating eyes, he looked down at his sister. Her long blond hair splayed over her shoulders and the furry hat on her head made her look like some Nordic fashion model. Kat was his twin, his only sib, and even after all this time, he and Kat sometimes finished each other's sentences.

As teenagers, they had fought like alley cats, and they still gave each other a hard time now and again, but he thanked God for good, solid Kat, the only true touchstone in his life.

"What?" Kat flicked her hair back. "What are you staring at? Do I have lipstick on my teeth?" She moved her tongue under her lips.

"You're fine. I'm just thinking, in line with Thanksgiving season and all, I'm really thankful that you're my sister."

"That's sweet, Bug. Are you grateful enough to be my labor coach?"

He held up both hands to stop her. "Already told you, that's a little bit closer than I want to be. I'll be there for you, but you gotta find a girlfriend to take care of that business. Or get Brendan back here." Kat's husband, a captain in the army, had been sent on special assignment to North Korea two months ago.

"You know that's not going to happen. He'll be gone for the holidays, gone for the baby's birth. If he didn't really like his job, I would throw a pity party for myself."

"You can still throw the party," he said. "I'll come."

She poked him in the ribs with her elbow. "Come to Nanna's with me tomorrow. Everyone wants to see you."

"Can't do it. I need to be back at work Friday morning. Black Friday's a big day for Halfway. Well, big for Lancaster County. We snag the tourists who get lost on their way to Paradise or Bird-in-Hand."

"What if I promise to drive you back tomorrow night?"

He folded his arms. "Still can't do it."

"You really are done with Philly, aren't you?"

"Yup." When Jack had followed his sister here to Halfway, he had told her he was never going back to Philadelphia. "As far as I'm concerned, there's a big red X on the map over the whole metro area." Although Kat had pointed out that he still had friends and family there, he had insisted it was over. He knew his sister understood why. It wasn't just about the chance meeting with Lisa; it was about the way his ex-fiancée had tainted everything he had once loved.

"Okay," Kat said smoothly. "As long as we're on the subject, have you heard from Lisa?"

"Nope."

"Well, I have. She keeps calling me. Leaves messages in this high-pitched baby voice, as if we're friends."

He winced. "You don't talk to her, do you? Is she off her meds? You know she's using you to get to me."

"Give me some credit, Bug. I have not spoken with her. No idea about the meds, and no way am I letting her get to you again."

He let out the breath he'd been holding and slung an arm over her shoulders. "Thanks." Breaking up with Lisa Engles had been Jack's undoing for a while, partly because Lisa had made it that way.

"Where does she get off acting like we're friends?" Kat asked. "She's got some nerve. I'll never forget what she did to you."

Jack still didn't know what was worse—the public disgrace or the broken heart. Most days, he thought the latter was worse, but that wasn't the sort of thing a guy owned up to around his buds.

"I will never forgive her," Kat said, smoothing down the fringe of her scarf.

"Whoa, whoa. That's not the Christian thing to do. You gotta forgive, Kat. Wipe the slate clean and move on. Let it go, and you'll feel better."

"It's hard to forgive someone so vindictive and . . ."

"It's not her fault," he said. "When she's off her meds, she's another person." Lisa had been diagnosed with bipolar disorder, which made her mood swings extreme and erratic when she wasn't on medication.

"Well, on that we can agree to disagree." Kat turned toward him and planted a kiss on his cheek. "Love you, Bug."

He grinned down at his sister. "Back at you."

14

Meg didn't mean to spy. It just sort of happened when she went to hang her down vest on the rack by the door of the Amish diner in Halfway.

The couple seated behind the cover of coats didn't notice her; they were too intent on each other, so in the moment. And though their faces were blocked by the apparel, Meg saw the man pull the woman close as she told him she loved him and kissed his cheek.

The intimacy of the moment pinched at her. Meg had loved plenty of people in her life, but she'd never been in love.

She jammed the hanger with her vest onto the rack and stepped back out of sight, telling herself that she was just feeling wistful because the holidays were here and the closest thing she had to a boyfriend was a text buddy who didn't even know she was in town.

She turned to find her brother-in-law, Tate, chatting up the diner's hostess while Zoey worked the crowd, greeting acquaintances, introducing herself to strangers, and making small children smile. That was Zoey, such a social butterfly. Tate had started calling her the mayor of Halfway. Meg was glad she'd made the trip. This was one of the worst weekends on the road, but at the last minute she had decided it was worth braving the traffic to help Zoey and Tate celebrate their first Thanksgiving in their new home.

The Amish hostess stepped forward and called out: "Jack Woods? Is the deputy here?"

Meg's heart pounded. *Her* Jack? *Here?*

"Right here!" came a shout from the area by the window. The coatrack rocked a bit as the couple rose and came out into the open.

Meg's jaw dropped when she recognized Jack, looking handsome and very official in his uniform. But he had his arm around a beautiful, very pregnant blonde. Around eight months, Meg guessed, sizing her up.

Well, he worked fast. Meg pursed her lips together, chilled by betrayal. He had been flirting with her back in July. Definitely flirting. And he was the one who'd started texting her. Three or four times a day. That implied interest, right? A relationship of sorts, if only in the cyber world?

Wow. This guy had some nerve.

"We're here," Jack called. "Don't give our table away now, Susie. You know I'm gonna eat a few platters of your best fried chicken."

"Well, hello, there!" Zoey opened her arms wide and went belly to belly with the pretty blonde for a hug. "How are you, Kat?"

Meg watched with slight annoyance as the two women exchanged pleasantries while Tate and Jack shook hands. One big party.

"Meg." Zoey waved her over. "Come meet Kat and Jack Woods. Kat's in my childbirth class, and Jack's one of our deputies."

"Hi. I'm Meg, Zoey's sister." Meg shook Kat's hand. Drawing herself up straighter, she confronted Jack with a forced smile. "And I know Deputy Jack."

His sparkling gray eyes opened wider as he smiled. "Meg! You are the last person I expected to see here tonight. You said you weren't going to make the trip."

"Change of plans," she said. "And I see I've caught you off-guard."

Jack was about to respond, but the hostess diverted his attention, pointing out the table—a corner booth. Jack suggested they all share the table, considering the crowd and all, and Zoey jumped right on it, thrilled to have a chance to catch up with Kat outside class.

"And Meg here is a midwife. Remember, I told you she was coming to stay in December?" Zoey asked Kat as the group filed into the main room of the restaurant.

"We definitely need to talk." Kat put a protective hand on her belly as she slid into the large booth, then patted the spot next to her. "Sit here. That is, if you don't mind talking shop during your leisure time."

"Not a problem for me." Meg decided it would be best to take a professional tack with this woman, whom her sister genuinely liked. "I'm a magnet for pregnant women. They're attracted to me because I know what's what and I'm not afraid to talk about it."

"I would love your opinion," said Kat. "I am no fan of hospitals. I would love to have this baby at home, but I was told I'm high risk because of my age. Thirty. Can you believe that?"

Meg went through her routine screening questions with Kat, who answered dutifully.

"I'm a healthy woman," Kat summarized. "And I am not going to be forced into a situation I don't want because some doctor wants to avoid liability. So I fired him and found a new one. Do you know Dr. Trueherz? His office is in Paradise, but he makes a lot of house calls to the Amish in this area."

"I've heard his name before," Meg said.

"He's agreed to help me with a home delivery, as long as I keep up with my prenatal visits. And I've got my eye on that new birthing center the Amish people are opening. That might be a nice compromise. Have you seen it?"

"Not yet."

"It's over at the Lapp place, right next door to the inn. Fanny Lapp is going to run it, and they've got an older Amish midwife. Dr. Trueherz told me he's thrilled about the birth center. Fanny said you don't have to be Amish to go there, but they don't deal with insurance. I just hope they get it open in time for me to deliver there. I'm due at the end of December."

"Okay, ladies over there," Jack said from across the table, "let's not be articulating the biology of reproduction while we're eating here. Right, Tate?"

"I've learned not to censor Zoey," Tate said, placing his hand over his wife's. "But I'm all for some lively dinner discussion on any other topic tonight."

Zoey chuckled, and Kat rolled her eyes.

"You're such a wimp, Bug," she told Jack, using a term of endearment. "He won't be my labor coach. Can you believe it?"

"Really?" Meg's eyebrows rose as she faced Jack. "Didn't you say that you had delivered a baby before?" She remembered it vividly. He said it was a miracle. What a fake.

"I did, and it was an awesome event, but that was a stranger, and this—" He nodded toward Kat. "It's different when you know the person well."

"Ya think?" Meg fought to keep venom out of her voice. She had half a mind to launch into her lecture on the benefits of a partner's participation in childbirth. She never forced the father to be in the room, but in the end nearly every man wanted to be by his wife's side, supporting her. She had totally misread Jack Woods the first time she'd met him. She focused on the menu, determined to take a backseat during this dinner.

After they ordered, the conversation turned to Halfway, where Christmas decorations had been hung earlier in the week. Tate said he thought November was too early, but Kat and Zoey loved the holly garland and white lights strung across the main street. Jack mentioned that the holly was real, harvested by a local Amish nursery. He had chatted with the workers while they'd been setting up.

"And the white candles that the shopkeepers put in the windows are so inviting," Kat said. "I know they're LED lights, but there's something about it that reminds me of an old-fashioned country Christmas."

"It is very quaint." Meg was happy that Zoey and Tate had found a serene, greeting-card picturesque community to live in. Despite the cold, Meg, Zoey, and Tate had walked here from the inn, and Meg had to admit that the twinkle of lights in the dark winter night inspired hope and cheer in a person's heart. Meg's home in the suburbs of Pittsburgh had a more strip-mall, transient atmosphere.

The arrival of the food brought a sense of relief for Meg; it meant this awkward dinner would be over soon. At Jack's insistence, she had ordered fried chicken, and she savored the crisp, buttery crust and moist meat, along with au gratin potatoes and salad.

"It's a good thing we're walking home," she teased as she wiped her mouth with a napkin. "I might have to take a few extra laps around Main Street to burn this off."

"Told ya," Jack said. "Molly's fried chicken is to die for."

"Delicious," Kat agreed. "I don't know how the Amish stay so thin with foods like that on the menu."

"I think they burn off a lot of calories with physical activity,"

Zoey said. "And without television, there's less temptation to be a couch potato."

Glancing up, Meg caught Jack studying her with a look of interest in his eyes . . . a look of longing. Closing her eyes, she swallowed and tossed her napkin on the table. "Excuse me," she said, ducking out to the ladies' room.

"I'll come with!" Zoey called, following.

Meg didn't wait for her sister; she felt sickened by Jack the creep, and wanted some alone time for self-examination. Was she sending out the wrong signals? Giving Jack the impression that she would get involved with a married man? Well, she wouldn't. Not in a million years. She locked herself into a stall and sat down to think.

"What a fun dinner," Zoey said as the door closed on the stall next door. "I'm going to invite Jack and Kat to Thanksgiving dinner tomorrow. I don't think they have any other family in Halfway, and I noticed the way Jack was looking at you. Well, we know he's interested if he's texting you and all that."

Meg winced. "Okay, time for a reality check. Jack is a married man with a pregnant wife."

"He's what? Oh, honey!" Zoey snorted. "He's not married. Kat is Jack's sister! *Sister.* Her husband is in the military, stationed over in North Korea right now. Did you really think . . . ?" Zoey's blustery laugh filled the restroom. "Jack is definitely very available."

"But wait . . ." Then that intimate moment she'd witnessed was a family moment, a sibling thing, not . . . "Are you kidding me?"

"I kid you not, but I think it's a hoot that you thought they were together. Really, honey, would Tate and I hook you up with a cheating snake and his neglected wife?"

"Well, no, but . . ." Meg went to the sink to wash her hands and check her teeth and hair. Suddenly, her appearance mattered.

Back at the table, Meg viewed everything with a new perspective. She dug into the fried chicken with a revitalized appetite.

Warm light glimmered on the content faces around the table. Zoey and Kat glowed with the happiness of expectant mothers. Tate leaned back in the booth, relaxed by the conversation, and Jack . . . well, Jack had the sort of wide-open, friendly face that would look handsome in any light. She felt a new respect for him as he talked about the town's preparations for holiday shoppers.

"All the Amish towns in Lancaster County have a boom of shoppers this time of year," Kat said. "That's why Jack has to work this weekend while I head off to Philly on my own." She explained that she would leave in the morning for their grandmother's house.

Zoey turned to Jack. "And you're going to be alone for Thanksgiving?" When he nodded, she wagged a finger in the air. "Oh, no. That's no good. You're coming to have dinner with us. It's going to be a small gathering. You know Shandell, the young woman who works for us? She'll be there with her mother. We have some guests staying in the inn, but they're here to connect with family. So come anytime after five. We'll eat around six." She patted his arm. "You can be our unbiased judge. Meg and I are doing a stuffing challenge—sausage-and-apple versus oyster."

"Hey, when there's sausage involved, I'm totally biased."

"Yes! Points for me." Meg pumped a fist in the air, causing quiet laughter around the table.

"Well, then, I guess I'll see most of you tomorrow." Jack excused himself, rose from the table, and slid his jacket on. The shiny gold deputy's star flashed bright, in contrast with his navy jacket, and Meg was reminded of the star in the heavens that led the three wise men to the newborn Savior. It was a Bible story close to her heart, especially since she was in the business of bringing babies into the world.

"I've got to get back to work, but this was a nice surprise." He placed a twenty onto the bill and headed out, stopping to acknowledge and shake hands with a few other diners on the way to the door.

Everyone seemed to like Jack, though that was no surprise. His friendly manner, earnest concern, and ready smile appealed to young and old. And personally, Meg had always found something downright attractive about a man in uniform. She knew her sister was trying to do a bit of matchmaking, but that was just silly with Meg living so far away. Still, Jack's presence at dinner would make Thanksgiving a bit more interesting. Meg was looking forward to it.

⊙⊙

"What a feast!" Jack said, looking over to the sideboard laden with platters of turkey, stuffing, vegetables in cheese or butter, mashed potatoes, and rolls.

Jack didn't know the half of it. Meg and Zoey had gotten up early that morning—even before the Macy's parade had begun on television—to get their birds in the oven. They had used the double ovens in the inn's kitchen to roast two turkeys with sage stuffing, one of which Tate had shuttled over to a shelter in Lancaster while the sisters continued cooking their evening meal. Dear Zoey had a good and generous heart.

Meg took her seat at the table festively adorned with candles, orange mums, and white roses. "You've really outdone yourself this year, Zoey."

"I couldn't have done it without your help, sis. But you know I love to do things up over the holidays, and this year, we've got so much to be thankful for." Zoey placed the brocade napkin on her belly and gave it a pat. "So I guess I'll start off the thankfulness and say how grateful I am to be living in this wonderful little town with the man I love and a baby on the way." She clasped her hands together and turned to her husband.

"And I'm grateful to Zoey for getting me out of the Wall Street jungle and into the land of milk and honey." Tate's graying brows lifted as he surveyed the dinner guests. "Every day I thank the Lord for my growing family and this good life He's led us to."

"And I'm thankful to have a job that I love and a chance to go back to school," Shandell said.

Shandell's mother, Chelsea, was grateful to have found a new start here in Lancaster County after a few years in Maryland that she described as "trying."

"I'm thankful to be here sharing this awesome dinner," Jack said. "And Chelsea, in many ways you and I are on the same road. Halfway has been a fresh start for me, a do-over. God gave me the chance to start with a clean slate in a small town where folks look out for their neighbors and lend a hand to strangers. Living in Halfway, I've got reason to give thanks every day."

"Okay, then." A gust of emotion made Meg's eyes blur over the burst of color in the flower arrangements. She wasn't one to expose her feelings, but there was no dancing around the facts of the past year. "I am thankful to be able to keep doing the job I love, delivering babies. It's been a rocky road this year. I . . . I lost a baby . . . one of the infants I was delivering and . . ." She took a breath to steady her nerves. "I thought they were going to kick me out of the profession and throw away the key. But they didn't."

"Of course they didn't," Zoey said. "You're good at what you do. The best."

"Thanks. I know my heart is in the right place. So I'm grateful to be working as a midwife. And very grateful to be here with you all tonight."

Tate nodded. "You're always welcome, Meg. Now . . . the blessing?" He closed his eyes and clasped his hands together. "Good bread, good meat, good God, let's eat!"

"Oh, honey." Zoey rolled her eyes. "Boys will be boys." She reached over and took the hands of Tate and Meg on either side of her and bowed her head to thank God for the bountiful meal.

After dinner everyone pitched in. The large industrial kitchen made cleanup easy, and Zoey was excited to try their mother's recipe for turkey noodle soup with the leftovers. Shandell and Chelsea left for a late movie—their Thanksgiving tradition—while Tate, Zoey, Jack, and Meg settled into sofas in front of the inn's broad stone fireplace.

"Isn't it nice that Shandell and her mom have that movie tradition on Thanksgiving?" Zoey snuggled closer to Tate on the sofa. "We need some tradition, sweetie. Something to pass down to the baby."

Tate lifted her hand as if she were royalty. "It's not enough that you get up at the crack of dawn to cook for the mission supper? Or the family gathering for dinner?"

"Well, that's sort of a tradition," Zoey said, yawning.

Meg could see that her sister was fading. "It's a wonderful way to start Thanksgiving, even if it does require getting up so early."

"Sorry, but the early morning is catching up with me, and baby needs sleep." Zoey sighed. "I'm going up to bed. But you guys stay. Eat, drink, and be merry."

Tate wasn't far behind his wife, and soon Meg found herself nursing a cup of tea by the fire, alone with Jack. There was something very freeing about being away from the commitment to her expectant mothers, something so comforting about spending time in the Halfway to Heaven inn. Zoey and Tate had made a peaceful retreat here. Although this had all the makings of one of Zoey's grand matchmaking schemes, Meg reminded herself that she and Jack had actually been the ones to initiate a relationship. And they weren't starting from scratch.

"I have to say, it's nice to have a conversation with you that can extend beyond three lines of text."

He nodded. "Nothing like face time. But with you living hundreds of miles away, you gotta make some compromises. Besides, I'm an awesome texter, right?"

With a chuckle, she leaned back into the plush sofa. "You do make me laugh. I look forward to your messages."

He grinned. "Snap. I was going to text you from across the table tonight at dinner, at the beginning. You looked so mad at me, I was glad we were separated by the salt and pepper."

She pressed her eyes closed. "I don't want to talk about it."

"What was that? Let me guess. I wasn't hip to it at the time, but now I'm thinking that you thought Kat and I were married."

She shot him a look. "I was so furious. Mad and disappointed with you."

He grinned. "Meggie-Margaret. I'm not that guy. And I'd never do anything to make you mad at me. At least, not deliberately."

Thinking back on the swell of anger and anxiety in that moment, Meg let out a sigh. "That was a near disaster. I'm so glad you redeemed yourself," she teased.

"I didn't do anything wrong!"

She turned to him, and they both fell into laughter. It was easy to laugh with Jack, easy to snuggle against him on the couch and ask him questions about his family, his dreams. There were so many stories to tell, so many blank pages to fill, and she was hungry for the details of Jack's life.

"So I got my training with Philadelphia's police force," Jack was saying, "and when I wanted to come out this way to be near Kat and Brendan, it just so happened that Halfway was looking for a deputy. I figured it was meant to be. Hank offered me the job, I said giddyup, and here I am."

"And that was in January? So you're coming up on your first year here. How do you like it?"

"Let's just say I stepped into a Norman Rockwell painting. That's Halfway: good folks, good neighbors. People following the Golden Rule. Let me tell you, it's a long way from Philadelphia, in more ways than one."

"A Norman Rockwell painting. Freckle-faced kids and dogs and a smiling milkman?"

"Exactly. I'm the cop in the diner, trying to talk the little kid with the hobo sack out of running away."

She squinted at him, pretending to assess his broad jaw, wide mouth, and warm eyes. "Yes, I see the resemblance. A cop with a good heart."

He smacked a hand to his chest. "Shucks. I try not to let it show." He put his mug down on the end table. "How about you? What brought you to Pittsburgh?"

"My mom and stepfather live there. It's where I went to nursing school. I still have friends there, but you know how that goes. People get married, have kids and jobs. It's hard to get together, especially with the demands of my job. You try to schedule things, and the best-laid plans go up in smoke."

"I hear you. Believe me, I used to hear a lot of complaints when I had to work weekends or holidays."

"From your girlfriend?" she asked.

"Fiancée, but that's over now."

From the way his gaze sank back toward the fire, she sensed that she'd hit a nerve.

"Was it a difficult breakup?"

"You could say that. We grew up together. Lisa and I were together for more than fifteen years."

Fifteen years . . . it made Meg feel like a novice in the world of relationships. "You definitely earn points for that one. I haven't been in a relationship for more than a year. That's a tough one."

"Yeah. It was good for the first ten years or so. After that . . . I don't know. Her family just about adopted me when I lost my parents. My grandmother loved her. We were a couple for such a long time that when it ended, it was hard to delineate that line between us."

Meg was reminded of the many couples she had worked with

over the years, people from varied backgrounds and ethnicities. Many shared a common bond—a love that brought them close together. It was always a pleasure to work with a cohesive couple like that. Others . . . well, when there was an obvious dysfunction, Meg was not surprised to learn, years after she assisted in a birth, that the parents were no longer together. "Do you ever want to go back? I mean, maybe it's not really over."

"Oh, it's over all right. There's no going back." She sensed the wound then, a sore spot that had not completely healed over. What had this Lisa done to him? She craved details, but it wasn't her place to dredge the channels of his former relationships.

"Is it still awkward when you run into her?" she asked.

"I'll say. Fortunately, she's back in Philly. I got me a fresh start out here in Halfway. No ghosts of girlfriends past lurking when I come around the corner."

She chuckled softly. "I doubt your fiancée was lurking."

"Oh, she was a lurker, all right. But that's all past. How about you? I'm not seeing any bling on that ring finger."

"I'm still footloose and fancy-free."

"A beautiful girl like you? Where you been hiding yourself?"

"You are such a sweet-talker, aren't you?"

"I've been called worse."

"As I mentioned, my job is not very relationship-friendly. Childbirth is unpredictable; it makes for a highly erratic schedule. When you cancel two or three times, guys get annoyed."

"I have an irregular schedule, so I would get it."

"Maybe you would. Too bad you don't live in Pittsburgh."

"Nah. I wouldn't do a big city again. I'm thinking you might want to step up your visits here. That way we could spend some time together. See if this hunch I have is right."

She smiled up at him. "A hunch?"

He nodded. "And I have pretty good instincts. It's a cop thing."

"And what do your instincts tell you about me?"

"That I can trust you. That you've got your feet on the ground and your eyes on the sky." He took the empty mug from her hands and set it on the end table. "That there's something sizzling like a live wire between us."

"Did you just take my tea away?"

"It's cold, and I don't want it to spill when I kiss you."

"Is that where this is going?" She drew the question out in a low, teasing voice.

"Yeah, girl," he said in that south Philly, bluesy way.

She almost laughed at being called a girl, but wasn't that how he made her feel? Young and spontaneous and free. Giddy and smart and pretty.

She could feel the heat of his body as he moved closer, resting his arm above her head on the sofa. He smelled clean, a lemony scent, and when his lips met hers she tasted coffee and yearning . . . such tender desire in that short but heated contact.

Without words, she pressed against him for another kiss and gave him the answer that burned deep in her heart.

15

*T*wo days after Emma and Gabe King's wedding, Zed was at the Lapp house, trying to get back to work. There was still much to do to finish the place by January, and he'd been off the job for a few days on account of the wedding. He'd been happy to be included among the group of people helping out at the Kings' dairy farm. There'd been all sorts of tasks that needed to be done, including landscaping, setting up furniture for the wedding, and wrangling horses for the guests. On the wedding day, Zed had been happy to have tasks that kept him away from the social gathering and the likes of Dorcas and Becca. It was getting harder to fend them off without hurting their feelings, but he kept turning down their dinner invitations or notions that he might attend a bonfire.

Today Zed had thought he might finish priming the trim around the carriage house doors, but when he saw Gabe trying to balance a set of box springs on the cart, he knew the younger man needed help.

Zed looped the rope around the runners of a rocking chair, pulled it taut, and tied a knot. "Ya, that's not going anywhere." He stepped back and looked up at the mountain of furniture piled onto the cart.

Gabe King tested the edge of the wooden rocker and found that it was secure, despite the fact that it hung precariously over the edge of the cart. "It's good and tight. Where'd you learn to pack a cart, Zed?"

"Here and there. I've helped my brothers and sisters move out of the house."

"I told Emma we needed some furniture," Gabe said as he pushed a basket in behind a mattress. "I didn't know she'd find us so much."

"It's just a few things Fanny said we could take," Emma called from behind the cart, where she was tying up plastic bags filled with books. "And you'll be happy tonight when you're sleeping on a real bed instead of the hard floor."

"You're right about that," Gabe called back to her. "How's it going with those books?"

"I think I've sorted through all the ones I want to keep," she said, coming around the side of the cart. "These others I promised to pass on to Leah."

"Giving them to my sister?" A slow smile spread on Gabe's face. "So either way, they need to get packed in the cart." He shot a leery look at Zed, and they both chuckled.

"Maybe we can stuff a few more things under the mattress," Zed said, frowning up at the top-heavy cart.

"I don't think we can add a single feather to this heap," Emma said. "How about if I follow in the buggy? There's plenty of room for the books in there."

"We're going to need a buggy for sure," Gabe said. While he headed off to get the buggy, Emma went inside to say good-bye to

Fanny, who had been working on wash with Elsie's assistance. Moments later, everyone filed out of the house to marvel at the overloaded cart for themselves.

"Oh, my . . ." Fanny pressed a hand to her mouth, her eyes bright with mirth. "Looks like you've packed everything but the kitchen sink. But there's not an inch to spare. Where will you sit?"

"Right here." Gabe scurried up onto the mound and wedged himself into a spot between the chest of drawers and the washing machine. "See that? There's room for one."

"And I'll follow in the buggy with Elsie," Emma said. "We'll need help setting things up, and you have a good eye," she told her sister.

"Can I go along?" Will asked, trying to climb into the cart behind Gabe.

"Me, too." Beth took Emma's hand. "I have good eyes."

"You can ride with us in the buggy." Emma pointed to the bags of books. "I'll put you to work carrying the small things."

"Unless you need our help here," Elsie told Fanny. "I can stay behind."

But Fanny waved off the idea. "Go on, help the newlyweds. Most of the washing has been hung, and we've got a good dry day for it. The chores will be finished in no time."

Delighted to have an adventure ahead, the children got to work toting the sacks of books over to the buggy. Zed and Gabe hitched two horses to the heavy cart, while Emma and Elsie supervised the loading of the buggy.

Minutes later they were ready to go. In his niche atop the heap of furniture, Gabe might have been riding a wild elephant down the road.

"Look at Gabe," Fanny said with an amused smile. "He's having fun driving that cart."

"Gabe likes a challenge."

"Then he'll be good with Emma. She likes to push folks to the next step, whether it's reading and writing or opening a business."

Zed and Fanny watched as the bulky cart lumbered down the lane like a lazy cow. The buggy followed at a safe distance, the children turning back to wave just before they disappeared behind the nearest house.

"Off to their new life. I'm going to miss having Emma here." Fanny gave a sigh. "I'd better check on Tommy."

Gravel crunched under her feet as she went around the side of the garage, leaving Zed to wonder if he should go after her. He could tell that something wasn't quite right, but it wasn't his place to pry. If Fanny wanted to let him in, she would tell him her troubles as they went over the renovation or shared coffee in the morning.

Rooting around inside the garage, Zed found the can of primer and a clean paintbrush. It would be good to cover the new wood before the weather got too wet. He headed over to the carriage house, passing the rose, green, purple, and blue dresses, pants, shirts, and curtains hung on the lines, like rows of thick trees in the Lapp orchard.

As he neared the back porch, he saw Fanny's feet emerging from a forest of laundry hanging over the porch. He opened his mouth to tease her about finding her way out of that maze of cloth when he heard the muffled whimper.

She was crying.

He paused, not sure what to do. Let her be, or offer her consolation?

Switching the can of paint from one hand to another, Zed considered. Despite his time out among the English, he was not a "smooth operator," as one of the other truck drivers used to call himself. He found it hard to even talk to most women, let alone a woman in tears.

But Fanny was different, and he couldn't walk away without trying to ease her pain.

"Fanny?" He put the paint and brush on the ground and lifted a shirt and blanket and dress, working his way in toward her.

"Oh, Zed. I didn't hear you out there." He got a flash of her red, swollen eyes before she turned away from him, unpinned a dress, and folded it in her arms.

"What's the matter?"

"I was just thinking of Emma, and . . . it's such a small thing. I shouldn't be upset, I know that. But . . . I didn't even get a chance to say good-bye." A sob escaped her throat, and she pressed a fist to her mouth.

"She's just moving down the road a ways," he said gently. "You'll probably see her later today."

"I know that, but . . . but it won't be the same. She's gone off to live with her husband now, Zed. She's taken her bed and her clothes. I was just thinking, Emma's dresses won't be hanging in this yard anymore. She'll be hanging wash for two over at the Kings' place."

Zed looked right and left at the laundry that surrounded them in a cloth cocoon. Was this not enough washing for one woman to take care of?

"She won't be far, but it will be different. At dinner, we won't be hearing Emma's stories of her scholars who memorized their times table quick as could be or struggled to hold a pencil right. And at Christmastime, when she teaches her students songs and stories to recite, Emma starts singing around the house."

It was hard for Zed to imagine the serious schoolteacher humming a light tune, but he knew that people were different inside the privacy of their home.

"She was just a girl when I met her." Fanny took down another dress and pressed it to her heart. "Only ten years old. Smart and well-behaved, but skittish as a colt. It's hard to believe that time could fly so quickly, but suddenly that girl is married and leaving home. I know this is the way it should be, that young people marry and move on, but it still gives me such a tender pang in my chest when I think of the little girl she used to be and ..." Her voice broke and the dress dropped from her hands as tears flooded her eyes.

At a loss as to how to comfort her, Zed touched her shoulders gently, and then folded her into his arms. *"Geh lessa,"* he said softly.

Let it be.

Let it go.

Let it be what it is.

"Geh lessa." It was an expression Amish folk used in daily conversation, the simple desire to accept Gott's plan. To submit. To yield to His way. Right now, it was all he could think of to bring her comfort.

A sudden memory flashed in his mind—the way his mother had held him close while he sobbed over Pepper, their family dog, who had been killed by a car on the road. He had loved that dog, and the loss had made him crumble inside. Remembering the reassurance of his mother's arms, he prayed he might extend the same comfort to Fanny.

A knot of sympathy twined in his chest as he considered the source of her distress. He didn't think this was just about Emma moving out to start her married life. Fanny was still fragile from Thomas's death—still recovering—and she wasn't quite ready to deal with the loss of one of her chicks.

As her whimpering breaths began to even out, he became aware of the flowery sweet smell of her, the smallness of her pink fingers on his broad chest. The way she folded into his arms so neatly, like a puzzle piece that fit just right. He held his breath, afraid that the smallest stir would unravel the moment.

"Look at me, crying over such a happy thing as a wedding. It must be a sin, not to appreciate the good things Gott has brought to us."

"We take the bitter with the sweet," he said. "But you haven't always had the sweet. You're still mourning Thomas, and when the heart is mending, it lacks the strength. The strength a mother needs to push her baby from the nest."

"You're right. *Geh lessa.* I knew that this wedding would be a strain for me. I forgot to brace myself when the wave of emotions hit." She drew in a steadying breath, and leaned back to look up at him. Her teary eyes were bright as stars in the night sky. "I'd be so lost without you."

Did she mean that? Did she mean to say that she needed him, that she wanted him near? He studied her eyes as if they might chart the way, but the answer wasn't clear.

Geh lessa, he told himself. *Let it go, at least for now.*

Fanny sniffed and swiped at her tears with the back of one hand. "Well, I reckon that's enough crying for one day. Especially a busy wash day."

He reached down for the fallen dress and handed it to her. "And you're worried about having one less to wash for? Five still left at home. Is that not enough for you?"

She let out a laugh. "I know. I've got plenty to keep me busy."

He nodded and then forced himself to turn away before he revealed too much. Her scent still clung to him as he peeled his way out of the maze of laundry and got back to work.

16

"The frost is on the pumpkin!" Will said for the umpteenth time that day as he came through the doorway with an armful of firewood. It was an expression his father had used, and now young Will had taken a liking to it as autumn gave way to winter.

"Ya, the frost will be back tonight. And that's why we need to keep our stove burning," Fanny said. "You can put the wood down in the basket in the corner, and bring me a few pieces."

"Can I throw it into the fire?" he asked.

Fanny used the poker to open the door of the wood-burning stove. "I'll let you add it gently. We don't want to throw it in and make the embers fly." Arming Will with thick padded oven mitts, she let him add wood, one split log at a time, and showed him how to move it with the poker. "And always keep the mitts on until you close the stove door and put the poker away."

Beth watched from the table where she was playing with an embroidery set. "Careful, Will," she warned.

"He's being very careful," Fanny said.

The fire cast a glow on his eager face as he soaked up her instructions. He was a good learner, this one. Emma had said he was doing well with his lessons when he managed to control the "ants in his pants." Hard to believe that her boy was in school now, and Beth wouldn't be too far behind him.

Time did fly, and Fanny hated to see it slip away like sugar through her fingers. She wished she could be more accepting of the changes Gott brought His children. Granted, she had weathered some difficult storms, losing two dear husbands, but she had begun to realize how the small changes pinched at her. There was Emma, a married woman now, no longer under this roof. Elsie would probably follow her next wedding season. And Caleb! He didn't speak of his girl at all, but Fanny knew there was someone special in his life. Next year at this time, she would most likely be living here alone with her three younger ones.

The thought of so many turns in the road sent her over to pick Tommy up from his playtime on the floor and hold him close. He chortled as she rained kisses over his chubby cheek. *"Meine liebe,"* she cooed, and he answered with sweet gurgled words.

"You're all getting so big," Fanny said as she sat in a rocker with Tommy in her lap.

"Not me, Mamm," Beth said. "I'm still little."

Fanny chuckled. "That's right."

"Someone's coming!" Will announced, and he and Beth hurried to the window of the front room. "It's Elsie and Caleb."

"It's about time they got home. Our dinner is almost done." She peeked in the oven to check the Yummasetti. The hot gust that emerged from the oven smelled of beef and mushrooms and melted cheese. This casserole was a favorite, and a good one to ward off the cold from inside.

The kitchen door opened to Elsie and Caleb, who had greetings for all.

"Our hard workers have returned," Fanny said cheerfully.

"I just spoke to Zed," Caleb told Fanny. "He's still working, but doesn't want to stop to eat. I told him we'd come out to check his progress after supper."

"He's working late today," Fanny said as she added chopped apples to a bowl of slivered carrots.

"Finishing up the floor, I think."

Meanwhile, Elsie was entertaining the children with tales of her day. Some travelers from Australia had come into the Country Store, and Elsie explained that they had opposite seasons because they lived below the equator. "For them it's springtime, while we're going into winter," she said.

"Did you tell them the frost is on the pumpkin?" asked Will.

"I didn't, but I don't know if they have pumpkins in Australia. But they do have kangaroos and koalas. Do you know what they look like?"

"I'll find a picture." Will and Beth went to the bookshelf to find an animal book, while Caleb and Elsie washed up for dinner.

Everyone enjoyed a plate of steaming casserole and an autumn salad made with carrots, raisins, mayonnaise, and the last of the apples. Little Tommy worked intently to pick up some noodles and chunks of ground beef between his fingers, though some of the food fell on his bib. When Fanny turned to him at the end of the meal, he had dozed off in his high chair.

"Fast asleep!" Fanny said, getting up to get a wet cloth.

Elsie giggled. "He's got a Yummasetti beard. But he looks so peaceful. Sometimes I wish I could fall asleep right in my chair."

"Me, too," Caleb agreed, straightening his tall frame. "Of course, I'd need someone to carry me to bed, then."

"No one can carry you! You're too big," Will exclaimed.

"I'll carry you," Beth offered.

"You sure about that?"

"Ya. I'm strong."

Fanny smiled at their banter as she wiped Tommy clean and lifted him from the high chair. This one would get a good night's sleep. Her shoes treaded lightly on the floor as she took him into her bedroom and paused at the bassinet. Tommy was heavy in her arms, and he had gotten so big she couldn't really contain him in her arms anymore.

Her baby boy wasn't a baby anymore. His little round face had thinned. Gone were the folds of skin under his chin, where she used to bury her lips to plant kisses.

"Oh, Tommy. I think you've outgrown your cradle."

Frozen in place, she bit her lower lip. She'd always considered herself to be a practical woman, but lately, when she had to acknowledge that it was time for a change, Fanny stalled.

"I don't want to give you up," she said softly. "But a mother really has no choice." Wasn't that how the saying went? If a mother did her job well, she lost it. Shifting the boy in her arms, she turned away and headed up the stairs. Well, at least she had a good eighteen years or so until this youngest son of hers rode off with his bride.

"You're going to like your new bed in here with your brother and sister," she said as she brought him into the room shared by Beth and Will. The crib in the corner was larger than the bassinet downstairs, a better fit—at least until Tommy started climbing out of it.

Settled in the crib, her boy looked peaceful and content with his belly up and his arms stretched out on the mattress. Fanny might have stood there watching him sleep if she hadn't heard male voices outside. She went to the window and saw Caleb and Zed talking outside the carriage house. Zed probably wanted to get home, and here she was, mooning over her little one. She kissed Tommy's forehead, grabbed a coat and lantern, and headed out.

The brisk cold air of the November night helped to clear her head as she hurried to the carriage house. The new windows glowed from the kerosene lantern inside, and even in the pale moonlight she could see how much this building had been transformed over the past few months. Zed and Caleb had decided to nail the old carriage doors shut and seal around them to minimize drafts. That work had been done, and Zed had put a new coat of white paint on the door trim, which made the whole building seem clean and new.

Fanny opened the side door and paused on the threshold at the sight of a smooth wood floor. It was quite a change since she'd peeked in a few days ago. "The old dirt floor ... it's gone." She blinked up at the two men. "Zed ... you did this part so quickly, and what a difference the floor makes. It looks like a house now."

"It's just a subfloor," Caleb pointed out. "We'll need to cover it with linoleum or hardwood."

"Ah, but we've come so far." Fanny smiled up at Zed with grate-fulness in her heart. She would not let Caleb's concerns taint her joy over the way Zed had breathed life into this sagging building. "You've done good work here, Zed, from top to bottom."

The answering glimmer in his dark eyes told her that he, too, was pleased with the results of his handiwork. "The subfloor went faster than I expected. It does make the place look more like a home for people than for buggies. But I wanted to talk to you about the next steps. It's time to make some choices about the finishes." Zed picked up a notepad from his worktable and handed it to Fanny. "Here's a list of the materials we'll need. The floors and walls have been measured, and that list includes the half walls you want to build over here to make a separate area for each bed."

"So we need to get some prices to see what we can afford?" Fanny said, scanning the list.

Zed nodded. "This is the expensive part. The flooring and walls, the plumbing and tile for a bathroom and kitchen area. None of that is cheap."

"We have some money set aside," Fanny said, though she wasn't quite sure it would stretch far enough.

"I talked to Dutch at the lumberyard. He'll give us the builder's discount, which will help." As he spoke Zed slid his hammer out of the loop on his belt and bent down to the floor to drive in a nail. He moved in one fluid motion, as if he had been born swinging a hammer. "And I haven't asked anyone yet, but I think some folks would make donations. People are looking forward to having a birth center here. I think they'd be happy to pitch in to make it a reality."

"But we're not a charity," Caleb said, hands on his hips. "We can't go begging for money."

"No one's going begging." Fanny lowered the supply list. "But if we put the word out that the center will open sooner if we get help, I think folks will lend a hand. The last few times I went to a quilting bee, all the women wanted to hear about the progress we were making on the building. This is important to women around here. They want their center."

Caleb shook his head. "Asking for money ... it doesn't feel right."

"You won't have to ask," Fanny said. "Zed and I will spread the word. Some of the women at quiltings have already told me their husbands would be willing to help. Lovina Stoltzfus said Aaron has the time, and there's Gabe and his brothers. And Bishop Samuel favors our plan to build a center. A few words from him would go a long way in letting people in the community know what it's going to take to open our doors." She felt lighter, as if a weight had been lifted from her shoulders. "And it's not money we're after. People might be able to donate a cot or a stove. Some of the women could help me sew curtains."

"That's what I'm thinking." Zed turned to Caleb. "It's not just about asking people for charity. It's about pulling the community together. Folks feel good inside when they do for others."

Moving the lantern to cast light on the cavernous space, Fanny felt the possibilities in this building. "It reminds me of the Bible passage. 'Ask and you shall receive. Seek and you shall find.' I think this is one time when the Almighty would want us to ask around."

The lines in Caleb's brow smoothed as his worry gave way to resolve. "All right, then. We'll see if anyone wants to pitch in."

With that decided, they talked about the floor plan of the building and the possible finishes. Fanny knew there wasn't money for tile, but she hoped they could afford a nice vinyl floor, durable and easy to clean. Tomorrow she would talk with Lois Mast, the bishop's wife, and put the word out about the things they needed for the center.

While Zed continued to talk with Caleb, Fanny tested the new floor, placing one foot in front of the other. Not a single creak or soft spot! Excitement fluttered in her chest when she imagined this renovation completed and occupied by mothers in labor. God willing, her own daughters would be here someday, giving birth to their own babies. Emma might even be here within the next year! What a blessing this birth center would be. It was really going to happen, and all because of Zed.

She kept her gaze on the floor to keep herself from staring at him in wonder. He was more than a handyman; he had a talent for building dreams and soothing the heart. Gott had blessed them in so many ways when He'd sent Zed here, and day by day she was growing attached to him. He was a good friend, almost like family. Too bad folks in the community didn't understand their relationship. Fanny knew if she spent too much time talking to him after church or at a fund-raiser, people would gossip. Ya, those older single women like Dorcas watched Zed like a hawk.

This was a time to seek gelassenheit, the resignation to bend to Gott's will. A good Amish person needed to surrender inside and be content with calm, simple ways.

Geh lessa, Zed had reminded her.

Breathing in the smell of newly cut wood, she thanked Gott for the joy in her heart and the secret friend she had found in Zed.

17

$\mathcal{D}$ressed in blue scrubs and a mask, Meg sat silently in the Pittsburgh hospital's operating room and tried to channel love and strength through Terri Fanelli's icy hand as she gave it another squeeze. It was the last day of November, a bleak day all around.

"I didn't want this," Terri sobbed, a tear rolling down her cheek.

Meg leaned closer to the young mother and nodded with sympathy, though she didn't speak. She believed Dr. Walters's threat that he would throw her out of his OR if she uttered one more word, and at this point, she figured Terri was better off with a silent companion here during her cesarean than no friend at all.

Four months ago, Terri and her husband, Blake, had come to Meg with a very specific birth plan. When her first child was born, the attending physician had insisted that Terri undergo an emergency C-section, and this time, for their second birth, the couple wanted to avoid a cesarean.

"They call me a VBAC at the doctor's office. As if I don't even have a name. I'm just a problem to them because I don't want a C-section," Terri had told Meg when she had first met with the couple. "I don't want the drugs or the incision. I don't want to be incapacitated for days. I want our baby's birth to be a beautiful experience for all of us."

Although many doctors would have insisted on a scheduled C-section for Terri, Dr. Taylor had reviewed her records and given his approval for her to try a home delivery with Meg as midwife.

"Of course, there are risks," Meg had told the couple. She had wanted them to know the facts and possibilities. But Terri and Blake had done their research, and they were passionate about making the birth process as natural as possible this time.

Most of Terri's pregnancy had gone well. She'd been two weeks away from her due date when she went into labor while her husband was away on a business trip.

When Meg had arrived at Terri's house, there had been a mood of joy and celebration that included Terri's mother and young daughter.

"Mom's going to take care of Patsy, and Blake is getting on the next flight out of Denver," Terri had told Meg. "Do you think you can convince this baby to stay put until her daddy gets back in town?"

"I have many skills, but that's not one of them," Meg said with a smile.

There was no stalling the delivery, and unfortunately, as Terri's labor progressed, complications arose that made it necessary to transport her to the hospital. "I don't think you're going to need a C-section," Meg had assured the young mother. "But we want to access the other technology that's available—for your safety and the baby's."

Although Terri had been disappointed, she had agreed. They had made the quick trip to the hospital, where the skilled maternity nurses had helped Meg get Terri settled in with everything she needed. Dr. Taylor was on his way, and Meg sent him a text with an updated status for their patient.

For two hours, Terri's room was a sea of calm in the storm of the busy Pittsburgh hospital. And then, Dr. Walters had penetrated the safe harbor, strutting into the room like an angry peacock.

"Where's her doctor?" he had demanded.

"Dr. Taylor is on his way. But I'm a licensed midwife."

Walters scowled at her as if her credentials and experience were a ludicrous insult. "As chief resident on the floor, I am now responsible for this woman. Where's her chart?"

"Everything is under control," Meg had said, keeping her voice low. She didn't want to disturb Terri, who was breathing through a contraction.

But Dr. Walters didn't care. He demanded the notes, which Meg offered to let him review out in the hall. That seemed to infuriate him all the more. Then, when he saw that they were doing a vaginal delivery after cesarean, the doctor pushed past Meg and, without a word of introduction, began to examine Terri.

"What's going on?" Terri cried, peering at the doctor through eyes puffy with exhaustion.

"Dr. Walters, please. Dr. Taylor is on his way, and until he arrives, we're monitoring mother's and baby's heartbeats. It's under control."

"Under whose control?" The edges of the doctor's mouth turned down in a sneer. "Aren't you the midwife who lost her license?"

She opened her mouth to tell him that she had been cleared of all charges, that her license had never been revoked, simply suspended. That she was damned good at what she did. But any response right now would take precious peace and attention away from the laboring mother.

"This woman needs a C-section now," he insisted. He peeled off his gloves and crossed to the door. "Get her to the OR stat."

"Wait." Meg held up her hands, keeping calm but firm. "That's not what she wants, and I'm—"

"You are not a physician with privileges here," Walters interrupted. "And patients do not call the shots in this hospital."

"But patients have rights, and I've been working with Terri throughout her pregnancy."

The doctor made a note on Terri's chart and strode out the door.

Meg followed him. "Dr. Walters, please. We can give Terri what she wants . . . what she deserves . . . without risk to her or her baby."

"There are always risks," he insisted. "It's my job to minimize them."

"But—"

"Why are you out here arguing with me when you should be with your patient? Go. Be a midwife. I'll even let you in my OR if you promise to keep quiet."

Meg fought him politely, and when that didn't work she asserted herself, stepping out of her comfort zone. But the doctor wouldn't budge.

Regrouping with Terri, Meg put in a desperate call to Dr. Taylor, who had scrubbed in for an emergency procedure across town. She tried to talk to another doctor in his practice and looked for support from the maternity nurses in the ward, but no one dared to cross Dr. Walters's path. As one nurse put it, "When Walters is on duty, we walk on eggshells around here. One wrong step and you're out."

When the aids came to wheel Terri into the OR, Meg had exhausted every resource. She and Terri were both crying, but Meg dashed away her tears, determined to remain calm and provide support to her patient, her friend.

"I'm so cold," Terri whimpered. She was shivering, maybe even a little bit in shock.

Fortunately the anesthesiologist, a silver-haired woman whose kind eyes shone over her mask, seemed sympathetic. She leaned over Terri and took her temperature with the wand. "It's almost over, honey," she whispered. "You'll forget all this and put it behind you."

That's the problem, Meg thought. A forced cesarean was a trauma that was best dismissed, unlike the natural birth experience that could empower a mother. Western medicine had a long way to go to embrace the art of birth.

Later, when Meg was alone in her apartment, she stepped into a hot shower and bawled like a baby. She cried for Terri, who had been robbed of a beautiful experience. She cried for Terri's baby daughter, whose mother would not be allowed to hold her for the first forty-eight hours because she was on a morphine drip to alleviate the pain from her incisions. She cried for every mother giving birth at that hospital, being pushed through like widgets on a factory conveyor belt. There was a better way, and she knew it. Why wouldn't the hospital administrators respect the organic stages and patterns of human birth?

And she cried for herself . . . her own failures and disappointments. Her time with Jack had underlined the fact that she was alone here in Pittsburgh, alone and often lonely. How had her daily schedule devolved into a string of battles with hospital administrators? Right now she felt miles away from her purpose in life.

When she stepped out of the shower and bundled up in a towel, her cell phone was buzzing on the bathroom counter. It was a text message from Jack, who knew what she was going through.

No one is strong enough to bear her burdens alone. Lean on me. I'm off tomorrow and I got vacation time. Should I head your way?

With a calming breath, she texted back: *Yes, please.*

His answer made her smile. *Look out, Pittsburgh.*

"I'm sorry, Meg," Dr. Taylor said when she met him in his office the next day to go over the chart notes for Terri Fanelli's case. "You know I would have done everything possible to respect the Fanellis' birth plan."

"I know that." Too antsy to sit, she paced in front of Larry Taylor's desk. Jack had counseled her over the phone, helping her to sort through the conflict calmly. Although she still had issues with Dr. Walters and his beaten staff, she felt no malice toward Larry Taylor. "You're not to blame, Larry. It's the administration at the hospital, stuck in the Stone Age." She paused, circling the doctor's desk and peering through the slatted blinds. "Actually, the Stone Age would be an improvement over their maternity practices. At least women were free to squat, and no one was cutting them open and pumping drugs into their veins."

Dr. Taylor sat back in his chair and drew in a deep breath. "The only thing I can say in defense of hospital protocol is that they have an extremely low mortality rate for mothers and newborns."

"But a high rate of C-sections," Meg pointed out. "One of the highest in the country. How is it that you became affiliated with them, Larry?"

"When I started practicing, they were the best game in town. And though doctors like Vic Walters may be lacking in bedside manner, most of the staff is well trained and conscientious. But old-school."

"Very old-school." She thrust her hands deep into the pockets of her fleece jacket. "When I mentioned the patient bill of rights, this big vein popped in Dr. Walters's neck."

"Sounds like you hit a tender spot."

She turned back to him and sighed. "Larry, I think I'm done here. The hospital rules are so restrictive, they might as well be handcuffing me. And after my showdown with Doc Walters, I'm probably barred from the facility, anyway."

"Not quite, but it's becoming clear that our hospital is not a good match for your skills."

She plopped into the chair opposite his desk. "It's a relief to hear it put into words. So, did they tell you I wasn't welcome back?"

"Not in so many words, but I'm under the gun for supporting a midwife. It's not you they're after as much as the notion of any midwives delivering babies in the hospital. I've spoken to the other doctors, even tried to call in a few favors, but they won't be swayed. They're holding strong on this. The other doctors don't want midwives on staff."

With a deep breath, she leaned back in the chair. "So the hospital administration wants to end their affiliation with me."

He nodded. "You don't fit in with their future plans for the hospital. As long as I back you, they won't suspend your privileges, but you've already seen how difficult it can be to work in an environment where the staff is less than supportive."

"Yes, indeed. I learned that lesson at Terri Fanelli's expense."

"Have you thought of starting a country practice?" he suggested.

"I've delivered some babies in rural areas. Some farm folk and Amish people." She had found the people to be cooperative, though the thought of being a country midwife brought her memory screeching back to that cold, icy night when everything had gone wrong. Relentlessly cold weather, impassable roads, uncooperative mother, and an innocent baby in distress.

"Plenty of women in rural areas are grateful for the help of a midwife. Maybe you should move beyond the 'burbs."

"I can't do it."

It was only when Larry looked up from his case notes that she realized she'd said it aloud. "Meg." He put the pen down and flattened his palms on the paperwork. "You're a capable, experienced midwife. Any woman would be fortunate to have you as a professional caregiver."

She frowned, still lost in the darkness of that winter night.

"And while it's good to learn from your mistakes, your actions in the Collier case were completely responsible, and the board agreed. You did nothing wrong."

She let out the breath she had been holding, and the shards of memory fell away. Larry was right. She had learned ways to free herself from regret and focus on the present, focus on the job that allowed her to nurture the rich, ripe cycles of new life.

"I don't know," she said. "I don't know where I belong. But it's becoming eminently clear that Pittsburgh is not the place." She thought of what Jack had said about the possibility that she might move to Halfway. At the time she had thought he was pushing things, but now she wondered if it was a real possibility. It would be nice to live close to Zoey and Tate, and she knew there was a need for licensed midwives in that area. To live in the same town as Jack . . . right now that seemed too good to be true.

"Look . . ." Larry interrupted her thoughts. "You're going on a break to deliver your sister's baby. It might be a good time to put some feelers out. Check out other institutions. Research their attitudes and policies on home births."

It was a plan that made sense. "I'll be staying in Lancaster County for a good six weeks. I'll scope out the situation there." She pushed out of the chair, tilting her head to the side. "I have to thank you for all you've done, Larry. You stuck by me, against all odds."

"Well, you're trying to do a good thing. Someday, the rest of the medical community will see that." When he came around the desk to shake her hand, she realized that he was a little thinner and grayer than when she had met him years ago, as a nursing student, and she felt a tender spot in her heart for the doctor who had supported her. "God bless you, Meg."

"Thanks, Doc. So long." There was a sense of finality in their good-bye; Meg had a feeling she wouldn't be back. There was a sad wisp of closure, but also a trembling anticipation of the future. She was at a turning point, a crossroads, and as Jack had emphasized, it was important to keep moving ahead.

☙❧

"Be the change that you wish to see in the world," Jack told her as they shared green curry noodles in a Thai restaurant near her apartment. "That's what Mahatma Gandhi said. And if that pearl of wisdom is too dusty for you, I've got a few others tucked up my sleeve."

She grinned over a mouthful of noodles. "You are never at a loss for words," she told him. "But I get the point. I've always been proud of the fact that I'm a careful, cautious person. I never realized that my steady approach would make me so resistant to change." It seemed that change was inevitable. Her position here was fizzling out, and there was opportunity in Halfway. Potential clients, her close sister, and Jack . . .

"The sweet part of the deal is that you don't have to make any big decisions right now. You're going to be in Halfway for a while. You can give it a test drive, see how that goes before you close up shop here."

A stained-glass piece in the restaurant window came alive with a burst of sunlight, and Meg realized that the entire room, with its old wooden booths and fake ferns, seemed more vibrant and alive with Jack here. How did he manage that?

Over the next two days, she saw the city in a new light. The mummies and gems at the Carnegie Museum were wondrous finds through Jack's eyes. A little French bistro at Penn Place transported them to Paris, with soft light and music, buttery croissants, and a fireplace to chase off the winter night. They held hands under the table and talked about their childhood years, their old neighborhoods, their hopes, fears, and dreams. Her heart ached for the boy who had lost his parents so young, and yet, from Jack's enthusiasm and joy in the moment, it was clear that his grandmother had raised him in an atmosphere of love and support. He was wise and impetuous, tough and sensitive; a study in contradictions that she hoped to spend a lifetime exploring. On Sunday morning, they shared the newspaper over waffles and fruit at Waffallonia. In the afternoon, they became part of a crowd of roaring fans at a riverside sports bar, where they cheered the Steelers on to victory.

"I wish you didn't have to leave," she said as he pulled up in front of her apartment.

"Me, too, but I need to drive back early tomorrow. My shift starts at three."

"Boo. I'll be coming to Halfway in two weeks. But I guess this is good-bye for now." As she looked up at him, a rush of emotion overwhelmed her. She reached for him and he pulled her into his arms.

"I'm gonna miss you, Megs." His kiss stole her breath away, igniting a flame of longing deep inside her. She wanted to stay in his arms . . . to never let go. When she was with Jack, Pittsburgh was a rich, hospitable city—not the ogre she had thought to be responsible for her sadness. Jack was the key. Wherever he went, that was where she wanted to be.

She couldn't get to Halfway soon enough.

PART THREE

ॐ

Geh Lessa: Let It Be

Blessed are the merciful:
for they shall obtain mercy.
—MATTHEW 5:7

18

Although Fanny had come to the hardware store for a roll of insulation, as she waited for Mr. Hennessey to fetch it from the storeroom she kept doubling back to a soft pair of men's suede work gloves and thinking about Zed's fine, skilled hands. Strong hands, with slender fingers but a good bit of meat on the palms. She had seen those hands lift heavy beams and rub sanding blocks over wood planks. Those hands had pulled her close to comfort her. They had lifted Tommy away from a bucket of nails and guided Will's hand on the hammer. There was power and grace in those hands.

Fanny blinked, trying to snap herself out of such a daydream. Zed had spent the past six months working at her place, so it seemed only right to thank him with a gift this time of year. She knew he would put these gloves to good use. If she bought them for him as a Christmas gift, would anyone think twice about that? Would it start tongues wagging?

There was no denying that she had become attached to Zed over the past few months. Each morning when she came downstairs she looked forward to seeing him. He worked on the carriage house by himself Monday through Friday. In the afternoons, he let Will tag along and learn how to do carpentry and projects. How Will enjoyed doing a man's work!

An Amish plumber had donated his time to install the kitchen sink and bathroom fixtures. On Saturdays, groups of men had been coming out to help Zed, climbing over the lumber pile like ants on a log. They had finished the flooring and interior framing in two Saturdays, and now they were cutting and installing drywall. Such good work! At this rate, they would be finished before the New Year.

But the thought of finishing made her a little sick. Would Zed stop coming once the place was done? That was a change she wasn't prepared for. In her heart she knew the truth: She didn't want to give Zed up. She had come to see him in a different light, as a woman viewed a man. And it seemed that after one glimpse with loving eyes, there was no going back to being strictly friends.

It was getting harder and harder to hide her emerging feelings for Zed, and it was not something she could talk about with anyone. She was a widow in mourning, her Thomas not gone a year yet, and Zed was still working his way back into the community's good graces after being gone and lost to the faith for so many years. Already the two of them stood out like sore thumbs, and right now a match between them would be pure scandal.

Taking the gloves from the rack, she slid one hand into the soft kid leather and pressed it to her troubled heart. A flame still burned there for her Thomas. It always would. She knew she was not ready to marry again, and yet the joy she felt when she was with Zed was so strong and sure. Conversation flowed easily between them, and he was as reliable as the sunrise each morning. They needed time, and the clock was clicking too fast. Once Zed finished his work at the carriage house and took a job with a builder, the single maids would pounce on him like barn cats on a mouse. Tamping down those jealous thoughts, she moved around the corner of a display and spotted Tommy, who was feeling his way along the edge of a stack of doormats. He grabbed on, pulled himself up to his feet, and started to toddle away.

"Where are we going now, little man?" she asked with an amused smile.

"I got him, Mamm," Beth said, gently shepherding Tommy along. She followed close, easing his fall when he plopped down to the floor. "Oops-a-daisy. You want to get back up? Here. I'll help." Beth lifted him up and propped him on his feet again. For a four-year-old, she was a good little helper.

"Here we are." Mr. Hennessey put the roll of insulation down beside the counter. "Anything else I can get for you, Fanny?"

"These gloves." She put them on the counter and paid for her purchase.

"Let me load this into your buggy for you," he said, lifting the bulky insulation. "I'm guessing this will be the last roll?" Mr. Hennessey had been keeping up with the progress on the center, and he knew they had already purchased most of the insulation.

"This should be the last one. They've already started closing up the walls, but they were a bit short." Fanny picked up Tommy and motioned to Beth to follow her out the door.

"Well, you tell Zed to let me know if he needs anything else. Sounds like they're getting close to the finish line. When are you planning to open your doors?"

"January. But we've already had one baby born at the center. A surprise for all of us."

"I heard about that. Deb and Gideon Yoder had their fourth, right?" he asked as he hoisted the roll into the back of the buggy.

"Word travels fast." Deb always had quick labors, and when her husband couldn't locate Anna, he had loaded Deb into the buggy and driven her to the closest place where he could get help. Fanny had caught the baby, and she still thanked Gott that everything had gone well.

That day with the Yoders replayed in Fanny's mind as she drove the buggy home. She recalled the shocked look on Zed's face when she and Gideon had helped Deb into the center. Looking back on it now, she could laugh. But Zed had been genuinely confused.

"But we're not open yet," he'd insisted. As if that would make Deb's labor stop for a few weeks.

"Open or not, we need Fanny's help!" Gideon had said firmly. "Our baby is coming, and it's coming right now."

That had made Zed put down his tools mighty quick. Fanny had asked him to keep an eye on the children, and told him that there was still coffee on the kitchen stove.

Fanny showed the couple to the one finished bay, where a new cot sat covered with a tarp. As she folded the tarp from the bed, she was glad that this small area was ready. She hadn't thought they would be using the cot anytime soon, but Fanny had covered it with plastic sheets, doing a little nesting of her own in the building. It was also good to have heat from the wood-burning stove that had gone in last week—a donation from Nate and Betsy King, who owned a successful dairy farm in Halfway. She put Gideon on the task of maintaining the fire while she tended to Deb.

When Deb had told Fanny her babies came quickly, she wasn't kidding. Within the hour Fanny had washed and wrapped the newborn and placed him in Gideon's arms. Deb was sitting up on the cot, so pleased to have her baby here.

"Look at his little hands. Such tiny fingers and nails." Deb folded the blanket back from the baby for a better look, and the baby let out a squall that made both parents laugh. "He's got a good set of lungs!"

Fanny left the three of them for a bit and went back into the main house, where Zed had heated up soup and made sandwiches for everyone.

"The children seemed hungry, and I figured the folks over there would want to eat eventually." The color had returned to Zed's face, and he looked so comfortable sitting at the table, bouncing Tommy on his knee.

It was clear he had recovered from being pushed out of the work site so abruptly. He was relieved that the Yoders' baby had arrived safely, and he helped Fanny bring back a tray of food for them.

Gideon had soup and half a sandwich, but Deb polished off three sandwiches, which was no surprise to Fanny, who understood the voracious appetite of a new mother.

"Next time you have a baby, you'll be welcome to stay a night or two," Fanny said as she ladled out another bowl of soup for Deb. "We'll be set up to take good care of you then. But I'm afraid we're going to have to send you home today so that Zed can get back to work."

"I have to say, you took me by surprise," Zed said from his perch atop a sawhorse. "I didn't even have a minute to sweep up the sawdust."

"A little sawdust never hurt anyone." Gideon leaned forward and rubbed his knuckles gently against his son's chubby cheek.

"I'm grateful that you opened up for us today," Deb said. "Homemade soup, sandwiches, and a new baby to take home . . . this has got to be one of the best days ever!"

"We appreciate it, Fanny," Gideon added. "But I can't help wondering what happened to Anna. It's not like her to leave without telling anyone."

Later that day, after the Yoders had left and Zed was back to work, Fanny drove into town and heard the news at the Country Store.

"Dear Anna broke her ankle," Elsie reported. "She tripped and fell while she was feeding the chickens. She's in a cast, and she'll need to stay off her feet for at least a month. Susie King is going to move in to take care of her since Anna's daughters have all moved out of the area."

"Poor Anna. She's not going to like being laid up, but that explains a lot about this morning." Fanny and Elsie decided to make a casserole and cookies to take over to the midwife.

"But I guess it means that, at least for now, you're the midwife around here," Elsie said. "It's a good thing you're here for the mothers who need you."

"And a good thing that we're opening the birth center," Fanny agreed.

&ℭ

When Fanny arrived at home, she got the children settled in the house and hid the gloves in the back of one of her dresser drawers. When she went back to the buggy, Zed was toting the roll of insulation on one shoulder.

"I'll unhitch the buggy for you," he said. "But if you have a minute, I want to show you something in the kitchen."

"I always have a minute for you," she said, following him into the carriage house.

He propped the insulation in the corner and led her to the kitchen area, where the refrigerator and stove that had been donated by Amish folk gleamed in the light of the kerosene lamp. "Down here, under the sink." He opened the cabinet drawer and dropped to his knees by the sink.

She gathered the skirt of her dress and kneeled beside him.

"It's the valve for the water supply," he said. "Do you see that blue lever?"

It was dark under the cabinet, and she couldn't see much beyond the pipes. "I don't think so."

He switched on a flashlight and leaned in beside her, so near that his arm brushed hers. The mixed smells of wood smoke, lavender, and sawdust awakened her senses. "Right back there. Can you reach it?" He pointed the light on it.

"Let me try." She reached into the cabinet to touch the lever, and in the tight space she had to press against him. Her fingers brushed the handle right away, but she lingered there, savoring the closeness of him.

"Got it?" he asked.

"Ya." Letting the air from her lungs, she leaned out and sat back on her heels, suddenly face-to-face with him, so close she could see a small patch on his neck that he had missed with the razor this morning. How she longed to touch the stubble with her fingers, to run her hand along his smooth jaw and burrow her fingers into his thick hair.

Her face was suddenly warm with embarrassment, and she cast her eyes down. "Do I need to keep an eye on this water valve?"

"Only if there's an emergency. If you turn this valve, it will shut off the water supply to this building. It's a good thing to know."

"Mmm." She could feel his breath and smell the scent of fresh cut wood on his skin. "But you'll be here to turn it off if there's any problem." She blurted the words out before she realized it was not true. Although Zed seemed close as a family member, he didn't belong here. Not forever. And the thought of a morning without Zed left her feeling empty and lost. Although Fanny knew her emotions were not practical, she wanted Zed to stay, for good.

"I'll be here a few more weeks." In a heartbeat, he was on his feet, reaching down to her. "After that, you'll be in charge. It would be wrong for me to leave without teaching you how things work."

"I see." She took his hand, surprised by the warmth of it on this December day, and held on to him as he helped her up. His touch sent tingles down her spine, but she couldn't speak of that. Those feelings had to be stowed away for now. "I will always remember the water valve lesson."

"Your hands are like ice." He pressed her hands inside his, then rubbed them gently, trying to infuse warmth. "Is it really getting that cold outside?"

It's the thought of losing you that leaves me cold. Please, don't ever go. Take me in your arms and warm me from head to toe . . .

It was wrong to have these feelings. She was in mourning, still wearing black. When guilt weighed her down, she kept telling herself that it was natural to become attached to someone you see every day. Besides that, the Millers were family. Family. Maybe she would come to love Zed like a brother. Maybe? No, that would be a lie. *Dear Gott,* she prayed, conscious of the heat of Zed's body radiating through her hands. *Teach me patience and help me appreciate solitude.*

A knock on the door broke the moment between them, and they both pulled their hands away as if caught doing something wrong. Zed turned to the sink and Fanny went to the door, crossing the invisible line back to their separate lives.

"I wonder who that is." Fanny pressed the backs of her hands to her hot cheeks, hoping that her face would not reveal the fiery longing that burned inside. With a deep breath she opened the door to two Englisher women. It was her neighbor Zoey Jordan and Zoey's sister, Meg, the midwife who was ever so helpful delivering Lizzy's baby.

"Hey, there!" Zoey's cloud of hair was like a golden halo around her head. She wore a fancy red coat with a big pin shaped like a

Christmas wreath, with little red lights on it that blinked on and off. "Sorry to drop in on you like this, but Meg just got here and I was hoping to show her your new center." She tilted her head, peeking inside. "Mind if we take a look?"

Fanny opened the door wide. "Come in." It was impossible to say no to good, kind Zoey, and Fanny was still grateful to Meg, who had taught her many things in the brief hours that they had worked together. A week or so after that difficult birth, Fanny had received a package in the mail from Meg—a little suctioning tool like the one Meg had shown her how to use. Anna had marveled over it, and Doc Trueherz had told her that it would be invaluable in her work as a midwife.

"Hi, Fanny. It's good to see you." Meg wore a blue quilted coat with a green scarf, and her copper red hair was nearly covered by a green, fleece-trimmed cap that made her look as young as a teenager. "I'm so glad the center is coming together for you."

"Folks seem to want it," Fanny admitted. "There's not really much to see. But we hope to open in January."

"I'm going to take care of the horse," Zed said, slipping past the women to go out the door.

Fanny nodded to him gratefully.

"Hi and bye, Zed," Zoey said. "You're doing a great job here. Everyone's excited about it."

He gave a tight smile before pulling on his black hat and stepping out.

"I didn't mean to chase him out. Was he afraid you two might talk shop?" Zoey said.

Fanny frowned. Well, of course Zed didn't want to hear about that.

Meg nodded. "I don't blame him. So tell me about your birthing center. Zoey tells me that you've been working on renovations since the summer."

"We have. And already one woman had her baby here."

"Really?" Zoey put her hands on her hips. "How'd that happen?"

Fanny told them about Gideon and Deb Yoder. "Luckily, it all turned out fine. A baby boy, strong and healthy."

"Excellent." There was a warm glow in Meg's smile, and Fanny was reminded of the midwife's knowledge. This was a woman who understood the peaks and valleys of childbirth, a woman who knew the joy of the final outcome, a healthy baby and mother.

"See?" Zoey wagged a finger. "That just shows you that women need this place. When I found out that I was expecting, I was shocked to learn that Halfway didn't have any medical facility to speak of." Zoey patted her belly in that way English women had of showing everyone that they were pregnant. Amish women kept such things to themselves. "I'm so glad you decided to build this, out here in the country."

"And I imagine that a lot of local women plan to use the center," Meg said.

"That's what we're hearing. Doc Trueherz says that most of his Englisher patients go to the hospital in Lancaster, but he thinks some will want to come here. And in January Doc will come out one day a week to do prenatal visits with his Amish patients in the area. The women will be glad to save a trip to Paradise and back, especially with the cold weather and icy roads this time of year." Fanny explained that the doctor wanted her to get involved, since Anna was still laid up with a broken ankle.

"So I take it this will be a little sitting area near the kitchen." Zoey walked over to the sink, the heels of her shiny boots clicking on the vinyl floor.

"It's smart for the front door to open up to a group area like this," Meg said. "It makes the delivery area more private."

"It's also a good place for Doc Trueherz to sit to do his paperwork." Fanny crossed to the sink and opened the door of the refrigerator with a smile. "Both of these appliances were donations from Amish families who support the center."

"Wonderful! See? The community is behind you, Fanny." Zoey leaned into the fridge, then frowned back at Fanny. "Umm ... it's not very cold."

"It's not hooked up yet, but the stove and refrigerator will be powered by propane tanks out back. And through this doorway are the beds." Fanny led the way, showing them the three areas separated by half walls. "We'll hang curtains for privacy, but from what I've seen, most mothers enjoy socializing after the baby is born." She pointed out that they had a bathroom with running water, but no electricity. Lights would be operated by battery or kerosene. "Nothing fancy here. We won't have any of those big machines they have in hospitals, but we'll have plenty of light and simple instruments."

"I've seen fancy and high-tech"—Meg's voice was firm but quiet—"and for most deliveries, I would prefer simple."

"Oh, look! You've already got a bed set up!" Zoey crowed. She sat on the single cot and patted the tarp. "Isn't this wonderful? I could just put my feet up right now and take a nap."

"No naps for you," Meg teased her sister. "We are walking into town. Exercise first, then nap, honey."

"Oh, dear. That's right. Time for aerobics, and we need vanilla to bake our cookies." Zoey pushed up from the cot. "My little sister has always been bossy."

Fanny smiled at the banter. "You two remind me of my own sisters back in Sugar Valley, Mary and Ruth Ann—the three of us are close in age, and we did everything together." How wonderful it had been to share chores with them, washing the windows together or baking a big batch of cookies. Fanny missed that closeness, but with chores and children and babies to birth, there wasn't a lot of time to spare for quilting bees and socializing.

"There's nothing like family," said Meg. "My sister may complain, but I know she's glad I'm here."

"Thrilled. I'm absolutely thrilled, and who's complaining? I just know that if we're walking into town, we had better get going if we want to get home before sundown. I'm moving a little slow these days. Fanny, do you need anything from the stores in town?"

"Not today."

"And I'm sure Fanny has plenty to do." Meg put a hand on her sister's shoulder and steered her toward the door. "Thanks for giving us a look, Fanny. I can't tell you how encouraged I am to see your clinic. I've been living in a place where doctors want women to have their babies in hospitals, with drugs and surgery."

"Oh, we wouldn't want that," Fanny said. "Most women here have their babies at home with a midwife. But the birthing center will make it easier on the doctors and the midwives, too. This way, Anna and I can share the responsibility."

"Well, your place is absolutely charming," Zoey declared, "and once you get all the beds and furnishings in, it's going to be downright cozy. If I didn't have Meg to be my midwife, I would love to be a patient here."

Fanny followed the two women, feeling as if she were walking on a cloud. Not that she usually paid much attention to the opinion of the English, but Meg was special. She understood the miracle of childbirth and she was skilled with the mechanics of it, too. And Meg had only good things to say about the birth center.

Ya, it felt good to have her approval.

Inside the kitchen, Fanny gave Tommy a wooden spoon, which was better to chew on than a pencil. She bent down to kiss Beth's forehead. Children were such a blessing. Would she have more?

She took a pot down from its hook and held it to her heart for a moment. *Please, Gott, let there be more children.*

19

As she followed her sister down the lane, Meg took one last look back at the Lapps' newly converted carriage house. From the freshly painted carriage doors, you would never know that it was about to become a birthing center. "I have a really good feeling about that place." There was something intriguing in the mingled smells of kerosene and sawdust, the cozy sitting room with its donated appliances and furniture, the spacious clinic room with separate bays for privacy. And Fanny herself, calm, unassuming, but bright as the North Star. "Of course, it would be nice to have electricity and some of the technology that comes with that. But I think it will serve the Amish community well. As a demographic, they're the largest group in the U.S. to advocate for home births and midwives."

"Oh, I knew you would love it." Zoey clapped her hands together. "I'm excited about it myself, not just for the service it will provide to the community, but also for the financial security it can give the Lapps." She lowered her voice and walked a little closer. "Fanny lost her husband last winter, and the family has been relying on small salaries and the money they bring in from the Country Store in town. Tate says their budget is probably a little tight, but the birthing center should provide financial security once it gets going. And you know Tate and his money sense. He's got a knack for numbers."

Zoey's husband was a financial wizard. He had prospered as a financial broker until a heart attack in his forties had convinced him to slow down and opt out of the fast-paced business. Meg tested the ground along the roadside with her boots. Frozen solid. With a little precipitation, they might have a white Christmas.

"That's sad about Fanny's husband," Meg said. "And with a new baby ... such a heartbreak. I'm glad the birth center could be a profitable business for her family."

"And a real financial aid to the community. For a pregnant woman, a birthing center is about one fifth of the cost of going to a hospital. And from what I hear, Fanny is a dedicated midwife. *And* this is an acceptable business for an Amish woman to be running. Fanny says the church leaders have been very supportive. You know, she doesn't have the career opportunities you and I would have. So that place is a win–win all around."

"Listen to you. Last year when you guys were scouting properties for a B and B, you didn't know anything about the Amish. Now you're an expert."

"You know me. I'm always sticking my nose in everybody's business, but it's all about community—neighbors need to help each other. And that's one of the reasons I'm so glad we landed in Halfway. People care about each other here, and they'll go out of their way to lend a hand. Not that they're all touchy-feely or anything. The Amish can be downright brusque and sometimes they come off as cold. But I persisted, and I've made some friends."

"In your Zoey way. Corner them with kindness and cookies."

Zoey wiggled her eyebrows. "My trade secrets. When I look at how things have worked out, well, it was just meant to be. We needed to hire someone at the inn, and Shandell landed on our doorstep. And her mother's moved here and loves it. Now you're here, and look at that—a birthing clinic is opening right next door. It's all falling into place. Next time I see Fanny, I'm going to ask her if she could use your help."

"Let's not make any assumptions," Meg objected as they walked past some clods of horse droppings that seemed to have frozen in the road. She was definitely not in Pittsburgh anymore and it was thrilling to be here in Halfway. She couldn't wait to see Jack, though she'd have to wait until he got off work tonight.

"It's just a simple question, and I'll bet she says yes. You heard what happened to Anna. She's going to be off her feet for a while, and with all the babies born around here, Fanny can't handle it alone." A gust of wind lifted the soft curls of her blond hair away from her face. "You can talk to Dr. Trueherz about it when we go for my appointment tomorrow. He is going to love you. That poor man travels all over this part of Lancaster County to deliver babies and make house calls on the Amish, and everyone knows he's spread way too thin. His wife, Celeste—she works in his office—she worries about him, and I can't blame her. Who can get a moment's rest when your sweetie is out there negotiating icy roads, sleep-deprived, and missing meals?"

Meg gave a quick laugh.

"What's so funny?"

"You just described my work schedule. But at least I don't have anyone at home to lose sleep worrying about me."

Zoey's lower lip jutted out in a pout. "That's sad. But I don't think you're going to be single too much longer. We both know Jack is crazy about you, and though you play it close to the cuff, I can tell you're into him. And once you move here? That deal is going to be sealed."

"Zoey! Stop that."

"You know it's true."

"I've been here two hours and already you have me moving here and married off. It's all a little premature, and I'd like to think I have a choice in two of the most important decisions of my life."

"You know I just want you to be happy."

"You think I don't want to be happy? Of course I do. But I don't need any added pressure. And Jack . . ." She sighed. "Jack's a great guy, and he's become a really good friend. But our relationship is still new and tenuous." To be honest, she had high hopes for the future of that relationship. But right now she didn't dare arm her sister with that information.

"Don't be silly. True love doesn't fade away."

Meg gaped at her sister. "Listen to yourself. My life is not a Hallmark card."

Zoey linked her arm through Meg's and leaned her head close. "Don't be annoyed. Look, I know I have tunnel vision sometimes. But Tate and I are so happy here, and the only way it could be better would be for you to be living nearby and happy, too."

Meg softened inside. "I'm not mad. You want a happy ending for everyone." And she hoped that Zoey was right. She felt optimistic about herself and Jack, and a new life in this quaint country town. Wouldn't it be funny if all those dreams came true? Her sister had such a gift; somehow Zoey always knew how to melt the iciest heart. That was the power of love. As they reached the main street of town, Meg was struck by the scene that resembled a Christmas village on a train set. Holly twirled around lampposts and candle-style bulbs shone from the shop windows. Fat silver bells dangled from glittery streamers strewn over the streets. The life-size Nativity scene in front of the church was complete except for the statue of baby Jesus, which Meg knew would be added to the manger after the Christmas Eve service. In the distance, the tall spruce in front of the town hall glowed bright with multicolored lights. Its tall peak pointed to the heavens, reminding Meg of the source of all this Christmas wonder.

"Halfway looks so festive," Meg said.

"Doesn't it? The only thing that would make it more Christmassy would be if we had snow."

"That's possible." Meg pulled her scarf closer as she noted the white puffs that formed in the air whenever they talked. It was chilly, all right.

"We need to cross here." Zoey moved toward the intersection, tugging her sister along in that direction. "I think you should go down and see the tree in front of city hall while I duck into the Little Apple Grocery. It's quite a sight from close up."

"Why don't you come with?" Meg asked.

"I've got to use the little girls' room. You go ahead, and I'll catch up."

"You okay?" Meg asked, sensing that her sister was holding back.

"Yes, of course. Just go. I'll buy what we need and meet you down the street in a few minutes."

As her sister ducked into the small grocery store, Meg returned her attention to the town's main street, where horses nickered at hitching posts, a line of gray-topped buggies behind them. Cars cruised slowly and people moved through the brisk cold. Red-cheeked shoppers lingered at shop windows and hustled into stores, and Amish folk bundled in coats or capes walked with purpose.

The charming scene was a welcome relief from Meg's neighborhood in the suburbs of Pittsburgh, where there were no decent shops or restaurants within walking distance. Lately there had been a rash of stolen cars in her area, and she had begun to feel wary whenever she had to pass through the grounds of her apartment complex in the dark. She passed by Ye Olde Tea Shop, a small tidy space with lemony yellow walls and cute little tables. It looked so warm and inviting; if they weren't aiming to get home before dark, she would stop in with Zoey and have a warm cup of tea—spicy chai for Meg, and a cinnamon spice tea for her sister. The Country Store seemed equally charming, though a bit crowded with shoppers. A small furniture shop would be worth investigating one day, and the bakery smelled heavenly.

Yes, she could see herself living here in Halfway. Compared to her current situation, this would be like a trip to Disneyland. How had Jack described it? Like stepping into a Norman Rockwell painting.

Jack. Something fluttered in her chest at the thought of him. Although she had always been skeptical about long-distance relationships, Jack had proved her wrong, endearing himself through his phone calls and text messages. His unwavering faith in God had shed light on her darkest moments, and his sense of humor always helped her keep things in perspective. While she was practical and pragmatic, sure to keep two feet on the ground, Jack was quick to take off and soar with his dreams. While he saved her from being stuck in the muck, she kept him grounded. They were quite a complement. Meg was looking forward to seeing more of Jack over this longer stretch of time.

A Salvation Army Santa was set up down the block with his boom box and red bucket, and strains of "I Heard the Bells" filled the air, adding to the poignant atmosphere: "... with peace on earth, good will to men."

Digging her hands deeper into the pockets of her quilted coat, she lifted her gaze to the tall tree that loomed ahead, the glow of its bright lights blurring in a lovely display of blue, green, red, purple, and yellow. How she loved Christmas! There was such a joyous spirit in the air. Granted, the lights and trimmings were a palpable sign of the commercial holiday, but every year around this time she saw hard hearts soften. At Christmastime the message of hope from the birth of the Savior reached many people who ordinarily looked the other way.

She was mulling over the true meaning of the holidays when she heard him call her name. She glanced away from the tree and there he was, as if she had dreamed him there. In his navy jacket and slacks with a black stripe down the side, he looked lean and authoritative. There was something about a man in a uniform that made a girl want to salute and wrap her arms around him, all at the same time.

When he spread his arms wide, she rushed forward and threw herself into a big bear hug. His arms closed around her, and joy burst inside her as he lifted her off the ground. Soaring in Jack's embrace, she laughed at the thrill that bubbled forth.

"Meg! Look at you! It seems like forever."

"I know, I know." She had never experienced such a feeling of sparkling delight and excruciating tenderness at the same time.

He planted a kiss on her temple, then lowered her to her feet. "You're a welcome sight, girl. How was the trip?"

"Good. I didn't think I'd catch you until later."

"Same. I'm usually rolling on patrol, but I just happened to be back there in the office, catching up on paperwork when I got this text from your sister." He took his phone from his pocket and tapped it to open the message. "Go to the Christmas tree for a holiday surprise," he read. "So I stepped out and you know what? Zoey's right. I'd be happy to find you under my tree any morning of the year."

"Well, then, Merry Christmas. Zoey strikes again."

"You gotta love her."

He leaned close, his voice low and husky. "Missed you. It's hard to let you go, but I don't want to put it all out there in the center of town." He rubbed her shoulders, then let his hands slip away. "You got here ahead of the snow. They say it's coming tonight."

"I planned it that way. Didn't want to get stranded on the turn-pike."

"We couldn't have that."

It was still there . . . the spark of energy between them. The ex-citement in the air around them. The irresistible impulse to smile at him. She forced herself to breathe deeply in an attempt to slow her racing pulse. Oh, she had it bad for this guy.

"So what's the plan, girl? You gonna pencil me in for some ice-skating or a movie or whatnot?"

Amazing how the heart could soar over the prospect of a few dates. "I'm counting on it," she said.

He told her he was working until eleven, but would text her when he got off.

"I'll be up," she said. *And waiting for your message.* Jack filled her vision, her mind . . . her heart. It was time to tamp down the doubts that always nipped at her when happiness came her way. Time to step away from the roles she was so comfortable with—midwife, caretaker, responsible sister. Time to nurture her own hopes and dreams. Time to push that naysayer out of her mind and take a chance on love.

They chatted awhile about a charity event Jack was working on and Jack's sister, Kat, who was due at the end of the month. They were talking about the glittering tree, which Jack said was deco-rated every year by Halfway's volunteer fire department, when Zoey arrived. She was sipping contentedly from a steaming cup.

"Well, look who you ran into!" she said, grinning up at Jack.

"The jig is up, Zoey. I saw the text message you sent him."

Zoey smacked Jack's well-padded arm. "You weren't supposed to tell her."

He shrugged. "I never was any good at lies."

Perfect, Meg thought. She was a person who lived in the truth.

Zoey cocked her blond head to one side. "I just figured, since we were taking a walk to get some exercise, maybe Meg could catch up with you."

"I like the way you think, Zoey." Jack nodded, lifting the cuff of his coat sleeve to check his watch. "Look at that! I gotta get back to work. But I'm glad we caught up. And thanks for dragging her into town, Zoey."

"Actually, we came in to get vanilla," Meg said. "We're doing some baking. Trying to re-create the old family Christmas cookie recipe."

"That's right. The vanilla." Zoey pointed at her forehead. "I'm telling you, pregnancy does affect the brain. I can't remember anything these days. I hope that changes after the baby's born."

"So you ladies are going to bake some cookies?" Jack's eyes, those kind, earnest eyes, had a direct line to Meg's heart at the moment.

"That's the plan," Meg said. "We'll save you some."

"Mmm. I got to get me some of those, hot right out of the oven."

"So come over tonight," Zoey said, forging ahead, as usual. "What time do you get off?"

For once, Meg wasn't annoyed by her sister's persistence. "Eleven." She and Jack said it at the same time.

Meg smiled up at him. "See you then?"

"Will do."

As Jack headed back to the police station, a small snowflake twirled before her eyes. "It's snowing," she said.

"Naw." Zoey looked up from her cup of tea and blinked. "You're right. It is!"

Suddenly the air was filled with lacy flakes. Zoey stretched her arms out and lifted her face to the sky. "I love snow when I don't have to drive in it."

With a chuckle, Meg held out a hand and looked up toward the heavens. White flakes floated and danced, suspended in the light from the streetlamp. Flakes dropped on her cheeks and clung to her lashes—a baptism of snow. It was as if all the hardships and grief of the past year were being washed away, and God was delivering her, shiny and new, to her dear sister and a tender new love.

"Don't you just love Christmas?" Zoey exclaimed.

Meg had to agree. "It's the best time of year."

20

The kitchen was warm with the smell of fresh-baked cookies, and the lingering glow of the stove made the room cozy. Fanny held Tommy in her lap and read the story as they paged through a children's book about the birth of Jesus. Kneeling on a chair beside them, Beth leaned on the table and carefully cut out paper stars with the blunt children's scissors that had been used by her older siblings years ago. Scissors were very good practice for little hands, and Fanny saw the makings of a patient quilter in Beth.

"Da-da-da-da." Tommy pointed to the figures in the book, as if he had a very important message to give her.

"Yes, liebe. That's Jesus, the son of our heavenly Father. And Christmas is all about celebrating His birth."

"I like the part about the star that shined so bright," Beth said. "And the wise men saw it and followed it to baby Jesus. That's why I'm making stars."

"That's right." Fanny glanced over at the stars. Some had uneven edges, but bit by bit, Beth was getting more skilled with her cutting. "That will make a fine paper chain."

"Da–da–dah," Tommy repeated.

"Why do you always say the same thing, Tommy?"

"Because that's what babies do when they're learning to talk." Fanny pressed a kiss onto his chubby cheek. Not even a year old yet and this one was babbling all the time. Fanny knew that the "Da" syllable was one of the first things most babies said, but she knew if Thomas were here they would joke that the boy was already asking for his dat.

This would be their first Christmas without Tom, and so far every tradition, large and small, had brought him to mind and heart. After Thanksgiving dinner, when they had put all the adults' names into a hat to pick for the gift exchange, she had wanted to put Thomas's name in. When she and Elsie had wound some pine greens and cones into a swag, she had wished Thomas was there to hang it in the front room. When Will practiced his lines for the Christmas program, over and over again, oh, how Tom would have enjoyed hearing it! The boy was not built for memorization, and Teacher Emma wanted him to say the lines exactly as they were written.

She could imagine her husband's amusement over that. Thomas would joke that rambunctious Will had met his match in Teacher Emma, and Fanny would have to hide a smile so as not to rile Emma and Will.

How she wished Thomas could have been there to be a part of their lives. But Gott had other plans for her good husband, and she was beginning to accept it all: the cold, empty spot in their bed, the need to step up and make decisions for this household. This was no mistake; she was right where Gott wanted her to be, and lately He had granted her the grace to see that.

And the wisps of longing for Tom did not make Fanny blind to her many blessings. She had six children, a roof over her head, a side business that was about to open up, and some new friends in Anna and Zed. There was much to be grateful for.

Two casserole dishes sat atop the stove—one for tonight's dinner and one to take over to Anna, who was still using a walker and was unable to make the trip to Ohio for the holidays. Fanny knew they had best get the dish over to Anna before the day got away from them.

On the way to hitch up the buggy, she stopped in at the carriage house, where Zed was working on the stairs. A box of new laminate flooring was open, and Zed was piecing together panels with a shiny, dark finish.

"Looks like real wood," Fanny said with an approving nod. She knew it was easier to install and clean than hardwood floors. Cheaper, too. Tommy leaned out of her arms and reached for the piece of flooring, and Zed held it steady, letting the baby boy inspect it.

When Tommy grasped the edge and pulled it toward his mouth, Zed took it away with a grin.

Zed held up two grooved boards. "See how they snap together like puzzle pieces? With the way these panels fit together, it will only take me a day or two to finish the stairs."

"That's good progress. At this rate, we might be open by the first of the year."

"Though unfinished stairs are not going to stop anyone from coming in if she needs your help," Zed said. "I've learned that."

"Sometimes Gott has surprises in store for us all," Fanny said as she surveyed the welcoming new space. Last month, with so many young couples getting married, her eyes had been opened to the path that Gott had been leading her along. So many weddings! And within the year, there would be many, many pregnant women needing help delivering their babies. Large families were the Amish way of life, and often when you looked around at church or other gatherings, there were babies, babies everywhere. She smiled. This center couldn't open soon enough.

She told Zed that she was off to visit Anna, and he assured her that he would keep Will busy if he got home from school before Fanny returned. The center was Will's usual place to go after school. Zed had the boy working on a project—a secret that brought a delighted smile to her son's face. Fanny didn't know what it was, but she enjoyed watching the bond grow between Will and Zed, who seemed to enjoy having the boy around while he worked.

Anna's door was answered by Susie King, a bright-eyed teen with the agility and energy of a chipmunk. When Fanny had heard Susie would be working for Anna while she recovered, she had thought the cheerful girl a good complement to Anna's no-nonsense personality.

"Come in, before you catch cold." Susie motioned them in and quickly closed the door behind them. "It was only twenty degrees when I left my house this morning. I was shivering! But Remy set some warming bricks in the buggy to take the chill off."

"It's warmed up a bit, but I think we're due for some light snow." Fanny set Tommy on the floor. He toppled over on his side, weighed down by his bulky snowsuit, but rolled onto his belly so that he could peer up at them like a turtle peeking from its shell.

Susie took the casserole dish from Beth. "And what is this?"

"Yummasetti," Beth answered. "Still warm from the oven. It's for Anna's dinner."

"Smells delicious," Susie said, straightening.

"Put the dish on the oven," Anna called from across the room where her leg was propped up on a stool. "That'll keep it warm."

"You can make a few meals out of this, Anna. Oh, it's making my mouth water!" Susie carried it into the kitchen, following Anna's instruction.

"And how are you doing, Anna?" Keeping one eye on her little crawler, Fanny took a seat in the rocking chair beside the elderly woman. "How's the leg feeling?"

"Stronger every day, though I don't have the pep that I once had. The thought of taking a horse and buggy all over the district to deliver a baby makes me weary. It's a good thing you've got your clinic ready to go. You're ten minutes by horse and buggy. In good weather, I could even walk or take a scooter."

The thought of dear old Anna riding a scooter warmed Fanny's heart; the woman was a dedicated midwife.

"Do you need anything from the bulk store?" Fanny asked. "I'm planning to go tomorrow."

"The pantry is full, thanks to a sunshine box that was delivered yesterday." When Amish folks were sick or injured, a sunshine box was usually set next to the checkout in the store. As folks paid for their purchases, they added donations of flour, peanut butter, or coffee for the party in need. "Susie just finished unloading everything." Anna patted the arms of her chair. "So much generosity in our community. I never thought I'd be needing charity, but here I am, grateful for the help."

"It must help in your recovery to know that groceries and housework are all taken care of."

"That it does."

Beth dropped to her knees beside a low table containing a Nativity scene. "Aw. A little lamb."

"Don't touch," Fanny warned. Beth loved to play with the statues in the crèche, lining the characters up like ants marching to the manger under the star.

"It's all right," Anna said. "Just be gentle."

"I will." Beth picked up the baby sheep and set it outside the manger scene. "I'm lost, and I don't know where to go," she whimpered. Then she picked up a wise man and set him down facing the lamb. "Just follow the star," she said.

Anna shot Fanny a look of amusement, and Fanny nodded. "Beth enjoys playing with the manger scene, more than any of her dollies. The story of the Savior's birth always fascinates the children."

"It fascinates young and old alike," Anna assured her. "How's young Will doing at school?"

"He's getting on better. We hear him practicing for the Christmas program at night."

"He's a little candle," Beth added. "And he says, Oh, no! I'm too small. And then he blows out his candle."

"Something like that," Fanny said, leaning forward to pick up Tommy. "Teacher Emma wants Will to memorize the lines exactly because they rhyme, but he has trouble getting it right."

"The poem about the little candles?" Tenderness softened Anna's craggy face as she gazed down at Beth and Tommy, who was crawling up beside his sister. "I remember that one from when my children went to school. How does it go? 'Ten little candles, Jesus bade them shine, but selfishness snuffed one out and then there were nine.'"

Beth's eyes opened wide in amazement. "That's it! That's the one."

"It's surprising what sticks in the memory and what time washes away," Anna said. "It's a very good story. Do you know what happens in the poem?"

Beth's lips were pursed as she gazed up at Anna and shook her head.

"There are ten candles, and each one makes the mistake of turning away from Gott's love. And when that happens, the candle's flame goes out. So one by one, the candles are blown out."

"And then what happens?" Beth asked.

"The last little candle is brave. He keeps his light shining, and his good example spreads to the other children. So at the very end, they share his light, and all ten candles are lit again."

Susie came in with two mugs of tea. "Oh, ten little candles? That was one of my favorite parts of the Christmas program. My brother Simon is a candle this year. He used to dread the Christmas program, he was so quiet. But now he's got lots to say. Adam said it's as if someone pulled the plug on the tub."

"How wonderful for Simon," Fanny said as Susie set down her cup of tea. It was good to know that the members of the King family were thriving after what they had been through.

"He's a good boy," Anna agreed, accepting one of the mugs. "I remember when he was born." She tapped her chin, giving Susie an assessing look. "Actually, I was midwife when you and your sister were born. Twins! That can be tricky."

Obviously at a loss for words, Susie gave a shrug and a wan smile.

Fanny thought it best to change the subject. "Everyone is looking forward to the school program. It really brings out the meaning of Christmas."

"It helps build confidence when children recite prayers and poems," Anna said. "But not every child excels in school, and it's good that Zed is teaching Will how to do repairs. A young man should know how to use a hammer and saw."

"Will is learning a lot, and he sticks to Zed like glue. You should see the way he follows him around." Fanny rose from her chair to fetch her son away from the manger scene, but Susie dropped down to her knees and said she would watch Tommy.

While Susie sat between Tommy and Beth, entertaining them with stories about the animals in the manger, the older women had a chance to talk quietly. Fanny invited Anna to join her family for second Christmas. "Many folks are stopping in on the twenty-sixth. Some of the new parents are bringing the babies. Why don't you join us? Caleb will come 'round in a buggy to pick you up."

Anna lowered her mug, explaining that she had already accepted an invitation to join Bishop Samuel and his family for second

Christmas. "But I'm grateful, Fanny. You've taken on quite a lot of work while I've been down with this injury, and you've gone out of your way to watch over me. I just got a letter from my daughter, and she says she can rest easy knowing that I'm being well taken care of."

Fanny brought the mug to her lips to hide the beam of pleasure that warmed her. A tender bond had been woven between them, but it wasn't something most Plain folk put to words. "We must keep you on the mend. The women of our community need you."

"And you. You're a capable midwife. What would you say if I told you I'm thinking about retiring?"

"No." Fanny's jaw dropped. "You can't go, Anna. Women need someone with your experience, and I still have a lot to learn. Besides . . ." She lowered her mug. "I was looking forward to the two of us working together. The fun's just beginning."

"I'm not going anywhere right now." Anna shifted, scowling down at her heavy cast. "I can't get far with a heavy weight like that on my leg."

The matter was too important to let it dwindle away in a joke. "Please, don't leave Halfway now, Anna. There've been so many changes in the past year, my head is still spinning. I can't imagine trying to open the birthing center without you."

"Changes can shake us up, but sometimes for the better." Anna reached over and patted Fanny's hand, an unusual show of affection for the older woman, but a treasured one. "Just when the caterpillar thought the world was over, it became a butterfly."

Although they were interrupted by the children, Anna's words echoed in Fanny's mind, like a call through the hills.

&c;

Excitement and snowflakes swirled in the cold night air as carriages arrived at the one-room schoolhouse. For Fanny, the Christmas program at school was one of the highlights of the season, and this year her hopes were high since Will was participating for the first time under the guidance of his sister and teacher, Emma. Will had been subdued during the ride, understandably nervous about getting his part right. Although Elsie and Caleb had tried to distract him by singing some Christmas carols, Will kept peeking out the side of the carriage. The merry songs did amuse Tommy and Beth, who tried to sing along.

"So you'll watch for me, Mamm?" Will asked Fanny, his brown eyes opened wide. "Remember, I'm one of the little candles."

"I'll be watching and listening, too," Fanny assured him, patting his shoulder. She longed to bend down and fold his lanky body against her in a hug, but she knew that would be a mistake here, with other parents and classmates watching. Such displays of affection were best kept in the home, anyway.

Will skipped ahead, climbing onto the schoolhouse porch amid a rush of parents and children.

The sight of families flowing into the schoolhouse filled Fanny with joy. Adam King corralled Simon, Ruthie, and little Katie inside, and Remy was right behind him, their petite baby Essie bundled in a blanket and knitted pink cap. Fanny called a merry Christmas to Thomas's cousin Edna, who was watching her son James make the step onto the porch.

Such a wonder, to see James walking. He quickly adjusted his crutches and strolled into the school smoothly, followed by his wife, Rachel.

"Gott is healing him," Fanny said quietly.

Edna patted Fanny's shoulder and nodded. "Gott is great." Gentle Edna was so easy to talk to, but somehow they rarely found the time. An Amish woman's life was chock-full of chores and children, cleaning and cooking. When the growing season ended, it was time for canning. When the garden produce was put up, it was time for holiday baking. One season rolled into the next in an age-old rhythm, sure and steady as the sun rising in the east.

Inside the big room, conversation popped and crackled like a roaring fire. A few Englishers were sprinkled through the crowd. Two of them were Fanny's invited guests.

"Hey, there!" Zoey Jordan waved from a bulletin board that showed a big tree with a student's name on each leaf. With her wild blond curls and bold red coat, Zoey was easy to spot. She seemed to stand out in any group, and yet Fanny had developed a fondness for her neighbor and for her sister. All Zoey's color and fluff was simply the frosting—the outward trimmings on a person who made the folks around her smile and feel good about themselves. Meg's gifts were heavier—more substantial—but just as welcome. In a world where many danced around the truth, it seemed to dwell within Meg, steady and burning.

Fanny sidled around a group of children to greet them. "I'm so glad you came."

"Are you kidding? We're thrilled to be here. I've never been in a one-room schoolhouse before, and I told Will I'd be watching for him." Zoey paused to wiggle her fingers at Elsie and Beth. "Hello, there, ladies."

"This is quite a turnout," Meg said, glancing around the room, which was quickly filling with people.

"It's a big night for families with children. The Christmas program comes but once a year." She motioned the English women over toward an empty bench. "We'd best find our seats before it's too late."

As the women sat down beside Elsie and Beth, Zoey asked how Emma was doing. "Just last month, we attended Emma's wedding," Zoey explained to her sister. "Our first Amish wedding, and it was quite a festive day. You wouldn't believe the array of food, and the cookies and cakes? Delish." Zoey scanned the room, and then pointed Emma King out to Meg. "Emma is the schoolteacher," she explained. "Fanny's oldest daughter."

Fanny smiled as she watched dear Emma walk up and down the line of pupils, who were far more quiet and organized than the family members settling into seats. With her open smile and watchful eyes, Emma was the perfect teacher. So many little eyes stared up at her with respect and admiration. Fanny felt a flush of pleasure, just observing her daughter at work. Well, Tom's daughter. Though she'd been mothering Emma for so long, a person would be hard-pressed to tell the difference. Fanny missed having Emma around the house, but she and Gabe had made their home in a small outbuilding on the King farm that had been converted to a living space. Gabe said they'd be moving to a real house as soon as they saved the money. Those two were hard workers, so Fanny reckoned they'd be moving to a house in no time.

The program got started when Davey King stepped forward. He was Will's age, only six, a small, nimble boy with a freckled nose and two teeth missing in the front. But, oh, what a booming voice he had!

"I may be small and very young, but I can still be heard. I'll raise my voice to welcome you and shout out every word. Merry Christmas!"

Laughter rippled through the room as Davey stepped back, and then the entire group began to sing "Joy to the World." Fanny bounced Tommy on her knee in time to the song, as Will caught her eye. He looked so nervous. She gave him a firm smile of support.

His lips were a stern line as he looked away, off to her right. Then, his brows rose as he spotted something. Or someone.

Curious, Fanny turned to follow Will's gaze.

A few yards away, Zed sat with his arms folded, his steady dark eyes on Will. How wonderful good of him to come! She had wanted him here, but thought that folks might start talking if she invited him as her guest. Perhaps Will had asked him, and Zed had wisely brought his mother, Rose, who had a way of smoothing out the social creases.

Next came a little play about sweet honeybees, and all the positive things folks could "bee." Seven children each had a picture that showed a bee and a word. Ruthie King said that a person must be generous. Hannah Lapp said that folks should be charitable. Be reverent, be kind, be unselfish—all such good messages for young and old alike. The last little bee brought it all back to the meaning of Christmas when he talked about being appreciative of God's love and the Savior born on Christmas Day, and then the little bees buzzed back to the larger group of students.

When ten children came forward and Emma went down the line lighting their candles, Fanny knew this was her son's big moment. Elsie took a squirming Tommy from her arms so that Fanny could give Will her undivided attention. She beamed with joy as an older child began the poem and blew out his candle. Down the line the story went, telling of ways that the little candles lost their faith, lost their light.

At last, it was Will's turn. Fanny studied her boy, noticing the many changes in his face and manner. His chubby cheeks were gone, as was his rambunctiousness. He no longer barreled into the kitchen or pushed his sister to the ground in a fit of temper. Will was finding his way, not an easy path without a father.

"Two little candles, and now we're nearly done," Will spoke clearly, with good expression. "'I'm too small and weak,' one said, and then there was one." He blew out his candle with a big sigh. Then he dared a look at Zed, and a grin lit his face.

Was there any gift greater than seeing joy on your child's face?

As the last little candle lit the others and the children sang "Silent Night," Fanny turned to her right and caught Zed's eyes. This man had been so good to her children, so good to her. Would there ever be a place or time when she could let him know how she felt toward him? Oh, but the eyes of the community were upon them, ever watchful, and it was sad when love and hope were tainted by guilt and shame. These matters of the heart were so complicated.

21

Silver and red glitter sparkled under the light of the kitchen counter as Meg tied a ribbon around a box of cookies she had baked for Jack. It was hard to believe that there was a special someone in her life this year after such a long dry spell, but lo and behold, she and Jack were an item. This would be a first—spending Christmas Eve with a guy she really cared about.

"So that's your Christmas gift for him?" Zoey leaned back on the kitchen stool and folded her hands over her wide belly. "Sweet and personal. I like that you didn't panic and grab for a last-minute safety like a scarf or cologne."

"I wish I could come up with something else. Something special." Meg plumped the bow. "But I didn't want a token gift, and I know that Jack isn't really into presents. He says that he's lucky to be able to afford the things he needs. So what can you give the man who has everything?"

"That's profound." Zoey broke off a piece of one of the extra cookies on the counter and took a nibble. "Mmm. Spicy ginger-bread."

"Jack's favorite."

"Well." Zoey brushed crumbs from her hands. "I know something Jack could get *you* for Christmas." She waved the back of her left hand in front of her ample bosom. "As in, diamonds are forever."

Meg bit her lower lip. "It's not the diamond I want . . ."

"It's the forever." Tears sparkled in Zoey's eyes as she reached over to squeeze her sister's arm. "Oh, honey, I'm so happy for you and Jack. It's been so much fun watching you two get to know each other. Ice-skating and movies and walks down Main Street. This is a love story right out of a Hallmark movie."

"I know, but we're not in any rush to get married. We just met last summer, and we've been living hundreds of miles apart. Right now we're both just grateful to spend time together." Meg rubbed Zoey's shoulder. It was a little scary how in tune her sister was with her emotions, but once again, Zoey had gotten it right. She could not get enough of Jack, and he felt the same way about her. Over the past two weeks they had spent almost every available hour together, sometimes on dates, and sometimes just hanging out at the inn, making a meal in the big kitchen or talking by the fire or watching television together. "Sometimes I can't believe it's happening to me, after so many years of having no one."

"So many years. And at last, true love. I would jump up and do a happy dance if I wasn't toting around a fifteen-pound belly."

"A little aerobic happy dance would be okay," Meg teased, always an advocate of exercise for her sister.

"Stop that. You are my labor coach, not my personal trainer." Zoey slid from the seat and opened one large door of the industrial-size fridge. "You know, when Tate and I moved here, I had a feeling you'd be joining us. I knew Halfway would be your kind of place.

And now you've fallen in love, and you've been welcomed by my neighbors, the local sheriff, and the doctor." She pointed a baby carrot at Meg. "Was I right or what?"

"You were right." Last week Meg had met with Henry Trueherz to undergo a diagnostic test, and, of course, the conversation had turned to the need for a midwife in the area. "The situation around Halfway will be eased when the birthing center is open," the doctor had told her, "but there are many outlying areas in need of midwives. Most of the Amish in Lancaster County choose to give birth at home; that makes life challenging for country doctors like me. I'd be thrilled to have you covering routine births. As for the Amish women, well, you've already worked with Fanny. Her recommendation will get you more clients than one woman can handle."

It was all falling into place; after she delivered Zoey's baby, Meg would collect her belongings from Pittsburgh and relocate to Halfway. With Dr. Trueherz as her consultant, she would start working with clients, both English and Amish, who wanted home births. She had also agreed to fill in at the birthing center when needed.

For now she would stay in her room here at the bed-and-breakfast; eventually, she would find her own place and give Zoey, Tate, and their baby more space to become a family. Granted, they had guests coming through all the time, but she suspected that was different from having your sister or sister-in-law breathing down your neck.

"Hey, there." Jack's low purr brought Meg back to the present. He stood in the arched doorway, his jaw shaved smooth, his hair fluffed from a shower. He wore gray slacks, a black shirt, and a lavender print tie, which was very dressed-up for Jack. "Shandell said I'd find my two favorite girls in here."

"You don't need to butter me up anymore," Zoey said as he leaned down to kiss her cheek. "I like you, Jack."

"Good news for me." His smile stirred something deep inside Meg. "How about you?" he asked Meg as he stepped closer and dropped a kiss on her lips. His touch was light but electric. "You need any buttering up?"

"I like you, too, but I figure it never hurts to grease the pan."

One eyebrow lifted. "Never hurts. So what's your plan tonight, Zoey? You and Tate want to come to Evensong with us?"

"That sounds like a lovely Christmas Eve ritual, but Tate is taking me out to dinner in Paradise. Soon, we won't have much opportunity to dine out, just the two of us," Zoey said as she twisted the bag of carrots closed.

"Well, you guys will enjoy that." Jack turned to Meg. "You'd better bundle up. I figure the best way to avoid traffic around the church is to walk."

"I'll get my coat." Meg went into the main entry to grab her blue quilted coat. She had left her hair down today, and it made her feel pretty and feminine to have it swinging over her shoulder as she returned to the kitchen.

"Don't stay out too late, you two!" Zoey called after them. "You might catch me kissing Santa by the tree."

"I do get a kick out of your sister," Jack said as they started down the lane.

"She'll keep you on your toes." Some men were really thrown by Zoey's mischievous sense of humor, but Jack seemed to get her. Meg reached out a gloved hand and he clasped it and pulled her closer.

"Let me hold on to you, in case you slip."

She knew it was an excuse to stay close, since Tate had gone over the paving stones in front of the inn with a snowblower. She liked the way that Jack found excuses to warm her up, rub her shoulders, or keep her close.

The evening was cold but clear, with a scattering of stars overhead. An oblong moon glowed silver just over the distant hills; it was a craggy moon, with gray and white spots that resembled the face of a wise old man. They had reached the end of the lane when she noticed the bright silhouette of the inn behind them. "Look at the way the lights outline the building," she said. "It looks like Santa's workshop at the North Pole." The white lights cast muted reflections on the snowy lawn.

"Sure does." They paused a moment to soak up the winter scene, and Meg felt caught up in the hope and wonder of Christmas Eve.

"Such a special night. Little kids hang their stockings and listen from their beds for sounds of Santa."

"I could never sleep on Christmas Eve," Jack admitted. "One time when I was supposed to be asleep in bed, I heard something on the roof . . . this scraping noise. It was probably squirrels, but I was sure it was Santa's sled making a landing. I yanked on the string of the blinds, ready to see Rudolph, and the blinds fell off the window."

"Oh, no!" Meg pressed a hand to her lips to stifle a laugh.

"Oh, yes. And I was supposed to be asleep. Needless to say, Gran wasn't too happy about that, but she understood. You can't keep a boy from meeting Santa."

"Your grandmother was very understanding."

"Putting up with me all those years? She's a saint."

"I've got to meet this dear woman," she said.

"You will. She's already heard about you. We'll hook up a trip to Philly after Kat has the baby."

"Perfect." Snow crunched underfoot as they headed off under the glittering ceiling of stars. The distant glow was the town of Halfway, where a line of lampposts seemed to point the way to the little church. Like the star of Bethlehem, guiding the wise men.

"So answer this," Jack said. "What was the most memorable gift you got from Santa? Answer quick. If you have to dig it out of your memory, it doesn't count."

"In-line skates," she said. "But it's a bittersweet memory." She shared the story of the Christmas after her father had died. She had been six, Zoey ten or eleven. "Before Christmas, Mom sat us down and warned us that we would each get just one gift. She kept saying how sorry she was. I remember thinking that she was wrong; I knew Santa would give me everything my heart desired. Boy, was I surprised on Christmas morning when it turned out that my mother was right."

"See that? The Santa thing does a number on kids' heads."

Meg admitted that she'd acted a little bratty that morning. She had pointed out that Zoey didn't get the sand sculpture kit that she wanted. Mom had said that maybe Zoey would get it for her birthday, and she had added that Christmas was really about celebrating the birth of Jesus.

"Well, little crumb that I was, I didn't want to hear that. I got dressed and went next door to see what the neighbors got for Christmas. All very inappropriate, because they had family visiting and I don't think they wanted the neighbor kid playing with all their new toys while they were having Christmas brunch."

He smiled down at her. "Stubborn little thing, weren't you?"

The memory of that Christmas used to make her feel awful, but she had forgiven herself for acting like the petulant, grieving six-year-old that she was. "And you know what Zoey did? She came next door with the skates we'd gotten and lured me outside. She helped me get the skates on and got me started rolling on the flat part of the sidewalk. We ended up spending the whole day out there. And Zoey kept saying how glad she was that we both got skates, so that we could play together."

"Seriously? She made you look really bad, my friend."

"I know. I've gotten over it, but it took a while." As they drew closer to town, other pedestrians bustled through the cold along the quiet streets. Although all of the Amish shops were closed, LED candles burned bright in the windows. "How about you?" she asked Jack. "What was your favorite toy?"

"Probably the rapid-fire Nerf gun I got when I was ten or eleven. The thing had foam bullets, but I hounded my sister with it. I think she ended up throwing out the bullets while I was asleep one night."

"So you were interested in law enforcement from an early age," she teased.

"Exactly."

"Holidays always bring out memories, good and bad." A cluster of three-dimensional stars shone bright in the dim window of the hardware store, offering light in the darkness. "Those stars are so pretty. I see them all over town," she said.

"They're called Moravian stars. They're Advent symbols for the Moravian church, a religious group that came here from Germany."

"Just beautiful," she said, admiring the fat stars that were illuminated from within.

They were walking along Main Street now, passing the small grocery, the tea shop, and Kraybill's Fish and Game. Since Meg's arrival Halfway had taken hold of her, and she had learned the shops and side streets. Ahead of them loomed the tall Christmas tree, a graceful tower of hope and light.

The sight of the festive town hall reminded her of the gathering where she and Jack had volunteered last week. They had spent two afternoons sorting donations of food and toys before setting out to the back roads between farms to distribute the goods to people who didn't have enough for the holidays. The charity drive had introduced Meg to some of the poor families of the town, and she had enjoyed talking with many of the women about their families and their favorite holiday recipes. The experience had also allowed her to see a different facet of Jack: his commitment to the people of Halfway. Jack was a helper, just as she was. It was an important thing to have in common.

They slowed their pace and stared up at the cone of colored lights, whorls and swirls of floating gems. The twinkling tree stirred emotion inside her, memories of Christmases past and hopes for the holidays of the future, with church pageants and cookie decorating and children of her own excited about the arrival of Santa Claus. There was something poignant about the cluster of warm colors sparkling beneath the indigo sky, like a symbol of God's love, shining in the darkness. Christmas trees caught her every time.

"It's all so beautiful," Meg said.

"Yeah." Jack slid his arm over her shoulders and pulled her into his warmth. "Halfway knows how to do Christmas right." He sighed. "I gotta tell you something, something that's been weighing on me this past week. I know I can talk up a blue streak most of the time, but this is hard for me to say because . . . 'cause it means so much to me."

Meg studied his face, patient and trusting.

"I'm blessed to live in this town," he said, "and I'm so grateful to be here with you right now. You're the best thing to rock my life for a long time. You've got to know that's true. I know it's kind of soon, but I've got to say what's in my heart. I love you, Meg."

She sucked in a breath, overwhelmed. Those three words . . . they changed everything . . . rocked her world, as Jack had put it. "Oh, Jack." She turned to him, her palms flat against his coat. "I love you, too, but I'm a little scared at how fast this is all happening."

"Yeah. Like lightning," he said.

She nodded. "I've never felt this way about anyone before. And it's amazing and wonderful. Fireworks and a river of deep emotion. But . . ."

"Oh, no. There's a but?"

"I'm a pragmatic person. Grounded. Responsible. I don't want to make any rash decisions with my head in the clouds."

"Okay, yeah. That's all good. No rush, Megs." He pushed the

edge of her cap back slightly and placed his hands on her shoulders. "We've got plenty of time to ease in and take it slow. I'm not going anywhere . . . at least, not without you."

"I'm really happy to hear that." Joy radiated through her. The colored lights blurred behind him as she swallowed back the knot of emotion growing in her throat. "Merry Christmas, Jack."

He leaned down so that his forehead pressed hers, so close, so intimate. It was as if they were the only two people on the busy Main Street. "Merry Christmas," he said before he swept her into a kiss that warmed her down to her toes.

⬥⬥

Later, during the Evensong service, Meg melted into the rosy glow of a hymn and tried to absorb it all. Most of the service was bright, festive music—a celebration of the Savior's birth—and the lovely songs gave Meg a chance to process the events of the evening.

Jack loved her. His words had been the finest Christmas gift she could imagine—brimming with joy and commitment, and yet no pressure.

We've got time, he'd said. They could take it slow.

Part of her wanted to simply revel in his lovely pronouncement, but the presence of a family in the pew in front of them brought the issue back with all the comfort of cold water. The three kids, who looked to be between ages eight and twelve, seemed to enjoy one another, sharing a hymnal and smiling up at their parents. Oh, to have a family like that! Meg wasn't sure that was possible for her, and she hadn't told Jack about her endometriosis yet. Not that it was life-threatening, but it could have some bearing on her ability to have children. And, dear Lord, they both wanted kids. She vowed that she would come clean with Jack on the topic as soon as she got the latest test results back from Doc Trueherz.

The smells of candle wax and evergreen reminded her of the church back in Pittsburgh, where Mom and Kip would attend services tonight. Meg had to press her lips together to suppress a sudden grin. Most Christmases she felt like a third wheel, tagging along with her mother and stepfather, but not this year. This year, she had found love.

Jack took her hand, and she sat a little closer to him and soaked up the sweet harmonies, fragrant evergreen garland, and candles trimmed in ribbon. There was such an air of expectancy in the church. Like the hymn that spoke of the thrill of waiting: "The world in solemn stillness lay to hear the angels sing."

The minister called for a moment of reflection, a time to think over the past year, and Meg knew she had so much to be grateful for: a loving sister, a chance to pursue the vocation she loved, a new home here in Halfway, and a man she loved dearly.

And none of this would have come about if she had not just endured the worst crisis of her career. She thanked God for clearing her name in the investigation. The silver lining in that horrible experience was that she had seen it was time to shake up her life. All signs pointed to Halfway being a much more hospitable place for a midwife, a fine place to settle and raise a family. Jack squeezed her hand as the choir began to sing "O Holy Night," and in that moment, Meg knew she was in the right place.

❧ 22 ❧

Christmas morning dawned with a pale sky and snow flurries. Fanny dressed quickly in the cold, grateful for warm water to splash on her face. She lit the kerosene lamps downstairs, started a fire in the kitchen stove, and woke her children with the good news that Christ was born in Bethlehem.

"He was? Again?" Will peeked out from under the blankets and swiped at the edge of his mouth.

Fanny chuckled. "I'm talking about the first Christmas, liebe. This is the day that we celebrate Jesus's birth. Come downstairs and we'll read the story together."

Beth sat up in bed and pushed stray hairs from her face. "Is Jesus in the manger?" Fascinated by the Nativity scene, Beth had been anxiously awaiting the arrival of the infant statue, which Fanny kept hidden until Christmas morning.

"Come downstairs, and you may put him in his crib," Fanny promised.

They assembled in the warm kitchen, where Fanny had set out a small pile of gifts covered with a bright dishtowel in front of each child's place. Beth was excited at the prospect of gifts, and Will wanted to take a peek but agreed to wait until after breakfast, as usual. Fanny put the crèche on the table in front of the children to distract them from their curiosity over the Christmas goodies.

Caleb had just come in from feeding the horses; wisps of snow-flakes were melting on his shoulders. Fanny slid a freshly diapered Tommy into his highchair and placed a handful of Cheerios on the tray.

Still wearing pajamas and slippers, Beth and Will sat in front of the crèche, their elbows on the table, their cheeks flushed with excitement.

"Mamm, we need to add the baby Jesus," Beth said.

"I didn't forget." Fanny fetched the small figurine from the top shelf of a cupboard and handed it to her youngest daughter.

"There you are!" Beth's tiny fingers cradled the statue and carefully placed it in the small wooden manger.

Elsie sang "Christ the Savior is born," as she slid an egg-and-bacon casserole into the oven and took a seat at the table. She opened the Bible, smoothed down the pages, and looked up at Fanny. "Who will read this morning?"

The question pointed to the one missing from the table—Tom.

The tradition was to gather around the head of the household and listen as he read the story of the first Christmas. In their family, Tom had read the scripture. In most Amish families, it was usually the father or doddy—the grandfather—who did the reading.

Fanny lifted the Bible with a soft, loving smile. Throughout the morning Fanny had been mindful that this was their first Christmas without Thomas. It would have been easy to fall into a trough of sadness, but she knew that was not Gott's will. "It's up to Caleb now," she said, sliding the good book over toward him. "It's from the book of Luke, chapter two."

He lifted his chin, a bit surprised, though he didn't object. "I think I know it by heart from hearing Dat read it all these years."

Caleb began softly, like a rustle of wind in the trees. "'And there were in the same country shepherds abiding in the field, keeping watch over their flock by night. And lo, the angel of the Lord came upon them, and the glory of the Lord shone round about them: and they were sore afraid. And the angel said unto them, Fear not: for behold, I bring you good tidings of great joy, which shall be to all people. For unto you is born this day in the city of David a Saviour, which is Christ the Lord.'"

Now Caleb's voice was strong and sure, steady as the ground under their feet.

"'And this shall be a sign unto you; Ye shall find the babe wrapped in swaddling clothes, lying in a manger. And suddenly there was with the angel a multitude of the heavenly host praising God, and saying,

"'Glory to God in the highest,

"'And on earth peace,

"'Good will towards men.'"

Quiet and contentment wrapped around the family for a moment. Will held an angel over the crèche, as if acting out the story, and Beth had sunk against Fanny, who folded her close and rested her chin on the little girl's dark hair.

"That story always stirs my heart." Elsie clasped her small hands to her chest. "Even the simple shepherds were visited by angels. Gott sent his Savior for all men, rich and poor."

"That was a very good reading," Fanny said, nodding at Caleb.

"I wish Dat was here to celebrate Christmas." Will's comment seemed to come out of the blue.

With a deep breath, Fanny reminded herself that Thomas was still in their thoughts. Mind and heart took a while to heal.

"I still miss him, too," Caleb said, putting a big hand on Will's shoulder. "Dat used to read to us on Christmas morning. And when I was little like you, he read from the Bible each day after breakfast."

"I remember," Will said thoughtfully.

"I remember Dat's gentle voice." Elsie lifted the statue of Joseph from the crèche. "He always had kind words."

It tugged at Fanny's heart to see her children missing their father. In some ways, the pain of loss was still tender, but so much healing had taken place in recent months. Will had gotten past his tantrums and bouts of anger. Elsie had learned to trust and taken a brave step, dating for the first time. Emma had taken on a wife's responsibility. And Caleb had become a capable sheep wrangler at the Stoltzfus ranch. The healing had begun, and Gott wasn't done with them yet. His love would see them through; that much Fanny was sure of.

"We all miss him," Fanny said gently. "But Gott didn't make a mistake when he called him to Heaven. I don't understand it, but every day I'm trying to accept it."

"That's all we can do," Elsie said, her broad cheeks puffing in a tearful smile.

"Dat used to say that a journey of a thousand miles starts with one step," Caleb said. "And I think we've got a good start."

❦

The mood was merry after breakfast when they opened gifts. Everyone was pleased to find homemade goodies—cookies, candies, and nuts. But there were personal gifts, too.

"Yarn for my knitting, and look at these colors! Blue to match Bethie's eyes. Chili pepper red. And sunset orange. These will make wonderful good caps or mittens." Elsie had never really taken to quilting, but she enjoyed knitting and embroidery.

Will was very pleased to receive a Jenga game, which he deemed to be "the noisiest game ever" when the wooden tiles came crashing down.

A set of colored pencils kept Beth busy, especially with the little sharpener that created fascinating curls of paper-thin wood.

Elsie and Beth were all giggles when Will told Fanny that she needed her coat to see the Christmas gift that he'd made for her. When she asked him why he didn't bring it in, he said it was too big.

"Too large?" she teased. "Did you build a new buggy?"

"No," Will insisted. "Just get your coat, Mamm."

Everyone bundled up, and Will told Fanny to close her eyes while he guided her out to the spot.

"Okay, now you can take a look."

Fanny opened her eyes to find a birdhouse sitting on the porch of the carriage house. It was large—probably three feet wide—with brown shingles on the roof and two arches on the side that echoed the carriage house doors.

"What a wonderful birdhouse!" Fanny moved closer to inspect it. "Real shingles on the roof! Did you really build this, Will?"

"I did. Well, Zed helped me. He built most of it. But I put a lot of the nails in. And I painted it and glued on the shingles."

"It's really something!" She rubbed the crown of Will's head and pulled him into a hug. "I reckon we'll have birds coming from far and wide just to visit."

"Do you think the birds will use the carriage doors?" Caleb teased.

"They're not real doors," Will pointed out. "Zed put them there to match the carriage house."

"Well, I think it's a good match," Elsie said. "And I think the birds are going to be happy to visit, once you put seed inside."

"Zed is going to mount it on a post," Caleb said. "He would have done it already, but Will wanted to surprise you this morning."

"And I am surprised." Fanny was pleased by the gift, but her true delight was the sight of Will's face, beaming with happiness. "Denki."

&&

For Christmas dinner, Fanny roasted a large chicken in the oven and Elsie helped her prepare mashed potatoes, gravy, stuffing, a Jell-O mold, and two kinds of salad. It was a delicious meal for all, though Fanny was aware of the two who were missing—Thomas and Emma.

"Why couldn't Emma have Christmas dinner with us?" Will asked.

"Because she's married now, and she and Gabe are having dinner with his family," Fanny answered.

"But we'll see her tomorrow," Elsie pointed out. "Emma and Gabe are coming for second Christmas."

Will held a chicken drumstick aloft as a grin lit his face. "And what about Zed? Is he coming tomorrow?"

"Ya. His parents, too. And Jimmy and Edna Lapp's brood will be here as well."

"It will be good to see all of them," Elsie said. "I've also invited Ruben, and if it's all right, Rachel King will stop by."

"Everyone is welcome," Fanny said.

"I've invited someone, too." Caleb ran his hand along the suspender strap of his pants, a gesture that reminded Fanny of his father. "And, well, I think she's going to bring some of her family."

That caught Fanny's attention. Caleb had never before spoken of the girl he was courting, and Fanny reached for another roll to hide her surprise. "The more the merrier," she said.

"I know you'll welcome Kate," he said, "but I wanted to warn you about the Fishers. Her mother, Lydia, will be here, and probably her aunt Joan, too."

"Joan Fisher?" she said aloud. Her former mother-in-law would be coming into her home? She could hardly believe what she was hearing. Caleb was dating one of the Fisher girls, a member of the family that had turned its back on Fanny after David had died. Of all the sweet young women Caleb might have chosen in the Amish community, why had he picked from a vat of sour pickles?

Not that she held a grudge. She had made her peace with these matters long ago. It had hurt to be rejected from the Fisher family, but that rejection had made her turn to Thomas Lapp—and wonderful good things had come of her meeting with him. When Gott closed a door, He truly did open a window.

"I don't mean to cause any problems, Fanny." Caleb's eyes held a golden glimmer of tenderness, so like his father. "But I don't even know why we always avoid the Fishers. What started this mess?"

"It wasn't any one event," she admitted. "I came here from Ohio, and I knew no one except David, but his sisters and cousins were kind and accepting toward me." But all gestures of comfort and friendship ended when the accident took David.

Looking down the table, Fanny was relieved to see that the little ones were more interested in their food than the conversation. Elsie watched attentively, but then Elsie was certainly old enough to hear Fanny's story.

"After David died, I felt very alone. I thought about returning to my family in Ohio."

"Did the Fishers convince you to stay?" Elsie asked.

"They were one of the reasons I wanted to leave. They offered me no small jobs in the bakery, no chance to pay my way. I was unsure of my place in their family. In some ways, I think they blamed me for what happened to David. Some were more angry than others. Lizzy was always kind to me, but David's mother, Joan . . ." She shook her head. "Joan was telling people that I would be on the next bus to Ohio."

"But you didn't go," Elsie said. "Why did you decide to stay?"

Fanny looked from Elsie to Caleb. "Bishop Samuel got me a job with a wonderful family here. A family that had plenty of Gott's love but needed a woman's touch in their home."

"Oh, Fanny." Elsie clucked her tongue, seeming far older and wiser than a teen. "We needed a lot more than that. But you came along and brought hope back into our home. Light and laughter."

"And your recipe for Yummasetti," Caleb teased.

Fanny smiled. "That, too."

He tore a roll and slathered butter onto one half. "I hope that from now on there can be peace between the Lapps and the Fishers."

"There is peace," Fanny assured him. "Gott does not abide grudges. Only forgiveness." Once she had put a little bit of distance between herself and David's family, it had been easier to move on, to forgive and forget. Of course, she was never too far from her former mother-in-law, owner of Halfway's bakery. David had a large family, and one couldn't live in this town without rubbing elbows with the Fishers. And Fanny had maintained friendships with some of David's family members, like dear Lizzy King.

"I think you're right, Caleb," said Elsie. "I'm going to ask Gott to bless this new bond between our families."

"That would be mighty good." Fanny would pray for smooth relations and a pint of patience when she came face-to-face with her former mother-in-law.

❧ 23 ❧

The inn looked like a picture on a Christmas card. The clear lights strung along the roofline and windows and doors were reflected in the snow, all cool shades of silver and white and blue. Out here in Amish country, where night usually meant dimly lit homes without electricity, Christmas decorations could really light up the horizon.

As Jack turned his truck up the drive, he had to smile. Zoey and Tate had done an amazing job turning this old Amish home into a hotel. They'd spent more money on it than Tate had intended, but the man took it all in stride. Good people, Zoey and Tate. And Meg . . . Meg was pure gold.

He parked the truck off to the far side of the small lot and checked his cell phone. Almost midnight. When he'd signed up to work the four-to-midnight shift on Christmas Day, he had figured he would cover for the guys with kids who wanted to do the big family dinner. He'd never imagined that he'd have someone special to spend Christmas with. But there she was, waiting inside the inn for him.

Well, he assumed that the golden glow from the front windows was Meg waiting for him. Dang. He'd never had a girl wait up for him without complaining—especially on a holiday like Christmas. Police work could be inconvenient, a sacrifice for cops and their families. But Meg got that. Her line of work required sacrifice, too.

The paving stones had been cleared of snow. As he walked to the front door, he tapped her name on his cell phone and held it to his ear. Better to call than to ring the bell and risk disturbing anyone.

"Jack." She sounded happy to hear him. Her voice melted something inside him, something that had long been frozen in place.

"Ho, ho, ho. You know you got a fine-looking man waiting on your doorstep?"

"Santa?" she teased.

"Naw. He came by last night."

He heard the click of the lock and saw light emanate from the crack. "Oh, this guy's much better looking than Santa."

Now he heard her voice in stereo, from the phone and from the doorway. The light behind her rimmed the edges of her red hair with a golden glow, even as it outlined her frame, that hourglass shape that couldn't be disguised by a bulky cable-knit sweater and blue jeans.

"You waited for me." Somehow that meant so much to him. "Were you dozing off by the fire?"

"Are you kidding me?" She stepped forward into the splash of illumination from the Christmas lights and pulled him into her warm, sweet glow. "I am an expert waiter. I wait on mothers. I wait on reluctant, sleepy babies who come into this world on their own, very particular schedules. I'll never have any problem waiting for the man I love."

Man, she had a knack for choking him up. "Good to hear. So it looks like I'm just in time to be the last person to wish you a Merry Christmas. At least until next year."

"Oh, you don't know my sister. In Zoey's house, Christmas is a state of mind that lasts through the year."

"I like that. How about one more Christmas kiss?"

She cocked her head to one side. "Any excuse for a kiss." She rose onto her toes and pressed her lips to his, a light sweep, then more of a commitment. He answered with a deep, tender kiss that just about drained every ounce of control from his body. He let his fingers curl into her silken hair, then glide down her shoulders, evoking a sigh from deep inside her.

He ended the kiss slowly, but held her in his arms. "You gonna invite me in, or we gonna build a snow castle out here?"

She pulled him by the arm. "Come on in."

A middle-aged couple nodded a greeting as Meg introduced Dave and Karen Balfour. They were visiting Halfway from their home outside Boston, spending Christmas with good friends who had just moved to the area.

"My kids," Karen said, explaining that she had kept in close contact with the children she had provided day care for. "And now that they have kids of their own, well . . . it's the great circle of life."

"We were just heading off to bed," Dave said, opening the French door that led to the hallway. "We've got a big day planned tomorrow."

"More shopping and ice-skating," Karen added. "And a lot of good eats. You guys have great treats here. We love those whoopie pies."

Jack agreed. "The Amish know how to do desserts."

The couple said good night and headed off to their room. Meg closed the French door behind them as Jack shrugged out of his leather jacket and took a seat on the couch in front of the flickering gas fireplace. Meg nestled in beside him, and they talked about how they'd spent the day.

After a brunch for the inn's handful of guests, Meg and Zoey had gone online for a video chat with their mother, who kept squinting at the camera suspiciously. "She always worries that she won't be able to turn the camera off," Meg explained. "That it's going to keep watch over her like Big Brother."

"I get that," he said.

"And how was work?"

"The real kicker was this neighbor dispute. One family's hound dog, old Toby, got loose and moseyed next door to where Mrs. Maresh was letting the roast rest. The dog got in the door, darted to the table, and had that boneless beef roast devoured in a matter of minutes."

"You're kidding me." Meg's eyes sparkled with mirth.

"Total truth. Mrs. Maresh came back downstairs in her Christmas sweater to find her husband still napping and their dinner gone."

She chuckled. "That must have been disappointing, but I can just imagine the dog's delight. He scored a Christmas feast."

"But the best part is the happy ending." He told her how relations had been chilly between the two neighbors. That was why Mrs. Maresh had called to lodge a complaint against the dog's owners. But in the end, the dog people invited the Mareshes to come over and share their prime-rib dinner. "So the complaint was dropped, everybody got a good dinner, and the neighbors might just become friends. Toby was relegated to the garage, but he got a nice Christmas dinner out of the deal."

They talked about pets they had been fond of as kids. Meg had grown up with cats in the house—mostly strays but one Siamese that had an affinity for barbecue-flavored potato chips.

"My grandmother wouldn't let me take in a dog," Jack said, "but

I totally bonded with this little long-haired dachshund named Odie. Lisa and I found him at the dog rescue shelter one day, and she pushed her parents until they said yes. That Odie, he was a good watchdog. Barked at most men. Didn't really like Lisa's dad, but he loved me. I'd lift him up to the couch to watch TV with us. I made sure he got fed and watered and walked. Yeah, Odie and me, we bonded."

"Wait. How old were you when you had this dog?" she asked.

"I don't know. Fifteen or sixteen. I think I'd just gotten my license."

"And you were seeing Lisa back then?"

He nodded. "We were childhood sweethearts who ended up getting engaged. You know how that goes."

"Not really. I don't think I ever dated anyone for more than a year."

"Oh, well, the teen couple thing can be a trap. We were best friends first. I was really tied into Lisa's whole family, and I know they liked me. They thought I was good for her, and maybe I was."

You're so good for our Lisa, her mother had said. *I don't know what we did before you came along, Jack. Our girl is a lost lamb without you.*

At the time, it had felt good to have someone relying on him. He thought he could be strong for the two of them. He would be the foundation, the pillar that held things up, while she was the soul of the relationship, the whimsical, beautiful dancer who made each moment count. But time had taught him that one person could not save another from herself. After so many years spent at the edge of the pond, reaching for Lisa in yet another attempt to save her, he'd had to let her go.

"So how did it end?" she asked. "I mean, you dated her for years, right?"

"Yup. We were engaged, planning the wedding."

And then, yet again, she'd gone off her medication. The meds, she claimed, stripped her life of all excitement. The drug that was designed to moderate mood swings had left Lisa feeling like her life was an endless succession of mediocre moments. "It makes me boring," she'd insisted. So she had gone off the meds. And she'd gone into crisis mode. She'd barricaded herself in the apartment and called the cops when he tried to come near her. She'd come to his workplace and blasted him with accusations: cheating and lying and assault. Although none of her charges was true, the department took it seriously when one of Philly's finest was accused of assault.

"I can see I've hit a nerve," Meg said, drawing him back to the present.

In the glow of the fire flickering on Meg's skin and lighting her hair like a copper penny, he needed to be giving his attention to her—not to the nagging ghost of Lisa.

"We don't have to talk about it if you don't want to," said Meg.

"I just don't feel comfortable sharing all her personal details," he said. "Lisa suffers from a disorder and . . ." He stopped himself. "I've probably said too much already. I really cared about her. I always will. But it's over between us. I got out of Philly so she could have her space. I've moved on, and I wish her well."

Meg tilted her head to the side, assessing him in her thorough, concerned manner. "Healing takes time," she said. "Sometimes it helps to talk. Sometimes a wound heals faster when you don't pick at it."

He snickered. "That's the medical terminology? 'Don't pick.'"

She gave a confident nod. "Yup." She moved from the sofa to open one of the wooden cupboards beside the fireplace. "I say we crack open one of the board games. You choose. I'll go get us drinks. Hot chocolate or sparkling cider?"

He chose the cider and started setting up the Game of Life, which had always been his sister's favorite. "Kat always wanted to play so that she could buy herself a carload of kids," he told Meg, once she'd returned with two goblets of sparkling apple juice.

"Definitely a girl thing," Meg agreed. "We girls were all about love and marriage while you boys were always trying to get great jobs and insurance policies. So boring."

"Yeah, well, most of us guys come around to the kid thing," he said. "Now I see how important family is, and I think, you and I, we'd make pretty good parents."

Her eyes opened wide as she put her goblet down. "Yes, we would. Definitely. I . . . I really want to have kids."

He sensed her awkwardness. "Here I go, pushing ahead. Sorry about that."

"It's okay. It's something couples need to discuss . . . just not right now." She spun a six. "Woo-hoo! I am going to take my husband and twins and move ahead six spaces."

He took a swallow of cider and watched as she moved the little plastic car. There was something mesmerizing about Meg, even her simplest movements: the way she tilted her head, pushed her hair over one shoulder, and then flashed a look up at him.

"Your turn," she said.

Dang if she wasn't the best thing that ever rolled into Lancaster County, into his life, into his heart. He had it bad and he didn't even care. If this was love, then, good Lord in Heaven, bring it on.

24

$\mathcal{A}$ny worries about smoothing things over with Joan Fisher flew out of Fanny's mind when guests began arriving the next day to celebrate second Christmas. Joy filled the house as family and friends shared Christmas greetings and personal stories and hearty jokes. A chain of Beth's hand-cut stars hung over the door. Emma had shown the children how to string up the cards the family had received from Englisher friends, and it made for a cheerful design over the kitchen sink. The kitchen table was nearly overflowing with casserole dishes, bowls of fruit, platters of cookies, and melt-in-your-mouth cakes.

Besides delicious food and good conversation, the house was bursting with so many little ones! Many of the Plain folks whose children Fanny helped deliver dropped by with cookies or sweets or nuts.

"Oh, let me have a chance to hold little John!" Fanny reached out and Lizzy swung the five-month-old into her arms. "You're getting to be such a big boy!" Fanny told the baby, who studied her with his father's keen, observant eyes. She couldn't resist running her fingertips over his doughy cheek. "Are you the light of your mamm's life?" she asked.

"Ya," Lizzy answered, "but his dat can't get enough of him, either. Joe talks and sings to him all the time. He's been sleeping through the night for two months now."

"Such a blessing." Fanny smoothed down the baby's dark hair and passed him back to his mother, as Remy King waved from across the room. Adam gently touched his wife's shoulder and guided her over so that Fanny could see baby Essie, a sweet thing with hair as bright as a copper penny, just like her mother. Adam's sister Mary joined them. She had little Nathan perched on her shoulder, and Fanny shared a few tips on burping that she had learned from her own children. How Fanny enjoyed the sweet cries and bright eyes of the babies!

When the Millers arrived, many of the guests spilled out of the house to have a look at the new birdhouse that Zed and Will had built.

"So how did it all go yesterday?" Zed asked Will, speaking in that low man-to-man banter. "Was your mamm surprised?"

Will nodded. "I don't think she expected anything like this."

"I didn't." Fanny folded her arms against the cold, though it felt a bit refreshing after the close warmth of the house. "I couldn't believe what I was seeing. So nicely built. And Will knows how I enjoy birding."

"This is a good thing for the center," Emma said. "When children come to visit, they can add seed for the birds."

"Very sturdy," said Zed's mother, Rose.

His dat agreed. "And the shingles will keep the roof from rotting. It's good to build something that will last." Ira nodded at the carriage house. "Let's hope you've made the new center as sturdy as this little house," he teased. "Tiles on the roof. Do the birds really need that? Don't they fly in the rain?"

Fanny chuckled along with Ira and Rose.

Zed had his hands on his hips, but from his smile it was clear that he also enjoyed his father's joke. "You see, Dat, the birds don't mind the rain, but if there's no roof, the squirrels will be jumping in to steal all the seed."

"A good point." Ira knocked on the side of the birdhouse. "Ya, good quality."

"I think the birds will like it," Will said.

Behind the group, Fanny noticed a gray buggy approaching, though she didn't recognize the driver. When Caleb came out of the house to greet the carriage, she realized that it was his friend Kate and the Fisher women, a group that would include her former mother-in-law. She turned back to the chatter about the birdhouse, determined not to stare, but soon she heard shoes crunching on gravel behind her. She braced herself to welcome the women who had caused some difficult times for her.

"Fanny," Caleb called, "the Fishers have brought some treats from the bakery."

"That was kind of you." Fanny smiled at the three women, but only two returned the warm greeting. What was it about Joan Fisher's mouth that kept it too stiff to curve into a happy expression?

Although she knew these women and saw them at church every other week, she did her best to avoid most of the Fisher clan. She was glad that Kate's mother, Lydia, had come along, as the woman had a gift for gab and kept the conversation rolling like a smooth marble.

As Fanny chatted with the visitors, she caught a thorough glimpse of Kate Fisher, a tall young woman with a broad face that seemed to be lit with a permanent smile. It was as if the joy inside her shone out to the world through her face. Fanny could see why Caleb liked her. Strong, serious Caleb kept his eyes on the ground while plodding ahead. He needed someone to help him look up at the sky and find joy in each day, and Kate's smile was contagious.

"That's quite a fancy birdhouse you've got there," Joan said, speaking up for the first time. "Must have cost you quite a bit."

Will glanced up from the birdhouse, where he was showing Ira how the floor slid out for cleaning.

Fanny suspected that Joan was joking, as Amish folks did not spend much money on decorative things like birdhouses. But Joan's expression was unreadable, flat as a stone.

"It was a Christmas gift from my son," Fanny said.

"I made it," Will piped up.

"With some help from Zed, of course." Fanny glanced up at Zed, who watched with a cool expression.

"Makes a person wonder why you didn't make something Plain." Joan's lips puckered in disapproval. "You could get a small, simple birdhouse at the hardware store, probably for half of what this cost to make."

But you can't put a price on the tender care that went into its preparation. The attention showered on a young boy. The quiet time together. The learning of a skill. Fanny was on the verge of pointing these things out to Joan, but she didn't want to cross the woman. She had promised herself that she would try to smooth things over, for Caleb's sake.

"Look at those curved doors." Joan's face puckered with disdain. "Birds don't need doors."

"But they're just like the doors on the birthing center," Kate pointed out, a gentle glimmer in her eyes. "It will serve the birds well, and I think folks will smile when they see it."

Kate's words swept over the group like a spring breeze, bringing ease to the conversation. It was simple to see why Caleb enjoyed spending time with this bright-eyed young woman.

"There's nothing like birdsong in the morning to brighten your day," Lydia said. "We have a seed cake in view from our kitchen window, and I enjoy watching the small birds swoop down on it, their little heads bobbing as they peck away."

"Isn't it wonderful, Gott's creatures all around us," Rose added, folding her arms against the cold.

"You're shivering, Rose." Fanny patted the older woman's arm. "Let's all get inside where it's cozy. I'm ready for some hot apple cider."

As the group made its way in, Will came to Fanny's side and took her hand. He waited until the Fishers ducked inside, then turned up to her and whispered, "Is the birdhouse too fancy, Mamm?"

"No, Will. It's as Plain as our carriage house. You worked hard on it, and there's no shame in that." She squeezed his shoulder, reassuring him. "It's a wonderful good gift."

With a grin, he stepped over the threshold and bounded over to play with his cousins, leaving Fanny relieved that she could undo the damage Joan had done. At least this time.

⬡⬡⬡

Although Fanny enjoyed having family and friends visit, she knew all good times had to come to an end. Already Gabe and Emma had gone home, as Emma and the children would return to school in the morning. Tom's brother Jimmy had gone out to get their buggy, and Fanny was wrapping half a chocolate chip pie and some cookies for them to take home.

"Don't forget the crybaby cookies," Edna said. "They're my favorites."

"And to think I almost didn't make them," Fanny teased. The simple cookies, flavored with leftover coffee, were not traditional holiday fare, but they were easy enough to bake. She added a few extras for her dear friend and covered the plate with tin foil. "There you go."

"I'm sorry to see the day end." Edna smoothed her fingers over the little pink scar on her chin—a habit from childhood, when a fall from a scooter had required stitches to heal the cut. One day, when Edna had confided that she was self-conscious about the scar, Fanny had taken a red pen and put a little squiggle of ink on her own chin, just to show Edna that the mark was barely noticeable. "It's been good to spend time with family and friends that we don't get to see often," Edna added.

"I hope we don't wait until next second Christmas to get together again," said Fanny. "Though both of us have had a busy year. You've been caring for James, and I've been trying to make do without Tom."

"A sad year, indeed, but I'm glad to put it behind us. And I'm back to my old daily routine now that James and Rachel are married. Rachel takes James to the clinic every day, and he's learned to move about with only crutches or a walker, thank the Almighty. You know, he came here tonight without a wheelchair, in the buggy. He's a determined young man."

"Gott bless him," Fanny said. "And does he get around the orchard, too?"

"Oh, he's been out there ever since he could move his own wheelchair, though there's not much need for it this time of year." Edna cradled the plate of cookies. "Let's get together soon, Fanny. Bring Beth and Tommy over and we'll do some sewing. Or I'll come help you finish setting up the birth center. I'm sure there'll be windows to wash and curtains to hang."

"That would be wonderful, Edna. It'll give us a chance to catch up." As Fanny squeezed her sister-in-law's shoulder, she realized she did have some women here in Halfway who were like sisters to her.

She simply had to find the time to enjoy some fellowship with them.

She walked out, arm in arm with Edna. Edna's daughter Verena was shepherding the younger ones into the buggy. The teens, who were now playing games in the buggy garage, would be staying on for a while. With the noise contained in a separate building, Fanny didn't mind if they extended the celebration.

"Tell Zed I'm serious about donating that newel post to the center," Jimmy said when Fanny approached the buggy. "We had to take it down to fit the wheelchair and ramp, and now it's just sitting out in our barn, no good to no one."

"I'll be sure to tell him." Fanny smiled and watched as the Lapps' buggy rolled down the lane. Her arms were crossed against the chilly night, but she didn't feel the cold so much. Not quite ready to return to the crowd in her house, she gazed up at the sky with its gleaming stars. It had been a good Christmas, and she was grateful to have a loving family and kind friends.

So grateful to be loved.

Edna had been right about putting the sadness behind her. A new year was coming, a year of many miracles, if she could count the babies about to be born in their community.

The first year that they would have the birthing center. She gave a happy sigh at the sight of the old carriage house with its sparkling white trim and shiny windows. Inside those walls, good things were about to happen.

A dim light flickered from the window of the carriage house; someone was inside. Of course, it would be Zed. She hadn't noticed him in the house for a while. Having been away from the community for so long, Zed sometimes felt uncomfortable at big gatherings. And with so many tasks still to be completed in the center, he would have retreated from the gathering to tinker a bit.

She had half expected that. This morning, when she had come across the gift she had wrapped for him, she had decided to leave it in the carriage house. That way they would avoid the eyes of folks who didn't understand that Zed had become a part of their family.

The cold night, the relief of a gathering that had gone well, and the excitement of Zed finding his gift made her giddy as she hurried to the birthing center and pushed open the door. "Merry Christmas," she called.

"So you found me." He held up his hands, revealing the kid leather gloves. "And I found these. A perfect fit. Denki."

Somehow she'd known they would fit. She had watched him work for so long that she carried the image of his hands in her memory. "I thought of you when I saw them. They might come in handy for some of the rough jobs."

"These gloves will get plenty of use." He slid one of them off. "But I'm not doing any heavy work tonight. Would you hand me the tape measure from the workbench?"

She found the yellow case and brought it to him.

"I need to measure the stairs. There's an old newel post that Jimmy Lapp is giving away, and I think it would fit fine right here. We need something to anchor our handrail, but we can't afford much more than a wood post."

"Jimmy mentioned that. He was hoping we could use it."

Zed retracted the yellow metal tape with a nod. "It would be the right height. I'll pick it up from the orchard tomorrow."

"A newel post." Fanny rubbed her cold hands together as she stepped back from the stairs. "I didn't think we'd have anything so nice." She held her arms out, encompassing the floors, the walls, the kitchen. "It's all so wonderful good, Zed. From floor to ceiling, the place is neat and tidy, but cozy, too. And we have you to thank for making it so."

"I'm just the handyman," he said, leaning back on the sawhorse.

"You came up with the notion of making the building a birthing center. A very good idea, but I hope the other mothers wait until I'm done with the renovations before they come in here to use it."

The light laughter came easily between them. "The mothers need this place," she said as she perched beside him on the sawhorse. "And it's really going to happen. It does my heart good to know that something wonderful will come of this building, thanks to you."

The kerosene lamp sizzled for a moment, and when they both turned to look at it, she caught his profile: square chin, bold cheekbones, and dark ridges of shadow around his eyes. Zed had thoughtful eyes. Her mamm used to say that eyes were the window to the soul. If that was true, Zed was a man who cared for others, a man who chose his words carefully so they didn't hurt anyone. He was such a part of her life, such a part of each and every day. How could she let him go?

"The work is almost done here," she said, giving voice to her fears. "You must be eager to move on. Take a real job on a crew. A job with good pay."

He rose to check the lamp, then turned back to face her. "I haven't thought that far ahead."

"I'm sure you'll get some offers soon." It was harder to say these things when she was facing him; he was sure to recognize the truth behind her words. He would know she didn't want him to leave. "Now that you're baptized and folks have begun to bring you back into the flock. It takes time for some folks to warm up, but they'll come around. And once they get a look at the quality of work on this place . . ." The thickness in her throat was making her hoarse. "After this, the best builders will want to hire you."

"There are good jobs out there," he admitted, "but I'll never find a job as good as this, working for you. Your house has been a good fit for me, like those gloves."

"Oh, Zed . . ." Sorrow was a bitter, flat taste on the back of the tongue. It welled up inside her and she pressed her hands to his broad chest, as if she could stop him from leaving. "I don't want you to go."

His eyes, the color of dark, sweet molasses, held her rapt. "If I had a say in the matter, I would never leave." He slid his hands down along her arms, then encircled her waist and drew her against his warm body. "I can't leave you, Fanny. What can we do?"

"You have to stay," she whispered.

His dark eyes told her that the answer was not quite so simple, but when he tipped his head down and pressed his lips to hers, all her worries dissolved in a magnificent kiss. She closed her eyes and reveled in the touch of his mouth on hers, the secure feeling of his arms around her.

The click of a door latch seemed loud as a shotgun blast. The noise jarred them, and the kiss ended as they turned to the source of the sound.

The door was open and there were voices.

Before they could move apart, Elsie's voice penetrated Fanny's daze. She was describing the way the building had been set up to care for mothers and babies. Oh, no! Not now!

Embarrassment splashed over Fanny like a pan of cold water as she and Zed faced Elsie, Ruben, and a very shocked Joan Fisher.

Ruben and Elsie shared a look of concern, but Joan snorted and glared at Fanny and Zed. "I knew it," she said. "I always knew you were this way. Such a disgrace."

"I'm sorry." Fanny pressed a hand to her flushed face, which seemed to be on fire.

But Joan was not accepting apologies. With her lips pursed in disgust, she swung around and strode out the door.

"I'm sorry," Fanny repeated, feeling stranded on the work bench. Zed had stepped back, quiet and distant.

"No need to apologize when you did nothing wrong," Elsie said.

Oh, but I did. I let my emotions run wild, without a lick of common sense for time and place, Fanny thought in despair. *And now, everyone will know my mistake.*

Ruben apologized for bringing Joan back. He wouldn't have thought of it, but it was one of the few things Joan seemed interested in.

"You couldn't have known," Zed told him.

Fanny curled up with her head in her hands, silently praying for Gott's mercy. It would have been shameful to have a private moment interrupted by anyone, but for Joan Fisher to see her in Zed's arms . . . She didn't want to think about the number of people who would hear of this mistake. When she felt a touch on her shoulder and looked up, it was Elsie, asking if she was all right.

She nodded, saying that she would be back at the house in a minute. There were guests to send off, leftovers to put away, and a kitchen to tidy. But as the door latched behind Elsie, Fanny heard a soft rustle beside her. Zed stood just beyond her reach. He rubbed his chin, his mouth a taut line of tension.

"Fanny, we can weather this storm."

She turned away from him, even more embarrassed by the tears that stung her eyes. His soft voice and quiet strength were soothing as a whispering snowfall, but she could not let him comfort her anymore.

"Please go," she said. "Leave me be. We don't need anyone else finding us together, adding wood to the fire."

"But I'm not afraid of what Joan might say."

"Please . . . I can't talk about this. Just go."

"All right. We'll talk in the morning. Everything looks better in the light of day."

She spared him a nod, then buried her head in her hands when the door closed behind him.

She imagined that most of the guests were leaving, but all the animated laughter and joy of the Christmas gathering faded in the wake of fear. What would Joan Fisher do?

To be caught in the arms of another man while still mourning her husband ... Fanny was sickened by her own actions. This terrible shame would cast a pall over her relationship with Zed. People would think less of them both. And poor Caleb. How would he gain the trust and approval of the Fisher clan when his stepmother showed no respect for the dead?

It was as if this mistake would prove to the Fishers that Fanny never had been quite worthy of dear David. And that was not fair, because Fanny had loved David Fisher with all her heart.

She bit back her fragile emotions and turned down the kerosene lamp until the room grew dark. She never meant to be disrespectful to the memory of Thomas ... or David. Gott knew she had barely made eye contact with a man until a year after David was gone, even if she was working in Tom Lapp's house then.

Oh, what a mistake she had made tonight! She prayed, for Caleb's sake, that Joan would be charitable and keep this to herself. Perhaps she would forgive Fanny and welcome Caleb into her family.

No matter what Joan decided, Fanny would keep a safe distance from Zed for the next two months—well into February, when the grieving period would be over. It was the least she could do out of respect for her dear Tom.

25

"Thanks for squeezing me in between the holidays," Meg told Dr. Trueherz. "I know it's hard for you to get time off to spend with your family."

"That's the life of a country doctor." With his silver-streaked hair and twinkling eyes, Henry Trueherz exuded a mixture of warmth and authority. "You'll learn that lesson soon enough once you take on clients around here. Be sure to carve out some personal time for your family and stick to it. You'll need to have another midwife to cover for you, but believe me, it's well worth it. Everyone needs a break now and then. Just ask my wife."

She laughed . . . a forced, nervous sound. The impending test results loomed over her like a bundle of black clouds. After years of dealing with cramping and heavy periods, she wasn't concerned about the discomfort of endometriosis. But when the tissue that normally lined the uterus began to grow outside the uterus, it often scarred and swelled, blocking the fallopian tubes and preventing pregnancy. And for Meg, that was the scary part.

"So let's see how the CT scan went." He lowered his glasses to the tip of his nose so that he could read over them. "Good. They didn't see any sign of a cyst on the ovaries."

"That's good news, though I never worried about developing a cyst. The disease runs in my family. My mom and aunt. My sister, Zoey, has it, too. And no one has ever developed cysts or cancer."

"You've researched this, so there probably isn't anything new I can tell you about the science of it." The doctor closed her folder. "And you're right; family history can be a strong indicator. So how's the pain? Do over-the-counter medications give you enough relief?"

"I'm usually good with ibuprofen. But I'm concerned about the possibility of infertility. I know that these imaging tests don't tell us much about the growth of the endometriosis implants."

"That's right. Are you trying to get pregnant?"

"Well, not right now. But . . . I'm seeing someone and it's getting serious. Looks like we might be talking about marriage soon." She felt herself blushing. "Wow. It feels funny to say that."

"Congratulations. Do I know the lucky guy?"

"Jack Woods."

"Halfway's deputy? Well, good for you. He's a fine man, an asset to the community. So you two are planning a family. Have you discussed your situation with him?"

"Well . . . no. Not yet."

The doctor rubbed his chin thoughtfully. "Don't you think you should be honest with him?"

"I do. Of course. I'm going to tell him." She pressed the palm of one hand to her forehead and sighed. "I should have told him already. Usually I'm a very honest, down-to-earth person. In my occupation, you can't be squeamish when it comes time to talk about the female reproductive system. But whenever there's been a window of opportunity with Jack, I've choked. I'm so afraid of disappointing him."

"Because he wants children, and you're afraid that won't be possible?"

"It's a worry," she admitted. "The thing is, I've kind of let it go too long with Jack. But really, when is the socially correct time to tell a guy you might have reproductive issues?"

There was a hint of a smile on the doctor's face. "I'm afraid that question is beyond my realm of experience. Have you encountered this dilemma before?"

She told him about Lloyd Corrigan, a guy she had dated a few years ago. Once, when she'd suffered crippling cramps while they'd been attending a Pirates game, she had mentioned the endometriosis. "From the look on his face, you would have thought I had bubonic plague. That ended that relationship."

He chuckled. "I'm glad you've come to terms with this, but it's too bad about the boyfriend."

"Trust me; it was a blessing in disguise." Zoey used to say Lloyd could have been the poster child for the "me" generation. Unlike Jack, who could win an award for compassion. The other night she had learned more of the details of Jack's wayward relationship with Lisa, who was a very troubled soul. He'd been reluctant to tell Meg about it, but the way she interpreted the story, Jack had given up his home and his good friends for Lisa.

"I'd rather that you heard this all from me," Jack had confessed. "I didn't come out to Halfway just to be close to my sister. I had to get out of the department in Philly, fast and furious. Halfway had a job opening, and I figured this town is far enough from the city to buffer me from the bad drama there."

"Drama involving Lisa?"

He'd nodded. "She was off her meds, having some episodes. We had broken up, not even seeing each other, and she shows up at my precinct and freaks out. Says she wants to press charges against me for assault."

"Oh, no."

"Oh, yes. It got pretty ugly. The police department takes that stuff seriously these days. Lisa managed to swing the assistant district attorney around to her side. She's an amazingly convincing storyteller. Landed me in jail."

"You are kidding me!"

"Nope. They took away my gun and badge for a while. Those were dark days."

Kind, gentle Jack . . . how could anyone accuse him of violence? "How did you get your name cleared?"

"My coworkers had my back. Turned out I was working a double shift at the time of the alleged attack. The charges were dropped, and I was taken off administrative leave. Even Lisa's family apologized and told me they would get her back on her meds. My minister got the congregation to rally around me. That helped me feel human again, but the damage had been done. Lisa made things end so badly between us. I wasn't feeling good about my job anymore. It was like a shadow was following me around, a bad rep. I knew I had to make a change."

"So you came here."

"I came to visit Kat and Brendan one weekend, and Kat shanghaied me into the sheriff's office to meet Hank. And here I am."

Meg knew that Jack had suffered over sharing that story. His honesty made her feel wimpy by comparison; she would have to tell him about her condition. Soon.

"Well . . ." Doc Trueherz's voice brought Meg back to the moment as he leaned back in his chair. "If you want to get pregnant in the near future, I would recommend laparoscopic surgery. And considering your age, time is of the essence."

Meg's thumbs pressed into the leather arms of the visitor's chair. "I was thinking along those lines. I mean, I've been told I have moderate endometriosis, but the extent of the blockage is a guessing game unless you can get a look through the scope."

"Exactly, and as procedures go, it's not too invasive. It's usually done under general anesthesia, but you can opt for a local or a spinal. I don't do it, but I can refer you to a gynecologist or surgeon in Lancaster. Or east of here, toward Philadelphia. It's up to you. The laparoscope requires a small incision. If they find any visible endometriosis implants or scar tissue, they'll remove it. But then, you know all this."

She nodded. "I've worked with clients who've had the procedure. I also know that it can take a week to fully recover, so I'll need to schedule it after my sister has her baby."

"February or March, even April would be fine. It's no rush, but the surgery will give us a definitive diagnosis, and if you have moderate endometriosis, the procedure will improve your chances of pregnancy."

Her grip on the armrests relaxed. "The sooner the better. If you give me some referrals, I'll get the ball rolling." It was a relief, having a plan. "That's one problem down. Now I just have to figure out how I'm going to dump this all on Jack."

"Knowing Jack, I don't think he'll be too fazed by this. Worried about you, yes, but not daunted." He mentioned how Jack had championed Halfway's Christmas food drive, and how he continued to push to set up a year-round food bank. "Jack's not the kind of guy to turn around when he comes to a roadblock."

That was the Jack she knew. It was foolish to think that he would abandon her because of her medical issues, but sometimes there was no logic to human emotions.

"Have you talked to Fanny lately?" he asked. "I'm wondering when the birthing center will be ready to open."

"I saw her just before Christmas Eve, and it sounds like they're doing the finishing touches. The major construction is complete. I'd say you'll be doing deliveries there in the next few weeks."

"Wonderful." The doctor's demeanor changed, his professional reserve giving way to delight. "That's quite an accomplishment, opening a place like that in your own backyard. I'm confident that it will serve the community well, and I'm glad Fanny has you involved. Takes some of the pressure off me."

"I'm itching to get back to work. As soon as Zoey has her baby, I'll begin doing prenatal care and helping Fanny with deliveries. Do you think Anna will want to midwife again after she's recovered?"

"That I don't know. She's been devoted to helping women give birth, but she's older, and her family has left Halfway. I'm thinking she might want to follow her daughter to Ohio."

"Whatever she decides, with the number of pregnant Amish women I've seen around Halfway and Paradise, there will be plenty of work for all of us."

"Indeed. The Amish have large families. The women of Lancaster County will certainly keep you busy."

Meg grinned. "Music to my ears."

26

As Fanny shoveled the freshly baked cookies into a basket for distribution at church, she thanked the Lord for the distraction of hard work. It cleared the mind, tired the body, and brought a sense of satisfaction when a task was completed. The chores of cooking, cleaning, and tending to the horses helped to ease the worry that nibbled at her conscience.

That kiss. Oh, how could something so sweet and tender sour into a moment of disgrace?

She could not undo the damage now. All she could do was hope and pray that Joan kept the knowledge she had gained from passing her lips. That was the only way Fanny and Zed could avoid a full-blown scandal.

Fearing the worst, Fanny had spoken with her older children. "I just want you to know the truth," Fanny told Caleb and Elsie one night after the little ones were in bed, "in case gossip starts."

Caleb took the news with stoic grace. He had already heard bits and pieces from Kate, who had suffered through the story from her aunt on the way home from the gathering. "Kate's mamm told her that it's no reflection on me," Caleb said, "though she wishes that Kate would date someone from a better family."

"A better family?" Elsie's face puckered in consternation. "We're all sinners on this earth. I wish those Fishers could see that we're not in competition for Gott's love."

Elsie's reaction eased Fanny's embarrassment. "You are so right, dear girl."

"I know Joan doesn't take kindly to you, Fanny." Caleb frowned, running his knuckles over the scarred surface of the table. "She doesn't know you the way we do."

"She doesn't know you and love you," Elsie said.

Caleb stacked his fists on the table, a twinkle in his eyes. "It made me bristle when I first heard about it. But I remembered what Dat used to say about pointing out people's faults. Before you point to someone's faults, take time to count to ten—ten of your own."

"He did say that," Elsie said with a delighted smile.

"Oh, I'm sure I can count way past ten," Fanny added.

They laughed together, easing the tension in Fanny's muscles. Laughter was truly the best medicine.

Fanny and Zed had not spoken of the incident, but how could that happen when they were never alone? Fanny made sure of that, taking little Tommy out to the carriage house with her when she checked on Zed. In the mornings, Elsie and Caleb were here to provide a buffer, but that wasn't necessary since Zed stopped inside for a mug of coffee and then ducked out just as quickly. Perhaps he was respecting her request to be left alone. Fanny had not been able to meet his gaze, and she longed for the mirth or warmth or compassion that flowed from Zed's molasses brown eyes. While the embarrassment of being caught stung, the loss of her connection to Zed knocked the life out of her.

She missed him. Her heart seemed to break just a bit more every day, and yet, she could see no end to the pain. She could not imagine a way back to his arms.

In the four days that had passed since second Christmas, Fanny had not heard much of anything from outside the walls of her home. Sarah Beiler had gone into labor, but the birth had been handled by Doc Trueherz and Anna, whose cast had been removed. Anna had wanted to be there, since Sarah was her grandniece.

Fanny would need to venture beyond the safety of her cocoon today; everyone in the Amish community would be attending church at the home of Dave and Lydia Zook. Oh, she was afraid to step out of the buggy and face the curious eyes! But one could not miss church. Besides, she might be making a mountain out of a molehill. Maybe Joan had cooled off after she'd vented a bit on the ride home. Maybe she hadn't told a soul.

"Flicker is hitched up and ready to go," Caleb reported. "And there are two warming bricks on the woodstove for the ride."

"Sounds like the cold spell has started." Fanny handed him the basket of cookies. "These can go in the buggy. And, Will, don't forget to put the milk back in the fridge."

Will looked up from the table and wiped a mustache of milk off with his sleeve. "Yes, Mamm." When he crossed the room with the pitcher, Fanny had to bite back a smile. "You're growing like a weed. Look at those pants!" The hem of his pants was a full two inches above his shoes. "There's some sewing to be done this week."

Will shrugged. "They're fine."

Boys could be so easy, Fanny thought, sweeping Tommy off his feet for a diaper change before church. They didn't seem to be tempted to gossip as much as women were.

Bundled together under lap blankets and singing carols with the children and young people, Fanny felt her worries fade. Family was the blanket of love that surrounded a person.

Memories of family life rolled through her mind. Digging in the garden, the whole family working shovels and spades to turn the soil. Grooming the horses. Helping Elsie clean the Country Store so that the windows and floors were shiny clean. So much activity to be shared in the kitchen, the center of their home. Canning berries and tomatoes with the girls. Baking and cooking. Playing board games and working puzzles.

And the joy when work became play! A few weeks ago, while Tommy was napping, Fanny had wrapped a kerchief on her head and put the children in old clothes so that they could help paint the center. Zed had pitched in, and fortunately he'd had the foresight to tape off the edges and cover the floor with a drop cloth. A good thing, because Beth didn't seem to notice when her brush dribbled paint from the can to the wall. Will was put to work on the corners, Beth on the taped edges, and Fanny smoothed a roller over the walls. Zed painted the ceiling, cutting in the edges by hand.

The laughter started when Zed straightened and brushed the ceiling with his head. That left him with a streak of white in his dark hair.

"You're a skunk!" Beth proclaimed.

"Do I smell so bad?" Zed had teased.

That had started the children laughing. Inspired, Will pushed his head against one of the walls and came away with a smear of pale blue in his hair. "I'm a blue skunk," he proclaimed.

Then Beth dipped a finger into the paint and dotted her arms with it, proclaiming that she had blue chicken pox.

Fanny had noted the paint spatter on her own arm. "I see that it's contagious," she said. But really, the only thing that had been contagious was the laughter. By the time they were through, Fanny found that her sides ached from laughing so much. But the center got its coat of paint—and so did the children. Fortunately, the water-based paint washed off easily in the tub.

Ya, family life was the way of the Amish, and Zed had folded into their family so effortlessly, Fanny had come to believe that was the way Gott intended it. She still prayed that other folk would come to understand that; that they might recognize the love that lived in Zed's heart, love he shared with Fanny and her family. That was nothing to be ashamed of. Jesus himself had said that there are three gifts that last—faith, hope, and love. "And the greatest of these is love."

By the time they arrived at the Zooks, an easy smile had settled on her face. With Tommy in one arm, she handed off the basket of cookies and found dear Edna, who wanted to come by to help set up the center.

"I've heard so much about it, Fanny, and I want to see it for myself," Edna said, her breath a puff of white in the air. "How about Wednesday?"

The offer of help was much appreciated, but more than that, Fanny was relieved that the gossip hadn't seeped out to poison her friendship with Edna. "Wednesday morning would be fine," Fanny said. "I could sure use some help hanging curtains. It's a two-person job."

They chatted for a few minutes, but then it was time to file into the house for church. Like many Amish homes, the Zook house had removable walls that had come down so that the entire ground floor of the house could be used for the service. Fanny took a seat beside Edna and settled Beth on the other side. As she pulled Tommy on her lap, she noticed that his nose was running. "Blow," she said in his ear, pressing a hankie to his nose. He just gave a little whimper. Probably teething again. His four front teeth had come in, but he was approaching the time when he'd be getting more.

A hush fell over the hundred or so people, who were all dressed in their Sunday best. The silence was broken by a voice that rose from the men's section—the *Vorsinger,* who led the group in song. Church had begun.

After a few minutes, Tommy's whimper made it clear that he was not feeling well. Trying to comfort her boy, Fanny held him close and swayed a bit. Soon the warm, sad music of the Loblied washed over the rows of Plain folk, and she let out a breath and lost herself in song and prayer.

Throughout the service, Tommy was fidgety. He did not seem warm with fever, but his cheeks were flushed and his little nose was dripping. "Either it's teething or a cold coming on," Fanny told Edna as they filed out of the house. Beth and Will skipped ahead to find cousins and friends.

"Poor thing. From the look of him, I say it's teething," Edna said, patting Tommy on the back. "When you get home, give him a big, cold carrot. He can teethe on it to his heart's content."

"A good idea," Fanny said, wiping Tommy's nose once again.

There was no barn, as the Zooks leased their land to other farmers and pursued other businesses. However, a large tent had been set up outside, and two space heaters did a nice job of taking the edge off the cold. Under the tent, men, women, and teens were congregating in different locations, chatting while the hosts and their helpers rearranged the church benches around tables for the fellowship meal. Small children played on the fringes or outside the tent, where they could run about without bothering anyone. With Tommy calling to get down, Fanny thought it best to get him away from the large crowds. While Edna went into the house to help set things up, Fanny took her son out.

At the door of the tent, she nearly ran into Joan, who was marching inside in a hurry. "It's awfully cold out there," Joan said crisply. Although she didn't look Fanny in the eye, it was clear she was talking to her.

"And from the sky, I'd say it's going to snow," Fanny said cheerfully. "I like it when the ground is pure white with snow, and the family can stay cozy by the fire."

"Not me." Joan rubbed her hands together and scanned the crowd. "Snow clogs up everything. Bad roads and bad for business."

"Maybe I'm wrong. We might just have a cold, clear night," Fanny said pleasantly.

"Let's hope so," Joan said, moving toward a group of women clustered near a space heater.

The sting of cold outside the tent was nothing compared to Joan's brisk manner. Well, at least she had paused to speak with Fanny. That had to be a good sign.

Seeing Will and Beth, she headed toward a group of children playing near a picnic table. But she didn't go three steps before she spotted Zed talking to the bishop and some men.

Dark-eyed, humble Zed. Since that shameful night, he had filled her thoughts. From looking at him now, she couldn't tell if he missed her, too. His face was calm as a summer lake under his black hat. The dark eyes that seemed to peer into her heart were fixed elsewhere. And the hands that could drive a nail or gently rub a bump on Will's head, those hands were hidden away, tucked into his black coat for warmth.

She had to steel herself to keep from staring, but she noticed that one of the men was Tim Ebersol, the builder. Hadn't Zed mentioned getting a job with him? And there was a woman in the group—Tim's daughter Sarah. Known as a chatterbox, Sarah wrote a regular column for one of the Amish newspapers, and more than once the bishop had warned her not to share personal stories from the community, but to keep things general. Fanny had to tear her gaze away and focus on her children.

Tommy seemed content to toddle around the picnic table and play in the midst of the older children, so Fanny took a seat there and braced herself against the cold. The table backed up to a tall boxwood hedge, and female voices traveled through it. Fanny tended to her little boy while one of the women revealed her recipe for cheddar apple pie and another talked of the lovely quilt she had received for her hope chest at Christmas. Then she heard someone mention Zed.

"He's going to be working for my father," a woman said, "so I'm sure I'll be seeing a lot of him."

That was probably Sarah, Fanny thought.

"Do you fancy Zed Miller?" someone asked.

Someone answered that she might, if she could get him talking. "Whenever I see him, it's as if his mouth is glued shut."

Fanny grinned. Zed was not one to waste words, but he had plenty to say to her.

"I think Sarah and Zed would be a good match," another woman said. "She can fill in the blanks when he's not talking. Which is most of the time!"

Laughter twittered through the hedges like chirping birds, and Fanny felt a twinge of annoyance that these girls would poke fun at a good man like Zed. Were matters of the heart a game to them?

"I see him at least once a week, sometimes more," came a booming voice. Dorcas Fisher. "Zed has a weakness for good bread. I suspect he'll be coming around more, once he finishes that center and gets himself free from Fanny Lapp."

"I didn't know he was hitched up to her buggy."

The words went through Fanny, sharp as a knife.

"Didn't you hear?" Dorcas's voice thumped like a heavy shoe. "They were caught kissing. Think of that. She's still wearing black, mourning one husband, while she's moving in on the next."

Fanny rose quickly, not wanting to hear another word. She scooped up Tommy, who was happily cruising around the seat of the picnic table, and marched toward the tent to find Caleb or Elsie. She needed to go home. Away from here. Now.

Shame burned hot on her face, but she swallowed hard to stave off tears. She would not cry in front of the community.

Tommy was fussing, upset at being torn from his fun. "Hush." She pressed a hand to his cheek and looked him in the eye. "We're going home now. We'll get you a nice fat carrot for your gums. How about that?"

His brow still furrowed in determination, but he stopped moaning and touched the string of her kapp. Not even a year old, and he knew when to give up.

Why hadn't she learned that lesson?

Stung by humiliation, she slipped into the tent to find a way home.

27

onday morning, Zed sat at the table in the Lapp kitchen and thought about the old saying to keep your boots under the table. It meant that a man belonged at home with his family, a message he had never really understood until he'd started coming here to work. Sitting with his boots under this table, it just felt right.

The coffee, hot and black, was just what Zed needed to sharpen his focus. He sipped quietly, occasionally chiming in while Caleb told Will and Beth about his own days in school with a different teacher, Miss Marian.

The story of a frog in someone's lunch pail had Will giggling, but Zed could only smile. He was too preoccupied with Fanny to chip in on the conversation.

He'd lain awake for most of the night, trying to build a plan that would keep Fanny safe from the scorn of gossipers, a plan that would protect them both from disapproving eyes until the time came when it would be acceptable for Zed to court her in February.

The plan would begin with a simple talk after the others had gone. They could not go on this way, with Fanny staring at the ground, with him walking on eggshells whenever they were together for fear of someone seeing them and fanning the fires of gossip.

He took another sip of the coffee, letting the bitter taste roll on his tongue. It was their timing that was bitter. Ya, it would have been far better to fall in love with her a few months down the road. Once a mourning period ended, folks believed that Gott wanted a person to marry again.

But who could stop an early frost or keep the sun from shining in the summer? Some things just happened the way they happened. Gott had brought Zed here. Gott had brought Fanny and him together. And Gott didn't make mistakes.

The sound of light footsteps on the stairs drew him back to the moment just as Fanny came into the kitchen with Tommy on her hip. The boy held a large carrot in his hand, while Fanny had one finger poked inside his mouth.

"Look what I found poking through," she announced. "A little nub of a tooth." As she brought the baby closer to the table she noticed Zed sitting with the others.

"Zed. Good morning. I didn't know you were here so early." Her gaze flickered immediately back to Tommy. "Show your brothers the new tooth that's coming in."

But Tommy recoiled, hiding against Fanny.

"At least he likes his carrot." Caleb rose from the table and pinched Tommy lightly on the chin.

"But he's not eating it," Will said. "Why doesn't he eat it?"

"It's for teething," Fanny said, explaining how it felt good to press the cool, hard surface against sore gums.

Just then Elsie came in from outside, bundled up in a coat, hat, and gloves. "Let's get a move on, folks," she said. "It's not getting any warmer out there."

Will and Caleb bundled up, collected their lunch pails, and headed out.

"Fanny?" Zed was on his feet as soon as the door closed behind them. "We have to talk."

She dared to look directly in his eyes, and he saw that her blue eyes were rimmed with red. "All right, then."

He followed her to the front room, where Beth was playing contentedly, introducing her doll to the figurines in the Christmas manger. With Tommy content in his playpen, they returned to the kitchen and she picked up the coffeepot.

"I have no words," she said, pouring him another cup. "Sorry doesn't really cover the shame I've brought upon you. And just when folks here were beginning to accept you."

He wanted to tell her that folks were also beginning to trust him, that he'd had a very good offer to work for Ebersol Construction. After a rough patch back here in Halfway, Zed knew he could find steady work now. But he also saw through some of the offers. He wasn't blind to the bishop's matchmaking, pushing him toward Sarah Ebersol. Or his mother's attempt to spark a romance in the bakery between him and Dorcas Fisher.

Fanny poured a mug of coffee, and then lowered the pot to the burner with a clang. "I'm sorry, Zed."

"You don't need to apologize. I'm the one who should be protecting you, and the memory of your husband. I'm sorry that Joan saw us together. But I'm not sorry to be in love with you."

Speechless, she pressed a hand to her mouth and shook her head.

He started to rise to his feet to go to her, wanting to hold her, to comfort her, but he couldn't. He couldn't chance someone walking in and seeing them, and he didn't want to add to Fanny's regrets. If she thought it was disrespectful to Tom's memory, Zed would abide by that.

"I'm afraid I've spoiled our chance at happiness." She sat at the table beside him, but now she would not meet his eyes. "I'm so ashamed, Zed. Joan has told others, and the terrible story is out."

He winced. From the way that Fanny had left church so abruptly yesterday, he suspected as much.

"And though I was cross with Joan, I can't deny the truth." Her voice was low, thick with emotion. "I loved Tom with all my heart, and yet I wasn't able to mourn him properly without falling into another man's arms."

"You're making it sound like a bad thing that Gott has led us to each other. Ya, you must mourn your husband for a full year. And we made a mistake, not waiting. But no crime was committed. We did not violate the Ordnung, Fanny. If you feel it's a sin, ask Gott in Heaven for forgiveness. Seek and ye shall find."

She smoothed her fingertips over the surface of the kitchen table. "I feel like there's a mark upon me, a scar that will never heal." Her palm stretched toward the center of the table, fanning over the wood's surface. "See these scratches on the table? Some from scissors; this is where we cut out patterns. This is where the children do homework." She ran her fingertips over a matted area. "They press hard when they write with a pencil. A gouge from the skillet. Sometimes I think this table is like a history of our family, a time line. I don't mind the scars, but it's just a table. It's different to know that people look at me and see so many nicks and scars."

He shook his head. "Nay, Fanny." He wanted to tell her that she was beautiful through and through, clear as a mountain spring, bright as the summer sun. That was how he saw her. But he knew she was beautifully flawed, too. That was how Gott made mankind. And Zed could not erase the scars that others saw.

He ran his fingertips over the table, finding a series of grooves cut into one corner. "Someone forgot to use a cutting board?"

She nodded, tears sparkling in her eyes.

"It's a very nice table. Practical and clean. Plain and simple. It brings the family together for meals. That's the Amish way. It supports the daily routine of a family. Isn't that all that Gott asks of us?"

She closed her eyes and pushed away from the table. "I'm sorry, Zed. I can't live with this shame." A kitchen drawer squeaked open, and her hands burrowed through it. "You can't be coming here anymore. I . . . I'll always be grateful for the fine work you've done on the center. Everyone in Halfway is thankful for that. But most everything's done now. Doc Trueherz said we should open our doors."

"But the trim isn't finished in the—"

"I'll ask Caleb to do it in his spare time."

They both knew Caleb had precious little spare time, and most of that was spent with his girlfriend, Kate. But Zed simply watched as she took the envelope of cash from the drawer and began to count out twenty-dollar bills on the table in front of him.

"No, no, Fanny. Don't do this."

"That's for the last two weeks." She swallowed, staring at the stack of money. "Please, take it and go."

"Fanny, liebe, take a deep breath. There's no tangle here that can't be undone with a little time."

She stared at the money, blinking back tears.

Zed rose from the table, coffee cup in his hand. "I'll go. But I'm not giving up. When your mourning is over, I'll be back. And when the time is right, I hope that you'll marry me and be my wife."

"That would be wrong."

"I've made plenty of mistakes in my life. But loving you is not one of them. I won't give up on you. I know Gott means for us to be together." He crossed the room and put his empty cup in the sink. "Just not quite yet."

28

That afternoon, just before dinnertime, an ice storm passed through the valley, tinkling the skylights and windows with beads of frozen rain. Meg was glad to be at the inn with no place to go. The kitchen was warm, suffused with mouthwatering smells of baking rolls and potato-leek soup, Mom's New Year's Eve tradition. By the time she and Zoey had a chance to step out of the kitchen, the outside world resembled an ice kingdom with trees, streets, and fences shining in silver.

"It's a winter wonderland. Everything is an ice sculpture," Zoey said as she and Meg stood at the big picture window staring out at the crystallized world of white and silver hedges, trees, and fences.

"Beautiful but slippery as all get-out," Tate said from his favorite chair, where he was reading *The Wall Street Journal*.

"He's right. Everything is glazed with ice. Not so good for New Year's revelers." Meg pulled her cell phone from the pocket of her kitchen apron. "Jack's out there working. Let's see how the roads are."

Jack texted back that the roads were *Icy chaos. One fender bender after another.* When he added that he probably wouldn't be coming over tonight as planned, Meg understood.

"Better safe than sorry," Tate said as the three of them sat down to their dinner of soup, rolls, and salad.

Although Meg had been looking forward to ringing in the New Year with the man she loved, the knowledge that Jack was safe and thinking of her was enough to sustain her through the night. Champagne gave her a headache, and it was no novelty to stay up past midnight, since her job often required her to remain awake through the wee hours of the morning. The prospect of curling up in bed with a book was inviting.

By ten she had soared through the first three chapters of a novel when a call came from Jack.

"Looks like I'm going to be seeing you tonight, after all," he said. "Kat's in labor, and I need to bring her over to Fanny's birthing center. Can you meet us there? Doc Trueherz is going to try to get there, but he's all the way over in Paradise. That's a treacherous route. I'm going to pick Kat up right now."

"Pregnant women have the worst timing," she murmured. "Are you okay driving over in this?"

"I got me a four-by-four with studded tires. This here's an icy monkey."

"So you want me to meet you at Fanny's?" She was already out of bed and staring out the window at the sugar-glazed tree limbs. Her feet curled reflexively from the cold, and she whirled around to grab a thick pair of socks from a dresser drawer.

"I'm counting on you, girl."

She got Kat's cell number from him and was already pulling on jeans when Kat came on the line.

"How's it going, Kat?"

"Slow and painful." Kat's voice lacked its usual confidence.

Meg went through a series of questions, trying to coach detailed responses from Kat, who had to stop to work through a contraction. "I can wait," Meg told her. "Keep breathing." Since Kat was Dr. Trueherz's patient, Meg needed to get up to speed on her history and background, preferably before Kat arrived at the birthing center.

"Have you been able to time the pains?" Meg asked. From Kat's response, she wasn't that far along; the pain shouldn't have been intense yet. But Meg knew that childbirth affected women in different ways.

As Meg pulled on her parka, the glimmering icescape beyond the window stopped her in her tracks. Just like the night that went so wrong, the night that was too icy for an ambulance to reach the mother, too cold and slick for Meg to transport the mother herself.

Wincing, she pressed her eyes closed. "Stop. Just stop it." This was a different night. Every birth was different, and this time, she would have support. Fanny and Jack would be there, and the doctor was on his way. She needed to approach this birth with patience, openness, and all the knowledge she'd gained from helping other women in childbirth. With a glance at her polar-bearish reflection in the mirror, she gave herself a nod. "It's go time."

Although she was trying to slip out quietly, she found that Zoey and Tate were still up, watching the Times Square festivities on TV. Tate insisted on walking her over to Fanny's, and she was grateful for his help carrying her two suitcases. Although Fanny had some supplies, Meg's stock of medical instruments and drugs was more extensive.

"It's sort of like ice-skating," Tate said as he slid a few feet down the driveway. He caught his balance and hopped onto the frozen grass, where there was traction in the snow below. The night was silent but for the whistle and jangling clash of ice-covered branches. In the stark beauty, Meg decided that this was the perfect way to start the New Year, jumping back into the vocation that suited her so well.

Fanny answered the door with a small LED flashlight in hand. In her nightgown, with a braid that fell down her back, she looked like a teenager at a pajama party. "Go on and get settled in the center," she said, handing Meg the flashlight. "I'll be right there to light the lamps and set up."

∽∾

As Jack's Jeep pulled up, Meg opened the door and went outside to help Kat maneuver over the ice. "You made it," she said in a calm, welcoming voice.

Jack looked over from the driver's seat, his face strained. "I'm glad you're here. She's in a bad way."

Kat's face, puffy and streaked with tears, revealed her misery. "I can't do this," she sobbed as she shifted out of the backseat. "On a scale of one to ten, my pain is ninety-nine. Sheer agony."

"Let's get you inside and we'll see what we can do for you." Meg helped Kat to the door, where Fanny received her, guiding her over to a cot.

"As I was driving over here, I kept thanking God that you were you." Jack slid one arm around Meg's shoulders as they watched his sister kneel on the cot. "It kills me, seeing her in pain like that."

"It's part of the process," Meg said quietly. "She'll be fine."

Fortunately, Kat seemed relieved to have arrived at the center, where the earthy smell of wood smoke from the stove mixed with a hint of kerosene from the lamps. Without thought Meg slipped into professional mode, taking Kat's vitals, checking to make sure she was hydrated. Based on the contractions, Kat seemed to be in active first-stage labor. When Meg placed her hands on Kat's belly, she suspected posterior arrest: The baby was in the wrong position to descend.

"I'm going to need to do an exam," she said, then looked up at Jack. "Kat? Do you want Jack to stay by your side? Or should he step into the kitchen and wait this part out?"

"Out. I want to be alone," Kat said. "Just go, Jack."

Hands up, Jack backed away with relief. "I don't have to be told twice."

Fanny stood by quietly, rubbing Kat's back as Meg slipped on surgical gloves and did an internal exam. It was just as she had thought. "Well, no wonder you're in so much pain," she said. "You and your baby seem to be fine, but the baby's turned the wrong way."

"Back labor," Fanny said with a nod.

"That's right." Meg kept her voice level as she explained. "Often a posterior baby can't descend into the birth canal, and it puts tremendous pressure on the mother's lower back. They say it's ten times as painful when the baby is positioned this way."

Kat let out a whimper. "What can I do to make it stop?"

"Sometimes you can turn the baby by moving around," Fanny said.

"That's right." Meg helped Kat to her feet. "Walking is good—like the pacing you were doing before. You can try rocking your hips, rotating them. Or there's a position we can try on the stairs, whenever you feel up to it."

"Show me. Now." Kat clung to a thin thread of focus amidst the pain.

"This will look sort of like a runner's lunge," Meg said, leading her to the stairs, where the old newel post anchored the railing. "You're going to put your left foot on the second step and lean forward as far as you can. That's it. Good." She explained that this position opened the sacroiliac joint, giving the baby more room to turn.

"My grandmother had a treatment for back labor," Fanny said. "She used to send the mother for a buggy ride on a bumpy road."

"And did it work?" Kat asked.

"Sometimes."

"It's the same principle as rocking," Meg explained. "Sometimes the movement coupled with gravity causes the baby to rotate."

When it was time for a break, Fanny pressed a hot water bottle to Kat's lower back for pain relief. They encouraged Kat to drink and eat, and Fanny brought her a cup of a hydrating tonic she had made from water, lemon juice, honey, salt, and baking soda. To calm Kat and reduce swelling, Meg found sepia and arnica in her bag of homeopathic herbs. Every half hour or so, Meg checked the baby's heart rate.

About an hour after Kat's arrival, Dr. Trueherz called to check in. Meg relayed Kat's vitals and gave him her assessment.

"Back labor? That's too bad. Are you schooled in the Hamlin technique to rotate the baby?"

"I am, but I know it's painful for the mother and not always successful."

"That's true. Stick with the stair stretch and other exercises for now. I'm afraid to tell you this, but I don't think I'm going to make it there through this storm. I just pulled into an empty parking lot, and I'm not sure if I should continue. The roads are so slippery I've had to inch along. I haven't even made it out of Paradise yet, and there's no telling what's ahead. Do you think you can handle this one without me?"

Meg glanced over to the stairs, where Kat was in position again, whimpering, while Fanny applied counterpressure and coached her in a soothing voice. It was going to be a long night, and there would be no emergency crew if there was a problem.

But what was the point of making Doc Trueherz drive for hours, in dangerous conditions, when he would most likely miss the birth, anyway?

And she could handle this. Meg's instincts told her that she and Fanny could help Kat have her baby. This was labor—painful, messy, tiring, but rewarding. "I think we've got this one," Meg told the doctor.

It was a long night of labor for Kat. Although Meg worried about the drain on the laboring mother's stamina and energy, Kat managed to escape to that distant frame of mind during the worst moments. Meg thanked the Lord for the trance that fell over women when they transitioned in labor.

There were many times when Kat wanted her privacy, and Fanny and Meg respected that space, moving away to a wooden bench near the door. They watched and whispered like two friends in a dimly lit movie theater.

"Is Jack dozing off in the kitchen?" Meg asked.

"He's playing a game on his cell phone." Fanny smoothed her apron down, letting her fingers twirl one of the pins. "And what about the baby's father?"

"He's in the army, stationed overseas."

Fanny nodded. "It's hard to have a baby without the father there. But she's lucky that he'll be coming back."

Meg let out a sigh of agreement as she realized that Fanny's last child had been born shortly after her husband had died.

"I've noticed that most Amish women in Lancaster County wear beautifully colored dresses," Meg said. "Deep gem tones like emerald green, sapphire, aqua, or purple. But you're still wearing black. That's to mourn your husband?"

"Ya. A widow wears black."

"And do you dress that way for the rest of your life? Or until you meet someone?"

"A year." Fanny's voice was hushed, quiet as a whisper. "A wife mourns her husband for a year, but . . ."

When Fanny paused, Meg turned to her and noticed the tears streaking down her cheeks. "Oh, I am so sorry. I stepped over the line, didn't I?"

Fanny swiped at her cheeks with the back of one hand. "It's not anything you've said. It's a mistake I made. I've disgraced my family. And my dear Tom . . . I've been disrespectful."

"What did you do? I mean, if you don't mind my asking."

"I . . . it's not something to talk about."

"I'm sorry." Meg rubbed Fanny's upper arm. "I don't mean to pry. I'm tired and I'm sure you're tired, too."

"I am, but being a part of a baby's birth, that's worth losing some sleep."

"You are so right about that, my friend." Meg yawned. "It's amazing to be part of a birth, but sometimes it's the moments in between, the waiting periods, that bring us back to ourselves."

"The waiting can be a wonderful thing. My dat used to say that sometimes we are too busy climbing mountains when we ought to be resting."

"That is a good way to describe childbirth, don't you think?"

Fanny nodded. "But we don't talk of it. Sometimes a mother will talk with a daughter, but usually we keep it to ourselves. When you live in a farm community, birth and death are all around us, a fact of life. We see it, but don't need to speak about it."

"But you're an exception, Fanny. You're learning the language of birth. And you built this center to make it easier and safer for women."

"Oh, I did none of the building. Zed and Caleb and some of the other men did that work, and we got so many donations from Plain folk. All of the kitchen appliances were hand-me-downs. It's really a community center, not mine at all."

Meg simply nodded, realizing it was a waste of breath to praise Fanny's efforts. Taking credit would be a gesture of pride, which the Amish censured. Still, Meg was beginning to understand the ebb and flow of Amish conversation: the tug of humility that gave way to the expression of joy in the simple things. And then that joy was once again tempered by humility and acceptance of God's will. Humble and Plain. Such was the enigmatic grace of Amish culture.

∽∾

In the early hours of the morning, they succeeded in rotating the baby.

"Good," Fanny said, stroking back Kat's damp hair. "It will be much easier for you now."

"Let's try to keep you leaning forward," Meg advised. "We don't want the baby to revert to its original position." She checked the fetal heart tones with every contraction, assuring Kat that the baby was descending quickly now.

With the baby turned, Kat's labor moved more rapidly. Everyone breathed a sigh of gratitude when a baby girl was delivered at 5:04 A.M.

While Fanny tended to Kat, Meg saw that the baby needed resuscitation. *Secondary apnea,* she thought as adrenaline shot through her. Instantly awake and alert, she grabbed the bulb syringe and oxygen tank, as well as towels that had been warming on the woodstove.

"Come on now," Meg cooed to the baby as she rubbed her back. "You're here at last, and we're going to keep you safe and warm. And your mom is eager to meet you, baby girl." She could feel Fanny and Kat watching in wary silence.

After a few minutes that seemed like an eternity, the baby gave a squall and the heartbeat was on pace. Her color was good and she became active. "That's what I was looking for." Meg soothed the tiny baby swaddled in a warm towel and blanket. "That's right. All pinked up. That's it, sweetie."

"Thank the Almighty, she's awake at last," Fanny said with a sigh.

Meg went to release Jack from his kitchen confinement, but he was already on his feet. "You got a baby out there? All good?"

"It's all good." Lulled by relief and pleasure, Meg took him by the hand and led him out to meet his new niece.

As sunlight touched the winter sky, casting a silvery glow over the frozen landscape, they sat around Kat's cot, sharing coffee and hot rolls that Elsie had baked in the house. Kat was treated to a tray of scrambled eggs, sausage, rolls, and canned peaches—a true feast!— which Fanny insisted any new mother had earned. Meg smiled as Kat dug in with enthusiasm, finishing every scrap while she admired the infant sleeping in Jack's arms.

"You know how you couldn't think of a Christmas gift for me?" Jack told Meg. "You're off the hook now. You just delivered the perfect gift. Because I am in love with this baby girl."

"She is amazing," Meg agreed.

"Remember that feeling when it's time for you guys to babysit," Kat teased them.

It was a wonder, the sight of Jack with the baby. For a thirty-one-year-old bachelor, a man who'd been eager to run from his laboring sister, Jack was very much at home with an infant in his arms. The copacetic image reminded Meg of the prickly news she had yet to deliver to him. She vowed to tell him about her medical issue. She would tell him this week—but not today.

Today was bright with celebration, with new life and newly forged bonds and glittering snow confetti beyond the window of the former carriage house.

Jack had sent a text to Kat's husband, and now he was able to connect to Brendan so that Kat could do a video chat.

"Hey, there, Daddy," Kat said, levering the phone so that Brendan could see the rosebud mouth of the baby in her arms. "Meet your little girl. Baby Abigail."

PART FOUR

☙❧

In His Footsteps

Yea, all of you be subject one to another,
and be clothed with humility:
for God resisteth the proud,
and giveth grace to the humble.

—1 Peter 5:5

29

*H*umming a song, Fanny traipsed through the backyard, grateful for the dawning light that turned the sky pearl gray. In one hand she held the wooden platform of the birdhouse, which she had just scrubbed clean with disinfectant. In the other was a sack of seed, which needed to be added daily. It was a chore that the children often forgot to do, but Fanny didn't mind. Local birds had discovered the new birdhouse quickly, and the small effort of putting out sunflower seeds and millet was worth the joy of glancing out the kitchen window to see mourning doves, chickadees, titmice, and dark-eyed juncos land in the little house.

Fanny found joy in the routine of small chores and simple pleasures. The pleasure of clean clothes at the end of wash day. The savory smell of a warm stew bubbling on the stove. A cozy night spent with the family, heads bent over a jigsaw puzzle, fingers working pieces to find the right fit. Whenever she longed for Zed or worried about what some of the other women thought of her, she had only to turn to the task at hand, the child at her side, the adult child telling her a story of their day. Family was the meat and potatoes of a good Amish life, and she thanked Gott for blessing her with a full plate.

She slid the platform into the base of the birdhouse, reached into the sack, and scattered seed inside the miniature carriage house. What a lovely gift it had been, a way to feed Gott's creatures and enjoy nature in their own backyard.

A daily reminder of Zed's fine building skills.

Despite her shame, she had not been able to push him from her thoughts these past few weeks. She found herself wondering about him throughout each day. Did he still wear the gloves she had given him? What was his new daily schedule? Was he enjoying his work for Tim Ebersol? Did he think of her, too?

He had told her that he wouldn't give up on her—a promise branded deep in her memory, but not a practical one. It was obvious that there was a lot of matchmaking going on. Fanny was sickened at the prospect of Zed being pushed toward other women, but as there was nothing she could do to stop it, she had to let it go . . . *geh lessa.*

She brushed off her gloved hands and lifted the seed sack. "There you go, little birds," she called, though there were none in sight. She had no doubt they'd be congregating by breakfast, when Will would be at the window, helping his sister tell the difference between a goldfinch and a titmouse. This birdhouse had engaged the whole family, sending Caleb and Elsie paging through Tom's old birding guide.

She stomped her boots on the mat in the mudroom, and stowed the seed in the cupboard. Off came the boots and gloves, and her jacket went on a hook by the door. A cloud of warm air greeted her when she opened the kitchen door, and her two girls smiled up at her from the kitchen table, their faces tipped up like sunflowers.

"Elsie made my favorite oatmeal," Beth said. "No raisins." Little Beth was at the stage where she didn't like raisins or nuts inside things.

"There's more on the stove," Elsie offered.

"That sounds good." Fanny gave a playful tug on Beth's braid, then glanced up at the kitchen calendar. January was passing slow as molasses, but maybe that was because the anniversary of Tom's death was approaching. Odd to mark someone's passing, but Fanny had begun to look at it as a day that the family could remember Tom and remind the children of the love and light their father had brought to the family.

With a bowl of oatmeal in hand, Fanny joined the girls and listened as Elsie talked of how much of the shop's inventory had sold out over Christmas. She had already spoken to some of the women who supplied Amish crafts for the stores. "Over the holidays we sold out of cloth dolls and lavender soap," Elsie said. "Some of our shelves are bare."

Beth finished and hopped down from her chair.

"Put your bowl in the sink and go get dressed," Fanny prompted gently.

With a cloth doll tucked under one arm, Beth cleared away her bowl and skated across the kitchen floor in her slipper socks.

"Such a dreamer, that one," Fanny said, gazing up at the calendar once more. In eight days, it would be one year. Tom's seat at the head of the table still remained empty during meals, and no one was in a rush to change that.

"I see you looking at the calendar, every time you pass," Elsie said.

"Do I do that?" Fanny dared to meet Elsie's eyes, and was warmed by the glimmer of sympathy there. "Ya, I'm always checking now."

"January. I thought I never wanted to see this month come again, but now that it's here . . ." Elsie shrugged. "It's not so bad. I forgot how cozy the winter months could be. It's fun to take the children out in the snow, sledding and ice-skating. And the best part of the cold is warming up by the fire with hot cocoa and the little ones."

"You always do see the sunny side of things." Fanny dragged a golden streak of melted brown sugar across her oatmeal. It was delicious, but sorrow made her appetite sag. "I have dreaded this month and the memories it brings. Gott has healed us in many ways, but we will always miss your father."

Elsie nodded. "So many memories of Dat linger."

His loss had created a hole in the world that had seemed impossible to fill, a hole that Fanny had found herself jumping over constantly. In the first few months, she had winced when she made Tom's side of the bed each morning or passed his empty place at the head of the table. But Gott eased the pain, day by day.

"We'll never understand why Gott took him," Fanny said softly. "All we can do is thank Gott that we have family to fill our days with joy and challenge." The little ones kept her busy and amused while the older ones constantly took little Tommy from her arms for a diaper change or a snuggle.

"The day of the accident, Dat told me some things I'll never forget." Elsie cupped her coffee mug in two hands. "We were standing outside the Reading Terminal Market, and I wanted to talk about my big plans for the shop, but Dat kept pulling the conversation back to talk of marriage. He so wanted me to marry and have children."

"It's what every father wants for his children."

Elsie took a sip from her mug and gazed off with a tender smile. "I never told anyone, but I had given up on ever marrying. I was afraid to have children, so I bowed out of every singing. I always had a reason to miss the youth events. Dat knew that."

"Thomas didn't miss much," Fanny agreed. Although Fanny

hadn't discussed it with Tom, she had always worried about Elsie finding a man who would love her, on account of Elsie looking different from other girls, being a little person.

"Dat was so sure that a fella would come courting. 'Just give it a chance,' he told me." Elsie shook her head. "I had no plans of doing that, but Dat was certain a young man would fall for my sunny disposition if I just gave it a chance. He was positive someone would see past the ways I'm different. He believed I would be having my own family one day. Standing there, outside the market, I looked up at him, so sure that he was wrong." Tears glimmered in Elsie's eyes. "It turned out, Dat knew what he was talking about."

"Your dat had faith in Gott's plan for you." Hearing Tommy fuss from the front room, Fanny retrieved him from his playpen and settled him on the kitchen floor with a pot and wooden spoon.

"What's all that about?" Elsie asked the baby, kneeling on the floor beside him. "Are you going to do some cooking?" She put the spoon in the pot and stirred.

Rising to his feet in a wobbly stance, Tommy watched her with rapt attention.

"Here. You do it." Elsie offered him the spoon.

Tommy clutched it and pointed it at the pot. He had to bend his knees a bit to reach the pot, but when he did he grinned with satisfaction at the clanging noise.

The two women laughed, and Fanny felt a tug of pleasure at the prospect of Elsie having children of her own. Elsie had not mentioned marriage yet, but Fanny was sure that event would come around next wedding season.

In the aftermath of the accident, Elsie had become friends with Ruben Zook, who'd also been a passenger in the van. Although older than Elsie and probably three feet taller, Ruben had helped Elsie in so many ways, taking over the heavy lifting in the shop and keeping the Country Store open for her when she needed time to grieve.

"Who would have thought a year ago that I would have a beau? Especially a prankster like Ruben." Elsie rolled her eyes. "Do you remember how he used to play tricks on everyone? He took every joke too far. I never would have guessed at what he was really like."

"Ruben is a godsend," Fanny said. "Thomas would be very glad to see the good changes in your life."

"Ya, we've all been through some changes." Elsie kept her attention on the baby. "With many changes to come. Soon it will be time for you to put away your black dress, Mamm."

A sadness trembled inside Fanny. In some ways, she had longed for her mourning to end, but now . . . now she wasn't sure she was ready for that.

"Do your old dresses still fit?" Elsie asked. "I'd be happy to do some sewing if you need a new one. There's plenty of fabric in the shop for you to choose from."

"I haven't tried them, but the old dresses are probably fine," Fanny said warily.

"You'll want to do that this week," Elsie advised, sounding like the mother instead of the daughter. "You've got some changes ahead, too. Now there'll be no worries about you being seen with Zed."

Embarrassment washed over Fanny as she quickly looked down at the table.

"And don't you think Zed wants to come back to finish the work on the center?" Elsie looked up from the floor. "We could have him come for supper. Will and Beth would like that."

"Oh, Elsie, I don't know." Fanny wanted to get off the topic, away from the emotions that were more tangled than a neglected batch of yarn.

"Everyone misses Zed. Don't you, Tommy?" she asked, tweaking the baby's chin. "And I knew you favored him long before second Christmas."

In the quiet pause in the warm kitchen, Fanny wasn't sure how to answer. Honesty was deeply ingrained in her, and if she was to tell the truth, she could not deny her love for Zed. "There may be a better match for Zed out there," Fanny said. "You can never know what Gott's plan is."

"That's true, but I think Zed would be lucky to marry you. And what fella could resist stepping into such a wonderful good family like ours?"

Footsteps bounded down the stairs, and Beth and Will scurried into the kitchen.

"Will found a spider in the bathroom!" Beth reported as she followed him to the mud porch. "He's letting it go free."

The muscles of Will's face were clenched in concentration as he tramped through the kitchen with his cupped hands in front of him. "Just a little one," Will said bravely.

Just then Caleb appeared at the back door. "Will? Elsie? You two ready to go?"

All at once, Tommy rattled the spoon on the pot, Beth squealed when Will opened his hand to show Caleb the spider, and Elsie fell back onto the floor beside the baby, doubled in laughter.

Just another morning in the Lapp kitchen. Fanny thanked the Almighty for the blessing of family.

❧ 30 ❧

The January day was cold and crystal clear with a sky so blue it could have jumped off a paint sample card. Compacted snow crunched under Meg's boots as she and Jack walked glove in glove down the path to the frozen pond. Although the temperature was in the upper twenties, Meg felt toasty and warm, though a bit puffy in the layers of thermal ski gear borrowed from Zoey. She was glad to have the day off to spend with Jack. If a local woman went into labor today and wanted to have her baby at Fanny's birthing center, Dr. Trueherz was going to make the trip in from Paradise to handle the delivery.

"I like that big smile on your face," Jack said.

"I'm happy to be with you, Jack."

He grinned. "Same. You've been one hard lady to pin down this week. What did you guys have, three deliveries? You worked through my day off."

"I know, and I wasn't planning to be working this much yet. Not really." Women were starting to come to the birthing center for their prenatal visits, but the facility wasn't quite prepared for that yet. Dr. Trueherz had been laid up two days with the flu, and Anna had told Fanny she wasn't feeling quite up to doing deliveries yet. That left Meg and Fanny to cover the prenatal visits as well as three deliveries in one week. At one point, they'd had two women in the center, both in labor at the same time. "You know I love delivering babies," Meg told Jack, "but man, I wish they would cooperate with scheduling."

"But it's all good in the end, right?" He slid an arm around her waist and pulled her close, so that they were walking in sync. "When that little baby gives a holler, you know it's all good."

"True. And I'm getting to know Fanny really well." During the lulls in labor, they had talked, quietly and slowly. She learned that Fanny was struggling with guilt over some wrong she had committed, but Fanny wouldn't say any more about it. When Fanny expressed an interest in Meg's record-keeping, Meg showed her the way she tracked how each mother's labor started and how it progressed, as well as the mother's vitals and the fetal heart tones. Noting Fanny's interest, Meg loaned her two books—an anatomy textbook and a midwife's guide. Fanny was grateful and curious, but she explained that she would keep the books in the center, out of reach and sight of little hands and eyes. The contradictions in Amish culture intrigued Meg. While the facts of life were all around Amish children, with animals mating and delivering their young, human reproduction was not discussed, and women did not acknowledge their pregnancies, even to their children. Meg tried to be discreet, even as she armed her patients with facts when discussing their pregnancies.

However, Meg could not complain about the Amish women who had delivered at the center. So far each and every client had been cooperative and calm. They remained active until the last stages of labor, and their deliveries were swift and routine. They commented a few times on the pain, but did not complain. If these women were any indication of her new practice here in Lancaster County, Meg was more than "halfway" to Heaven.

After each delivery, Fanny had taken to complimenting Meg on her handling of newborns. "The way you talk and coo over the babies is so natural," Fanny said. "I believe Gott intends for you to be a mother because you already know all the right things to say."

If only it was that simple, Meg had thought. *If only my body would cooperate.*

The pond was occupied by more than a dozen Amish youth. At the far end, a hockey game was in progress, and the boys skated fast and hard as they called out to team members to pass the puck. A few slid down to their knees to keep from falling. Closer to the path, a handful of young women skated in a wide circle, chatting as they went along.

Meg tried to ignore the knot forming in her lower belly as she sat down and pushed off her boots. Cramps. She knew they were coming on, but she figured she would power through them.

She and Jack laced up their skates and took to the ice. From his days of playing street hockey, Jack liked to skate fast with knees bent, staying low to the ground. Meg had only been skating in rinks with groomed ice.

"Whoa." She held out her arms for balance. "Pretty bumpy."

"You get used to it," one of the Amish girls said.

"After you learn where the bumps and ridges are," said another girl.

On closer inspection, Meg realized she was a woman, a little person. Fanny's daughter. "Hi, there, Elsie. Do you skate here often?"

"Only in the winter," Elsie answered with a smile. She wore a black coat with a blue scarf that wrapped around her neck and under her black bonnet. "My friend, he likes to come and play hockey. I like to get out in the fresh air, but not for too long."

"Yeah, you'll turn to a snowman in this weather," Jack interjected.

Elsie giggled, covering her mouth with a mitten. "Or a snow woman," she answered before she skated off.

"Hey, girl." Jack skated up to Meg and took her arms. "You're really pale. You feeling okay?"

She held on to his forearms as pain tugged at her abdomen. "I've got cramps. Bad ones."

"Okay. You just hang on to me and I'll be your guide over the bumps." And just like that, he began to skate backward, pulling her along slowly like a tugboat.

"You can skate backward? I never learned to do that."

"Yeah, I got mad skills."

She relaxed a little, relieved to let him propel them and keep her steady. Face-to-face, she could bask in his eyes, which spoke of love and concern for her. It was highly romantic, a close, personal dance.

But their bliss was short-lived.

"I'm just going to sit down for a while and swallow some ibuprofen," she told him.

"Poor kid. I'll sit with ya. We got that thermos of hot chocolate."

The snow pants and puffy coat gave her plenty of padding as she maneuvered into a comfortable spot on the log. Being off her feet helped ease the pain immediately, but the cramps usually held on. When Jack perched beside her and opened the thermos, she realized this was her chance. Her teachable moment.

"I've always had a problem with cramps," she told him.

"Female stuff?" They both watched the steaming cocoa gush into the cup.

"Actually, it's a little more extreme than that. Have you ever heard of endometriosis? Because that's what I have."

He capped the thermos and handed her the cup. At least he

wasn't racing off through the snow yet. *So far, so good.* "So tell me about it."

She swallowed the pills down with a sip of cocoa and handed the cup back. "It could limit my ability to have children."

He stared off over the pond as she spilled out the details. It was hereditary but not usually serious. She often suffered painful cramps, but only during her period. Zoey had it, too, and she'd managed to get pregnant. She told him about the laparoscopic procedure, which she had scheduled for February. "The doctors think surgery will improve my chances of pregnancy."

"Well, that's great. I mean, bummer that you've got this thing, but it sounds like you've got it all figured out. And then you've got a window of fertility for a year or so?"

She nodded, relieved that he comprehended the situation immediately. "That's what studies indicate."

Jack put the empty cup aside and rubbed his chin, a thoughtful light in his eyes as he processed it all. "Okay, then. What's your thinking on a time line for the next year? For us."

"I don't know. Mostly I wanted to give you an out. I know you really want kids, and it's a deal breaker for a lot of people. I want kids, too, I really do, and I'm going to do my best to make it happen. But you can't ignore science."

He squinted at her. "You're giving me an out? Come on, Megs. I'm not giving you up. Get that through your pretty head." He pretended to knock on her knit cap. "I'm in this for the long haul, for better or worse."

She looked up at him, wanting to laugh and cry at the same time. She didn't think she would ever love anyone as much as she loved him in that moment.

"I'm not going anywhere." He angled his body toward hers and took her in his arms. "I'm gonna stick with you and take my chances."

When he kissed her, the light touch of his lips awakened something inside her. The tenderness he stirred in her gave birth to a new vulnerability. The tough shell of stoic, practical Meg was cracking open to reveal a new woman—a playful, impetuous person—one who would take a chance on love.

Jack ended the kiss, hugging her close. "I don't want to give these kids any ideas," he muttered under his breath.

Meg smiled as she glanced lazily down the pond at the other skaters. No one paid any attention to them. "Mmm. I think they know the deal but, yeah. The midwife and the cop should not be setting a bad example."

"So . . ." He leaned back slightly so their eyes could meet. "How about that time line? I didn't want to rush you to get married, but now it looks like God's giving us a little push."

"A big push," she agreed, studying his face. "But I'm ready, Jack." It was the first time a huge decision in her life did not seem daunting and frightening. "I'm ready if you are."

He looked up at the winter sky. "Thank you, Lord. I couldn't have asked for a better segue."

"What are you talking about?"

He unzipped his jacket and fished out a small, blue velvet jewelry box. "Man, I've been walking around with this ring in my pocket, hoping and praying there'd be a time to spring it on you." Dropping to one knee on the well-packed snow, he lifted his eyes to hers. Jack had a way of captivating her with a simple glance. "Marry me, Meg. Marry me and we'll have a whole posse of kids. A house filled with joy and laughter. I know there'll be bumps in the road, but if we're traveling together, we'll make the most of it."

A pulse of joy thrummed in her ears. She could not have dreamed of such a beautiful proposal, under a canopy of snow-covered trees. "Jack . . . I can't imagine a life without you."

"My heart's pumping like crazy." He pressed the jewelry box to his chest with a smile. "This is like . . . an epic moment."

A moment Meg would never forget. She'd been so nervous about telling Jack; this was not the outcome she'd expected. "You are full of surprises."

"You should try this on." The ring's lavender stone glittered as he slid it onto her finger. "A perfect fit. How about that?"

Never a big jewelry fan, Meg was drawn to the ring's tooled silver setting and the way the flat stone was nearly flush against her hand. "It's beautiful, Jack."

"It was my grandmother's . . . a late engagement ring. My grand-father gave it to her on their tenth anniversary when their finances were on an even keel." He explained that his gran had popped it into the mail soon after Christmas because of her sense that Jack was getting seriously involved with Meg.

"How could she know that? You haven't seen her for months. She hasn't met me yet."

"Maternal instincts, I guess." He held up her hand, smiling over the twinkling gemstone. "If you want to pick out a diamond in-stead, I'm cool with that."

"No way." She tugged her hand away, coddling the stone. "It suits me well, and I like that it has a family history."

Still kneeling, he put his hands on her knees and leaned forward so that his forehead pressed hers, so close, so intimate. It was as if they were the only two people in this winter scene.

"Thank you," Meg whispered.

"You're welcome."

With a sigh of contentment, Meg closed her eyes and melted into his kiss. For a few moments they sat in silence, basking in the peace of the winter landscape and the contentment of each other's company. *Thank you, dear Lord,* Meg prayed silently. *Thank you for bringing love into my life when I least expected it.*

"How're you feeling?" Jack asked. "You okay?"

"Better, but I don't think I'll be competing for any figure skating medals today."

Jack chuckled. "There's always another Olympics coming down the pike."

The day's light was graying and a chill set in as they finished up the last of the cocoa and removed their skates. Meg moved tenderly, but pain no longer gripped her. As they walked up the path from the frozen pond, they held hands, chatting about how Jack had started putting together Abigail's crib and had to abandon the project after four hours.

"I was thinking we might head over that way, help Kat out."

"Sure. Though the baby really won't need a crib for a few weeks, it's good to have it all ready to go," she said. "And any excuse to see Abigail works for me." Although Meg routinely did postpartum care for mothers, she didn't always get to visit with the babies she'd delivered. But then, it would be different with Abigail . . . soon to be her niece.

Her niece. That had a nice ring to it.

For years she had resigned herself to being single and childless. And now? Now she was about to be a wife, an aunt, and maybe even a mother. God truly did work in wondrous ways.

ᏝᏨ 31 ᏨᎧ

It began when Zoey couldn't finish the breakfast frittata that Shandell had prepared. "It's delicious, as usual," Zoey insisted, maneuvering to lift her bulky body from her seat at the table. "But I'm just not that hungry this morning." She stretched her arms out. "My lower back has been feeling a little twingey. Is it too decadent to take a bath this early in the morning?"

Meg pressed a napkin to her lips as she studied her sister. All the signs were there. The baby had dropped two days ago, and Zoey had reported that she didn't sleep well. Of course, she would examine Zoey after her bath, but she had a strong sense that this was it.

"Take your bath, honey," she said. "When you're done, you and Tate might want to take a walk, just to the edge of town and back. That's really helpful in the early stages of labor."

Tate lowered his newspaper and Shandell rushed over from the kitchen sink.

"Do you think? Really?" Zoey scraped back her pale hair with a wan smile. "I'm not sure I'm ready for that."

"Of course you're ready. You've just about memorized *What to Expect When You're Expecting.*" Shandell started to clear the table. "This is so exciting. What do you want me to do?"

"For starters, you can take out those sheets that we wrapped up, and the drop cloths. In a little bit, I'll send you over to let Fanny know. Experienced help is always a good thing." Fanny had a wonderful way with mothers, and she seemed to anticipate what was needed. Working with Fanny, Meg often felt as if she had an extra set of hands to accomplish everything that needed to be done during a delivery.

Tate put down his *Wall Street Journal* and came to Zoey's side. "How about I escort you to the master suite?"

Zoey took his arm and leaned into him affectionately. "Well, it's just a few steps away, but you're so sweet, I can never say no to you."

Meg's suspicions were confirmed with a quick exam. All that morning, she thanked God for bringing her here to monitor and chart and savor her sister's progress. She kept watch over Zoey, sometimes just rubbing her feet. It was best to keep a low profile and allow Zoey and Tate their privacy and intimacy. Just after noon, Zoey transitioned into active labor, and just before suppertime, a baby girl was born.

Although the birth had gone smoothly, Meg felt supercharged with the surge of adrenaline that came with coaxing a baby into the world.

"Ten fingers and ten toes?" Tate asked.

"Yes, and she's beautiful and very alert. Aren't you?" Meg saw her sister's full lips in the infant, who stared up at her curiously. She swaddled her in a warm receiving blanket and handed her to Tate, saying, "Off you go to Daddy."

"Amazing Grace." Low-key, rational Tate actually had tears in his eyes.

"That's a wonderful good name," Fanny said, and she began to hum the hymn.

Tate brought the baby to Zoey and laid her on his wife's belly. With a slow smile, Zoey was now a picture of relaxation. "Come here, you little girl, you." She pushed back the blanket to examine her little girl, downy hair, wrinkly flesh, and pudgy thighs. "You are just perfect."

෯෯

Over the next two weeks, as Zoey and Tate settled into their wondrous, sleep-deprived role as parents of a newborn, Meg and Jack began to sow the seeds of their new life together. They picked a wedding date in the first week of March. A ceremony at their church would be followed by a small dinner at the Halfway to Heaven Bed and Breakfast.

Meg and Jack began a series of counseling sessions with their minister, Bob Palmer, whose home could have been an advertisement for family life, with sleds and snow forts on the front lawn, and kid art on the bulletin board in his office.

Neither Meg nor Jack was thrilled with the prospect of staying in his bachelor apartment. A local Realtor showed them a few places, but nothing suited them. In the end, they decided to rent one of three outbuildings that Zoey and Tate had turned into guest cottages. Some renovation was required to turn the tiny kitchenette into a full-size kitchen, but once the work was completed the two-bedroom cottage would be a perfect home for them. The cottage was full of country charm, and both Meg and Jack liked being close to town and just off a major road, in case they had to get to work in inclement weather.

"And you'll be right in our backyard!" Zoey exclaimed.

Meg chuckled. "Literally. Mom always wanted the two of us to stay close, but I don't think even she could imagine us living a few yards from each other."

"I'm so glad Mom's coming for the wedding." Zoey patted the baby's back. Grace was facedown in her lap, a good position for relieving gas.

It was Sunday, just after noon, and Zoey and Tate had just returned from church. Meg had gone with Jack last night, as he had to work today, and she had enjoyed spending the morning with her niece, who definitely favored a connection with a warm body over the flat, cool desert of her barren crib. Now that there were guests in the inn, they were using the private sitting room, just off Zoey and Tate's suite. Wearing a robe and spandex shorts, Meg was waiting for Shandell to return from the sewing area in the laundry room with the shell of her wedding gown.

"I can't wait to see your gown," Zoey said. "Shandell is really excited about it."

To her surprise, Meg had been enjoying the dressmaking process, too. For someone who lived in blue jeans, the prospect of dressing up had been daunting.

Wanting to keep things simple, Meg had been putting feelers out for local dressmakers when Shandell had volunteered to make her wedding gown. "You've chosen a really simple pattern; I could have whipped this together in junior high," Shandell had insisted.

"That young woman has hidden talents," Meg said. "I was a little worried when we picked out the material; it's so delicate. But she's a skilled seamstress."

"And do you know who taught her how to follow a pattern and sew a straight seam?" asked Zoey. "Rachel King." A young Amish woman, Rachel had helped Shandell when she was first stranded in Halfway. "Shandell is a treasure," Meg agreed.

The young woman was also going to be Meg's driver tomorrow, the day of her surgery. Shandell had been the obvious choice because Jack was working, and Meg didn't want to drag Zoey or Tate away from the inn and the baby for the entire morning.

Meg was cooing for baby Grace when Shandell returned with the dress.

"Okay." Enthusiasm flashed in Shandell's eyes. Her obsidian hair was braided and piled atop her head, giving her an elfin appearance. "The seams are done, but I can always take them in a little if need be."

"Oooh." Zoey's face was lit with approval as she smiled up at the dress.

Even on its hanger, the dress had a lovely shape. It was a basic A-line with an empire waist made of wide satin ribbon, which Shandell had stitched in on the top. "Let's try it on," Meg said.

"First let me unpin the back. That's where the zipper goes." Shandell helped Meg slide it over her head, then pinched the back together and slipped in some pins.

"Shandell! You have really outdone yourself. Meg, honey, you look beautiful!"

Meg turned to Shandell. "Does she think I'm usually ugly?" she teased.

Shandell laughed as Zoey sought to correct the impression. "No, no, it's just that you almost never dress up, and when you do, this is the look that works for you. A-line, sophisticated yet simple. I love it."

Facing the mirror, Meg took a breath and smiled. "I do, too."

"I would recommend adding some sleeves," Zoey said, dabbing at Grace's mouth with a cloth diaper. "You are getting married in March, and it's bound to be chilly."

"The dress has sleeves, gathered at the shoulder then tapered," Shandell reported. "So you really like it?" When Meg nodded,

Shandell pressed a hand to her chest and let out a breath. "I am so relieved! I've been reading so many stories of crazy bridezillas who change their minds, I was beginning to worry."

"Meg is no bridezilla," Zoey said. "If anything went wrong, she'd walk down the aisle in her midwife uniform. Jeans, cotton top, and down vest."

"I would not." Meg nudged her sister on the shoulder as a tap sounded on the door.

"Are you dressed?" Tate asked as the door swung open a few inches. "Meg? There's someone here to see you."

Zoey made a shooing motion with her free hand. "Don't let Jack in! He can't see the gown before the wedding."

"It's not Jack. It's a . . . a Ms. Engles."

"Who?" Meg hoped that a laboring woman hadn't dropped in on her, but she had no one by that name under her care.

The door opened wide, revealing a polished young woman with flawless skin and hair the color of spun gold. "Actually, you don't know me." Ms. Engles scanned the room, taking in the three women. She quickly dismissed Zoey nursing on the couch, eyed Shandell a minute, and then latched on to Meg.

"You're Meg, right?" she asked, shifting her pose the way models do on the runway. Dressed in that short leather jacket and skinny jeans, she wouldn't last twenty minutes out here in the Lancaster winter.

"I am." At a disadvantage in her scrapped-together gown, Meg lifted her chin. "What can I do for you?"

"I'm Lisa Engles, Jack Woods's fiancée. And I've come to ask you, *politely,* to back away from my guy."

∞ 32 ∞

As she chased little Tom down the path, Fanny was glad that this week's church was at Edna Lapp's home. The wide lawn and trails into the orchards gave folks plenty of room to stretch out, and with her good friend so busy hosting, there would be little time for personal conversation. In the few hours she had spent with Edna, Fanny had felt too ashamed to speak of her mistake, but also guilty that she couldn't trust in her friend. It was still hard to look folks in the eye, always afraid of what they had heard and what they were thinking of her.

Tommy toddled over to a flowerpot with a small evergreen shrub in it, and Fanny hovered over him, smoothing down his shiny hair. "You're going to want to leave that alone," she said. "It's prickly."

"Look at this one, working on Edna's planter." Rose Miller bent down and bussed Tommy on the chin. "He's getting big, Fanny. Walking already?"

"Ya, he keeps us on our toes. He'll be one this month." Fanny kept her eyes averted from Rose. This woman had shown her a world of kindness. When Tom passed, Rose and her husband, Ira, had managed everything for Fanny's family, arranging meals and taking care of the household so that Fanny and her children could mourn Tom.

"The years fly by us like a flock of birds. But look at you, skin pale as the moon. Are you feeling all right, Fanny?"

"Nothing wrong with me," Fanny answered, trying to sound cheerful.

"Maybe it's the black dress you're wearing. Still in mourning? It's been more than a year since Tom died, hasn't it?"

"Ya. About two weeks ago, on the anniversary of his death, our little family remembered him with prayers." She told Rose how Elsie and Emma had both read from the Bible, and Will and Beth had sung "This Little Light of Mine, I'm Gonna Let It Shine," which Tom used to sing with the little ones at bedtime. "Then we played a few rounds of Jenga, which Tom so enjoyed."

"That sounds like a fitting way to remember him." She leaned down to Tommy. "It makes me sad that you never got to meet your father."

Grinning up at Rose, he offered her a fistful of mulch from Edna's planter.

"No, thank you, boy. You can give that back to the bush." There was such a lighthearted lilt in Rose's voice that Fanny felt encouraged to face her. When she did, she saw Zed's eyes, warm and dark as molasses. Oh, how she wished she could sit with Rose over a cup of coffee and talk, really talk.

"Fanny?" A woman's voice called to her.

Both Rose and Fanny turned to see Anna Beiler walking along the path gingerly. "If you two wander any farther out, they'll put you to work in the orchard," said Anna.

Having come to appreciate the midwife's wry sense of humor, Fanny smiled. "How's your ankle, Anna?"

"Doc Trueherz says it's healed, but it starts acting up whenever there's a snowstorm coming."

"Saves you a trip to the window, I guess," Rose said, and the two older women shared a chuckle.

"I've been looking for you everywhere, Fanny," Anna said, a serious cast to her tone now. "We need to talk."

About the gossip. Anna had heard. She was disgraced.

Fanny dropped to her knees behind her son to hide the distress that weighed her down.

"It's time to see if there's any more coffee left," Rose said, heading back toward the house.

"There's something I think you need to know."

Anna's hand rested on Fanny's shoulder, probably because Fanny was still on her knees, and Anna wanted to maintain her balance. Still, the motherly touch stirred Fanny's emotions.

"Being laid up in a cast has given me plenty of time to think, and I can see that the life of a midwife takes more get-up-and-go than I have inside me. I've already cut down my schedule a lot, but I'm going to be sending all the women to the birth center from now on. I'm through."

"Oh, dear, no." Fanny rose to face Anna, taking her hand. "We need you at the center, Anna. Please don't leave us." Fanny had counted on working with Anna, partly to gain acceptance from the Amish community. "Doc Trueherz thought it was a good plan, and the center is close enough that you can even walk, now that your ankle is healed."

"Ya, it's nice and close. But these old bones can't take the cold and the long hours of waiting on mamms. You've got that English midwife, ya? And Doc is happy to come to the center. You'll be fine on your own."

Thoughts raced through Fanny's mind like a blizzard wind. So it *was* about the gossip. Anna was separating from her because of Fanny's bad reputation. "Is it . . . is it something I've done?"

Of course it is. Dorcas's cruel words pounded in her head as if they were being punched into a batch of dough. *Caught kissing a man when you've barely said good-bye to your husband.*

Anna's stern face softened as she blinked up at Fanny in surprise. "Nothing you've done, honeygirl. I can't do it anymore. Seventy-four and my legs and back are so sore, you'd think I'd been kicked by a mule. Doc says it's time I got off my feet, time to get some regular sleep."

"Ya, your health is important. It's just that . . . I don't know what we'll do without you."

"You'll do fine," Anna insisted. "Women love the place already, and you've been getting more and more experience."

Although Fanny was relieved that Anna had not turned against her because of the rumors, the prospect of running the center without Anna's help was frightening. Sure, Doc Trueherz and Meg would be on call to do most of the deliveries, but with her family to care for, Fanny could not handle being the only Amish midwife in town. And the chores at the center—the cooking and cleaning, not to mention sanitizing blankets and sheets in the oven—it was too much for one woman to manage.

"Please," she asked Anna, "won't you reconsider?"

"The Bible says, 'To every thing there is a season,' and my time as a midwife has run its course." Anna patted Fanny on the arm. "Don't fret, honeygirl. Gott will provide. Have faith."

∽ 33 ∾

Meg stared at the bold, beautiful woman who had made the trip out here from Philadelphia. *The ex-fiancée, "ex" being the important part of that word.* Meg had to hold on to that fact to stay on solid ground. "Why are you here?"

"I came to ask you a favor, woman to woman." Lisa pressed her hands together in prayer position and held them to her heart. "Would you please back off and give Jack and me a chance?"

Meg smoothed down her dress as she took in the elegant woman with earnest eyes. If nothing else, Lisa deserved an acting award. She had a knack for stealing the show.

But none of this was real, was it? Was this some psychotic episode that Lisa was having—or simply a master manipulation to end Jack's happiness?

"See, I've had a change of heart. I'm ready to make a go of it with Jack, gonna give it the old one hundred percent. Jack is thrilled, of course. Couldn't be happier. But you know how he is—such a marshmallow. He doesn't have the heart to tell you that it's over."

"Really." Meg wasn't buying any of it, but she wasn't going to argue with Lisa. There would be no coin toss or arm-wrestling tournament to see who won the boyfriend. This was not a competition for Jack's affection; Meg was secure in her relationship with him.

Lisa was moving through the room now, checking it out as if she was a potential buyer. Zoey pulled a receiving blanket over Grace's head, as if to protect the baby from a wandering menace. Meg didn't blame her.

"I'm hoping you'll be as gracious as Jack says you are. That you'll back off. Give us time to heal our relationship."

"You know what? I'm going to talk to Jack about this, and I'm sure we'll work it all out." Meg crossed her arms over the smooth bodice of her gown and stepped between Lisa and the other women in the room. "But right now, I think you should go."

"You're right. Jack's waiting for me." Lisa went to the door, then turned back to eye Meg. "That's quite a dress you're wearing."

Aware that she was being mocked, Meg simply nodded, her mouth a grim line as she followed Lisa out into the hall. She watched Lisa exit, and then bolted the big front door behind her.

"What was that about?" Shandell asked from the hallway.

Meg held up her hands. "I don't know, but I'm going to find out."

She grabbed her cell phone from the sitting room, but of course, Jack didn't answer. "He's at work. Murphy's Law." She shot him a series of texts.

"You know," she said as she was texting, "after he stops apologizing, Jack's going to find this whole incident rather amusing."

"Ya think?" Zoey asked.

"Yeah, one day we'll probably laugh about it."

"But right now . . . not so funny."

"So . . . do you want to finish with the dress fitting?" Shandell asked.

Meg held out her arms. "Absolutely."

An hour later, Shandell had fitted the sleeves and pinned up the hem. Then she headed over to her mother's apartment for their Sunday visit.

Having changed back into her jeans and a sweater, Meg collapsed on the couch beside Zoey and checked her cell phone. No messages, and the ringer was working. "Where are you, Jack?"

"I have to say, you took that very well today. If Tate's ex had stormed in like that, I don't know what I would have done. But I'd have been mighty tempted to throw something. Like pie. A dirty diaper. A candelabra. Anything handy."

"Zoey, the woman is not well."

"I know, but she's a button pusher. Just saying."

"Honestly? I'm a little sick inside. Maybe it was wrong to rush into this with Jack. We haven't even known each other a year."

"Oh, no, no. Don't let her do that to you," Zoey insisted. "Don't let her shake your faith in Jack. You know I've been a little wary of your rush to the altar, but that one has changed my mind. I know you and Jack are a forever couple."

"Unless Lisa has her way."

"Lisa, schmisa. I know you're upset, but just give Jack a chance to explain things. There are two sides to every story."

As Meg went out to the kitchen to make a cup of tea, she thought of calling Kat. Jack's sister was probably well versed on the Lisa story. But that seemed petty, calling her fiancé's sister for relationship advice.

Leaning on the kitchen counter, Meg broke down and called the police dispatcher. Trying to keep it casual, she told Cindy that she was trying to get in touch with Jack. "Would you have him call me?"

"Jack took the day off," Cindy said. "He said he had a family emergency."

Meg felt the bottom drop out from her safe world.

"Is everything okay?" Cindy asked.

"Sure. Fine," Meg said, thanking the woman.

Ignoring the hollow feeling inside, Meg sat down on the sofa beside her sister, who was napping in front of the television, the baby monitor blinking on the end table beside her. An old Christmas movie about a homeless man who moved in to an empty Fifth Avenue mansion was on, and for a few minutes Meg managed to lose herself in the heartwarming story. When the cops came into the mansion, she thought of Jack in uniform, and she remembered the day they had spent working on the holiday food drive. He was a good man, Jack Woods. A helper, not a cheater.

She was settling into the cushions with her feet on the sofa when a big boom rocked the house. From the rattling window glass and the vibration of the furniture, Meg thought of an earthquake at first.

"What was that?" Zoey shot up, instantly awake. "Where's Grace?" She grabbed the monitor, but found that the baby was silent.

Meg was already at the window. "I think it was an explosion."

"Did you hear that?" Tate called, appearing at the door. "I think it came from down the lane."

Zoey trudged toward her husband. "I'm going to check the baby."

"I just did. She's fine. I'm going to head outside and check it out."

"I'll go with you."

Meg and Tate threw on coats and boots and trudged down the lane toward a rising plume of black smoke.

"It looks like it might be coming from Fanny's house," Meg said, her words puffs of mist in the cooling air.

"Maybe it's just burning leaves or a bonfire out of control," Tate said. "It happens sometimes."

But as they rounded the house next to the Lapps' and the dense black cloud came into view, Meg began to run. It was the old carriage house that had caught fire, their little clinic that had already welcomed a handful of babies into the world. Orange flames danced in the upstairs windows, wicking into charred black smoke that engulfed the roof. She ran past a handful of bystanders, rushed up as close as she could get before the wall of heat made her skid to a stop. This couldn't be happening!

"I reached the fire department," Tate called to her. "Two trucks are on their way."

He tried to tug Meg back, but she couldn't take her eyes off the hungry orange flames and billowing smoke. Their beloved center was burning.

❧ 34 ❧

Although most folks had finished eating, the tables in the Lapp barn were still occupied and every corner was filled with groups of men or women gathered to chat and share a story or two. Over at the dessert table, Fanny rested Tommy on one hip as she surveyed the sweets. She and Elsie were about to share one of the last gmay cookies when Fanny noticed some folks at the door pointing her way.

An English woman stood there, framed by the light of the doorway.

"Is that Meg?" Fanny asked, handing Elsie the entire cookie.

As Elsie turned toward the door, Meg strode toward them. Her red hair swung wildly over her shoulders and her mouth was a grim slash. Why was Meg here, looking so frazzled? Even in the most complicated deliveries, Meg managed to remain cool as a cucumber.

"Something's gone wrong," Fanny said aloud as Meg reached them.

"It's the birthing center." Meg clutched Fanny's arm. "There's been an explosion, and the building caught fire."

Stung by alarm, Fanny fought the sick feeling in her belly. "Oh, Meg, no!"

Elsie's hand flew to cover her mouth, as folks around them surged closer.

"We'll all go," said a man's voice. "Kumm. Let's hitch up the buggies."

"I'll give you a ride, Fanny," Meg offered. "It'll be faster."

Fanny handed Tommy to Elsie and hurried out with Meg, grabbing Caleb on the way. He took the front seat beside Meg while Fanny settled in a fog in the back. Cold fear clutched at her, making her shiver. The clinic was empty, thank the good Lord!

"Your neighbor Marta told me you'd be at the orchard." Meg kept her eyes ahead as the car seemed to fly down the roadway. Snow mounds and farms and fences whizzed past them.

"Was anyone hurt?" Fanny asked.

"No. It's a blessing that none of our mothers were in labor. And Marta's son was able to look inside before the heat and smoke were too bad. He said it was all clear."

"That's very good news," Caleb said.

"Ya," Fanny said with a confidence she didn't feel. "If no one was hurt, then it's only wood and nails. Nothing that can't be replaced."

"We'll try to stop the fire before it does too much damage," Caleb said, turning to Fanny. "We might be able to save your center."

"And the fire department might be there already," added Meg. "Tate called them as soon as we saw the fire."

The sight that greeted them at the end of the lane stole Fanny's breath away. The old building seemed to have a different life now, with eyes of flame in the upstairs windows and a toothy look below where the fire had sprung through, burning the three solid carriage house doors.

Any hope of saving the building drained away the moment Fanny saw it engulfed in flames and black smoke. Even the steady stream of water from the fire truck seemed powerless against the hungry fire.

Somehow, the fire chief found them in the commotion of assembling folk. The tall man wearing the bright green coat and black helmet introduced himself as George Katcher, the fire chief. His voice was gruff, but his eyes were kind as he confirmed Fanny's fears. "When more than a quarter of the roof is in flames, we know we can't save the structure." He paused to turn back to the ball of fire and smoke behind them, then faced them with a frown. "I'm sorry. We've already hosed down the roof of your house and the nearby trees to prevent the fire from spreading. We'll stay on the site until the fire is out."

As Caleb thanked the man, Fanny stared at the orange glow and wondered how so many hopes and dreams could slip away just like that.

Rose Miller tapped her shoulder and gave her a hug. "I'm taking Tommy and Beth to our house. We'll keep them the night, give you two less little ones to worry about."

"Denki." Only after Rose left did Fanny realize that her cheeks were streaked with tears and soot. She swiped them away with her sleeve and focused on the friends and neighbors organizing into lines. The fire chief didn't think it would help, but at least it was worth a try.

As she went down the line, she passed so many familiar faces: Tate Jordan and Marta Kraybill. Bishop Samuel and his wife, Lois. Adam King, Jimmy Lapp, Gabe King, Ira Miller, and Zed. Her heart ached at the thought of all Zed's work burning to cinders, but Zed had no time for self-pity. He stood in line closest to the fire, tossing water and stepping back to dodge the heat.

Fanny took her place between Emma and Meg in one of the bucket lines. A line of men passed water from the house spigot to the burning building. Fanny was in the second line of women and children. They passed empty buckets back to the water source. The bucket brigade was slow and tedious, but it was better than standing back and doing nothing.

When the structure began to creak and sway, everyone had to move back. The fire truck pulled closer, allowing metal poles to push the debris inside the building's footprint. With a sad groan, the walls collapsed, leaving only the sad arched frame of the old carriage house doors.

Steeling herself, Fanny bit her lower lip and stepped out of the bucket line. The firefighters thanked everyone and sent them on their way home.

It was done.

ᏰᎨ

Afterward many of the folks who had pitched in stopped into the house for fellowship and rest. On Elsie's instruction, Will had gotten the folding chairs out of the storage shed and set them up in a wide circle in the front room. Ordinarily Fanny would have been on her feet, serving food and hosting guests, but this was no ordinary gathering, and the fire had knocked the life out of her. A dozen or so people sat out in the front room, but right now Fanny preferred the relative quiet of the kitchen, where she sat at the table, warming her hands around a cup of hot cider.

Zed sat beside her, and although neither of them had much of a desire to talk, she drew a silent comfort from his presence. His face was smudged with soot from working the line close to the smoke and fire. Throughout the terrible afternoon and evening, she'd been so glad that he was there to take action and make wise choices. The sharp prongs of the crisis had shaken loose the scales of shame and embarrassment and revealed the plain, strong foundation of love between them. She would not hide from him anymore.

Across the table sat Caleb with his friend Kate. The girl was not afraid to get her hands dirty; Fanny had seen her moving buckets in the women's line, working tirelessly for the hour or two that it had taken to douse the fire.

Meg had brought over a dozen doughnuts, and Elsie had baked a lazy woman's cake—a very basic sheet cake with cocoa flavoring. Elsie had also brewed a pot of coffee, and there was a pan of warm apple cider on the stove. Folks sure seemed grateful for a bit of something sweet and the chance to sit for a moment.

The fire chief and one of the firemen came in from the mud porch. They stowed their long flashlights in their belts and accepted cups of coffee from Elsie.

The chief took the empty seat at the table. "We're trying to track down the cause of the fire, and it's clear that it originated in the rear of the building—the kitchen area."

The other firefighter stared into his mug. "A couple of people heard the explosion."

Fanny nodded. "Our neighbors heard it and came running. What was it that exploded?"

"An older model gas-powered refrigerator," George said. "Looks like that was what caused the explosion. Sometimes all it takes is a spark to set something like this off. Where did you buy the refrigerator?"

Zed caught Fanny's eye, and she understood the need to keep this to themselves.

"All of our appliances were donations," she said. She knew full well that John Zook, Ruben's father, had donated that refrigerator, but she wasn't going to mention him by name. John Zook and his family weren't to blame. No one was to blame.

"These things happen," said Caleb. "Dave Zook was just telling me about a similar explosion a few years ago near Lititz. Things can go very wrong with gas."

"Thanks be to Gott that no one was in the building," Zed said. "No one was hurt."

George sat back in the chair with a heavy breath. "That's the silver lining in the cloud." He used his mug to point to the people in the room. "You can't replace people. But property damage? With enough time and money, it can be restored."

The fire chief's comment opened the door to talk of renovation.

Fanny closed her eyes and tried not to see the gaping black giant next door as they talked of clearing the lot and raising a new building. Costly building estimates were tossed back and forth as if they were as light as a Ping-Pong ball.

"There's no question about it," Caleb said, "we must rebuild."

Fanny opened her eyes to stare at her son. And where did he think their family would get that kind of money?

Kate talked about the high expense of a renovation done in the bakery kitchen a few years back. Zed and Caleb and the fireman debated whether one story or two stories would be cheaper.

When the conversation began to unravel and folks started leaving, Fanny was relieved. The incident had shaken her to the core, and she needed some sleep and time to consider Gott's plan for her family.

The firemen left. The front room began to empty out, and Caleb went outside to help Kate with her buggy. The bishop came into the kitchen to say good-bye, and then he slipped out the back door and it was just Elsie, Zed, and Fanny in the kitchen.

Fanny craned her neck, trying to twist out the kinks of stress. "So much talk about rebuilding. No one's paying attention to what's right in front of us. This fire was Gott's doing. Shouldn't we learn from that? I think Gott's telling us there shouldn't be a birth center in Halfway."

Elsie and Zed exchanged a look of surprise.

Zed's voice was laced with calm. "Sometimes bad things happen, and it's Gott's way of testing us."

"I think this is a challenge," Elsie agreed. "The center is a wonderful good thing for our community. Doc Trueherz says it makes for healthy babies and happy mamms."

"Change isn't always a good thing." Fanny's mind was a jumble of thoughts, a tangle of colorful yarns that just could not be sorted or straightened. First, Anna was quitting, and now the fire . . . the center was gone. Maybe Gott didn't mean her to have a successful center. After all, it was a business. Maybe she'd been a little too proud of the popularity and early success of the birthing center.

"It's a setback," Zed agreed.

Fanny pressed her palms to the table, trying to gain comfort from the nicks and scars of its surface as she faced Zed. "You remodeled nearly every inch of that building, and it's gone now," she said, struggling to keep the catch of emotion from her voice. "Can you really start all over? This time without even a shell? Without a roof over your head?"

"It's a setback, all right. A big disappointment. But the building was just wood and nails; it can be replaced."

"How can you bear it when you worked so hard?" Fanny asked sadly.

"One step at a time," Zed said. "Remember? It's like following a recipe. You trim some boards and hammer some nails. Work hard and at the end of the day, you see progress."

"But progress was not part of Gott's plan for the clinic," Fanny insisted. The harsh truth throbbed like a wound in her heart. "Gott burned it down, and Gott doesn't make mistakes. The dream is over . . . ashes to ashes, dust to dust."

ꙮ 35 ꙮ

*F*ive o'clock came far too early when you were up until ten or eleven trying to support and comfort a friend in need. Rolling over, Meg realized her hair smelled like the black smoke of the fire. She needed a shower before she left for the clinic in Lancaster. A shower but no food or drink—doctor's orders.

Tired, hungry, and thirsty, Meg pushed herself out of bed and checked her cell phone. Still no word from Jack.

Her worry had morphed into distress. What if something had happened to him? A slippery stretch of road, a moment of distraction while driving. Bad things happened to good people all the time, as evidenced by the fire at the birthing center.

As she stepped into the shower, her worry was compounded by the memory of the fire. What would come of Fanny's idea to have a place for the women of Halfway to go? It certainly would have been convenient for Meg and Dr. Trueherz, as well as the women.

Meg hoped Fanny could find a way to continue the good she had done for the community.

And Fanny herself . . . how was she holding up? Last night she had seemed dazed, understandably so. There would have been no insurance on the building, as it was not the Amish way. The fire would pose a huge hardship for Fanny's family. Right now Meg could only pray for her friend's well-being and peace.

Last night, when Halfway was in crisis, Deputy Jack was nowhere to be found. He had disappeared for an emergency, something involving Lisa; that much, she was sure of. But why was he out of touch? Last night, just before bed, she had broken down and called Kat. "I don't know what's going on with him, but I'm sure he's not dodging you. He's crazy about you, and Jack is extremely loyal." Meg's speculation that Lisa had been in crisis made sense. It all added up. They figured Lisa had come to town on a mission to win Jack back and then . . . what?

Insecurity needled away at Meg's faith in Jack. Whatever the circumstances, he could have at least shot her a few details in a text message. Was it too much to hope for a contrite phone call?

This wasn't the Jack she knew. Then again, maybe she didn't know Jack all that well, after all.

She quickly dressed and met Shandell in the kitchen. The Jordans' wing off the kitchen was quiet, and Meg was relieved that Grace was letting Zoey and Tate get their sleep, at least for now. Tate would be up soon enough, putting together breakfast for his family and guests.

With Shandell in the driver's seat of Meg's Subaru, Meg turned on the seat warmer and tried to sink down into herself.

"Are you okay?" Shandell asked as she braked for a light on Halfway's Main Street.

"Just tired." Meg watched the door of the sheriff's office, willing Jack to emerge and wave. No such luck. Except for the lights in the bakery and a few Amish buggies on the road, Halfway was still waking up at 5:30 A.M.

Shandell took a sip from her travel cup, then tentatively jabbed it toward the console, trying to find the cup holder without taking her eyes off the road. "Couldn't sleep last night?"

"I was up late last night with the fire."

"Fire? Was there a fire at the inn?"

Of course, Shandell hadn't heard yet. She'd been with her mother, and word among the English didn't travel quite so fast. "There was this explosion, and Tate and I grabbed our coats and went outside to check it out . . ." Meg let the story spill out, pacing herself. With any luck, news of the fire would take up the half-hour trip to the hospital in Lancaster, and Shandell wouldn't have a chance to ask her about the upshot of Lisa's surprise visit yesterday. Right now she didn't want to discuss the fact that she couldn't reach her fiancé. It was embarrassing and painful.

Chatting about the uncertain future of the birthing center, Meg eyed Shandell's travel mug with envy. How she would love a sip . . . if only to wash down her anxiety.

If the procedure went well, Meg would be checked out in the early afternoon and sent home for a week of taking it easy. Anxiety curled deep inside her at the prospect of being alone once Shandell brought her back to the bed-and-breakfast. Meg tried to imagine Jack waiting there for her, greeting her with a perfectly logical explanation, but that felt like a sugar-coated fantasy. In the real world, when people let you down, they were sending a very clear message of withdrawal and rejection.

But that wasn't Jack. Looking back on her time with him, she didn't see any signs of erratic behavior, nothing to indicate that he would let her down like this. With a deep breath, she sent up a little prayer that Jack was all right, and that they would find each other on the other side of this mountain that separated them.

36

Although both Caleb and Elsie had offered to take Will to school the morning after the fire, Fanny had wanted the time to herself. Few things calmed the mind like a buggy ride with its rhythmic rocking and the steady patter of the horse's hooves on the road.

"Why do I have to go to school?" Will lamented as they rolled down the lane. "Can't I stay home and help with the cleanup? Zed always says I'm a right good helper."

It warmed her to see how Zed had helped the boy find joy in daily tasks. "There'll be plenty of work for you to do in the next few months." The lot would need to be cleared, the debris hauled off. Beyond that, Fanny expected the land to sit for a good fifty years or so. There was no way their family could scrape together the money to rebuild in her lifetime. At least Will's birdhouse had survived, a reminder of the dream that had almost become a reality.

"Mamm?" Will rubbed the knees of his pants. "Are we going to be poor now?"

It was a thoughtful question for a boy who'd just seen part of his home destroyed by fire. "We have family and food and a roof over our heads. That's enough, isn't it? A man is only poor when he wants more than he has."

Outside the schoolhouse, she held the horse and watched as he bounded up onto the wooden porch. It was good for Will to stick to his routine. How she wished for routine in her own life, instead of the topsy-turvy day ahead.

When Fanny arrived at home, she had to brace herself to face the sight of the singed pile of rubble. The center was now nothing more than the charred ash she shoveled out of the woodstove.

There was a horse and buggy outside the house. Inside, Bishop Samuel sat at the kitchen table, talking with Elsie.

"Good morning," Fanny said, even though the morning wasn't so good at all. As a girl she had learned that a cheerful outlook could bring sunshine to a dreary day.

"Caleb went off to borrow some shovels," Elsie said.

Most likely he would return with plenty of shovels and volunteers. That was one of the blessings of the Amish way. Community was not a place, but a group of familiar faces and helping hands.

"Sit down, Fanny." The bishop's eyes were cool as gray river stones behind his spectacles. "Elsie is going to give us a few minutes, ya?"

Elsie nodded and headed upstairs as Fanny took a seat.

"There is something we must talk about." Samuel let out a heavy breath. "Something I overheard, though I don't go for gossip. This came right from the horse's mouth."

Fanny froze, a startled creature in the woods. "So you have heard the talk about Zed and me." Shame flamed on her cheeks as she stared down at the table. What could she say to him . . . a man? A man of high authority. Oh, she had to tell him the truth, of course. Honesty was the only road worth traveling. "I don't know what they're saying now, but I confess, part of it is true. I fancy Zed, and ... and I took a liking to him while I was still mourning Thomas."

Samuel's bushy brows rose above his glasses. "What's this?"

"It's true." She smoothed the skirt of her dress, tugging on the black fabric. "I meant no disrespect to Tom; I cared for him deeply. This attachment for Zed, it crept up slowly, day by day. Working here, he's almost become a part of our family."

He grunted. "And what are his intentions?"

I won't give up on you. How she had clung to those words, day after day. She stared down at her hands. "He wanted to marry me. But we can't, with the gossip and all."

The bishop pushed his glasses up the bridge of his nose and squinted at her as if she were a very unusual bird. "I think marriage would be a very good thing for the two of you."

It was Fanny's turn to squint. Had she heard him correctly? "Then ... then, it would be all right? We could marry?" Although Amish weddings were traditionally held in November, widowed folk were permitted to marry any time of year in smaller, quieter celebrations that required less planning.

"I hope you do, but I don't know this gossip you're talking about."

"It started when—"

"Nay, don't say it." He held up a hand. "There's nothing to be gained by stirring the pot. Gossip is a sin. Don't I preach that a few times a year?"

She nodded. "I have heard you speak about it. More than once."

"And yet, it goes on." Samuel sat back with a sigh. "I must pray that Gott will help me get His message across more clearly. Some church leaders think that a little bit of gossip helps keep members on the straight and narrow, but it's a danger. A little bit of pride changed the angels into devils. A little bit of sin ..." He shook his head. "It is already too much."

The booming thunder of tension began to drain from her, and

she found herself settling into the chair, lulled by the bishop's gravelly, soft voice.

"The Bible says that without wood, a fire goes out, and without gossip, a quarrel will die down." Samuel tapped the table with one finger. "Have you ever thought that if Zed and you become husband and wife, it takes the wood from the fire? No more fuel for the gossipers."

"I never thought of it that way," she admitted. Such a wise man, Bishop Samuel. He had a way of showing how Gott's plan was the pattern for even the most personal matters.

Fanny ran her hand over the scarred table. Could it be that simple? That the way to end the nuisance of gossip was the one thing she had been denying herself? She smiled, feeling a heavy cloak lift from her heart. To have Zed back, just a heartbeat away, a part of her daily life ... such a joy. Together, they would find their way down even the bumpiest road.

"Now, put the talk of gossip aside and let me tell you why I came back. Last night, when I was just outside putting on my hat and coat, I heard you say that the fire proves it is Gott's will for the center to be closed." He wagged a finger at her. "This is not what the Bible teaches us. When soldiers chased Gott's people across the desert, did they give up? Nay. When Joseph's brothers were cruel to him, did he lie in a ditch and let them break his spirit?"

"He did not." Fanny liked the way Bishop Samuel added up Bible stories and extracted meaning from them, like a cook squeezing every last drop from a lemon.

"That's right. It's one thing to surrender to Gott's ways in matters that are beyond our control. When death comes, we must accept the loss. But when there is a problem we can fix, we must give ourselves up to the needs of the community." He paused, his gray eyes magnified by the lenses of his spectacles. "So. Sometimes Gott puts things in our path to challenge us. Like the fire. Gott has no quarrel with giving women a place to have their babes. It must be rebuilt."

Fanny ran her fingertips over a groove in the scarred kitchen table. It was hard to imagine another building in the charred, withered frame where the birthing center had once stood. "Watching it burn was like . . ." She kept touching the groove in the table. "It was the end of a dream. There's no money to rebuild. Anna is retiring, and with a family of my own, I can't be the only Amish midwife at the center. And I don't have the heart or the strength to rebuild."

"Mmm." The growl wasn't so sympathetic. "What about the heart of the community? What about the women and families who need help bringing their babies into the world? The center may have been a source of joy for you, but it's not really about pleasing you, is it? Swallow your pride and thank Gott for the charity of our community. Your friends and neighbors will be there when you need them."

"I'm grateful for everyone's help. But to rebuild—I wouldn't know where to start."

Samuel leaned forward, his eyes intent. "The journey of a thousand miles begins with one step."

Fanny gave a little gasp; that had been one of Tom's favorite expressions.

"So you take the step," said the bishop, "and then another, and like little Tommy, soon you will find that you are walking, and the path is clear."

❧ 37 ❧

Jack stared at the pay phone in the corridor of the rehab facility and wondered how it worked. He hadn't used one of these things in a hundred years. A credit card. *Okay, then.*

He swiped his card and tapped in the number for Meg's cell. No answer. Well, yeah. She would be in the clinic, getting her procedure done. Cell phone off.

After that he was at a loss. He didn't know any other phone numbers by heart; they were all stored in his cell phone.

His mysteriously missing cell phone. *Yeah, thanks for that, Lisa.* He suspected that she'd tossed it out the car window or dumped it into a toilet at one of the rest stops they'd made on the way to Philly. He couldn't be sure where she'd stashed it, but he knew that she'd taken it. She'd admitted as much to the psychologist doing the intake interview at Gladstone.

He tapped his fingers on the shelf under the pay phone. Next step, see if 411 still worked.

He got Kat's number through information, and at least managed to reach her. "Jack, where've you been? Everyone's been looking for you."

"Everyone like who?"

"Meg. Lisa paid her a visit yesterday. I think it threw her, but things got worse when no one could reach you."

Poor Meg. Lisa had pushed too far this time.

"And the sheriff's office called. Apparently there was a big fire last night and they were hoping you could come in. Why aren't you answering your cell phone?"

"It was stolen. By Lisa."

"What's going on, Bug?"

"Long story. Tell me about the fire."

He winced over her description of the devastating fire at the birthing center. Tragedy had struck his town, and he'd been off chasing a disaster of his own. He heaved a sigh, laden with guilt. At least no one had been injured. He explained that he was at a pay phone and asked her to look up some numbers for him.

She gave him the information, then had to go. "Abigail sleeps so rarely, it's my only time to eat and nap."

"Thanks, sis. Later." He hung up, then swiped his card again for a call to the bed-and-breakfast.

Tate answered, but he didn't have any info on Meg's procedure. "Hold on and I'll get Zoey."

As he waited, he stewed over the way Lisa had messed things up for him. Driving all the way out to Halfway. Telling people lies. Stealing things from him.

"I'm doing this for you," she had insisted. "I love you, and I know you love me. You said you would always take care of me. You promised."

"I was fifteen years old when I made that promise. I was a kid . . . we both were. But those days are over."

"They don't have to be," she had pouted.

"Yeah. They do. I wish you no harm, Lisa, but it's time for you to grow up and take responsibility for your actions. Put on your big-girl pants and stop blaming other people for your unhappiness. Nobody else can help you if you don't help yourself."

That little lecture had shut her up for a good twenty miles. Man, he'd thought he was through being her caretaker, but he'd gotten a bitter taste of the past when she'd shown up at his door, glazed and manipulative. Definitely in crisis.

"How did you find me?" he'd asked.

"Dear old Gran," Lisa had said in a voice laced with sarcasm. "She's so proud of you. Told me all about your job in Halfway, and your new girlfriend."

That had steeled Jack's protective instincts. "You need to stay away from me and the people I care about."

Lisa had just laughed at that and pushed her way into his apartment. Furious, Jack had called her dad, who'd begged Jack to bring her back to Philly.

"She's been going downhill for a few weeks now, and her mother and I, we're at a loss. We've been trying to get her to return to Gladstone for rehab, but she refuses. If you can get her back to there, we'd really owe you, son. Her mother and I will meet you there to check her in. I think they open at eight-thirty."

"And what am I supposed to do with her till then?" Jack had asked, trying to keep his voice low. He was using Lisa's phone, talking in the men's room. He'd slid her cell out of her purse while she was driving. Yeah, two could play at that game.

Although Jack had threatened to dump her at her parents' place, he knew Lisa would freak if he went near that upscale neighborhood. So they drove, and ended up at an all-night diner.

At least Richard Engles and his wife had been good on their word. They'd been waiting at the clinic lobby, contrite and grateful.

Jack had told the Engleses, in no uncertain terms, that they needed to take care of their daughter. He warned them that if Lisa tried to contact him again, he would get an order of protection.

"It's time for a clean break," Jack had said. "That's the only way we can both start over. The only way your daughter can start to make a life for herself."

"I hear you," Richard had said. He had promised to take good care of Lisa, and he would bring up Jack's right to privacy in their family therapy session.

Raking a hand back over his head, Jack sighed. What time was it, anyway? He'd been up all night, trying to keep Lisa from hurting herself while they waited for the admitting office to open at Gladstone. He desperately needed to shower and shave and sleep. But even more, he needed to connect with Meg.

He snapped back to the here and now when Zoey's voice came on the line.

"Hello?"

"Zoey, it's Jack."

"Oh, honey, you are in the doghouse."

"I know, I know. That's why I need your help. Please. Is Meg still in surgery?"

38

The work of six men, hauling off charred beams and ash, had barely changed the look of the mound of scorched debris. Zed dumped the load of cinders into the bed of the cart and leaned on his shovel to take in the line of buggies coming up the lane. They were earlier than he had expected.

For Zed and Caleb, the morning had been spent going from one church member to another, filling in details they didn't know about the fire and asking for help rebuilding the center. It was the sort of task that Zed usually dreaded, talking and socializing with folks he didn't know well. But to his surprise, he'd found that the words poured out of him, his request earnest. He had learned the truth in his dat's advice to walk softly, speak kindly, and pray fervently.

The visitors parked near the house but assembled in front of the fire site, talking quietly and shaking their heads as they surveyed the damage.

Adam King, a skilled carpenter, had offered to do some of the interior finishes with Zed. Jimmy Lapp and Nate King had older sons who would work as laborers, along with other able-bodied men in the community. Folks like Aaron Stoltzfus and the Kings, who owned profitable businesses, had offered to donate money.

Zed was happy to see Preacher Dave and the deacon, Moses Yoder, who had helped Zed locate a master builder.

Caleb came up beside Zed. "Should I go fetch Fanny?" asked Caleb.

"Do you think she's done talking with the bishop?" Zed asked, rubbing his smooth-shaven chin with his knuckles.

"The real question is, did he convince her to rebuild?" Caleb smacked the arms of his coat, sending gusts of black dust in the air.

The birth center had been close to Fanny's heart. Once she got past the shock of losing the first building, she would see her way to building another. Besides, she wouldn't go against the bishop. No one wanted to do that. "I'm sure she came around," Zed said. "Why don't you go test the waters?"

Brushing soot from his pants, Caleb strode down to the house.

Zed used the time to meet the master builder, a thin man who was chugging on a pipe. "So you hired a car to come all the way from Bird-in-Hand?"

"I did. I've done barn-raisings in Halfway before, but it's been a few years."

When Zed looked up, he saw Fanny walking over from the house, flanked by Caleb and the bishop. Fanny wasn't wearing a coat, and although the wind billowed the skirt of her dress and lifted the strings of her kapp, her footing did not waver.

The sharp edge of fear was gone from her blue eyes, and in its place was a calm, easy peace. Gelassenheit. This was the woman he recognized, the woman he knew well. A nurturing mother, a kind and soulful friend, a calm and sympathetic midwife.

He watched as she walked past the dozen or so buggies in the lane and came to the circle of friends in front of the blighted building. The sight of Fanny with her faith restored was like the first purple crocus poking through the snow. A sign of springtime, a hint of hope.

"What's this?" Bishop Samuel spouted as he reached the group. "Have you all come to work? I don't think you want to be digging in the ashes with your broadcloth trousers on, Dave," he teased the preacher.

"We have come to lend our support for rebuilding the center." Joan Fisher was the first to speak up, much to Zed's surprise. As she went on to say that the center would help many women and families, Zed let his bitterness toward her fade. Ya, she had hurt Fanny, but forgiveness was long overdue.

"Your kindness is a blessing from Gott," Fanny said, tenderness in her eyes. "It would be wonderful to put up a new building, but right now there's just no money to pay for it."

"It's a good thing, this center," said Aaron Stoltzfus. "Lovina will be over this afternoon with some dinner for the workers, but she wouldn't let me miss this meeting. If it's donations that are needed to get you going again, you can count on us."

"And the King dairy cooperative," said Nate King. "Not to mention the labor we can provide. I've got a few strapping boys who could use some experience with a hammer and saw."

"There are emergency funds available in this community," said Moses Yoder. "We'll see you through."

"And I'll organize a haystack supper to raise money." Fanny's friend Edna came to her side and placed a hand on her shoulder. "Folks love having a night when they don't have to cook."

The outpouring of support brought tears to Fanny's eyes. "Denki. Thank you all so much."

"It's the way we live," said Edna Lapp, who had benefited from the community's strong passion for charity when her son James had been injured last year.

Zed bit his lower lip, moved by Fanny's gratitude and by his own awareness of Gott's blessings. To have been led back to this community after years among the English, years in an emotional desert, Zed knew he'd been blessed by Gott.

Meanwhile, Fanny was moving around the circle, speaking with each visitor and thanking them. When she came to the stranger, she paused, and Zed stepped forward.

"This is Joseph Stoltzfus, a master builder who came all the way from Bird-in-Hand." Zed introduced the wiry man who had come to take measurements so that he could start construction on the frame of the new building.

"Thank the heavenly Father!" Fanny turned to Zed, her blue eyes alight with pleasure. "You don't waste any time."

"This debris will be cleared away in a few days," Zed told her. "We need to be ready."

"The first thing is to decide on one story or two," Joseph said. "The original building had an upstairs attic, but Zed said it was not used. Do you need one story or two?"

"That's up to Fanny." Zed didn't want to step on her toes.

"There hasn't been much time to think on that, but I reckon one story is cheaper?"

Joseph nodded. "A lot cheaper."

"Then one story will do," she said, prompting a laugh from the center's supporters.

❧ 39 ❧

Meg woke up from surgery to the sound of his voice. He was humming "Amazing Grace," rather poorly, but the gritty melody was the sweetest music she'd ever heard.

"Jack . . ." She opened her eyes, feeling refreshed. The anesthesia used in the surgery had that effect, letting the patient snap back to full awareness.

"You okay? Feeling good? You look great. They said everything went well." He took her hand. His smile was crooked but contrite. "Man, you're a welcome sight. I've been through the wringer in the past twenty-four hours."

"Yeah." She squeezed his hand, happy to see him even if he was in the doghouse. "It wasn't so good for me, either. What happened to you, Jack? Why didn't you answer any of my messages?"

"I'm so sorry about that, girl. It was killing me, but my hands were tied. Well, not literally, but sort of. Lisa swiped my cell phone and I haven't seen it since. Do you know how lost you can be when your cell is gone? I still don't know what she did with it. And with Lisa needing a full-time watchdog, I couldn't really go off hunting for a pay phone."

"What's going on with her?"

"She went off her meds. Needed to be shepherded in. I heard she paid you a visit."

"She did. I'm afraid she got a sneak peek of my wedding gown."

"Whoa. I bet the fur was flying."

"No, it was all very civilized. She kept her claws retracted and I resisted the urge to pounce. Actually, she put up a good front, but I sensed that something wasn't right with her. Then when I couldn't get through to you, it had me worried."

"You don't need to worry about me."

"Yes, I do. That's what we do, watch out for each other. You're going to have to get used to that if you're planning to stick around."

"You're right. It's nice to know you've got my back."

She lifted one hand to scratch her nose and noticed the IV line and clip on her finger. Raising the other hand to her head, she felt the goofy surgical bonnet that kept her hair contained. One tug and it was off. "You didn't tell me I looked like a lunch lady."

"Girl, you always look good to me."

The thread of insecurity that had been twisting inside her for the past twenty-four hours now melted away as relief overcame her. This was Jack, solid, kind, so dependable that he wouldn't deny anyone help, even a woman who had done him wrong, hurt him deeply.

"So tell me the whole story," she said. "Everything. Spare no details. I'm stuck in this bed for another hour, at least, and I want to know what we're dealing with, in case Lisa decides to boomerang back into our lives."

"It's kind of a sad story, but here goes." And he told her how he had been Lisa's crutch, her enabler, for years. How her family had alternately supported her treatment through the years but couldn't offer Lisa a strong emotional commitment. Now, at least, Lisa was under the care of a psychiatrist, and she had been checked in to a program. After a long talk with the rehab staff, Lisa's parents had agreed to take better care of her in the future, and the doctor would try to adjust Lisa's medications so that she wouldn't resist taking them. "Unfortunately, there are no guarantees that she won't come back and hound me again, but I made it pretty clear that I'm not her hero anymore."

"I appreciate your loyalty to her." Fierce loyalty—that was Jack. It was one of the many qualities she'd fallen in love with. "If she ever shows up again, we can help her together. That might help her to see you less as a former boyfriend and more as a friend."

He nodded. "That's a good idea. And I like the idea of having you on my team."

They talked for another hour or so, interrupted only when the doctor came in to tell her how the procedure had gone. When the surgeon asked if Jack should step out, Meg shook her head.

"He should stay. Pretty soon he's going to be Mr. Meg Harper."

That got the surgeon chuckling. It was the perfect segue to the doctor's news of a successful procedure. "If Mr. Harper here is your ride home, you're free to go. Get something to eat and take it easy for the next five to seven days. We'll see you back in two weeks for a recheck."

After the curtain whisked closed behind the doctor, Meg took Jack's hand and held it to her cheek.

Good news, coupled with the joy of having Jack by her side after his mysterious disappearance. Meg felt something sweet and light glimmer through her. Happiness? Joy? It was all so fleeting, but such was the nature of life. When it shined on you, the moment had to be savored.

❧ 40 ❧

*I*t was late. The children had gone off to bed hours ago, and Elsie and Caleb had just gone upstairs. Jack and Meg had also just left after an evening spent going over three different possible floor plans for the new birthing center—three maps of the future, Fanny thought. With Meg's experience as a midwife, her feedback and suggestions were important. Now that they had a chance to start from scratch, it was a good time to improve the floor plan.

At the kitchen table, Fanny sat writing down figures in a notepad. It was a ledger, of sorts, for the new center. Zed and Mr. Hennessey at the hardware store had worked out estimates of what building materials would cost, and she was keeping track of everything. An estimate was coming in from the lumberyard, too, and Tim Ebersol was getting them a contractor discount.

Zed sat beside her, sketching out a revised floor plan based on Meg's suggestions. Good with a pencil, he drew straight lines and had a knack for figuring out how to fit things into the plan.

"How about a scrub sink for the midwives over in this corner?" he said, pointing to the paper. "That way, it leaves more space in the hallway."

"That would be good," Fanny agreed, watching as he formed a handful of lines that resembled a sink. Amid the sweeping and shoveling, she had been watching him all day, but she hadn't been the only one. Everyone had been looking to Zed for direction on the best way to clear the sad, crumpled building. In the past year, he had come to be a part of this community again, accepted and appreciated. He was so dear to her! She hoped and prayed for a lifetime of evenings such as this, with Zed by her side.

As she finished adding up some numbers in the ledger, her mind went back to the talk she'd had with the bishop earlier that day. Samuel had given his blessing for them to marry! Joy fluttered inside her at the thought of it. And all her worries over the rumors had faded in the light of the truth. There was no shame in a man and a woman who loved each other under Gott's blessing of marriage.

"That's a good offer from Tate and Zoey." Zed kept drawing as he spoke. "Have you seen the cottages?"

The Jordans had said that one of the guest cottages on their property could be used as a birthing center if needed in the next few months. "I haven't seen them, but Meg is going to show me. We'll see."

"Mmm. And I have one more question for you."

She drew a little heart in the margin of the ledger. "And what is that?"

"Will you ever let me court you?"

She couldn't help but smile. "Widows don't go on dates like young people. There's no time for that when you're as old as me with a houseful of children."

"Then marry me, Fanny."

Letting the pen drop from her fingers, she turned to him coyly. Her heart was racing, but she couldn't bear a repeat of what had happened on second Christmas. She rose from the table and extended her hand. "Kumm."

He squinted at her, curious.

"I have an answer for you, out on the mud porch." Leading him by the hand, they passed through the kitchen door and sank into the cold darkness of the porch. "It'll be more private out here," she whispered, although no one but Zed was around to hear. Leaning against a post, she peered up and waited as her eyes adjusted to the soft darkness and the smooth line of his jaw began to take shape. Some things were worth the wait.

"So, what was your question?" Reaching up in the dark, she found his shoulders and steered him closer. "The one I've been longing to hear."

"The one I've been longing to speak: Marry me and be my wife." His hands slipped around her waist, and she shivered with pleasure as he encircled her in his arms.

"Those are the sweetest words . . . like the song of birds. I do want to marry you. My heart is so full, brimming over with love." She blinked back tears. "Gott's blessings come to us in surprising ways, don't they?" Amid the heartbreaking accidents, the sorrow and pain, Gott's love kept shining through.

"The Almighty is a wonder." His fingertips traced the line of her jaw, sending sweet shivers down her spine. "Only He can make a broken man whole again. Only He could join a lonely man with a loving family."

"A family in need of a good man." She sighed against his broad, firm chest. "I thank Gott for every day with you."

"To be by your side through the night and wake up beside you in the morning, to raise your little ones to be good Amish men and women . . . it's more than any man could dream of." He leaned down to tease his lips against her ear. "And Gott willing, we'll have children of our own to teach."

"Gott willing," she said firmly. He lifted her chin and she swayed against him, feeling as if she could melt in his arms. Grateful for the privacy of darkness, she closed her eyes and lost herself in his kiss.

41

On her wedding day, Meg moved in a cloud of happiness. Zoey doted on her, straightening her bronze hair so that it gleamed. Her skin glowed porcelain under the makeup that Mom had applied for her. The dress Shandell had sewn was comfortable and so flattering that Meg had felt a jolt of surprise when she'd seen herself in the mirror this afternoon.

"I look like a bride."

"A *beautiful* bride," Zoey added.

"Oh, honey." Mom's eyes misted with tears, not for the first time that day. "I'm so happy for you."

"Happy and surprised," Meg said, giving her mother a reassuring hug. "Come on, Mom, we know those are tears of relief. Your spinster daughter is tying the knot. You thought you'd never see this day."

"Don't say that." Vicki fanned her eyes, as if that could dry the tears. "You know I've always wanted the best for you. And now, you've found him. Jack was definitely worth waiting for."

"Oh, yeah." Meg took a moment to bask in the smiles of her mother and sister, her family's joy a significant part of the celebration of life and love on this wondrous day.

Not one to fuss with hair, makeup, or clothes, Meg had smiled at the beautiful bride in the mirror. This was an unexpected blessing.

A delicate lace design seemed to border her thoughts in a whimsical, un-Meglike way that suggested that life as Mrs. Jack Woods was going to be full of surprises.

The first surprise had come that morning when Jack had appeared at her door with two paper cups and a paper sack of muffins. "Thought I'd bring my bride breakfast," he'd said, leaning against the doorframe.

She had waved him in and taken a cup of coffee. "Isn't it supposed to be bad luck to see the bride on the wedding day?" she'd teased.

"Nah. That's just the dress." He came around behind her and massaged her shoulders. "I just wanted to make sure you were feeling good and relaxed, and I figured it would be good to start things off with God's blessing. Want to pray with me?"

"Oh, Jack . . ." She could not have imagined a lovelier, more reverent start to their lives together. She bit her lower lip as she turned to him with a nod.

With clasped hands and lowered heads, they had joined together to commit themselves to walk together in God's love.

∞

Waiting in the church vestibule, Meg sniffed the lovely white roses in her bouquet and paced the length of the vestibule. She wasn't nervous about being married to Jack, but the idea of being one of the major players in this ceremony gave her pause. *All you have to do is walk down that aisle,* she reassured herself, *and Jack will be by your side for the rest.*

One of the big wooden doors opened and Sheriff Hank came through with his wife, Maybelle. "The big day!" he said with a twinkle in his eyes.

Maybelle touched Meg's sleeve. "You look gorgeous, dear."

She thanked the couple, and then they disappeared through the open door to the small church, just as Zoey rushed in. Wisps of blond hair that had pulled loose from the twist fluttered around her face like a cherubic halo.

"Well. Your niece has decided that she does not want to attend the ceremony. That is, unless the pianist wants to play along with a shrill soprano."

"Poor little thing. Where is she now?" Meg tipped her head to one side.

"With Elsie Lapp, bless her heart. That young woman has a magic touch. She's walking Grace around in the parking lot. Fanny offered to take her, but I didn't want her to miss the ceremony."

"Okay, then." Meg clasped her bouquet to her chest and took a deep breath. "I guess it's time to do this thing."

"Yes, indeed." Zoey stepped closer and slid an arm around her sister's waist. "And I am here to walk you down the aisle. I know, I know, you planned to go on your own steam, independent woman that you are. But every bride needs a boost from her family. A little send-off."

It was Meg's turn to blink back tears. "Thank you. I was beginning to feel like I was about to walk the plank. It has nothing to do with marrying Jack and everything to do with walking down a tiled aisle in heels."

Zoey's chuckle echoed through the vestibule. "Silly girl." She gave a quick hug, then linked her arm through Meg's. "If you're jumping ship, I'm right by your side. Sisters forever."

"And ever." Meg tipped her head toward her sister's shoulder, and then, with the synchronicity of sisters and lifelong friends, they stepped into the doorway together and began the wedding march up the aisle.

The ceremony was a new layer in Meg's billowing cloud of happiness. Grateful for the joy welling inside her, she was very in the moment as she joined hands with Jack and exchanged vows. The pragmatic part of her recognized that their journey would be marked by sorrow and disappointment, but there was also love—a boundless sea of God's love to keep them together and carry them over the tough times.

In preparation for the small reception, the inn had been festooned with greenery and small floral arrangements—festive yet simple, in keeping with Meg and Jack's wishes.

Jack's boyhood friend Skeets toasted the couple, wishing them love and happiness in five languages. "I don't know the Pennsylvania Dutch dialect, but I've been told by some of my new friends here to say, '*Geh lessa*,' which I think means go with it. Not a bad bit of advice for any married couple."

Meg felt Jack squeeze her hand under the table as Skeets lifted a glass to them. "Jack, my buddy, I have to say, I never saw this coming in the days of Slip N' Slide and action figures. By the way, I think you still have my Incredible Hulk. In any case, I love you, man, and I wish you and Meg a lifetime of love and happiness."

"Hear, hear!" everyone chimed in, and Meg nodded her thanks, then clinked her glass of sparkling cider with Jack's.

After a quick sip, Meg scanned the big table, wanting to soak up the friendly faces and the air, so thick with laughter and love. Skeets winked at her, and his wife, Lanie, lifted her glass in a toast. Zoey blew her a kiss, then placed a hand on her husband's shoulder. Tate nodded as he patted the bundle in his arms, searching for the sweet spot that would soothe baby Grace. Mom and Kip smiled, beaming their support. Kat held her glass high, her eyes shining bright with hope for her baby brother's happiness. Beside her, Gran tugged her dangly earring, a secret signal she used to send Jack across the room when he was onstage in the school show. Meg could feel the love from Elsie and Anna, Dr. Trueherz and his wife, Celeste, and dear Fanny and Zed, who had hosted their own wedding dinner just last week. It had been Meg's first Amish wedding, a solemn affair followed by a fine roast chicken dinner at the home of Zed's parents, Rose and Ira. Folks told Meg the celebration was smaller than most, as a huge fuss was not made when a widow wed, but Meg and Jack had counted nearly forty guests. Meg had been grateful to be included in the family gathering.

Meg knew that she and Jack were blessed to be surrounded by this wonderful extended family. Full of thanks, she turned to her handsome husband, whose face was animated with tenderness and joy. The clang of silverware on crystal rose around them.

"Okay, Skeets." Jack waved toward his friend, not taking his eyes off Meg. "We got this." He tipped his face toward hers. "Love you, Megs."

"I love you, too," she said amid the high-pitched clamor that competed with her racing pulse. She closed her eyes against the noise and kissed her husband.

42

The sounds of hammers, saws, chirping birds, and conversation filled the air as men swarmed over the platform that had already been built at the site of the old carriage house. More than a hundred Amish workers had assembled from nearby church districts for the "barn raising"—the construction of the new birthing center's outer walls and roof, which, the master builder had assured everyone, would be completed in one day.

Lugging a pot of fresh coffee just brewed in her kitchen, Fanny couldn't help but grin at the clusters of gathered folk. Like a colony of ants, men covered the work site. They marched in line carrying framed trusses. They pounded final nails into the platform. They huddled in groups, pointing and discussing the next step. Children played over by the beech trees, taking turns on the swing and ducking in and out of the little house Zed had helped Will build with wood scraps. Under the canopy, women set up tables and benches for the dinner that would be served around the noon hour. The large tent had been erected yesterday; however, the weather was cooperating nicely for an April day, with sunshine and a few blustery kicks of wind.

"Here's fresh coffee," Fanny said, approaching the serving table.

"Perfect timing," Meg said. She opened the lid of the large thermal serving vat so that Fanny could add the fresh coffee.

In the blink of an eye, four workers were lined up with paper cups. The women stepped back as the men served themselves, sipped for a moment, then quickly got back to work.

"They certainly don't waste much time," Meg said. "Quite different from your average American coffee break."

"The Amish know how to relax and have leisure time," Fanny said. "But when there's work to be done, there's no time for laziness."

Rose and Edna came over with Meg's photo album from her honeymoon. After their wedding, Meg and Jack had flown off to the Caribbean to spend two weeks on the beach. Upon their return, they had moved in to the renovated cottage on Tate and Zoey's land—very convenient for Meg, who had only to walk next door to help deliver a baby.

Now a handful of women clustered together to marvel over the photos of the turquoise waters.

"The color of the sea in St. Thomas is such a wonder," said Rose. "Is the water truly that way?"

"It is, and it's pretty warm for swimming," Meg said, flipping a few pages to show them the coral reef. "They say it's because the water is so clear and the bottom is mostly sand."

The women oohed and aahed over the photos, remarking on the unusual mangrove trees, the exotic flowers, and the fancy drinks with paper umbrellas popping out of the top.

"Such a small umbrella would be just the right size for a tiny mouse," Edna said, eliciting a round of chuckling.

Rose held up a hand, stopping the conversation. "Mind—they're about to raise the first truss."

A joyful silence fell over the women as the workers lifted and hoisted a huge piece of framing that had already been assembled. Fanny found that she was holding her breath as the large piece swung into the air, rising until it stood tall as a pine tree.

Such a sight! A true sign of people working together, a community assembled to help one another. Soon the hammering resumed, and everyone breathed a happy sigh.

"This is amazing." Meg's loose red hair glinted in the sun. "Not even an hour in and they're already raising the house frame."

"That will be the side wall," Fanny said. "The master builder has men to assemble the frame in advance. I've seen a few barn raisings, and it's always a wonder how everything fits together. By the end of the day, we should have a roof and four red walls."

They had decided on red so that the building would stand out for anxious fathers or visiting doctors. The little red house down the lane. In the past few months, Fanny had given up some of her original ideas for the birthing center and accepted the design and features that the community wanted. That was the difference between this building and the old carriage house: This center was not hers; it belonged to the community.

Soon the second truss was raised, and then the third. Men straddled the rafters, hammering and hoisting boards.

Edna left to go back home and fetch the coleslaw and pickles she was contributing to the lunch. Soon Fanny and the other women would need to fire up the grills and start cooking chicken for the men. Sixty roasters! Good thing they had borrowed the big grills used in charity events.

"Mamm! Mamm," called a young voice. Nearly every woman under the tent turned toward the young caller. It turned out to be Fanny's Will, running up the hill. In his arms was a pitcher of lemonade, which he gingerly tried not to spill. He brought it to Fanny. "Elsie says to give this to you."

"Denki. And where are you headed?"

"Back to work. I've got to help Dat."

Her lips tugged into a smile. Since the wedding in March, Will had started thinking of Zed as his father. "Denki. Back to work with you."

As the boy raced off, Fanny set the pitcher on the table and reflected on how her marriage to Zed had been a good thing for their family. Tommy had taken to Zed, following him around like a little duckling. And it felt so natural for Zed to sit at their supper table and then read to the children and tuck them in to bed.

They had married quickly and quietly, after a few meetings with the bishop. Fanny would always look back fondly on the small ceremony that had included just a few family members and friends. Afterward, there'd been a supper at Zed's parents' house with chicken prepared by the girls and some of their friends, a celebration similar to a holiday meal. And then, their blessed wedding night.

After the children were down, they had rocked together by the fire and talked softly. Then she took him by the hand and led him into her bedroom—their bedroom—and Fanny thanked Gott for bringing her Zed. Funny, but she'd been a little nervous at first. "You're shaking like a leaf," he'd told her, and she'd remarked on the low temperatures outside. But after they'd slid under the covers, after the kerosene lamp was turned down, they had found each other. Oh, they had kindled a warmth that would chase away the frostiest winter chill.

An Amish man came up to Fanny and Meg, his face pale. It was Amos Fisher, whose wife, Mary, was due any day now. "Mary is in the buggy," Amos told Fanny. "She needs your help now. I'm taking her over to the Jordans' cottage."

Up the lane, a single gray-covered buggy sat. A woman waved from the front seat.

"Tell her I'll meet her there," Meg said, raking her hair back into a ponytail. She gave Fanny's arm a squeeze. "I got this."

"Back to business," Fanny teased.

As Meg headed off to care for Mary, Fanny turned back to the construction site. Which one of the tall Amish men was her husband? It was a bit hard to make him out amid the hundred or so men in similar clothing with black hats covering their heads.

Then she found him, straddling a rafter with Will beside him. He was showing their son something to do with the hammer.

She smiled as Zed drove a nail into the plank. Dear Zed. Such a good man. They were truly blessed.

ACKNOWLEDGMENTS

I am ever grateful to my editor, Junessa Viloria, for her gentle hand in shaping a story, her understanding of human nature, and her bright enthusiasm.

Many thanks to Dr. Violet Dutcher, whose nurturing advice and lifetime of relationships with Amish family and friends were invaluable to me. Her knowledge of Amish culture and literature is a winning combination.

And as always, thanks to the people of Lancaster County, the inspiration for these characters.

ABOUT THE AUTHOR

ROSALIND LAUER grew up in a large family in Maryland and began visiting Lancaster County's Amish community as a child. She attended Wagner College in New York City and worked as an editor for Simon & Schuster and Harlequin Books. She currently lives with her family in Oregon, where she writes in the shade of some towering two-hundred-year-old Douglas fir trees.

Facebook.com/pages/
rosalind-lauer/131734543591674

ABOUT THE TYPE

This book was set in Bembo, a typeface based on an old-style Roman face that was used for Cardinal Pietro Bembo's tract *De Aetna* in 1495. Bembo was cut by Francesco Griffo (1450–1518) in the early sixteenth century for Italian Renaissance printer and publisher Aldus Manutius (1449–1515). The Lanston Monotype Company of Philadelphia brought the well-proportioned letterforms of Bembo to the United States in the 1930s.